THE FACE TRANSPLANT

R. Arundel

ISBN: 9780991979905
ISBN: 0991979907

To my family for their enduring support, encouragement and nurturing.

TABLE OF CONTENTS

Chapter One

*G*uaarrr. It sounds like water draining from a very large bath-
tub, through a very large hole. *I just killed myself. I just killed
the patient.* Dr. Matthew MacAulay looks down on the operating room
table at the gaunt, graying man. Matthew quickly scans the operating
theater. Out of the corner of his eye, he can see the short wide man in
the observation area.

I just killed myself, Sarah, and Amanda.

They have been hijacked into performing a face transplant. The
patient is unknown. Mr. Glock, the short wide man, hovers in the far
end of the operating room. He made it clear that if the patient did not
survive, the three of them would be following him in short order. The
9 mm Glock with a silencer on the end gave credence to his profanity-
laced words of warning.

Matthew looks across the operating room table at Amanda Soto,
forty-two, an American of Spanish ancestry. She has been his scrub
nurse, assisting him in the operating room for the last three years.
Divorced, one child.

It will take a few more seconds for the monitors to tell everybody
what Matthew already knows. Amanda already knows. She is right
across the table. She saw him use the robotic arm to dissect the vessel
and mistakenly cut the large artery in the neck. An operating room
nurse of Amanda's experience has seen it all. When Matthew looks
into her eyes, they flash ever so quickly an acknowledgement that it is
all over. Instead of any words, she quietly unclamps the suction. Now
a dull hiss fills the air. To the casual observer, or the short wide man
holding a 9 mm Glock pistol in his fat stubby hands, nothing really

has changed. Amanda, anesthetist Dr. Sarah Larsson, and Dr. Matthew MacAulay act as if all is going well.

Matthew can not help but glance over to the man with the 9 mm Glock. In his mind he names him Mr. Glock. Adrenaline surges through Matthew's body and time slows. The short wide man, Mr. Glock, has gray eyes. Pale, gray eyes. Very pale, almost tired. Matthew remembers reading somewhere that people with gray eyes have the best visual acuity. They make the best marksmen, the best assassins. He wonders if this was true.

Guaarrr. Matthew tries to make eye contact with Amanda. He wonders whether or not she has ever heard this sound before. Probably not, he muses to himself with a wry smile. Amanda is bright; she hands him the instruments in the exact order needed. She is very observant. Not infrequently she puts the instrument in his hand that he needs, not the one he asks for.

Maybe she does know what that sound means. She could have heard it before. Matthew remembers his days as a trainee surgeon, a resident, at St. Mary's Medical Center in Chicago. Myles B. Neuwirth was the Professor of Surgery and his teacher.

Dr. Neuwirth said, "Matt, both you and I know you are well on your way to being a very rare commodity, a true surgeon, not a political animal that climbs the greasy pole."

To this day Matthew remembers his sophisticated British accent as he spoke. The trainees joked it was an affectation since he left the United Kingdom over forty years ago.

Dr. Neuwirth continued, "Maintain your passion to be the best, and keep your humanity. There is nothing more I can teach you. Go forth and prosper."

Matthew said, "Thanks for the kind comments."

A long pause ensued and Professor Neuwirth seemed to consider something before he made up his mind to speak.

Dr. Neuwirth said, "There is only one more thing I can teach you."

The entire operating room staff was silent. The medical students took out their pens to record the impending words of wisdom from the professor.

"There are only three types of bleeding that are important when performing surgery. One: bleeding you can't see. Two: bleeding that you can hear. Three . . ."

Silence filled the operating room theater as nurses, anesthetists, medical students, and visiting surgeons strained to hear.

With a sense of the dramatic, Myles lowered his voice. "Three . . ." Then he roared, "Your own!"

With the final comment, the operating room burst into applause and laughed; it was vintage Myles. He had a flair for the dramatic. The Professor pulled off his gloves with a flourish.

"Matthew, close up the wound."

The professor passed Matthew and whispered, "Unfortunately as you go through life, young man, you will learn: the heart bleeds the worst."

. . .

Guaarrr. Matthew is back to the present. All these thoughts and recollections shot through his mind in a fraction of a second. Time has slowed, must be the adrenaline. He is back in the here and now. Matthew cut the major vessel in the neck. The impossible had occurred. Blood flows at a ridiculously fast rate out of the patient's body. It is leaving at such a rate that Matthew hears the bleeding. The sound is distinct, once heard never forgotten. In sixty seconds at the outside, this man would be dead.

It's funny how all these things run through Matthew's head in less than half a second. It seems to him he has been daydreaming for a long time. The feeling of slowing time is due to the surge of adrenaline. It is a wonderful natural drug. He can now think more clearly and react instantly. Surprisingly, for the position he is in, he feels good. No, he feels great.

Who is this man on the table? Why does he want this transplant? Who is the man with the 9 mm Glock? Mr. Glock holds a shiny titanium container. There is no doubt in Matthew's mind that this contains the face to be transplanted. The container is only available in three centers in the United States: Houston, Palo Alto, and his center in New York. It definitely is not from his center. He always checks the faces to be transplanted; he is sure all the containers are accounted for. No worries.

The suction roars to life and Amanda begins to suction blood. Matthew needs to see. Blood flows like bright red water pouring out of a faucet. Out of the corner of his eye, Matthew can see Mr. Glock moving toward the operating room table. Matthew works to stop the bleeding; he notes Dr. Sarah Larsson did a remarkable thing. With two quick finger strokes, Sarah silenced the alarms. Brilliant. Our supervisor with the 9 mm Glock will not hear a thing. Sarah does not appear flustered. She does not make any move to increase the intravenous fluids or call for blood for an emergency transfusion. She just calmly switches off the alarms. She already knows they have a problem; the alarms aren't going to help her. They will only tell Mr. Glock they have a problem. Sarah continues like all is routine. Of course she doesn't call for blood. They are in the experimental wing of the university facial transplant facility in the middle of the night. Who would hear her?

Mr. Glock looks like a caricature of a thug. Short, muscular, but overweight. His face is like a square block. A wide short nose. Chopped black hair. Intimidating. The thing Matthew noticed first were his pale gray eyes. A watery gray from a washed out palette.

Amanda tries to keep the banter up. It is working; Mr. Glock has not detected anything is wrong yet.

Amanda asked, "Have you seen the play *The Spiral Staircase*?"

Matthew said, "Not yet, but I have tickets for next week."

Amanda said, "It was pretty good."

Sarah added, "I saw it a couple of weeks ago. I really liked it too."

Matthew works furiously to stop the bleeding. He is winning; the blood flow is slowing. The sucking sound lessens. He notes Amanda has moved her body ever so slightly to block any view Mr. Glock has of the suction canister. Even with the blood slowing, the canister will fill soon. Mr. Glock will realize things are not going as planned if the canister overflows and blood pours onto the floor. Matthew reminds himself, *Don't worry about that now. Concentrate on the task at hand. Stop the bleeding.*

"Everything okay?"

Mr. Glock's voice sends a bolt through Matthew. Sarah flinches ever so slightly. Maybe Matthew has misjudged Mr. Glock; maybe they aren't as slick in covering the bleeding.

"We got into a little bleeding. It's normal for a face transplant, no worries," Matthew replies.

Mr. Glock said, "When the incisions are closed and the recipient site prepared, I have some Steriazol to put on them."

Steriazol? The night turns surreal. Matthew is bewildered. A street thug just told him about the most secret compound in the Transplant Working Group's facial transplant program. It is being developed in Houston, Palo Alto, and New York. Only a few other highly specialized international facial transplant centers are working on this compound. No one is publishing data on this yet. They are all hoping to make a substantial breakthrough in the compound and then publish a blockbuster result in a prestigious journal. Steriazol is made to heal the thick incisions in face transplants. At the moment it still leaves a lot to be desired. The incisions are disfiguring and prominent.

"Don't worry, we have some and I will use it at the end," says Matthew.

"No, call me when you're ready. I want you to use mine," Mr. Glock takes his cell phone out of his jacket and punches in some numbers. One large hand remains firmly on the Glock. One more clamp and they will be home free. The vessel is deep and hard to see despite Amanda's suctioning. If Matthew can get this clamp on, they will live. The metal clamp is titanium, the best quality; unfortunately he has a bad angle. Matthew puts the clamp on the vessel. The sucking sound stops. His racing heart slows. Matthew now is aware of the sweat on his forehead. His surgical cap is wet; it now has a tie-dyed appearance.

Matthew looks into Amanda's brown eyes. Amanda's pupils are dilated. They have won. They will at least get out of this alive. The patient will live. Mr. Glock will not have to carry out his profanity-laced threat. Matthew quickly looks at Sarah; she peers over the drapes, looking at the wound. The twitching on the left side of her face relaxes.

Guaarrr. Matthew looks down at the neck. The clamp is at the bottom of the wound, and the vessel is open, like a large fish mouth. Open and frowning at him. There is no more to do. The patient is dead.

He looks up at Amanda and sees the panic in her eyes. The heart rate monitor continues a steady *beep, beep, beep.* The heart pumps two more dry beats and then stops. Even with the alarms off, Mr. Glock will know what happened. The patient is turning white, stark white. There is no blood in the body. The mystery patient is dead. Dr. Matthew MacAulay, Dr. Sarah Larsson, and Nurse Amanda Soto will soon follow.

Matthew and Amanda wait to hear the last beep. The adrenaline is wearing off. He and Amanda look exhausted. Amanda's shoulders are rounded, and he can feel himself slouching. *Keep your back straight. Think of a line of string going right through your back and out the top of your head. His mom, Caroline, has good advice.*

He begins to experience the events in real time. No more extra clarity of mind and focus that the adrenaline had given him. They wait for the last beep, and then as if by a miracle the heart rate picks up. A regular rhythm of seventy beats per minute. Matthew knows that the sound from the anesthetic machine is normal sinus rhythm. He doesn't need to look at the monitors. He peeks at the monitor showing oxygen saturation, 100 percent. That is better than before they started the operation. He closes and then opens his eyes. The patient is alive and fine; the heart is beating. He must have misjudged things due to the extreme stress. The clamp did stay on; in his hyperactive state, he misjudged it. Or was it the other way round? Is this all a very silly dream? In the time it takes to opens his eyes, he understands. He has a few minutes, but he must act fast.

Sarah realized the bleeding could not be stopped and the patient was about to die, so she switched the anesthetic machine to a pre-programmed patient record with normal heart beat, pulse, and vitals. It is the factory demo setting. It sounded like a routine operation for all who were listening or even looking at the monitors. She had bought them some time. Matthew is very grateful.

Amanda's daughter is off to the Australian university in the fall for an Environmental Studies program; Amanda is booked off for three weeks starting in September. Maybe Amanda will see her graduate. Sarah had anticipated this death, maybe as soon as she heard the bleeding. *Guaarr.* Maybe she understood what it meant to have bleeding so severe you could hear it. Maybe she knew the professor's Rules of Bleeding. She understood Rule Two. Before he went to sleep, the patient smiled at Dr. Sarah Larsson. She has pure white hair. It is the only thing people mention when they talk about Sarah. Although she is only twenty-eight years old, her hair has lost all color. Some people think she has dyed it this pure white, but it is natural. Her white hair seems to shimmer. She spent her early years pursuing her mother's dream of becoming a ten-meter diving champion. She rose to Olympic trials level but never quite made it to the Olympics. It was much harder on her mother than Sarah. The experience left her with a slim, toned body. And a relationship with her mother that was always uneasy. Her pure white hair makes her look like a ghost with her pale skin and blue eyes. Her father told her she looked like an angel. He was a good man. Her Swedish ancestry gave her a narrow, refined nose with a delicate upturn at the end. But it is the hair that everyone notices. The eighty-year-old hair on a twenty-eight-year-old woman. Truth be told it is genetic. Many in her family undergo premature loss of hair color. It is really an absence of pigment that causes this stark white appearance, but she doesn't bother to explain this to people.

When the patient tonight asked about the hair color, he asked if she was an angel to carry him to the other side. She made her usual remark about losing her hair color by studying too hard in medical school so he could rest assured she knew what she was doing. The patient was quiet for a moment and then said, "If I don't wake up with my new face, everyone in this room is joining me on the other side." As he drifted off to sleep, he quietly murmured, "Maybe we'll all be in a better place."

Matthew looks at Sarah and remembers these words. She is not as calm as he thought. Sarah has a tremor in her right hand and the twitch in her face has returned. She is desperately trying to get herself under control. Matthew notices the hand tremor when she tries to inject drugs into the IV. Matthew must act now.

"Looks like the worst is past," says Sarah.

"He's doing good now," says Matthew.

Sarah says, "We need to finish soon."

Amanda is still panicked and cannot play along with the charade. Matthew is afraid Amanda might start crying or try to run. At this range she will not get five feet before Mr. Glock cuts her down; then he will finish them all off. Amanda has to control herself and fight the natural urge to flee if they are to have any hope. Matthew looks directly at Amanda. He wills her to stay calm, hold it together. Small beads of sweat collect on her forehead; sweat dampens the collar of her surgical gown. Amanda's eyes fill with water. She is not going to be able to hold it together.

"Yes, we're almost there," says Matthew, scanning the room.

There are no weapons or potential weapons. Anything used correctly can be a weapon, and if all else fails, the human body is the best weapon. Matthew holds an 11 blade scalpel. Amanda picks up the 10 blade scalpel and hands it to Matthew. The 10 blade is the "harpoon." A big blade rarely used in facial transplant work. The knife edge is razor sharp. Matthew will have to strike Mr. Glock in precisely the correct spot. One clean cut. *There could be associates waiting outside the hospital. . Possible, but not a real concern now. Stay focused, one problem at a time. We can worry about later, if and when later ever comes.*

Mr. Glock seems preoccupied on the cell phone. He is giving or getting instructions. He grips the canister containing the face that is to be transplanted between his legs as he talks. The shiny cylindrical canister looks like a small garbage can.

"Sir, we're ready for the transplant," Amanda beckons Mr. Glock to bring the face.

Matthew recognizes the white bottle and red top. The red top peeks through the pocket of the black leather jacket Mr. Glock wears. This is the Steriazol being worked on in Palo Alto. Matthew notes the limp in Mr. Glock's gait. He is sure the right foot is shorter than the left, definitely an old hip fracture.

Mr. Glock moves to within two feet of the operating table. Amanda notices the thick black dirt under his fingernails. Matthew makes a smooth turn. Before Mr. Glock realizes it, the 10 blade scalpel stabs smoothly through his neck. There is no blood splatter, just a gurgling sound.

Matthew made sure that his strike severed both carotid arteries, the two main arteries in the neck that carry blood to the brain. The blood from the cut drains into the trachea and into the lungs. A clean, quick exit.

Matthew senses relief in Mr. Glock's pale gray eyes when he finally understands what has happened. As if he knew, sooner or later, it would end this way. Mr. Glock slumps to the floor. Amanda and Matthew catch him and gently lower the body to the ground. Matthew takes the Glock and puts on the safety.

The titanium canister holding the face to be transplanted falls to the ground and makes a loud clatter as it rolls to the entryway. It finally comes to a stop and the room is dead silent.

Amanda rips off her operating room mask and pulls out her cell phone.

"Amanda, what are you doing?" says Sarah.

"We have to call the police," Amanda screams.

Matthew pulls the cell phone out of her hand. "No."

Amanda says, "What?"

"No, let's just . . ."

Before Matthew can finish his sentence, a large pizza delivery van screeches up to the front door. Matthew, Sarah, and Amanda hide in the little used storage closet at the back of the operating theater. From this vantage point, they can see the entryway and the operating room. Old operating room equipment blocks the storage closet.

The pizza delivery crew go to the side room beside the surgical suite. The large pizza bag they open holds an array of equipment and supplies. The two women and one man immediately remove the pizza delivery uniforms and put on white overalls with head covers and latex gloves. The women are in their late twenties, both lean and muscled. They strip their clothes off with practiced speed. Sarah, Matthew, and

Amanda can see they are each very different in body types. The short woman has very thin thighs. She looks like a long distance marathoner. Lithe, taut, an endurance athlete. Strapped to her left inner thigh is a revolver with a silencer attached. The other woman is tall and voluptuous. Curvy, but hard curves, curves made of muscle wrapped by skin. She has thick thighs. The muscles in her back stand out like ropes. In the small of her back and the left inner thigh are two weapons, silencers attached. She has very full lips with a wide mouth.

The man is obviously in command. He has a nondescript appearance. He has brown, medium length hair. Not out of shape, not particularly fit. Average build. He wears an ear piece. He is in constant communication with someone, giving them real-time updates on the situation. Although he can't hear the words, Matthew can tell the situation is tense and the person on the other end is not happy. The man relays instructions to the two women and they begin to work with calm purpose. Matthew worries. If they are ordered to search the operating room, this group will find them. This is a professional team. Matthew looks around their tight space and finds an old screwdriver. He holds it tight. The cleanup crew will find them and kill them without much effort, but if he has to go down, he will go down swinging.

The cleanup crew begins to systematically cleanse the scene. Mr. Glock and the patient are placed in body bags. They grab the titanium canister that holds the face to be transplanted. The commander takes the canister. They cleanse the room and replace everything. Surfaces are wiped down. The blood is removed, suction hoses replaced. In the space of twenty minutes, there is no trace of any of the night's events. Before they leave the commander takes the hard drive out of the anesthetic machine and replaces it with a new one. Matthew, Sarah, and Amanda watch with eyes wide open as the crew silently change back into the pizza delivery uniforms, carefully avoiding the security cameras. The tall muscular woman bends to pull up her pants. As she buttons her pants, she looks right in Matthew's direction. He gets a good look at her face—the full red lips. The process is quick but unhurried. The pizza delivery truck drives off into the night.

CHAPTER TWO

The parking lot behind the hospital is empty except for a few cars belonging to the main hospital's late shift. No one is working in the research facility at this hour. The constant roar of the highway off in the distance punctuates the conversation of Sarah, Matthew, and Amanda.

Amanda says, "We're lucky to be alive." She keeps looking behind her and walking back and forth.

Sarah says, "I think they were in a hurry. That's the only reason we're alive."

Matthew breathes deeply, taking slow breaths.

Matthew says, "The night is cool; it feels good." He leans on the hood of his car.

Amanda says, "Did you see how they left that place? No chance of fingerprints, no blood, no fibers, no nothing. Professionals."

"King Kamehamehaaaa." The words are screamed out of a passing car.

"I don't know who did this," says Matthew.

"Precisely, that's why we call the police," says Sarah.

"You guys don't know the full story. I'm part of a special group, TWG."

Amanda and Sarah look at each other.

Sarah, "TWG?"

Matthew says, "The Transplant Working Group. TWG is a group of three centers of excellence in facial transplant surgery in the United States. One in Palo Alto, one in Houston, and the third is right here. Liam Rasulov probably mentioned it to you when he recruited you for the transplant team."

Sarah says, "Yes, Liam mentioned you were part of a group of transplant centers."

Matthew says, "What he didn't tell you is that we receive some covert funding from the US government. The military has a long tradition of funding robotics or other medical research that may have applications for them."

Amanda asks, "Is this a university program?"

Matthew says, "Some of our research is funded by the US government. We report directly to people in the military. The university is not aware of some of our actions."

Sarah asks, "How high up is this thing?"

Matthew says, "Transplant Working Group reports directly to Secretary of Defense. Some of our research is classified."

Sarah says, "You can't get any higher than that. They are obviously interested in transplanting a face of one person onto someone else for spying."

Matthew says, "If we can perfect the technique to transplant a face from one to the other with no scars, it would have many possibilities. We're far from that at this stage."

Amanda says, "So who came in here tonight?"

Sarah adds, "That's a very good question."

Matthew says, "I thought the guy with the gray eyes was some street hood who heard about the transplants and wanted a friend disguised with someone else's face."

Amanda says, "That's what I thought."

Sarah adds, "But that cleanup crew was not a group of street goons. That was special ops or someone in government."

Matthew says, "That's what I can't figure out. We are working for government, so what were they doing?"

Sarah asks, "Liam is the director of the facial transplant program here, correct?"

"Yes."

Sarah says, "Liam might know if something's going on."

"He might."

Amanda says, "This is crazy."

Matthew says, "I'm not sure what's going on."

Amanda says, "The cleanup crew was an elite military squad. It's the government."

Sarah asks, "But who would authorize this, and why?" She bites her lower lip. "I'm with Amanda now; we need to call the police."

Amanda says, "We need to call the police. They can get to the bottom of this. Our lives may be in danger."

Sarah says, "She's right. They could be waiting for us at our homes right now."

Matthew says, "I'm not sure we want to go to the police right now."

Sarah says, "So when you invited me tonight you had no idea of this?"

"Michael Coulson, the head of the Transplant Working Group lab in Houston, called me on short notice to do him a favor, meet with this guy. He told me to assemble a few people. He said the guy was an Italian facial transplant surgeon who wanted to discuss some aspects of setting up a program of his own. He was leaving to go back home in the morning and was only flying in tonight to New York. Mike said he wanted to meet me, my transplant anesthetist, and scrub nurse. I had no idea, and I'm sure Mike had no idea this was what was planned."

Another car rushes by and they hear, "King Kamehamehaaaa."

Matthew, "What are they yelling?"

Sarah says, "King Kamehameha, it's a hot new club that's opened up. It's not bad."

Amanda adds, "Wasn't the King Kamehameha club a spot in a really, really old action television show set in Hawaii?"

Matthew says, "It was, a very old detective show."

Amanda pulls out her car keys. "So what do we do?"

"We need to figure out who did this, to figure out what to do."

"Could it be someone in government acting alone?" says Amanda.

"Someone acting without authorization, that would make sense. It would explain a great deal." Matthew continues, "But the fact remains they took great trouble to cover their tracks."

"As we've seen tonight, these guys play pretty hard," says Sarah.

"Exactly. What I think we should do is go home and think about everything. Tomorrow we can make a plan."

Amanda says, "I don't feel comfortable not calling the police."

"If we go to the police with our story, we all lose our jobs." Sarah stares at Matthew. "I lose my license."

Matthew says, "Sarah's right—we all lose our licenses. We were involved in the murder of a man."

Sarah says, "We can argue that it was self defense, but bottom line, we have a lot of explaining to do. It would get messy. We tried to do a transplant on someone we did not know. It would take a few years to sort out. In the meantime, we would not be able to practice."

"We were forced," says Amanda.

Sarah says, "The state licensing body would suspend us at best, pending the outcome of a thorough investigation." She pulls on her hair hard. "Matthew would have to tell them about the military involvement in the research. Do you think anyone would believe we were not part of Dr. MacAulay's team? The university would have more than grounds for dismissal."

Matthew says, "I had no idea this is how it would all turn out tonight. But Sarah's right, the university would not want this kind of press. I'd go down, but I'd take you both with me."

Matthew continues, "Go home. We'll see each other at work tomorrow. If anyone asks, say you went to the lab to help me answer a few questions from an Italian surgeon who is setting up his own program in face transplants. Try to stick to what I told you to get you to come in. The best lies start with the truth; try to stay with the truth as long as possible."

Amanda looks at Matthew in silence as if she is seeing him from a fresh angle. She reluctantly gets into her car and drives off. He isn't sure if she will follow his advice. At this point, he doesn't really care. Sleep is what he needs now.

Sarah watches Amanda's car leave the lot.

The force of the slap twists Matthew's face. Sarah's open hand connects with his cheek squarely. She turns abruptly and hops into her electric car. She silently drives away.

Chapter Three

Matthew is happy to see his brownstone in the Meatpacking District of Manhattan. It is a three-level, detached home. He loves the architectural detail; the original brown brick still covers the exterior. He lives on a tree-lined street with a series of these detached homes, very rare for this part of New York. He parks in the garage and puts his head on the steering wheel.

Matthew hears a loud, constant ringing. It is coming from the left. He turns to his left and realizes nothing is there. At first he thinks it is his alarm system, or an intruder. He laughs hysterically. The ringing noise is coming from his left ear. Tinnitus. A constant ringing in his ears, a high-pitched buzz usually with no known cause. But not tonight, tonight the cause is known. A powerful slap to the left ear and face. Sarah hit him so hard his ear is ringing. The laughter just keeps coming. While he was a resident in surgery, he never had a symptom of any of the diseases he studied. For some reason he took pride in that fact. Well, tonight he has tinnitus. Patients always asked, "Have you ever had this?" Matthew always said no and waited for the standard response, "Then you don't know what it feels like." He is not sure why that is so funny tonight, but he just can't stop laughing.

The interior of his home is a study in contrast from the simple brick exterior. It is decorated in a contemporary style. Sleek and modern. However, the design is warm; many of his photos from travels are on the walls. When the laughing subsides, a deep feeling of unease takes hold of Matthew. He lies on top of his bed and closes his eyes, but he cannot sleep. He begins to think about the night's events. Matthew turns from side to side. He closes his eyes and opens them again. Finally, he picks up the phone.

The hospital dispatcher answers. "Hello."

"This is Dr. MacAulay. Can you give me Dr. Larsson's telephone number?"

"Dr. MacAulay, I can't give you Dr. Larsson's number, but I can connect you to her home."

"Do it. "

Matthew waits.

"I'm sorry. I reached Dr. Larsson and she said she doesn't want to take your call."

"Try again. Tell her it's important."

Matthew waits.

Sarah says, "What is it?"

"I couldn't go to sleep."

"You think you're the only one? None of us can sleep. I'm sure Amanda's up right now. What did you call me for?"

"I wanted to apologize."

"Thanks."

"Wait, don't hang up."

"What else?"

"Give me a chance. I wanted to explain myself."

"It's the middle of the night. It's the middle of the night of the worst night of my life. Forgive me if I'm not interested in explanations."

"I really want to explain."

"If it'll get you off the phone, go ahead. But I'm warning you, I may hang up at anytime. Don't call back."

"I just wanted to make a new contact in the face transplant world."

"How did Transplant Working Group come about?"

"Tom Grabowski, Liam Rasulov, and Michael Coulson were initially all working together in a lab down at Stanford. When they split, the three centers each created became the Transplant Working Group. TWG shares research. Liam set up in New York. Tom stayed in Palo Alto. Michael Coulson set up a lab in Houston. When they went to their own centers, they continued doing research in facial transplantation. It was not until later that the government approached them. The military applications of being able to transfer one face onto another was too big for the government to ignore."

Sarah lies on top of her bed, fully clothed. She goes to her dressing table and begins to undress. She puts Matthew on speaker phone.

"You don't have to justify what you did to me."

"Maybe I'm justifying it to myself."

"Are you going to tell Liam? I read a lot of his research when I was learning how to give anesthesia to transplant patients. Much of what we do in transplants is based on Liam's work. He seems like a smart guy."

"His early work in neurotubules enabled a great deal of the transplant work done today. It's very interesting."

Sarah puts on her flannel pajamas and plops onto her bed. "Wasn't it Tom Grabowski down in Palo Alto that developed the Steriazol?"

Matthew says, "That's right. He helped formulate the compound that helps the neurotubules join to allow the transplanted face to heal."

Sarah leafs through a travel magazine on her bedside table.

"Why did the three split up?"

"I'm not really sure. There were rumors, nothing specific."

"Do tell."

"Some say Tom and Michael turned on Liam. It just all of a sudden ended."

Sarah asked, "Were they jealous?"

"Liam was the real driving force. He was the star. Who knows?"

"They were probably jealous."

"Liam met with endless people to push face transplants back then. He was doing a great deal of basic research and all the administrative stuff. Liam got all three labs up and running. But I can't believe they were jealous. Tom is not the jealous type."

"I heard Liam is rich?"

"Rich and connected. Liam's family has been in the oil and gas business for generations. His family knows presidents, heads of state in foreign places. When the government took an interest in face transplants, they reached out to Liam. He smoothed the project along."

"So that's why you came to New York. You followed the money?"

"I wanted to be in the Big Apple. Enjoy the New York life. But eventually, I see myself in Palo Alto with Tom."

"Why did they get in bed with the military?"

"They just offered so much money TWG couldn't refuse. Right now the big problems are the thick scars and long-term stability of the face transplant. We're all working on the Steriazol compound to fix these things. It's really much better than the original, but it has a long way to go. We're about twenty-five years away. With the extra funding, we'll probably get there in fifteen."

"It makes that much difference?"

"Money is a big factor in research; most people don't realize it."

"The military is interested because they want to put someone else's face on their man for spying. Anyone can see that."

"It's true I meet with Quentin Taylor to update him on our progress, but we can help a lot of trauma patients with our research."

"Is that supposed to impress me that you meet with the Secretary of Defense to update him?"

"It wasn't meant to, but if you're impressed, that's great."

"The problem is other countries are doing this type of research. They're probably spying on you guys as well. I know you're going to say you're far ahead, but this stuff is so secret. Do you really know that?"

"I was thinking the same thing. And when I saw that canister, I knew it was obviously a face harvested from someone. The canister looked like it was from one of the Transplant Working Group centers, but who knows?"

"Maybe he paid someone in the military to set this up?"

"You're talking big money."

"To get that kind of plan together, big, big money."

"If I hadn't severed that vessel and killed the guy, the plan would have worked perfectly."

"Don't feel guilty. You were under stress. We all were. That was not easy surgery."

"I still hate to lose a patient. Even a criminal."

"The guy forced you to do this in the middle of the night."

"You're right. We all make mistakes, even the best surgeons."

Sarah sits up and laughs. "So you're the best now, are you?"

"You know what I mean."

Sarah laughs. "I was looking forward to a long sleepless night. You've made it a bit of fun, Matthew. If we weren't in such a bad mess, I would almost forgive you."

"All is forgiven?"

"I said almost."

"Almost is not too shabby."

"We're not sure what is going to happen. Whoever planned this might want to make sure we have no way of talking about it. This could be very, very bad. But I understand you really can't be held responsible."

"I'll take that as all is forgiven."

"Good night."

"See you tomorrow."

Matthew looks at the light blinking on his phone. He suddenly remembers his mom. Matthew listens to the voice mail.

"Good evening, Matthew, it's your mom, I was expecting you. Guess you got busy with work. Or maybe you're busy finding someone to give me that grandchild I want. Love you, call me."

He looks at his watch, it is four a.m. He will call his mom later today.

Chapter Four

Sarah is busy in the operating room alone. She is preparing her anesthetic machine. Today's list of surgical patients is short and she should be home early. The cases look routine; they should go to sleep with no problem. The modern anesthetic machine is now really at the level of a state-of-the-art fighter jet in terms of computerization and complexity. The modern anesthetic machine did everything. It recorded the blood pressure, heart rate, patient's oxygenation. It suggested when the vapors used to put a patient to sleep needed to be increased and then did it. It realized when the vapors were too low and the patient was awake while under anesthetic. A terror for the patient. With the new machines, this was eliminated.

The machine really was a super computer. It shared many of the components of the modern surgical robots. This machine could almost think. A computer with the power of these new anesthetic machines just ten years ago would have needed to be housed in a small warehouse. Today it came in a package the size of a washing machine. The anesthetist watches and lets the machine do its thing. In fact, some researchers have begun trials where the anesthetist is not even in the room for the surgery. They monitor the machine remotely and are available if some emergency occurs. One day humans will not be needed for any aspect of surgery. Robots will put the patient to sleep. Another robot will do the cutting.

Sarah looks out the window of the operating room and sees that Matthew has arrived. Sarah approaches Matthew as he washes his hands in preparation for surgery. Matthew notes how the slight curls of pure white hair peak through the sides of Dr. Larsson's operating room cap.

Somehow Sarah's pale skin seems to have color when placed against that hair.

Sarah says, "I was thinking about last night."

"I just couldn't sleep. I'm sorry if I bored you."

"I wasn't going to sleep."

"I got a couple hours."

"I was thinking about what I did in the parking lot. I had no right to strike you. I'm sorry.

"We were all frazzled."

Sarah says, "There's a lot going on in my life. I thought I had it under control. Now this happens. I'm not making excuses. I should not have slapped you."

"No worries. I just got off the phone with Dr. Coulson."

"What did he have to say?"

"He wasn't involved at all. A contact told him about this Italian transplant surgeon. The details were sketchy."

"Did you tell him about last night?"

"No. We don't want anyone else involved. The less who know the better."

Sarah says, "I was thinking about this all night; we are in some kind of trouble."

"Maybe. Maybe not." Matthew's hands are red from scrubbing so hard under the sink. "If this was a well-planned transplant of an organized crime type who wants to escape detection, he is dead. He's been expertly disposed of. Whoever was helping him wants this to go away."

"I thought about that, but with what you've told me about TWG, I just don't see this as some criminal wanting to change identity."

Matthew says, "Transplant Working Group may be involved, but whoever did this will want to keep it quiet. The guy who died could have paid a lot of money to arrange this. Whoever arranged this may want to make it look like it worked and the patient left our operating room and disappeared. The perfect job."

The circulating nurse calls them inside to begin the case. As Matthew passes she asks casually, "Did you have a good night? You were on call."

Matthew had forgotten that he was on call for emergencies last night. They rarely called him in, except for the most severe facial trauma. Residents and fellows handled almost everything.

"You wouldn't believe me if I told you."

Matthew gets down to the muscle and finds the nerves. His resident today seems uninterested. His senior colleague, Spencer Lambert, is also assisting him. They occasionally operate together on difficult cases.

A phone rings, and Sarah picks up the operating room phone.

Dr. Liam Rasulov is on the other end of the line. "Hello."

Sarah says, "Hello?"

"This is Liam. Who am I speaking with?"

"Hi, Liam, it's Sarah. You sound funny. Where are you?"

"I'm in my plane. I'm flying back to New York."

"You seem to be in the air quite a bit."

"Any chance I get. I told you I'd take you up anytime."

"Thanks for the offer. I've just been so busy settling in to New York."

"You're with Matthew and Spencer today?"

"Yes."

"The boys treating you well?"

"They're behaving."

"Good."

"They're almost finished."

"Tell Matthew I want to see him in my office in about an hour."

Liam presses a button on his head set; he is now connected to air traffic control. Liam looks out at the New York skyline. "This is Liam Rasulov preparing to land."

The air traffic controller has known Liam for many years. Liam is notorious for his many flights into and out of the airport at all hours. The controllers never have a problem with him; he likes to fly and takes great pride in doing it professionally.

Air controller, "Hi, Liam. Clear to land."

Liam is anxious to get back to the office; the recent news will make for a busy day.

. . .

"Dr. MacAulay, that was Dr. Rasulov. He wants to see you in his office. He said he will be there in about an hour."

Spencer says, "I didn't see him at the university meeting this morning. Where's Liam calling from?"

Sarah says, "His plane, Dr. Lambert."

Spencer says, "It's great that he's got all that time and money to fly. Some of us have to look after patients—do the real work."

Matthew steps in. "He's allowed to have a hobby."

Spencer says, "His residents do all his work."

Matthew remains silent.

Spencer says, "Let the resident close the case. I want to see that flap you did."

"No problem, I was going to get your opinion on that case."

Matthew rips off his gloves. Spencer takes off his surgical cap, revealing his thinning gray-brown hair.

Matthew and Spencer go directly into Ryan's room. Ryan Smith is a big man. His feet stick out over the bed, especially with the bandages. He is also very wide. Ryan has put on some weight since his injury. The wounds to his legs and back are healing slowly.

"Good afternoon, Doc MacAulay." Ryan's booming voice fills the room.

"Hi, Ryan, I brought a colleague of mine, Dr. Spencer Lambert, to get his opinion." "Nice to meet you, Dr. Lambert."

Spencer rips the surgical dressing off Ryan's face.

Ryan sucks in a breath. "Whoa, it's a little sensitive."

Spencer continues prodding the wound. "Sorry."

Matthew looks at Ryan's facial wound over Dr. Lambert's shoulder. "No pus."

Dr. Lambert says, "Not yet."

Dr. Lambert moves to the side so Matthew can see.

Matthew carefully examines the wound. "This may hurt a bit. I'll say sorry in advance."

Dr. Lambert says, "Not that great really."

Matthew wanted to respond to Spencer's comment, but it would not be a good move. Dr. Lambert was his senior colleague; he was on the hospital board that determines whether the facial transplant program proceeds.

Matthew asks, "Did my resident check the flap this morning?"

Ryan says, "Of course, you were the one missing."

"Sorry I didn't stop by this morning. I had a long night."

Ryan Smith's military uniform is freshly pressed and hung with great care. His private room has a large closet. . It will never be worn again. The uniform stands in memory of better days. Days when Ryan had comrades, when he could battle. Now he is a bedridden wreck with a mangled face. An invalid monster—that's how he thought of himself these days.

Matthew moves to the foot of the bed with Dr. Lambert. He notices the slight stoop in Spencer's shoulders. "I'm going to ask my senior colleague for advice. Don't worry if you hear some talk that's medical. I'm going to tell you the game plan as soon as we make it."

"No problem." Ryan picks up a magazine and begins reading.

Dr. Lambert says, "When you take off the dressing, it's a much bigger loss than I thought; his nose is completely gone."

Matthew says, "I rotated some tissue from his forehead to make a new nose and repair skin lost in the middle of his face."

"It's a little dusky."

"I agree. What should I do?"

Dr. Lambert answers, "Just wait and see what happens."

Matthew agrees. That is going to be his plan. Spencer has good clinical judgment, even if he sometimes lacks beside manner.

Matthew goes to the head of bed. Spencer leaves without acknowledging the patient or saying good-bye.

Matthew says, "Ryan, I think this flap was a good idea. The forehead flap is a workhorse. As I told you before, we took some skin from your forehead and turned it to fix the areas of your nose and cheeks that were damaged."

Ryan says, "I know. It's a flap that's been used for thousands of years, very reliable, first used in India."

"Correct, I see you do listen to what I say, and remember it too. I thought you were just a pretty face."

"Very funny, Doc MacAulay."

"I try. When we told you we were going to do this, I said there could be some problems. You remember my concern with the tissue and the blood supply due to all the damage to the surrounding skin. I was hopeful but not confident that this would take."

"I just want to be able to go to the mall and not have everyone look at me."

"That's our objective, but I am not sure this flap is going to get us there."

"Then what?" asks Ryan.

"Well, first we are going to follow this flap closely. We're going to start giving you medicines intravenously to help the flap live, but even with that it's touch and go."

"What happens if the flap dies?"

"We have other options, but let's just see how this goes. If we need to do something else, we will, don't worry. How's the physio going?"

"Great. My movement is improving." Ryan flexes and extends his leg.

"Looking good," says Matthew.

"My resident will be by later. If there are any concerns, he'll contact me," says Matthew. Matthew closes the door. Spencer is waiting for him outside.

Dr. Lambert says, "You keep a close eye on this. We want our department flap survival rate to be above 98 percent. I am publishing a paper soon."

Matthew says, "I'll be checking every six hours."

"No, every three hours. Around the clock."

"Not a problem."

Dr. Lambert asks, "How's he holding up? He seems chipper."

"Nurses say he seems upbeat."

Chapter Five

Matthew walks into Liam's office. It is a large square space. A little-used squash racket lies beside the wooden desk. Liam has a large computer monitor on his desk. Beside the desk is a picture of Liam and his wife with their twin daughters, smiling on vacation.

Matthew says, "Every time I see that photo it makes me smile."

Liam picks up the photo. "Me too. We took it while we vacationed in the Caribbean. Jamaica."

"I remember. You guys went to a high school track meet."

"Not just any track meet. This was the yearly event. All the great runners on the island of great runners come out. It was a blast. I loved watching those young kids run."

Matthew says, "Everyone loves competition."

"I tell you I had to beg the girls to go, but when they got to the track, they loved it. We all loved it. It was the highlight of our vacation."

"A lot of Olympic champions come out of that small island."

Liam says, "Yes, they do. I'm such a hopeless athlete, I don't know why I enjoy track so much." He puts the photo down.

Matthew points to the photo beside it. "New pic."

"Just shot that last week."

"That's you and the university president."

"We were at a graduation ceremony."

"And it gets the prime real estate, right beside your family. When is he stepping down?"

"I didn't ask him, but I heard any day."

"Rumor is you're the next university president."

Liam says, "I won't lie—I want the job. He asked me to pose with him. That's got to mean something."

Matthew looks at Liam's smooth narrow face. "You have my vote."

"You don't have a vote. You're not on university council."

"Well, you know what I mean."

"Now to more sobering business."

Matthew squirms in his seat on the old metal chair in front of the desk. The somber look on Liam's face leaves no doubt he heard about last night and the failed face transplant.

"How did you hear?" says Matthew.

"Got a call yesterday."

"I'm surprised you heard so quickly. I was coming to tell you the story."

"News of a death always travels fast."

"Who was he?" says Matthew.

"Who was he?" Liam is perplexed.

"I didn't recognize him."

"What are you talking about? Tom died last night."

Matthew gasps. "Tom Grabowski?"

"Yes, what did you think I was talking about?"

"How did he die?"

"An MI."

Matthew stares at nothing.

"I know it's a shock."

Matthew's eyes moisten.

"I know he was like a father to you."

Matthew recovers. "He was there for me and mom."

"Tom was a good friend to me as well."

"How did you get the news?"

"I was in Palo Alto visiting his lab. It happened in the night. I flew back to tell you."

"Thanks. Does my mom know?"

"Not yet. I know Caroline was close with Tom. Do you want me to call her?"

"No, I'll tell her."

"Sure."

"This is out of the blue."

"These things happen."

"I doubt that it was a heart attack."

Liam asks, "Why?"

"I was down in our lab doing a transplant last night."

"For who?"

"A very persuasive man carrying a very large gun."

"What are you talking about?"

"Mike Coulson called me last minute. He said a surgeon from Italy was in New York and wanted to go over some aspects of transplantation for the program he was setting up back home. He requested an anesthesiologist, scrub nurse, and transplant surgeon. He wanted to ask the team some questions."

"Why didn't he ask Mike in Houston?"

"I asked the same question. Mike said he never saw these guys, but the name the guy mentioned was of a guy in Italy where he had lectured, so Mike wasn't suspicious."

"Sound fishy. Why didn't he go to Houston?"

"He was flying into New York. He was leaving after a quick visit because he had emergency cases to do back home."

"I guess that makes sense."

"So I asked Sarah Larsson and Amanda Soto to join me. When we got to the lab, we were met by a very large gun."

After Matthew tells Liam the story, they both sit in silence.

Matthew asks, "Nothing to say? You've always got something to say."

"I'm still trying to take it all in."

"I was up most of last night, and I still can't make sense of it."

"I was down at the lab this morning; there is nothing out of place. There is nothing to suggest any of what you have just told me," says Liam.

"Like I said, the cleanup crew was professional. I remember the one woman. Tall, very curvy, but all muscle."

"The one with the full lips—you seem to remember her real well. Just remember if she had spotted you, I'm sure she would have had no problem taking that gun out of her back and putting a few bullets into you."

"I know."

Liam, "Did you recognize whose face it was? Did you recognize the man who you were going to transplant?"

"No."

"Are you sure? Think."

"No."

Liam says, "We need to call Quentin Taylor."

"Did it occur to you that Quentin could have been behind last night?" asks Matthew.

"I never liked him. Quentin Taylor most likely authorized this." Liam pauses. "The cleanup crew was definitely Special Ops. They may as well have had name tags, but you need to speak to the Secretary of Defense. If he is behind last night, you'll get some indication when you talk to him."

"Tell him about last night?"

"Don't mention last night, just listen. If it looks like he might know something, then hint that an item was left behind. The cleanup crew can't be sure they got everything. Hint that the item left behind points to the government."

"Then what?"

"See if you can draw him out."

"Who would do this?"

"I don't know for sure who is behind this. It could also be a rogue group of senior military personnel or one lone wolf after a big payday. There are many possibilities."

Matthew asks, "Who has the reach to do this on our soil? A foreign power?"

"Only the biggest players could even dream about doing something like what you described. It was well planned and executed. A foreign power does that on our soil? That's an act of war."

"Us?" says Matthew.

Liam says, "We don't kill our own."

"Don't we?"

"I can't see why they would kill Tom," says Liam.

"He must have been involved in harvesting the face they were going to use to change the identity of the patient. The canister with the face in it was one of the Transplant Working Group containers, a Palo Alto container, I'm positive. They may have done what they did to me; after he harvested the face, they killed him."

Liam, "I agree—that much is obvious, but why kill him?"

"No idea."

"It doesn't make sense. Think about it. If you had done the transplant, you and your team would have been killed. That would mean killing two transplant surgeons on the same day. No one would have believed that was coincidence."

"No, I think they would have made us disappear. No bodies. Then it would be an open question. What happened to the New York transplant team?"

"Still, that's pretty bold."

"I'll visit Quentin and see what he knows, if anything."

Liam says, "All roads lead to the Secretary of Defense. Use the death of Tom as an opener. I was told it was garden variety heart attack, not uncommon at his age."

"He did love his cigars. I remember I got him some Cubans for his fiftieth birthday."

"He had a little fun with me in the lab one time. This was the old days; you were a little thing. It was when we were all at Stanford. Me, Liam, Mike Coulson. Your mom was Tom's graduate student. I remember Tom in the lab puffing away one night. I said to him, 'How can you do that? You're a doctor.' He smoked those big fat ones."

"Same as now: the big fat ones with the dark black wrapper."

Liam smiled. "Precisely. So I asked him how a surgeon can indulge in such a bad habit. I remember he looked at me, took the cigar out of his mouth, and looked at it. Then he took a long puff, savored it, and blew smoke in my face. It smelled like a hit of rich dark chocolate. And then he said, 'Liam, never trust a man without a vice.'"

Matthew laughed "That's something he would have said."

"A fine man has passed, no doubt."

Matthew nods. "No doubt."

. . .

Liam walks down the hall slowly, his head bowed. The hospital is full of patients on stretchers moving along the hallway.

Liam almost walks right past Sarah. "Sarah. Sorry I didn't see you."

"I have to talk to you."

"No problem. "

"Somewhere quiet."

Liam takes her arm and leads her into an empty operating room. He sits on a stool. Sarah sits on the operating table across from him.

Liam says, "I know what kind of night you had. Matthew told me. I'm still trying to piece it together myself."

"It's like a film in my mind. Something that happened to someone else and I'm watching. The someone else just looks like me."

"Don't worry, I think whoever was involved is now more scared than you. You're fine."

"I'm not sure what to make of last night, but it definitely complicates my situation."

"Potentially, it complicates things for everyone. I think we need to push the pause button on this. At least until we get some clarity."

"You recruited me to come out here."

"I remember. You plan to spend six months with us and then travel the world. I had no idea something like this could happen; I couldn't have foreseen it."

Sarah says, "I'm not blaming you. I was happy to accept your offer."

"Good."

"I've come to a decision."

"That sounds final."

Sarah hands Liam an envelope. "I'd like to hand in my resignation. I'm going to leave the hospital effective immediately. The letter is my formal resignation."

"Sarah."

Sarah says, "I wanted to get a little extra money, doing the anesthesia here, before my trip. With things as they are, I feel I should leave now. They'll never be able to find me. They won't be bothered to look."

"You probably haven't heard yet, but Tom Grabowski, he headed the face transplant team out of Palo Alto, died yesterday. I was told a heart attack. He collapsed while running. But Matthew's convinced the failed transplant you did and Tom's death are related. The more I think about it, the more I think he is right."

Sarah says, "A transplant surgeon dies last night and we're forced to do a transplant the same night. That's no coincidence."

Liam returns the envelope to Sarah.

Liam says, "Why the attempted transplant and the killing of Tom, I have no idea. They happened at opposite ends of the country. Bottom line is: this is no amateur show. Whoever did this will want no loose ends. If you leave this place . . . They are going to leave no loose ends."

"So you're saying if I try to leave now, I'm as good as dead?"

"I suggest we all just lie low. Go about our business as if nothing happened. Stick together, and take precautions to be safe. In a few months if it all goes away, then you leave."

"This is not how I was planning this conversation would go."

"You know I'm right. Wait a few months. Finish your contract. You have your whole life ahead of you to travel."

"That's just it. I don't."

Liam asks, "What do you mean?"

"ALS."

Liam is silent for a long while. Then he nods. "When were you diagnosed?"

"Twelve months ago."

"The occasional facial twitches you have, it all makes sense."

"I have less than twenty-four months."

"ALS, Lou Gehrig's disease. I just can't believe it. Look at you. Beautiful, strong . . . I can't believe it."

Sarah, "I don't look like a person with a progressive neuro-muscular disease."

"Exactly."

"I don't feel like one either, not at this point."

Liam finally speaks. "So your plan to travel the world is in jeopardy with this new wrinkle added to your life."

"And time is short."

Liam repeats, "Time is short."

"I'm not going to end up on a ventilator. I'm going to travel. At least I was."

Liam gets up and gives her a hug.

"How long do I wait around to see what happens? I need to go on my world tour."

"I'm not sure what to make of them but the events of last night are connected. It's not safe for you to leave, not yet. You're going to have to wait to see what happens. But I promise you this, I will do anything I can to make sure that your plans don't get crushed."

Sarah puts the envelope back in her white lab coat. "I just had to tell someone. "

"Thanks for sharing."

Chapter Six

The quiet rap on his door forces Quentin Taylor to swallow a piece of grilled chicken breast much too fast. Quentin coughs. "Come in."

There is a large gray sofa and two chairs in front of the massive desk of the Secretary of Defense. Matthew takes his usual spot in the corner of the sofa.

Matthew says, "Sorry to interrupt your lunch."

"It's the only time I could squeeze you in. You want some? It's a Cobb salad. I got it at The Purple Tomato."

"The Purple Tomato?"

"It's a new restaurant. Read the fantastic reviews online. I just had to try it."

Quentin munches away as Matthew watches.

Matthew says, "Looks like it gets two thumbs up."

"This is the way a Cobb salad should be made. You can't have a Cobb salad without watercress and Roquefort cheese. Both are fresh."

"Bacon bits?"

Quentin says, "Yeah, real bacon. These guys know what they're doing."

"Maybe now you won't complain about all the shuffling back and forth you do between New York and Washington."

Quentin's mouth is stuffed with salad. "My grandfather introduced me to the Cobb salad. He spent some time in Hollywood. That's where the salad was invented."

"I didn't know that."

"My grandfather took me to the John Langston Estate to have lunch once a month. I was only nine years old when he started. We'd both order Cobb."

"Sounds like a great tradition."

"It was. We carried it on until I left town to go to college in Boston. My grandfather would say the same thing every time we lunched. 'Quentin, only men of breeding order a Cobb salad. This is a real Cobb salad. Never accept a substitute.'"

Quentin eats the last bits of Cobb salad. "That old man was something. We'd go for a Cobb later, when I was working, but not nearly enough. He was sharp as a tack until he died at ninety-one."

Matthew watches Quentin.

"So you heard the news?" says Quentin.

"I did, but I wanted to hear it from you," says Matthew.

"I know you were close. It's true, Dr. Tom Grabowski, one of the best research surgeons of his era, has died of a heart attack."

"Where?"

"Cypress Hill—a witness saw him running, and then all of a sudden, he collapsed. Paramedics were called, couldn't revive him."

Quentin takes a piece of lettuce and rubs it around the bit of salad dressing that remains. "Delicious."

Matthew asks, "Patricia is fine?"

"She's devastated."

Matthew frowns.

"I understand he was like a father to you; you have my sincerest sympathies."

Matthew looks at the photo on the wall above the massive desk. It is a large framed photo of Quentin Taylor, about age fourteen, with the future President of the United States of America, Carter Middleton. They are arm in arm, holding up a canoe between them. The young men are dwarfed by the large trees in the background.

"Nothing related to what we do?" says Matthew.

"Not on first blush. I'm having the body brought here for an autopsy at George Washington. I'm sending out Jason Cooper."

Matthew, "Jason Cooper?"

"Just to do some routine leg work, but it seems pretty straightforward."

• • •

The top is down. Jason Cooper is being massaged by the wind.

"Slow down, big fella. We want to get there in one piece."

Celerie puts her hand on his thigh and squeezes. She smiles and a row of perfect white teeth are bracketed by bright lipstick.

"Sure." Jason accelerates, and the car takes the sharp turn hard. He is exhilarated. Sitting beside him is his fiancée and he has a new assignment.

Celerie says, "Hey, cut it out." She is pushed back in her seat as they take the next turn. Her thick black hair is tussled by the wind.

"Okay."

Jason laughs and eases off the gas. Celerie is stunning. *Sounds like celery and good enough to eat.* Jason had made this play on words a little too often. Celerie doesn't like it, so he keeps silent. Jason looks down at his thigh where her hand lies. Her bare legs almost brush his.

"Don't get any ideas," says Celerie.

"Now what ideas would I be getting?"

"I'm already late."

"The wind protector's pretty good. We're ripping along and there's no cabin noise. We can talk in a normal voice." Jason finally applies the brakes. "I'm glad I got it."

Celerie says, "Yeah, you're right."

"It was well worth it."

"For what you paid for this car, it should fly."

Jason gets just a hint of her perfume and stiffens. "You smell good."

"Thanks, it's hard to believe in another two months we'll be husband and wife."

"I can't wait." Jason swallows hard. Her dress clings to her chest.

"How's the assignment?" says Celerie.

"Although it seems cut and dry, it may not be."

"You're just confirming a heart attack, dear."

"It may seem obvious, confirm a heart attack in a relatively old man, but you never know." "Dr. Tom Grabowski was no ordinary old man." Jason looks at his speedometer.

Celerie says, "You two fought all the time."

"No denying he was an arrogant old prick. He never liked the fact that the military was supervising his research. He let me know it every time I got an update, but he sure had no problem taking all the extra money for the research."

The car glides to a stop at the hotel entrance. Celerie is attending a show for fashion week.

"I'll call you tomorrow," Celerie says, exiting the car, "I'll be home very late."

Jason sees a passerby looking at Celerie's legs. He pulls Celerie close and kisses her. "Call when you get home."

. . .

It is early afternoon when Matthew returns from Washington. He takes a taxi directly to the hospital. Matthew is stopped by Dr. Spencer Lambert in the hallway.

"Matthew, did you check on your flap?"

"I did a while ago, looked the same."

"I just stopped by, and I suggest you look again. I can't talk. I'm late for a meeting with the university president."

"I'll go right now."

Matthew knows the flap is dead. Spencer is a good doctor; he is in the running with Liam to be the next university president. The smart money is on Liam. Matthew hopes the smart money is right. As Matthew walks to Ryan's room, the question is what to now do with the flap? The flap had been the best option to get Ryan back to his life as quickly as possible. The physiotherapy was coming along well and Ryan would be walking normally soon. But without a face to present to the world, the psychological effects will be devastating.

Aly Smith is sitting in a chair beside her husband. Ryan is telling a joke and she is laughing raucously. The kids run around the room.

Matthew enters. "Hi Aly."

Aly says, "Hi, Dr. MacAulay."

Matthew asks, "Can I get in on the joke?"

Ryan says, "Are you sure you want to hear it?"

"On second thought, maybe I'll pass. How are things going, Aly? You look great."

Aly wears faded jeans and a worn out T-shirt.

"I know everyone's saying I've lost weight. I haven't really been trying. We're getting by," says Aly.

Ryan says, "I'll be out of here soon and things will get back on track."

Matthew says, "I can see the kids seem healthy."

The four kids continue running around the room.

Aly says, "These kids are just too much. Their energy is amazing."

"You're doing a great job. Having four kids all under age eight is a real chore."

Aly jokes, "I think we should have canceled date night after the second."

Ryan says, "Now, now, Aly."

"I'm just joking."

"Aly, we're gonna get this great big lug home soon to give you some help."

"I sure need it."

Matthew goes over to Ryan and removes the bandages. Matthew keeps his body between Ryan's face and Aly so she cannot see the wound. The central portion of his face had been completely blown away by the injury. The forehead flap is not dead. That is the good news. However, the color is not pink; it is a bluish color. The blood supply is not enough for the flap to have a healthy color. It is not sure if it wants to live or die. The puckered, scarred tissue around it is becoming infected. Matthew searches Ryan's face intently. There is no other skin that would work to repair the large hole in the middle of his face. If this doesn't work, he will put Ryan into the facial transplant program. Matthew already has donor tissue ready. Ryan would need a partial face transplant.

Matthew says, "Unfortunately, the flap does not know what it wants to be, rock star or bum."

"I kind of figured that. It's starting to hurt."

"It is not what I had hoped. I'm not sure it will survive. I'll start antibiotics."

Aly asks, "What now?"

Matthew says, "We will take it one day at a time. I don't want to be too negative. If I was sure it was dead, I'd take him back to the operating room and remove the dead tissue and dress the wound. You'll look pretty much as you do now."

Aly says, "It seems we just keep getting bad news."

"I'm sorry for this, but we may need to consider a partial face transplant."

Ryan says, "Partial transplant, you mentioned that before."

Matthew says, "I think that is the best option if this doesn't work. Let's keep our fingers crossed. However, if the flap fails, the partial trans will give us the result we all want."

"Well, I just hope this works. Come on, kids, let's give dad some rest. Bye, Ryan." Aly and the kids quickly leave and the room is silent.

Matthew says, "Aly took it pretty hard."

Ryan says, "She's having a tough time."

"This can be difficult on a family. Remember to cut her some slack. How are you hanging in?"

"I'm fine. Roll with the punches, you know me, Doc MacAulay."

"That's great. It's hard for anyone to deal with major changes like this."

"I seem to be doing just fine."

"Good. If you ever want to talk to anyone, let me know. We have people who are very experienced in helping you deal with this kind of thing. People you can talk to. Keep it in mind."

. . .

Matthew likes his mother's brownstone. She bought it almost twenty years ago. With current real estate prices, she would be a very wealthy woman if she ever sold. He always remembers how difficult it was to pay that mortgage in the early days. Together they made it; it is a source of satisfaction.

Caroline says, "Tom's death's been keeping you pretty busy these last few days."

They sit in the kitchen.

Matthew says, "It's just so sad."

Caroline says, "He was a good man. In the old days, we were all so close. He really took you under his wing. I'm sure that's why you ended up doing transplants."

"He was a giant and a truly decent man."

"He was a decent human being. He lived life well. He was a little heavy, and he liked his cigars. I guess a heart attack is as good a way as any to go. Quick."

"I'm going to Palo Alto."

"Give my love to Patricia."

. . .

The meeting spot at the lake is quiet. At this time of the year, the area is deserted. The lake is tranquil. The trees hang low around the water, setting the mood. He thinks that is why the Secretary of Defense liked to meet here. It sets the mood. Quentin Taylor did like a sense of the dramatic. A few seconds after Jason arrives, Quentin pulls up.

"What does Tom's death mean, practically speaking?" says Jason.

"Nothing, the lab in New York is fine. I spoke to Matthew. His transplant research is proceeding on schedule, and the lab in Houston is doing good work. They were all independent."

"What do you think?"

Quentin waits to answer. "I was convinced it was a heart attack, but I got a visit from Matthew. He didn't say anything, but I'm sure he was fishing for something. He was hiding something. I could feel it."

"You think golden boy is involved?" says Jason.

"Not sure, but he was trying to see if I could tell him something. What, I have no idea."

"So who takes over Palo Alto?"

"We'll promote Kofi."

"Kofi? Is he an American?" says Jason.

"Kofi Adebayo, born in Bakersfield, California. As American as apple pie my friend. Parents from Nigeria."

"He's African-American?"

Quentin says, "Shouldn't the American come first?"

"I'm sure he'll do just fine. Where'd he go to med school?"

"One of those fancy Ivy League places. He's a double doctor, MD, PhD, doctor of medicine, doctorate in computer science. He stayed on faculty for a while, then left to do a start-up. Cashed in big time. Then started another and cashed in again. He owns an island in the Caribbean."

"An island?" says Jason.

"Serial entrepreneur. He's crazy rich. He's on that top four hundred list." Quentin continues, "A real brain, computer guy."

"Most of the transplant program is computer-driven now; the surgeons are really glorified technicians," says Jason.

"Kofi can take over from Tom. He worked with him closely. We have an alternate at each place for just this type of event."

"Does he know we're involved?"

"Yes. We've already done Kofi's background check; we'll put him in as new team leader. When you get back, send me your report immediately, then I'll schedule a meeting with the president. He'll want to know."

Jason says, "Tom was not really living up to his billing. He wasn't that far in developing the facial transplants. New York was showing more promise."

Quentin swallows.

Jason continues, "I told you Tom was hyped up. He was good thirty years ago, maybe even great, but he was living on his reputation. The last reports I got from him recently were weak. The other centers were pulling away from him."

"I personally reviewed his file. He was a very creative scientist and surgeon throughout his entire career. I appointed him."

"People peak in their creativity in their twenties or thirties. After that, forget it."

"What are you trying to say?"

"Our boy Tom was way over the hill. He should have never been given the lead in Palo Alto."

Quentin replies, "I heard that's not true. Experts say that creativity occurs at any age."

"Believe what you have to, mate," says Jason.

Quentin smiles and appears relaxed. "Mate? Last time I checked, I'm the Secretary of Defense of the United States of America. You'll address me as such."

"My apology, Mr. Secretary."

"Next time you speak to me like that again, you'll be sitting at a desk in the dirtiest rat hole office I can put you, far away from the bright lights of New York and that high society girl of yours."

"Yes sir, Mr. Secretary."

"Let me know how you get on in Palo Alto." Quentin jumps into his car and speeds off.

Chapter Seven

Matthew sips his tea in an oversized white cup. "Patricia, the tea is very good."

"It's mint, your favorite."

"It's been too long since I last visited."

Patricia, "You didn't come out to Palo Alto much after we got married."

Matthew sips the tea. "I should have come out here more. Sitting here, I now feel the loss."

"He was very fond of you."

"I still feel him with me . . . When I was sixteen, I got brought home by the police. It was two a.m. Mom was frantic. She called Tom. You know what? He came right over. He got up at that hour to come and speak to me. I don't even remember what he said to me, but I remember thinking, who would get up in the middle of the night to do this? He's not my father. I thought, you know what, I'm never going to make him ever have to wake up like this ever again."

"Tom was a special man."

"He was, and I should have come out here more. I wasn't there for him when he needed me."

. . .

The tall, thin man in the flat top hat has a great view of Matthew. He looks tired. Maybe Matthew will be sensible and realize looking for Dr. Grabowski's murderer is not the way a surgeon should spend his time. The man in the flat top hat prides himself on the careful manner in which he plans and executes his murders. This business was not for amateurs. A simple surgeon need not apply. Through the window, he sees Patricia. She looks good. Beautiful. He can not hear the conversation, but he is concerned. Unfortunately, he has a feeling they will both need to be dealt with. He is never wrong.

. . .

Patricia sits across from Matthew drinking her decaf coffee. She has a good view out the window. She thinks she sees someone looking at her from across the street. The Andersons had taken an extended vacation, and the house was vacant.

Matthew hasn't seen Patricia in some time. She is thirty-four, but doesn't look a day over thirty.

Matthew sees Patricia glance at the window and asks, "What is it?"

"Nothing, just a little paranoid I guess." She grips her cup tightly.

"You look great. Still working out?" "Two hours a day, rain or shine," says Patricia.

"What are you into these days?"

"I like to change it up. Always some cardio and then weights. I'm doing NR2."

"NR2?" says Matthew.

"Nature raw runs."

"I'm afraid to ask."

"You run on dirt trails and on uneven terrain. Periodically, you stop and do pull ups on branches, try to climb trees, jump over small streams, roll large rocks. By mimicking actions we would have done when we lived in the forest, we get a workout in tune with our natural rhythm. Our bodies develop into the shape nature intended."

"Well, it seems to be working. Keep it up."

"Thanks," says Patricia. She takes a big gulp of decaf.

"How much did Tom tell you about his facial transplant work?"

"Everything. There were no secrets. The Transplant Working Group, the Secretary of Defense Quentin Taylor's involvement, the special funding. He told me all of it."

Matthew isn't surprised. Tom adored Patricia. Matthew remembers the day they were married. Tom was very happy. Despite the crazy age difference, it seemed to work.

"Anything unusual the day he died?" says Matthew.

"He was going to jog at Cypress Hill after work at the lab. He was pretty regular about it, three times a week. He wore his jogging clothes to the lab on those days to force himself to run."

"Did he run alone?"

"Yes. He had a bit of a sweet tooth and he had gained quite a few pounds of late. He was trying to run it off."

"Did he have any of his files at home?"

"No, everything was on his work computers."

"Did his pattern change in any way that morning?"

Patricia plays with the white pearl necklace while she thinks. "No, everything was routine."

"Was he concerned about anything? I know he confided in you." Matthew puts down his cup of tea.

"No, all was normal. You obviously don't think it was a heart attack."

"I wouldn't say that; it's just that with what he was working on, I want to be sure."

"The loss hasn't really sunk in yet."

"I'm going to his lab. I'll see if anyone there knows anything."

• • •

The university campus has changed little since Matthew has last seen it. Large rectangular buildings around a central courtyard. White stucco walls with the red roof tiles. Matthew walks into the large central court-yard and through the thick clay arch that rises from wide white pillars. He remembers Tom's lab well. His mother had worked for Tom as a graduate student. They had remained close and it seemed only natural that Matthew would work summers as Tom's intern.

When Matthew finally gets to the lab, he notes the equipment has been updated, but the biggest change is the students. Over the years, Tom had built up an internationally known research laboratory specializing in facial transplantation. Now that facial transplantation is hot, he attracted students from all over the world. However, there is a certain style to his lab that Matthew has never seen in any of the labs he has been in. Times are changing if this is how the students in research look. The students are mainly in their midtwenties. They seem to all dress as if they have come off the fashion pages of a hipster chic magazine. Very stylish haircuts and clothing. Dark blue, gray, or black hues. Slim fit pants. Stylish footwear. Minimalist cool. They all are very well put together. They could be at home in any private LA nightclub. Intelligent hipster. The more he looks at them, the more he thinks that phrase describes them perfectly. Intelligent hipster. The style of dress fits perfectly with the new modern lab's sleek white drawers and polished aluminum accents. It is quite different from what he remembers of his time as a graduate student. It all seems to fit: the sleek computers, cutting edge equipment, cool researchers.

Matthew looks around. A tall, smiling man approaches. The first thing Matthew notices are the gleaming white teeth. They contrast with his polished ebony skin. The skin seems to have a glow. It looks like black lacquer with an undertone of pink. A smile is permanently etched on his face.

"Kofi."

"Matthew."

"Nice to see you again."

"You haven't been by the lab in a while."

Matthew says, "You know how it is. Work, work, and more work. New York's a busy place."

"It's a difficult time to meet."

"I'm taking it hard, real hard."

"He was a great man."

"Show me around the lab."

Kofi shows Matthew the surgical robot. They have the same machine in New York; it is the standard robot for facial transplantation. Matthew is a little disappointed. He expects more from Tom's robotic surgical suite.

The three large cylindrical rods are the basis of the robot's ability to operate. They are arranged in a triangle. Off to the side is an area where the surgeon can put his hands on the joysticks. The surgeon's movements are then translated to the robotic "arms" to do the procedure at points where precision and no tremor are essential. Even the finest surgeon has a measurable tremor. It looks like Tom had added a computer link to allow remote data transmission and possible experiments with remote robotic access. Except for these minor modifications, it looks like his robot.

Kofi places a lifelike model of a face on the operating table. He punches a button labeled demo. The robot hums to life. It expertly dissects the face, removing the original face. The donor's face has already been removed from its body; usually the donor is someone killed in a car accident who donated organs to help others. The robot then prepares the blood vessels for the transplant. Cutting and cauterizing tissue. Matthew sees that the robot is performing the surgery without human assistance. The robot in New York needs more human oversight. Maybe he was disappointed too soon.

Kofi speaks quietly, "Talk to some of the students. In thirty minutes leave by the west exit. I will be parked nearby. Walk into my car and lie down in the backseat." Kofi leaves.

• • •

Jason says, "How did you get us into this restaurant? Wait list is supposed to be years."

Celerie says, "Mom's on the board of directors with a woman who helped back this place."

"The place is packed."

Celerie says, "I've been to his previous place out in LA. This is totally different."

"I heard that place was a lot flashier."

"Glitz, but the sushi was mediocre."

Jason says, "This place is the opposite of flash. Just white everywhere."

"He grew tired of the lifestyle and moved to Manhattan. Everyone expected more of the same in New York. He surprised everyone."

"Some are calling this place the best sushi bar in the world."

"All the vegetables are grown nearby, picked daily. He flies the fish in three times a day, within three hours or less of being caught. The LA place was a real hangout, a place to be seen. This place is all about the food. The only color in the restaurant is the sushi on the plates."

"This guy has re-invented himself in a way no one thought possible."

"When he was in LA, no one thought he could do this. His creativity here is just amazing."

"Hats off to him."

Celerie says, "You seem particularly happy tonight."

"I love eating sushi."

"You are a pretty good sushi eater. But that's not it, I'm sure."

"Can't I be happy to be in a wonderful restaurant with the most beautiful woman in the world. The woman who will soon be my wife?"

"You probably should, but I'm sure that's not it."

"Remember my assignment?"

"Sure."

"You remember I told you about the Facial Transplant Program we're funding?"

"Yeah, the top secret program no one knows about. The one you're not supposed to tell anyone about."

"Yeah, that's the one."

"Nothing was really happening."

"Correct, but I think Tom Grabowski was murdered."

"By who?" says Celerie.

"Don't know, not yet."

Jason looks at the menu.

"I thought it was a heart attack?" says Celerie.

"Correct."

"It's all over the news; he died of a heart attack."

"That's the prelim, but I'm going down to Palo Alto to check it out." Jason can't wait to try the spicy tuna roll.

"Doesn't seem that unusual."

"Matthew MacAulay was talking to Quentin; he got a strange vibe, like Matthew was fishing for something."

"Matthew?"

"Yes, he may be involved."

Jason and Celerie are both hungry. Large white plates with sushi arrive. The waiter is wearing all white.

"How?" says Celerie.

"We're not sure, but I'm going to find out."

Jason watches Celerie for any reaction. Her face is calm. Jason lowers his head and eats a piece of sushi. Celerie looks at him.

• • •

Kofi stops the car, and Matthew raises his head. He is surprised at their location. They are in an old industrial park. There are large concrete buildings, some of which are still active while others wait for new business tenants. The area is gritty. A transitional neighborhood. Modest lower-working-class housing cheek by jowl to large warehouses. Many of the warehouses are boarded up. Matthew has no idea where they are.

Matthew and Kofi enter a warehouse. From the outside it looks like a deserted factory. The paint is peeling from the concrete walls. The windows are covered with an inch of dirt. They enter the pitch black building. The grimy windows are blacked out. Matthew can sense that they are in a very large room. Suddenly, the lights come on. Matthew is stunned at what he sees.

Matthew knows exactly what he is looking at, but even then, he cannot believe it. It is as if he has gone to some futuristic new world. His mouth opens, and his eyes widen. Standing in front of him are two fourteen-foot-high columns made of white lacquer. In the center between the two columns, which are four feet wide, is a surgical chair. There are three brushed aluminum steps to get to the chair. It is positioned with a perfect view of the operating table. On each wide arm of the chair are two joysticks. A large video monitor is five feet above the front of this chair. It is on a hydraulic arm which can be raised and lowered into place when operating. This is done by voice commands. Matthew marvels at the design. It looks like a Swedish design studio has created this robot. It is beautiful, a real work of art.

This robotic surgical suite is like nothing he could have imagined. Occasionally, they have international design competitions featuring ergonomics in the modern surgical suite. This looks like it was taken from one of those designs and implemented flawlessly. This is a true masterpiece of medical design and engineering. Matthew realizes he was holding his breath up until this moment. He then looks to the left and sees the operating room table and the three articulating probes positioned. He is looking at the next generation robotics facility for facial transplantation.

Matthew moves to get a closer look.

"Good afternoon, Matthew."

The voice is that of a young woman. It is calm, confident, and reassuring.

Without skipping a beat, Matthew says, "Hi, what should I call you?"

"I am Alice."

"Hi, Alice."

Kofi says, "I did all the computer programming. Alice has some facial recognition and voice commands."

"So this is what Tom was doing," says Matthew.

"He began to have some concerns about the military funding. That's all he would tell me."

"That's when he started to build this?"

"He would do all his real facial transplant work here. The university was a decoy."

"What was he afraid of?" asks Matthew.

"Tom was killed, man."

"I thought as much."

"I was there."

"What?" says Matthew.

"That's right. I was right there."

Kofi points to the area behind Alice. The area is hidden from view by the column of the robot. Matthew walks behind to see the hidden room. Then he comes around and stands looking at Kofi.

Kofi says, "T came to me that afternoon. I have been doing the transplants or first assists here with him for a while. He said we were going to do something different. I would stay hidden, and if I heard him say, 'I really need to think this through,' that was my signal to come out. If not, I was to stay hidden no matter what I heard."

"And you agreed to this?" says Matthew.

"It gets better—he hands me a gun. T says, if I have to come out, I'll need it." Kofi takes a deep breath and then continues, "I was in position and T comes in. I had a bad angle, but I saw one guy. He was mean-looking. You could see he was angry at the world, hair trigger. He was short, squat. He had the palest gray eyes."

"I've met those pale gray eyes."

"He looked frightening," says Kofi.

"Continue."

"I couldn't see any more. They either did a transplant or took the face off someone. I heard them take a titanium canister. After the procedure, I heard the voices raised. I could hear T was not happy. I heard the voices getting louder and then T said 'I really need to . . .' He just paused. I was ready to come out. I knew there was trouble. Then he said 'I really need to just get out of here.' He was telling me to stay put. After they left I went out. The place was clean, no trace they were even there. When I went to Alice, they had taken her hard drive and swapped it out with a blank." Kofi walks over to the large column and pulls open a panel. There are many different colors of wires. The circuits blink. "To know this module and have it ready to swap out . . . These guys were very well-prepared. I knew that when T did not show up. . ."

Kofi's voice becomes heavy with emotion, his eyes teary.

"T was a good man." Kofi snaps the panel closed. "I think he knew they were going to kill him. He didn't call me because he knew we would both be dead."

"How many people were there?" says Matthew.

"I only saw the short mean guy, but I heard T and four other men. One was the boss. He didn't talk much, and he had a hat on, a fedora."

"Tom had progressed further than any of the other two centers. Why keep it secret?"

"I am not sure. I told him we needed to at least share our Steriazol with the others."

"He had advanced the Steriazol?" says Matthew.

Kofi commands, "Alice, demonstrate transplant."

"With pleasure. Full trans?" says Alice.

"Let's show him the works, full facial transplant."

With that, the beautiful piece of architecture whirred into life. The robot produced a 3-D hologram of a face to be transplanted. For the next sixty minutes, Matthew watched as Alice demonstrated her capabilities. For the final closure, the robotic arm carefully poured the Steriazol on the suture lines and recipient bed. Matthew thought what he saw next was time-lapsed photography.

Kofi, anticipating his thought, says, "This is real time. This is a hologram of a real patient. This is what we can do."

Within minutes of pouring the Steriazol, the wounds seemed to heal as if by magic. The incisions disappeared and the blood, nerve, and veins were joined. Perfect healing. The patient got off the table and walked out of the operating room. The hologram was lifelike.

Matthew claps spontaneously. "Bravo, Bravo."

Alice says, "I'm so glad you liked my demonstration, Dr. MacAulay."

"Call me Matthew."

Matthew has his answer; this is why Tom was killed. Tom had done it. But how could he have been so foolish, so reckless? He had developed the robotic transplant technology and upgraded the Steriazol. Tom had brought in Kofi and his work eclipsed the other groups. Matthew was sure Houston had no idea of this; he sure didn't. He thought they were ten years away from some modest improvements, nothing like this. What Tom had developed was the perfect facial transplant. No scarring, no downtime. Presumably, this could be done on anyone, anytime. The possibilities were limitless. Tom had done it.

Kofi says, "I told him we could not keep this secret; it was too big. He finally agreed but said it was complicated. He wanted a little more time. He was going to bring you out to see it. He was going to call you, get your advice."

"It makes no sense. He had the breakthrough we were all after. Tom should have made his work available."

"He was going to hold a meeting. Just the Transplant Working Group: you, Michael, Liam. He wasn't sure he should turn it over to the military. He was considering publishing it all online. Make it available to all scientists throughout the world at once. Put the world on a level playing field."

"Are you sure your modifications of the Steriazol can do what I just saw consistently?" says Matthew.

"Guaranteed. Our tests confirm the healing and the ability of all microvessels to seek each other out and heal within minutes. It builds on the work of Dr. Liam Rasulov down at your institution."

"This is truly revolutionary. This is disruptive technology."

"There are some caveats. It has not been tested in all conditions. We were mainly doing midface and lower face."

"How about the more difficult complete facial transplant that you just showed?" says Matthew.

"We did very few complete trans. That was our next step, to do a few more."

"Complete trans would be incredible."

"Yes, the complete trans is the ultimate, but carries the ultimate risk."

"How so?" says Matthew.

"We know that the transplanted face must not be subjected to heat more than eighty degrees Fahrenheit for more than thirty minutes. If this occurs the protein bonds break down. The face completely separates from the patient. It will dissolve into a gelatinous mass."

"What happens?"

"We did a nose early on and the patient was from Florida. We got a call his nose had melted off."

"Melted off?"

"In a heat wave. His wife noted he was sweating from the forehead and nose, which was weird, for about thirty minutes. He felt nothing and then it just dissolved."

"Could you save it?" says Matthew.

"No, we had to do some local flaps to reconstruct the nose. We were lucky it was just the nose. If it were the whole face, a complete trans, it would have been a disaster."

"Why the sweating?"

Kofi, "The largest concentration of sweat glands on the face is on the forehead. When the temperature rises, the first sign of impending transplant failure is sweating from the forehead. We are not sure why, but the transplanted part of the face feels no sensation. We were working on that when T passed."

"No sensation at all?"

"No sensation on the transplanted face. They don't even feel the sweat on the transplanted forehead. When the temperature rises, the complete transplant recipient starts to sweat on the forehead. The sweating increases, and at that point, if the recipient does not cool the face, the breakdown begins. Once the process starts, it is irreversible. Just like the nose, but due to the size of tissue involved in a complete facial transplant, the result is far more serious. The vessels and tissue of the entire face just melt away."

"Tell me this has not happened," says Matthew.

"Thankfully, no, but we have not had a patient keep a complete trans for more than seven days. We always reverse them."

Matthew walks up to Alice and sits in the chair.

Kofi says, "Authorize Matthew, single use, model head."

Alice comes alive. The chair is very comfortable and in no time Matthew is immersed in the operation.

Kofi says, "Seventy-five minutes, not bad."

"That was fun. I could get it down to sixty."

"I think you could."

"Even right now, that was a full face transplant, no scars in seventy-five minutes!"

"We're not bad out here."

Matthew says, "Alice is amazing; this is no ordinary robot. The inputs are flawless."

Alice says, "Thanks."

Matthew says, "The pure fun of cutting and sewing—it reminded me of why I got into this business. Partway through I forget about everything. It was just me and the patient."

Kofi says, "We're surgeons. That's what it's all about."

Matthew says, "He called me."

"Tom called you?"

"The day he died. He didn't leave a message. If I had taken the call . . ."

"Don't play that game. I wonder should I have done things differently. Should I have even helped him in the first place? I should have stopped this when he handed me the gun. We're surgeons, man. If I had said we're not doing this, this is crazy, we need to go to the police, Tom may be alive today."

Matthew says, "If he had left a message, given me any idea his life was in danger, I would have been out here. I would have come out here."

"He knew you were there for him. He spoke of you all the time. He was proud of the man you had become. Maybe that's why he did it this way. He didn't want to involve us. He knew the dangers. I think he protected us to the end."

"What Tom has achieved here . . . I mean, it's just, I don't know what to say."

Kofi says, "We were doing big things."

"How were Patricia and Tom doing?"

Chapter Eight

"I want to know all the details surrounding Dr. Tom Grabowski's heart attack."

Quentin says, "Mr. President, at this point it appears to be a tragic heart attack. Nothing more."

The president looks over to the television. His college team is losing. A perfect season in the balance. He missed the last play and the mute button is on so he can't hear the play-by-play.

"I need to tell my Chief of Staff to make sure I get out to a few more games next year."

Quentin says, "Our college is going to lose their perfect season."

"It's not over til it's over." The President looks at Quentin. "Any intel?"

"We've had our guys pull his medical records; they were able to get into his doctor's electronic medical records. His cholesterol was up; he was prediabetic, a lot overweight."

Carter Middleton picks up the heavy briefing book and leafs through to a page. "Says he smoked?"

"Dr. Grabowski liked his cigars. I apologize for the briefing book. We couldn't get it any smaller."

"No apology needed. We're in the West Wing of the White House, the Oval Office. The most famous office in the world. It's my duty to serve the people. To serve the people, I need all the facts."

"Well said. I get no greater pleasure than sitting in this office with you, serving the people of the United States of America. It's funny how things end up. I never expected to be here."

"I never expected to have you here, old friend. The tragic death of your predecessor, George H. Brown, was very stressful. But you jumped in and are doing a great job."

"Thanks. I always get a rush out of coming into this office. I don't know what it is—the beautiful silk carpet with that big presidential seal, the furniture, the history."

The president looks out the east doors to the rose garden.

"It's the tradition. There's real power here. You can feel it."

Quentin nods.

The president says, "Nothing suspicious then?"

"Unidentified witness saw Dr. Grabowski collapse while jogging up Cypress Hill."

"Unidentified?"

"It was called in. We couldn't trace from where."

"When will the body be here?" says the president.

"It will be flown to George Washington and an autopsy conducted in a few days. We don't expect any surprises. I know how important this file is to you, so I've sent a man to do some on-the-ground investigating. He will report back shortly."

"Keep me informed. I don't have to remind you, Transplant Working Group is a game changer. TWG success puts us right back at the top."

"Yes, Mr. President."

"In a few years when they perfect the face transplants, we will be able to put any face we want on anyone."

"Yes, Mr. President."

"We will be the leader in intelligence gathering. We will develop a legion of perfect spies, able to impersonate anyone."

"Not quite, we have to take their face first. From the reports I have read, we're far away from creating transplants that have no telltale signs."

"I agree. I'll have long left office and been forgotten. But that's the greatness of this office. I will have started a program that will put America back on top, one of the greatest acts of a sitting president. And I don't even need to get the credit, but history will remember. True service to country."

Quentin says, "We're spending a great deal of money on this research. Some of it could be spent on projects that might have some benefits in the next two years. Face transplants may not generate anything more than research papers for these guys."

"That's not how a president thinks. I know re-election is two years away. You don't put a man on the moon with that kind of thinking. Greatness, that's what gets a man on the moon."

"Yes, Mr. President."

"The world will know to never again underestimate the resiliency, hard work, and creativity of the American people. We innovate. We lead."

As Quentin Taylor gets up to leave, the president unmutes the television.

He says, "Stay. Let's root for our alma mater."

. . .

Jason stops his rental car at the top of Cypress Hill. He then walks to the area where Dr. Grabowski collapsed. The hill is small, more mound than hill. The dirt path has been well-worn by runners, cyclists, and backpackers. It is not that steep a grade. But then again, for a man with a weak heart, it may have been just the tipping point to cause a heart attack.

Jason turns to go back to his car; about forty feet away, he sees a broken branch. He is looking in that direction because it is the exact spot he would have chosen if he were a sniper. The perfect spot to remain hidden but have a clear line of sight to a runner at the top of the hill. He walks over and looks at the branch. His first thought is that whoever was in this area had broken the branch walking by. He looks at the branch again. Then he bends over to smell it. It looks like it has been burned. Now a few days later, it has bent as the burned segment no longer can hold the weight of the leaves. Jason looks at the burn pattern. It is a regular sphere. Not from a rifle or other firearm.

Jason smiles to himself as he thinks, *We have ourselves a case.*

Chapter Nine

Matthew sees Aly outside of Ryan's hospital room.

"Doc MacAulay." Aly touches his arm and he stops.

"You'd like to speak to me?"

"If you don't mind."

"Of course."

They move to a hall a little farther away from Ryan's room.

Aly asks, "Do you have any idea when he's getting out?"

"As I told you both, I really can't be sure. I'm still trying to save the flap."

Aly has her hands tightly clenched in front of her in an awkward manner. "We have some money issues."

"How bad?"

"We're going to lose the house."

Matthew takes her hands. "You need him back working, I understand. I can put you in touch with social work. They might be able to help."

"It's too late for all that. I just need this to be over. We need our life back."

"Okay, I hear you. I'll get on with it. The flap is still alive. If it looks halfway decent, we're nearly home."

"We need to get out of here. I'm feeling trapped."

Matthew nods. "I get it. I'm going to try to speed things up."

"Don't tell him I came by."

"Aly, thanks. I needed to know this."

Matthew enters Ryan's room.

"Doc MacAulay."

"Ryan. You're looking a little too comfy in this room. "

"This room is nice, it's so big. I'm really glad you got it for me."

"You've earned it. You served your country with distinction and have paid a heavy price."

"I know you got my back."

"How's the pain on the face?"

"Pain's totally gone. I feel great."

Unfortunately, Matthew no longer needs to look at the wound. Ryan has told him all he needs to know. The flap is now dead. The nerve endings have died, so there are no fibers to transmit pain sensation to the brain. Matthew carefully pulls the dressing back. The blue-black mass of tissue in the middle of Ryan's face is swelling.

Matthew speaks softly. "It didn't make it." He replaces the dressing and slumps into a chair beside the bed.

"Doc MacAulay, you look like you lost your best friend."

Matthew gives a half smile. "Surgeons have fragile egos. We don't deal with failure well."

"We've got other options right?" says Ryan.

"Sure we do. I'll take you back right now for a quick procedure to remove this flap. I will put a dressing on the area and prepare for round two," says Matthew.

"We have not yet begun to fight."

"Who said that, a famous pop star?" Matthew jokes.

Ryan laughs. "My son told me he heard it said by one of his video game characters."

They both laugh loudly. Suddenly, Ryan becomes serious. He lowers his voice. "I have only one concern."

"What is that, Ryan?"

"When we do the face transplant, will I be as handsome as you?"

Matthew smiles. "We both know the answer to that. No."

They laugh again.

· · ·

"Why are you talking to me about this?" Sarah's jaw clenches as she speaks.

"There are not a lot of people I can talk to about it."

"I'm not really involved."

The operating room day has ended and only Sarah and Matthew remain in the room. The nurses have headed home. Matthew sits on a stool, while Sarah is at the anesthetic machine.

"We were involved in a murder and a patient died on the table. We witnessed the bodies being removed," says Matthew.

"I know. I feel bad, but it is what it is."

"How can you say that?"

Sarah says, "I'm tired. I just want to go home and stay low until this thing blows over."

Matthew says, "We need to find out who is behind all this."

"Did you see Mr. Glock? These guys are criminals. They may or may not be a part of some government, ours or foreign. It doesn't really matter. As soon as they realize we're not causing any trouble, this thing will go away."

"And we let them all go free?"

"People like this don't die peacefully in their beds of old age. They'll get what they deserve, if not today then tomorrow."

Matthew says, "Someone found out about our advanced transplant work. They tipped off someone. I knew it was going to be hard to keep our work secret."

"Hard. How in the world did you think you could take government funds and keep it a secret? Do you know how many people in government had to approve this thing to make it happen? The amount of people involved made secrecy impossible."

"It seemed like a good idea at the time."

"Any government bureaucrat who was signing those checks for the project would know that this was not regular university funding. I'm almost positive your extra money was coming out of some military or intelligence budget. Some committee had to approve that."

"I wonder who we were supposed to transplant. I think if I can find that out, I can find Tom's killer."

"Looking for the killer will result in a bad end. You're just a surgeon. I don't mean to burst your bubble, but you're not a detective.

You're not Sherlock Holmes. I'm not trying to be rude or put you down, but you cut and sew, that's it. You don't have the skills to investigate a complex murder."

"That's hard."

"It sounds hard, but it's the truth, Matthew."

"You might be surprised what can be accomplished if I put my mind to work on a problem."

"That's surgeon's ego talking. This time it will get you killed."

Matthew asks, "You want to hear my theory?"

Sarah puts away the drugs and her stethoscope in the cupboard beside the anesthetic machine. She punches in the codes to log out and lock the machine. "Sure, go ahead, Sherlock."

"To do what we saw that night, across two sites in Palo Alto and New York, requires vast resources. Kofi thought Tom transplanted or harvested a face in Palo Alto. My guess is Tom harvested a face from someone. That was the face we were going to transplant at our center. The person we were going to change the identity of had to be involved in something criminal, or was about to be charged for something criminal."

"That's probably right, but why would Tom do the harvest and then refuse to do the transplant?"

"That's what makes no sense. He'd either do nothing or do both."

"It's clear that the person we were going to transplant was trying to disguise himself. He was going into hiding."

Matthew says, "It had to be something that would put him away for the rest of his life. Otherwise, it isn't worth it. This drastically limits the people who we need to consider. Net worth is extremely high. Only a select few could even think of doing this. It's a small group of hedge fund managers, bankers, CEOs, computer guys, and senior leaders in foreign countries where they have stolen major dollars. That's it."

"I agree."

"The guy we were transplanting was not foreign. He was American or at least North American."

"Sure," says Sarah.

"So it's very simple. We go to the library and look for high-net-worth people in trouble or involved in controversial business activities.

They will have disappeared recently or just dropped off the media spotlight. That list can't be too long. As long as we investigate this in a library, nobody will know we're still pursuing it. They will assume we have decided to drop the whole thing. Nothing's happened so far."

"Correct," says Sarah.

"So we're safe. Trust me, these guys are long gone."

"So all we're going to do is visit the New York Public Library?"

Matthew, "Exactly."

Matthew was glad Sarah was going to help him with the investigation into Tom's murder. She was in just as deep as he was. She should take some responsibility.

The hallway outside the operating room is crowded. Usually there are a few relatives milling around. Today it is chockablock with people. Two healthy post-op patients have just died of unexplained heart attacks. Some relatives are loudly crying; others talking in hushed tones. They all have blank looks on their faces.

The man in the black fedora spots Matthew immediately. He has chosen well and been a little lucky. A few of the men from one of the grieving families wear black hats. No one pays any attention to the tall, thin man in the black fedora. It may be worn slightly lower than the others, but they are all distraught. No one will notice. Each family thinks the man in the fedora is with the other. He can't understand what all the fuss is about; both men were very ordinary. Nothing special. No real loss. In fact, Luka was an idiot. The world is a much better place without him.

Matthew forces his way through the hallway. The hospital will review all post-op procedures to see if anything was amiss. It is virtually unheard of to have two deaths, same cause, so close together. In his entire career, Matthew has never seen or heard of such an occurrence. Some relatives have already started talking lawsuit. The university president is on the scene. The hospital CEO is present. The university president can be heard consoling relatives and assuring everyone the university is doing everything in its power during this crisis.

Matthew passes the university president and nods hello. Matthew has too much on his mind to stop. Strange things can happen in surgery, but for two healthy men to die at the same time? Matthew would like to avoid this crowd. However, this is the only way out of the ward.

The man in the black fedora is going to kill Matthew MacAulay. It will bring him no joy. It will bring him no sadness. It is just something he has to do. He knows this one should feel different, but it does not. He sees Matthew and begins to approach him. He is very excited; it feels almost sexual. The small pin he carries in his right palm is a work of art. It is a two-inch-long needle with a hollow core. It is very difficult to have this manufactured. The mechanical specifications are exacting because the point is so fine it is invisible to the human eye.

He has to be careful with the point. If anyone looks closely at his right hand, they may notice a thick flesh-toned pad on his palm with a needle flat against it. As soon as he pushes the small button, the needle will become erect. The needle will penetrate Matthew's skin and the plunger will inject the microdroplets. The amount is less than two grains of salt. Eight hours later Matthew will be dead. It will be relatively painless. Matthew's muscles will violently constrict; it will be over in two minutes. Maybe it will not be so painless, but less pain than Matthew is causing him with his inquiries.

A relative thinks he recognizes the tall thin man in the black fedora. Sam is an assembler for a plastics company. Thirty-two years on the job, he rarely missed a day. Sam is sure that it is Joe Khan. He had retired a few years ago. Sam would recognize that walk anywhere. Sam needs a better look at his face. He pushes through the crowd.

"Joe."

Sam gently puts his hand on the man's right upper arm. Sam cannot be sure of the man's face; his black fedora is so low on his forehead.

"It's me, Sam Zoldt. Your old line mate."

The man with the black fedora is not expecting this. Sam nearly causes him to poke himself with the needle. What will he do if Sam puts out his hand to shake?

"No, I'm sorry. You must have the wrong person."

Matthew is almost through the crowd. The man in the fedora fears he may lose his opportunity. He puts his hand up to the fedora as Sam tries to get a better look at him.

Sam is unsure. He looks like Joe, but he seems to be cold, a little aloof. Sam could be mistaken.

"You did the evening shift. We'd sometimes overlap."

"No." The man in the black fedora moves quickly away.

Matthew stops to ask the charge nurse if she has any ideas how these deaths occurred.

The man in the black fedora is now close to Matthew. The pin is ready for insertion. The fact that now, if someone jostles him, the needle could prick his own skin adds to the thrill. He had tried to get his associates to do this job. They all refused.

Looking down at the erect needle is stimulating. The beauty of the needle is that the point is so fine it will penetrate clothing and skin, leaving no mark. Better yet, it will not stimulate any pain fibers. He is two feet from Matthew. He rotates his palm outward. Now anyone looking will clearly see the small needle in his right hand. It will only be visible for a few seconds. He moves to plunge the needle into Matthew.

Daniela is wracked with guilt. Mary and Luka are long-time family friends. Mary and Luka had been married for eight years. Luka had been kind to Daniela, comforted her when her own husband had left last year. Daniela would now comfort Mary in her time of need. Mary's husband had been a good man; Daniela was the one who had caused Luka to sin. She would do anything Mary wanted. In one way she was relieved. She had always worried Mary would find out.

"I'm sorry." Daniela's tears flow.

"It's hard on all of us. Luka was my world."

"He loved you so very much," says Daniela.

"He was a great father, a great husband. It's just such a sudden . . ." Mary is too overcome to talk anymore.

Mary's four-year-old daughter is dressed all in black. Too young to understand, she stands by her mom. Daniela remains silent, transfixed by Mary's grief. Daniela wants to confess, but how can she? It was a crazy time–her husband had just left her for a bartender barely out of high school. What good would telling Mary do anyway? The little girl looks up at Daniela, directly into her eyes. Daniela sobs loudly. Maybe this is the punishment.

The wages of sin is death. Daniela feels the pain. Luka is dead. Death cleanses the soul. Death frees all guilt. Luka was a strong man. Virile. He ate good. He worked out. The heart attack was out of the clear blue sky. The doctors even said so. What would be her penance? Daniela cannot bear the pain, the shame, the guilt. She begins to wail.

At the precise moment that the pin is going to enter Matthew's side, Daniela lurches upward. She doesn't feel a thing. The man in the black fedora looks on in shock but remains silent. Daniela has taken the needle right in the buttock. Even in his shock, he admires her firm round buttocks. The thin navy blue skirt fits Daniela well. Daniela hugs Mary.

Matthew is happy to be past the crowd. Matthew pushes the button and waits at the elevator. Beside him is a man in a black fedora. Matthew notes he is wearing his hat very low. The man is slightly tilted away from Matthew, hands in his pockets.

Can he strangle Matthew? It is a foolish thought. He is in a large group of people and could not hope to escape. Maybe in the elevator? The man in the black fedora knows he would stand no chance. Matthew is much younger. He knows everything about Matthew; he has done his research. They enter the elevator. Is there anything left in the needle? He knows the answer is no. It is a precision device, single use only.

The elevator opens. Matthew turns to exit and the man turns away from Matthew. For some reason Matthew gets a cold chill that runs down his back. Matthew quickly gets off the elevator. He has an urge to move away. The man in the fedora veers right to avoid the security cameras. As he walks down the street, he thinks that it is just as well. Maybe he shouldn't have tried to kill Dr. Matthew MacAulay anyways. It would bring too much police scrutiny. Fate has always been good to him. This is a sign. His mind wanders back to the woman with the nice firm buttocks.

Daniela hugs Mary tightly. Daniela feels much better. She didn't kill Luka; he died of a heart attack. She feels badly about her affair with Luka, but what could she do? It only lasted a year. He was young for a heart attack, but these things happen. No one is punishing Daniela for her sins. She releases Mary from the hug.

Daniela says, "Sometimes good people die. Sometimes it just doesn't make sense."

Mary asks, "But why did it have to be him? He never did anything bad. Why couldn't it be someone else?"

Chapter Ten

Erin Rogers is a middle-aged woman. She is bony with a lot of sharp edges. Her pleasant smile and short clipped speech show she is all business. She has thin lips, a small mouth set on a very wide face. Her face is not particularly remarkable, except for her pointy nose. She would have been at home in any university setting, maybe as a professor of literature.

"Mr. Cooper, your hunch proved spot on."

"Fantastic," says Jason.

"We ran some tests on the tree branch. It was a high-energy-pulse device that caused the burn pattern."

Jason subconsciously rubs his nose. The heavy smell of formaldehyde is nauseating. "A laser?"

"Not exactly."

"Then what?"

Erin says, "I have already communicated with some of your higher ups. I'm impressed, you're Yankee White, the highest security clearance given."

"You're Yankee White too."

"Yankee White through and through."

"So we can both talk freely."

"I'm sure you're not thrilled to be in the morgue of George Washington, so I'll be quick."

"What happened to Grabowski?" says Jason.

"The burn pattern on the branch was confirmed as a high-energy weapon, so I re-examined the heart."

"And?" says Jason.

"Have a look." Erin pulls open the drawer.

Tom's body lies naked inside. Jason tries to look only at Tom's chest. Jason looks around at the metal sinks and cabinets. The floors are smooth white, easy to hose down to remove bodily fluids.

Jason says, "I don't see anything."

"Neither did I until you found the branch. Now take a look."

Erin turns off the lights. She shines a light on Tom's chest. Immediately, the area of skin overlying the heart glows pale red. It is a perfect circle.

"This displays the mild tissue damage caused by the focused energy beam on the skin. It's undetectable to the naked eye."

"Someone focused energy on his heart?" says Jason.

Erin flips on the lights. Then she pulls back a flap of skin on Tom's chest. She casually reaches into Tom's chest and removes his heart. She puts the heart on a tray.

"The human heart is like a small grapefruit. It is a muscle with four chambers. The heart looks grossly normal."

Erin again turns off the lights and shines the light on the heart. "See the red glow. That's the left ventricle. The heart chamber that pumps the blood to the body. The same perfect circle."

"Wow."

"No doubt, Dr. Tom Grabowski was killed. A high-energy-pulse weapon was used to stop his heart. Unless you were specifically looking for it, this would be classified as a garden variety heart attack. That's what I thought initially."

"Who has this technology?" says Jason.

Jason's phone chimes, alerting him that he's received a text message.

"Sorry, I have to take this."

"No problem, you guys keep us all safe."

Jason moves to a corner of the morgue to read the text. Jason's fiancée, Celerie, sent him a text with a photo of herself. The text says: Get back to New York. Come over and make dinner. I'm the dessert. Jason takes a second look at the photo and swallows hard.

"Sorry about that; it couldn't wait."

"No problem. Whoever did this was cutting edge. They had to calculate the distance from the energy weapon to the subject. Too close and burn marks on the clothes and chest would have been a dead giveaway."

Jason cringes at "dead giveaway." Maybe it is her morgue humor.

"Too far away and the energy would have been dispersed over a larger area, no arrhythmia."

Erin plops the heart back into Tom's chest and replaces the flap of skin. She pushes hard and the body drawer slides closed. The clang echoes in the room.

• • •

"We are the only ones with this technology," says the White House Chief of Staff.

The implications of the statement hang in the room. "How can this weapon system induce heart attacks?" says the president's advisor on foreign affairs.

All the people sitting at the table have the president's complete trust. With the surprising developments, the president had no choice. He had to call this emergency meeting in the Oval Office.

"The weapon system develops pulsed energy waves that can be focused very precisely. When focused on cardiac muscle, the conduction pathways of the heart are short circuited. The signals that usually go to the heart and tell it to beat regularly are stopped. This leads to an arrhythmia, an irregular beating of the heart." Gilbert Lee rubs his left cheek and continues, "The heart cannot pump blood to the vital organs. Sudden death."

Gilbert Lee is the president's special advisor on physics and technology. He works closely with the military on innovation in weapons systems. Gilbert had been positive they were the only ones with this technology.

"I thought we were the only ones with this technology?" says Edith Clarke.

As Director of the CIA, Edith should know if anyone else has the weapon system. She seems clueless.

Gilbert Lee says, "We did as well; we knew a few of the other countries may have had intel that we had developed it, but we thought they were all at least ten years or more from developing their own system. It's incredibly complex."

In his early sixties, the president is still very trim and fit. Tall and thin, he looks the part of president, but these long meetings are beginning to wear on him. Gracie, his wife of thirty-seven years, wants him to slow down. She honestly wants him to quit after his first term, not run for re-election. He is popular, and although he grants her most of her wishes, he is running. He loves the job—they are working on things that will change the United States of America. He has to see it through.

President Middleton says, "So, Quentin, we know that Tom was murdered."

Quentin says, "The examination of the body is conclusive."

"We're lucky to have such a bright young officer as Jason Cooper on our team, or we would have been under the assumption that it was a heart attack."

"That's why I chose him, Mr. President, and why I took the steps to uncover this."

President Middleton asks, "Who is behind the murder?"

"We are actively pursuing some leads, Mr. President."

"We don't have any idea, is that it?"

Edith Clarke jumps in. "We have a number of scenarios. One, a foreign power has infiltrated our military, gained access to our energy weapon technology, and copied it. They also gained access to our facial transplant program."

"They gained access to two of our most secure programs?" asks the White House Chief of Staff. He looks directly at Edith Clarke.

"They would have needed help. We are operating under the assumption that someone within the transplant program or a high-clearance government employee is passing on secrets," says Edith.

"A spy?" says the president.

Quentin says, "We think that is the most likely scenario. We are investigating all the members as we speak. Nothing so far."

The president asks, "Do we think they know about The Binary Sequence?"

Gilbert Lee answers, "All indications are that it has not been compromised."

The Chief of Staff adds, "No one in the facial transplant program is aware of it. They couldn't pass on the information."

"Is the traitor in this room?" says the president.

All participants remain silent. Quentin bows his head. What an embarrassing comment for Carter Middleton to make. An awkward moment, but the president has a point. Only the people sitting at this table know the whole picture. Only they know the power of The Binary Sequence.

"No chance of that, Mr. President," says Quentin.

Edith agrees. "All in this room have been cleared."

The president says, "I don't need to remind any of you of the importance of this project. This is a game changer. This is as big as it gets. This is why the American people give us their incredible trust. Do this right and the world will once again understand the hard work, resiliency, and creativity of the American people."

The foreign affairs advisor turns to Quentin. "Looks like he is testing his election material. Isn't the election two years away?"

Quentin smiles.

. . .

"We know all these people." Sarah pushes her chair back from the computer and reclines.

The library is very busy. Matthew is bent directly behind Sarah's chair in a very confined space. They talk softly.

"You're right. All these guys with this kind of money have been in the news," says Matthew.

Sarah sits browsing the computer. She is looking at international newspapers. She scans the headlines at remarkable speed. Matthew's face keeps brushing into her hair as people pass behind him.

Matthew says, "This isn't getting us anywhere. Maybe you were right and this is a waste of time."

Sarah continues to tap on the keyboard. "Not so soon. We still have a few financial papers to look at."

"I'm sure the guy who died on the table was not one of these guys."

"I agree."

Matthew says, "Type in Eastern Europe money men. I think we need to look at expats farther away."

Sarah turns around, and her hair brushes across his entire face.

"Sorry, I didn't mean to do that."

"It's quite all right, we're in pretty tight here. We need to include Australia, South America, even Asia."

Matthew opens his knapsack. He has brought in a couple of orange sodas, and he offers one to Sarah.

"Can we drink that in here?"

"I won't tell if you don't. It's made from organic juices, my favorite."

"Thanks."

She looks at the label.

"Not right now," says Sarah and hands it back.

"Suit yourself."

Matthew drinks while Sarah vigorously types on the computer. Matthew notices that Sarah's white hair seems to glow under the lights of the library. It is the first time he can see it is pure white. He tries to remember the medical term for it. Premature something or other. Sarah gives a long sigh. Matthew's nose is almost resting on her head. Sarah turns around.

She says, "This is no use. I am not sure we are going about this the right way."

"It was a long shot, but you saw the patient yourself. He was white, male, late fifties, early sixties."

"I think we can't get too caught up on age, or even ethnicity. We could be off by a lot on the age depending on how he took care of himself."

"You could be right."

Sarah turns her chair around to face Matthew.

"Where'd you grow up?" says Sarah.

"Where did that come from?"

Sarah uncrosses her legs and lolls her head back.

"I don't know. I think we need a break, a change of pace."

Matthew says, "Early days near Palo Alto, so I'm a California boy. Yourself?"

"I grew up in Chicago. Lots of Swedes settled there. My parents are from Gullholmen."

"Small village in Sweden."

"How do you know it?" says Sarah.

"Aren't all villages in Sweden small?"

"Ha, Ha." Sarah continues, "No, my origins are from that small fishing village in Sweden. My parents took me back at fourteen, and it was beautiful. My hair was already all white by then. I stuck out like a sore thumb in Chicago. The thing I most remember is seeing all the village kids my age with white hair."

"I know what it is to be on the outs as a kid. I had it rough growing up. My mom was a single parent. I grew up quickly; kids can be cruel at that age."

"Kids can be cruel. The teasing was nonstop. My parents were really supportive. They told me my hair was a gift, that only special people had it. Mom and Dad's thirtieth anniversary is next year. I want to be there for it. I'm going to surprise them with a trip to Gullholmen. My brother and his wife are coming as well."

"My mom worked two jobs to make ends meet. It's the old cliché, hardworking single mom, barely making it. Tom was around a lot."

Matthew's cell phone rings. "Hi?"

Amanda Soto, his operating room nurse, is on the other end. When Amanda asks if he is alone, Matthew looks at Sarah and says, "No, I'm with someone."

Amanda tells him to come alone, immediately, and not to tell anyone where he is going. Amanda hangs up.

Matthew puts the phone back in his pocket. "Sorry, something's come up. Keep working, and I'll be back in an hour."

Within no time, he is on his way to Amanda's house, wondering what has prompted her mysterious call.

· · ·

Celerie has a modest apartment. It is eighteen hundred square feet. She bought the flat because of its stunning view of Central Park. She had the whole place gutted and a friend of hers did the interior design work for free. The results were impressive with high-end finishes throughout. The apartment was featured on a program showing how to maximize small spaces.

Celerie says, "You got back here pretty quick."

"Your photo had its intended effect. I couldn't stop seeing it in my mind all the way back."

Celerie sits on the sofa. Jason is making dinner.

"What are you making?"

"It's a surprise."

Celerie sits up to try to see the countertop. "All I can smell is red meat."

"It's Frogo."

"Frogo?"

"I'm experimenting. It's a North African dish. Basically beef in a rich sauce."

"Sounds good." Celerie browses a magazine.

Celerie, "We're going to my parents next weekend."

"Whose birthday is it?" says Jason.

"No one's, we're going to visit, have fun."

"With your parents?"

Jason cuts the large chunks of beef into cubes.

"Very funny, just don't forget," says Celerie as she flips pages.

"These models are all too thin. The clothes hang off them. They look like little boys."

"Seriously, I could be busy. The case is heating up."

Celerie looks up from the magazine. "Don't miss this—everyone will be there."

"I think Matthew is selling secrets."

"Come on." Celerie closes the magazine.

"I think he murdered his mentor."

"Matthew. Murder. No way."

"I can't go into details, but I think the guy is guilty. I have a hunch."

"Never," says Celerie.

Jason puts some garlic and oil into the pan. "How can you be so sure?"

"I just don't think Matt would be involved in anything like that."

"Pass me the coriander." Jason looks at her.

Celerie goes to the spice rack. "We're out."

Jason says, "Not good."

"I'll run out and get some." Celerie puts on her shoes. "Be back in ten."

As soon as the door closes, Jason goes to Celerie's bedroom. Behind the row of books, he puts his hand on the diary. Jason opens the diary. He quickly reads some sections; other parts he only reads a sentence or two. He grimaces. Thirty minutes later Jason hears the door open.

"Back," says Celerie.

Jason puts the diary back. He flushes the toilet and then goes into the kitchen.

Celerie says, "Coriander."

"Thanks." Jason finishes the meal.

Chapter Eleven

The modest bungalow on the street with no trees has aluminum siding that is peeling, but the grass is neatly trimmed.

Amanda opens the door, and it is obvious she has been crying.

"Hey, what's wrong?"

Her olive complexion is pale. Her eyes are red. She rejects his hug and leads Matthew to the kitchen.

The large window allows the bright sunlight to warm the room. Amanda is obviously upset, and Matthew decides that the best approach is to give her time. He puts his arm around her. She removes his arm and sits at the table.

"Hey, calm down."

She begins to sob loudly.

"I'm sorry—they threatened my Inez."

Matthew notes a flat top cap on the counter. Then he hears two soft *poof poof* sounds.

Two neat bullet wounds appear on Amanda's forehead before she falls forward. Matthew turns in the direction of the sound.

He feels a sharp pain in his head and hears a thump. He slowly watches the world fade to black. He wonders, *is this how it ends?* It feels like he is floating. He wonders if he will see the white light.

The tall, thin man is pleased with his work. He takes his flat top cap from the kitchen counter and puts it on his head. He pulls the front down low. To hit the medulla oblongata from his location is perfection. He knew his shot was on its mark when she immediately went limp. A perfect shot from a difficult angle in the house. The second bullet was for insurance. He knew the fates were with him.

The ringing will not stop in Matthew's brain. His eyes are still closed and all he can hear is this loud continuous siren going off in his head. He slowly opens his eyes. He looks down at his hand. There is a gun. The ringing in his head is getting louder by the second. As he stands up, Matthew realizes that it is not tinnitus. It is the sirens of the approaching police.

The man readjusts his flat top cap over his forehead. The fates were indeed with him. Killing Matthew would have been the wrong thing to do when he was at the hospital. Matthew lived so he could use him. The fates are always right. He quietly makes his exit from Amanda's house. The sirens get louder.

Matthew is very unsteady on his feet. He is still recovering from the powerful blow to the back of his head. He goes to Amanda and feels for a pulse. She is dead. He drops the gun. He has only seconds to get out of here before he is arrested for the murder of his scrub nurse.

Matthew's mind clears, and he realizes his dilemma. His prints are on the murder weapon. His car is out front. The telephone log will reveal Amanda called him. The sirens are getting louder, just seconds away. He picks up Amanda's telephone in the kitchen.

Liam answers on the fifth ring.

"It's me. I'm at Amanda Soto's house"

"What are you doing at Amanda's house?" says Liam.

"Someone just killed Amanda."

Liam, "Amanda's been murdered?"

"I was knocked out."

"What is the noise in the background?"

"Sirens," says Matthew.

"Wait for the police. Tell them what happened."

"No, they'll take me in. I'll be arrested."

"If you run, you look guilty."

Matthew says, "I can't be arrested. I need to find out who did this. Where are you?"

"In my car."

"We need to meet up." Matthew waits.

"Go to the Fox & Farmer bar. Dump your cell phone." The phone goes dead.

Matthew watches the police cars arrive out front. He is trapped.

. . .

Officer Frank Melky is a veteran. He has served the police department for eighteen years. As the most senior officer on the scene, he is in command. Officer Kathy Sanders has been on the force for five years. Kathy likes being Frank's partner; they get along. Kathy has two young boys. Frank has two older boys that are both off at college. Frank's boys play college football. Frank never misses a game. He drives down every weekend with his wife.

The second squad car screeches to a halt behind them. Frank signals them to cut the sirens.

"Draw your weapons," says Frank.

Kathy walks four feet behind Frank. The other two officers walk side by side, guns out in front.

"Cover the rear exit." Frank motions the two officers to go around the side.

Matthew's hand is still on the phone. He sees the two officers heading for the back. Frantically, he tries to race to the rear door. He is too late; he sees a heavyset young officer beginning to climb the step, gun pointing straight ahead.

Officer Melky never likes these types of calls. An anonymous tip that a man with a gun is on the scene, shots heard. It could be nothing, but it could be your last call. When he was younger, the adrenaline flowed and he loved it. Now, he just wants to make it home to see his wife, Adele, and his two sons.

Kathy says, "His car is still here." She points to the car in the driveway.

"Good chance he's still on premises. Exercise caution."

"Will do, sir."

"Just maintain position and be alert."

Officer Melky enters the front door. It is a neat and tidy bungalow. Nothing seems out of place in the family room. Kathy looks at the photos. The occupant is a middle-aged female. She has one daughter. There is no man in the pictures. The house is silent. Frank and Kathy proceed to the kitchen.

One look at the woman and officer Melky knows she is dead. He clutches his weapon tighter. This is no fake call in; this is the real deal. The veins on the side of his neck pop out, and his pressure rises. Frank Melky looks around the room.

Kathy is the first to spot the gun. She moves toward it. Frank feels Amanda's neck for a pulse. There is none. Officer Melky feels warm liquid on his hand. It is coated with warm blood. This is a fresh crime scene. Things are getting worse by the second.

Kathy says, "We have a weapon." She looks at Frank's bloody hand.

Frank shouts, "Neil. Kirk."

The two officers that had entered from the rear immediately appear.

Neil says, "No one left the rear."

Kirk adds, "We're sure."

Kathy's excitement rises. "Shooter's still here."

Frank already knows that. He had a bad feeling from the moment he took this call. He talks into the communicator on his left shoulder. "Send backup. Shooter on site. Any more updates?"

The dispatcher says, "The vehicle is registered to Dr. Matthew MacAulay, a surgeon. The house is registered to Amanda Soto, a nurse. They work at the same hospital. No weapons registered to either one. Stay safe."

"Thanks."

Probably a lover. Killed her in a rage. He's still here and he is dangerous. The murder weapon is on the ground. Killer probably brought a few weapons.

"Do we clear the house, Frank?" says Kathy.

Frank is tempted to wait for back up, but they will all realize he is afraid if he does this. He will lose face and never be able to work in the department. Being alive might be a good trade off to working in the department. He is near to getting full pension anyway. "Do we clear the house?" says Kathy, this time with more emphasis.

The other officers look at Frank.

Frank says, "Neil, Kirk, take the basement."

Frank nods toward the stairs, but they are already off. Frank worries the killer is planning to ambush them. Is he planning suicide? Death by cop.

"Don't take any chances. If anything moves, shoot to kill," says Frank. "Kathy, keep behind me."

Matthew hears the entire conversation. He had tried to escape through the back door but had been trapped. He hides in the closet near the rear exit, just past the kitchen. Matthew is not sure what to do. If he tries to surrender, they might shoot him in the confusion. Even if they do not shoot him, he will be arrested for the murder. Matthew needs to escape. If he is caught, he will be unable to find out who killed Tom and Amanda. Matthew knows the house intimately. It is a small bungalow. Frank and Kathy will clear the front rooms quickly because there is nowhere to hide. They will come back here and see the closet.

Frank and Kathy systematically begin to clear the main floor. The family room is not too large. The couch is worn but clean.

"Kirk," Frank calls down the stairs.

Kirk calls up from the basement, "Clear. Just checking some boxes."

Frank and Kathy make their way silently out of the kitchen to the back of the home. Frank points to the closet and motions Kathy to position herself on the opposite side. It is a brown wooden double door. It has a solid wood frame with thin plywood in the middle, small gold knobs for the handles.

It is clear the killer is in the closet. Frank looks around. It makes sense. The killer must have tried to leave from the back when they had arrived. They had been too quick, and the killer had to run back and hide in the first spot available. This closet is the only hiding place between the kitchen and the rear door.

Kathy is about to order whoever is in the closet to come out with their hands up. Frank beckons her to be silent. Frank and Kathy both have their weapons pointed at the closet. Kathy looks at Frank, her eyes asking, What's the delay?

Frank is tense. The killer could burst out of the closet firing. The two of them will surely get him, but a stray bullet could injure or kill either one of them. This guy may not be thinking straight. At this point he may feel he has nothing to lose; come out guns blazing. If they identify themselves, he will have an idea of where they are. This guy could be setting them up; he could have an automatic weapon.

Frank fires six rounds into the closet. Kathy is stunned, but she says nothing. The other two officers run upstairs as soon as they hear the gunfire. Kathy opens the closet.

• • •

Matthew moves quickly through backyards into a quiet street. The real assassin probably made his way out in a similar fashion. Matthew knows this area well. He often visited Amanda and Inez . He knew Amanda was looking forward to going to Australia next year when Inez began the Environmental Studies program at the Australian university. Amanda had a list of places she was going to visit in Australia. She felt like a sister to him.

Matthew quickly finds the laneway between two houses. He is sure the police will begin a foot patrol of the area and ask the neighbors if they saw anyone. He is fortunate that there are few neighbors about. He knew the area well enough that he is already merging on a busy main road with many people enjoying a casual evening stroll. Matthew has no idea how close he had come to being killed. As soon as he heard the two officers go down the stairs and the other officers move to the front of the house, he quietly slipped out the back door. That instinct saved his life.

Matthew passes a car ready to pull into traffic. The next thing he sees is the mother taking the young girl back inside for a minute. He takes out his cell phone and places it under the front seat. He has put the cell phone on silent mode.

After forty minutes, Matthew knows he is free. He also knows that there is a good chance the police will have alerted the entire region to find him. He is now a "person of interest." Police code for prime suspect in the murder of Amanda Soto. The police still have to operate on the chance that he, too, has been killed, assuming his body has been removed or not yet found.

Liam had given him a code. They never go to any pub called the Fox & Farmer. Mr. Farmer was a patient of Liam's a long time ago. He owns a luxury condo on the Upper East Side. Mr. Farmer lives in Rio de Janeiro, Brazil. Matthew can't remember his real name. Mr. Farmer owns one of the largest cattle ranches in Brazil, so they always call him Mr. Farmer. He uses the condo maybe one week out of the year. Liam was given keys and told to use it whenever he wanted. The building houses many international residents of considerable wealth. The doorman is discreet. Liam uses the place rarely, but they can talk freely and will not be found.

CHAPTER TWELVE

"**A**manda is dead," says Matthew.

Liam is watching TV. Matthew falls onto the sofa and stares straight up into the ceiling.

"Twenty minutes after you called, the university president called me. The police are actively looking for you. I told them you just called me and said someone killed Amanda," says Liam.

"Why?"

"They will have my phone records in days. If I didn't mention the call, they would be suspicious."

Matthew outlines in detail the events surrounding Amanda's murder.

Liam's face sags. His eyes narrow.

"We are dealing with a ruthless group. Amanda had no knowledge of the Transplant Working Group. They would know that. She was killed solely to frame you. Your inquiries into Tom's murder are making someone uncomfortable."

"Sarah." Matthew tries to pick up the phone, but Liam grabs his hand.

"Sarah was at the library with me. I said I'd be back in an hour."

"Forget about Sarah. For the time being, she is safe. You're the one who is in a bit of a spot."

. . .

Jason Cooper's sports car pulls up to the house. There is a complete forensic team and a large contingent of state, local, and federal police on site. The scene is controlled chaos. He has called ahead and three other military officers are waiting for his instructions at the site. The local police are aware that Jason has full control. However, he is not taking over the case. Jason comes in street clothes, trying to look like a detective.

The Chief of Police greets him immediately, "Mr. Cooper?"

"Chief Riggs?"

"Glad you're here. As you can see, we have a full house."

Jason surveys the mayhem which is the crime scene.

Chief Riggs asks, "There is a lot of interest. Can you tell me why?"

Jason ignores his request. "What does it look like so far?"

"Amanda Soto was at home. Dr. Matthew MacAulay was seen entering the house by a neighbor. They knew him because he visited fairly regularly. Later, we got an anonymous call that two loud gunshots were heard coming from this location. The neighbor didn't hear anything. When our men arrived, they found Amanda, shot in the head. Our men canvassed the neighborhood. Someone fitting Dr. MacAulay's description was on a street five minutes walk from here, fleeing the scene. His car is still in the driveway."

"Do we have the murder weapon?"

"Yes, Beretta."

The Chief and Jason walk over to the forensics team. Not an easy task with all the officials falling over each other. "Beretta, military issue." The forensics expert shows Jason the murder weapon.

"Carry on. Hand me that camera," says Jason.

Chief Riggs says, "No need, sir, you'll have full access to all our crime scene photos."

"I'll take you up on that." Jason continues to take his own photos. He has no doubt the forensics will confirm Matthew's prints.

Gotcha.

· · ·

Sarah is very fit, but when she is stressed and angry, she likes to eat chocolate. She knows that dark chocolate is all the rage, but she loves creamy milk chocolate. She long ago reconciled this guilty pleasure as part of her personality. Many people do this, but at least she admits it. She makes sure to swim six times a week, and she does weights four times a week. With her recent diagnosis of ALS, she has increased her fitness regimen. Her body is firm and muscled.

She tried to control her desire for chocolate during her competitive diving as a teen. She could not. Her mother always blamed it for her not making the Olympics. Sarah blamed her mom. Sarah doesn't keep any of the stuff in her house, but at times like now, when she needs it, she heads to the grocery store. All premium items, only the best. No more guilt, she decides. She is a human being, and she is allowed to indulge in chocolate.

Sarah jumps into her electric car. She had waited for Matthew for two hours at the library. She continued the research but could not find any leads on the identity of the transplant patient who had set this whole sorry tale in motion.

She was angry. He could have just told her where he was going. Why leave her to do the work in the library? She had little time left and each minute wasted on this nonsense was a minute of her short life that she would never get back. Sarah pulls the car out from her space. As she moves up the condominium parking ramp onto the main road, she sees a head emerge from the back seat of her car. A white man with dark hair. He moves to her. The predator must have been lying in her car, waiting to strike. She is too scared to scream. Her body shudders and stomach acid fills her mouth. She can't control the tremor in her hands. Her lower lip quivers and the right half of her face spasms.

"It's me."

Sarah becomes enraged when she sees Matthew's smiling face clearly. She grips the steering wheel. The right side of Sarah's face goes into a severe spasm. She tries to control it, making her lips quiver.

"Sorry to scare you, but there was no other way."

"You break into my car, nearly give me a heart attack." Sarah's voice quickly increases to a shrill pitch. The longer she looks into the rear view mirror, the more the anger becomes physical. Sarah feels the sweat on the back of her shirt. She breathes slowly, and soon the facial spasm goes away.

"I need an anesthetist."

"So you just expect me to jump and help you out."

"I'm going to go undercover and the only way to do it is to get a face transplant. You're going to give the anesthetic."

"I'm not interested. Remember what I told you, Sherlock Holmes. You do the investigating on your own. I'm lying low for awhile, then I'm off."

"Amanda's dead."

Sarah pulls the car over and stops in a parking spot at the side of the road.

"So it's started. They're coming after us."

Matthew says, "It was made to look like I killed her. She's the one who called me. The police are after me, and I can't be seen in public."

"So the killer told her to call you to come over."

"They threatened her daughter, Inez."

"I'm sorry that happened, but I can't help you. I don't want anything more to do with this thing."

"Don't you want to get whoever killed Amanda?"

"I'm not involved."

"Don't you see we need to stick together? Whoever is behind this will hunt us down one by one. We have no choice now."

"Please get out of my car."

"You're the only person who can help me. We can't bring in anyone else. I need you to do my face transplant."

"You're going to get us all killed."

Matthew says, "Liam and I have a plan. Liam's already got a plane that will take us to Palo Alto. There's a transplant facility there."

"Why not do it here?"

"The robotics at Tom's facility are superior. He also has a Steriazol that allows for the perfect transplant."

"Then you'll go undercover with your new face. You'll be a totally different person so you can go around and, in no time, solve this thing."

"That's about it."

"I will not help you. I am out. Now please leave my car."

Matthew gets out of the car and gently closes the door. Sarah watches him walk away. She puts her head on the steering wheel and begins to cry. The sobs get louder and louder until her whole body shakcs.

Sarah talks softly to herself. "Just let it out. Let it all out."

She wipes her face and takes her head off the steering wheel. Sarah starts the car and begins driving. After a few blocks, she sees Matthew. Sarah stops the car in front of him.

"Get in."

Chapter Thirteen

Liam says, "She's beautiful."

Alice answers, "I'm glad you like."

Liam asks, "The design elements are Swedish?"

Kofi says, "Yes."

Alice says, "I think Tom and Kofi were going for a fresh take on modern contemporary."

Liam chuckles. "You would be at home in the Museum of Modern Art."

Alice says, "Thanks."

"I love your voice. Young, perky, but also confident and controlled."

Kofi scolds Liam. "Don't flirt with my robot."

Liam runs his fingers over the brushed aluminum joystick controls. They are shaped with sensuous curves. The aluminum accents and the white lacquer finish surround the control chair. "I never believed in love at first sight. Now I'm not so sure."

Kofi says, "Alice can do a few tricks."

With that Kofi has Alice run through a 3-D hologram of a face transplant. Liam sits in the seat that is Alice's center. He puts his hands on the joysticks and runs through some basic transplant techniques. Then he goes over to Sarah, who is sitting in a chair by herself.

"On the plane ride over, you seemed upset. Can I help?"

Sarah says, "A simple six-month job before I started traveling the world has gone sideways. I'm now roped into doing a secret face transplant. Yes, I'm upset."

"None of us planned this. We're all in the same boat."

"I had already lined up some temporary positions in Europe. I was getting my trip finalized."

"I understand. Let's try to get this thing solved as fast as we can. Then we all go back to our lives."

"I know that. It's just hard. I feel caged. Caged in a body that soon I won't be able to control. ALS will rob me of every dignity. And I'm roped into a plan to find a killer. I have no choice. I have to help if I have any hope of avoiding Amanda's fate. I know that. Caged, with no way out."

Matthew walks over to them. "What are you two so intently talking about?"

Liam says, "We're trying to find a way to solve this thing fast. Let's get on with the transplant."

Sarah carefully checks the anesthetic machine. She signals she is ready. Matthew is already on the operating table, ready to be transplanted. Kofi puts the titanium canister with the face that will be put onto Matthew's body beside the operating room table. Kofi then goes to the control chair and takes a seat.

Liam will act as Kofi's assistant. Liam stands beside the patient. He watches the three mechanical arms whir and twist as Kofi maneuvers the joysticks.

Kofi says, "This is a complete trans. You understand the risks. Now is the time to back out."

Matthew answers, "Do it, complete trans, a new me."

Liam is amazed. The precise scalpel blade cut along Matthew's hairline starts at the forehead. The incision then goes behind his ear and curves just under his jawline. Slowly, the dissection removes the skin precisely, taking his face off in one nice sheet of tissue. The underlying muscles are left intact. Within fifty-five minutes, Matthew's face has been removed.

A titanium canister is raised from a place in the floor beside the operating room table. Matthew's face is gently placed in the canister. The lid is sealed and the titanium canister mechanically moves to the storage area. The precision and majesty of the process are awe-inspiring. Liam looks across at the second container, holding the donor face. "Do we know who the face came from?"

Kofi says, "Yes, he was a high school teacher, hit in a car crash by a drunk driver. He donated everything: kidneys, heart, liver, even corneas. I harvested his face. I promised his parents it would be put to good use."

The second canister slowly rises to the level of the operating table. The robotic arm gently removes the lid. The face is wrapped in a white cloth. It is gently raised out of the canister. It is clearly from a man in the same age range as Matthew, early thirties, but there the similarities end. He had thinner lips. His cheeks were very flat, his face square. Not ugly, not handsome. Comfortable would describe him best. He was very ordinary. Sarah thinks about the leader of the cleanup crew the night at the lab. Matthew is now that man, a little taller, but Matthew is everyman.

Liam is mesmerized by the robotic surgery. The new Matthew will need to be able to go anywhere unnoticed to investigate and ask questions. Liam sees their chances of success improving by the minute.

Alice whirs to life, occasionally reminding Kofi to clamp a vessel here, check the nerve anastomosis there. At the end, Liam squirts a clear fluid over the wound and the transplant bed where all the nerves, arteries, and veins lay.

Sarah is in awe. The anesthesia is going well and she has very little to do. As the Steriazol compound permeates the tissues, Matthew's blood pressure shoots up. Sarah reflexively jumps up to correct it.

Alice says, "Sarah, the rise in blood pressure that Matthew is experiencing is transient and due to the Steriazol. The neurotubules are connecting."

"Okay?" says Sarah.

"No action is required, Sarah."

"Thanks, Alice."

"No problem."

After five minutes, Alice speaks. "The blood pressure has normalized."

Liam watches the wound change. "If I was not a trained scientist, I would say this is magic. All the incisions have disappeared, and the wounds are completely healed."

Kofi laughs. "Magic. That's a good way to describe it. Our Steriazol compound allows wounds to heal like magic. No scars. Tom perfected it."

Liam shakes his head. "The incisions literally disappear before your eyes! Do you realize what you have here? This compound alone, forget the transplants, is miraculous."

"We had the same feeling when we saw it work."

"Tom's Steriazol is enough to kill for. Think of its value in all types of surgery. Surgeons can now do any procedure, place their incisions anywhere, knowing that at the end of the procedure, with the help of Steriazol, there will be no scars. The incision will just disappear."

Kofi says, "We are still doing clinical trials on the Steriazol. It isn't quite ready."

"My patients would now be perfect, not just good, not just passable. An invisible incision."

Sarah peeks over the anesthetic machine. "It was only a matter of time before researchers elsewhere perfected the compound. Quite often, similar scientific breakthroughs are discovered completely independently in different parts of the world. Why would Tom not publish these findings as soon as possible?"

Kofi says, "The Steriazol is not perfect. Patients have to stay out of temperatures above eighty degrees. Tom thought he could work that out very soon."

Liam says, "This was too big to sit on. This work needed to be published. Tom's Steriazol will change the lives of millions of people immediately. No more disfigurement. The fact that the patient has to stay in temperatures less than eighty degrees is minor. As soon as this compound is given to labs everywhere, that will be solved in no time."

Kofi agrees. "It was Tom's compound. I told him the same thing, but he thought he was close."

Liam says, "This discovery is among the most significant in the history of medicine. I'm not exaggerating."

"I know. We both knew. But the problem lies with the military applications. The extra funding paid off. Maybe a little too well. It will now be relatively easy to transplant a face and insert the individual anywhere. Our military will be able to kidnap someone, take their face, put it on our own man, and then re-insert that person. They would look identical to the real person. Think of the access to foreign powers' classified information. Think about the possibilities. The government funded us. Would they let us make this compound available to other researchers worldwide?"

"There is no way they would let this compound out. It's too valuable. The strategic advantage is too great."

Kofi says, "Now you see our problem."

Sarah speaks. "Matthew's waking up."

Sarah reverses the anesthetic quickly and Matthew regains consciousness immediately. Kofi gives him a mirror.

Matthew slowly moves his face around and looks at all sides in the mirror. "Amazing, absolutely no scars."

Kofi says, "Just like when you did the hologram face."

"The hologram didn't seem real. Looking at this face on my body. . . now it really hits home, the power of this Steriazol."

Liam asks, "How do you feel?"

"I'm not really sure. I feel like someone else, but I know it's me."

Kofi, Liam, and Sarah gather around Matthew, looking at his new face.

Kofi says, "The procedure went off without a hitch. You must be aware of the limitations of the transplant. The Steriazol is the key to this result. At temperatures over eighty degrees, the compound breaks down. The first sign of this is sweating on the forehead."

Sarah says, "That's the largest concentration of sweat glands in the face."

"Correct. Your facial sensation is also gone. Your face is numb. You will not be able to feel the beads of sweat on your face like you would have been able to pretransplant. This is very important; if you do not heed this sweating you will die."

"How long does he have to cool down?" says Liam.

"He has precisely thirty minutes. If he does not get to a lower temperature and cool the face before that time, the Steriazol breaks down. All the neurotubule connections break down. The proteins dissolve."

Matthew says, "My face falls off."

Kofi says, "No, your face melts off."

Sarah asks, "Can you replant?"

"No, once the process begins, it is a cascade reaction. It is irreversible."

Matthew says, "This seems like a significant downside risk. The transplanted face would be unusable."

"Worse than that, your face falls off but all the nerves, arteries, and veins that were micro-anastomosed with the Steriazol fall apart and die. This happens on the patient side as well as the graft side. So there is no hope to transplant your own face back onto your recipient bed, or any face for that matter. If the recipient bed is damaged, no face can be transplanted onto the person."

Sarah says, "So his face can't be put back on?"

"No face can be put back on."

Sarah asks, "And then what?"

Kofi pauses for a long time. "There is nothing."

Liam says, "So we just have to make sure he stays away from temperatures above eighty degrees."

Kofi says, "If he does get into a warmer environment, make sure it is for less than thirty minutes. I'm also not sure how long a face can stay on. We haven't done too many full face trans. We think it can stay on a long time."

Liam asks, "What's the longest a full face trans has stayed on?"

Kofi says, "Seven days." He brings out a beautiful hand-carved wooden box, and he takes out a watch. It is a custom-made timepiece. The wristband is platinum. The clasp of the band has a coat of arms engraved on it.

Matthew says, "I recognize this, a Scottish coat of arms."

Kofi, "It's my coat of arms. I have ancestors in Scotland. I did a family tree and found this out. Who would've guessed?"

Matthew asks, "Who wore the watch before me?"

Kofi says, "You are the first."

"The watch has a built-in thermometer." Matthew looks at the temperature reading seventy-two degrees Fahrenheit.

Kofi says, "It has been programmed to beep once as soon as it senses the temperature at eighty degrees. It will emit three short beeps continuously repeating if the temperature hits eighty degrees for five minutes. If you hear this sound, you must get to cooler temperatures immediately and cool your face with water. If you miss this warning, the watch will beep continuously at the twenty-minute mark. The tone will also change. It will not stop until the temperature falls below eighty degrees."

Sarah asks, "What happens at thirty minutes?"

"At thirty minutes a very high-pitched siren will sound until you get back to cooler temperatures; this is a critical warning you hope never to hear."

Kofi takes the watch back. He takes a match out of his pocket and lights a candle on the table. Kofi holds the watch over the flame. The digital readout quickly registers eighty degrees. The watch emits a very distinct beep. It reminds Matthew of a bird chirp. An annoying sound that can not be ignored. They all stand mesmerized as the watch is left in place for five minutes. The three short beeps are emitted continuously.

Matthew unconsciously feels his new face. They all seem transfixed, looking at the flame. At the twenty-minute mark, the beeping becomes continuous and the tone more piercing. At the thirty-minute mark, a screeching siren emanates from the watch. It fills the whole room. Kofi takes the watch away. He goes to a sink and turns on the cold water.

"Let's hope you never hear any of those sounds ever again, Matthew." He hands the watch to Matthew.

Sarah takes the watch from Matthew and turns it over in her hands. "It's beautiful."

Kofi says, "It is a functional work of art. It is a mechanical watch, but it is also fitted with a digital component for the temperature, alarm, and GPS.

Sarah admires the watch. The upper part of the watch is like any other handmade timepiece. The bottom of the watch displays the temperature, which is blinking. She hands the watch to Matthew; he puts the watch on his wrist. Then he gently feels his new face. They all turn

and look at the titanium canister storing his real face; it is neatly positioned beside four other canisters.

"How long can my face be stored?" says Matthew.

Kofi says, "It is cryopreserved. It can be stored for one hundred
years. As long as it is kept at the precise temperature, there is no
problem."

"How secure is this storage system?"

"State of the art. Double power backup. Highest level of security,
better than my own house."

Alice says, "I monitor the harvested and preserved faces. The temperature control is to within 1/100th of a degree.

Kofi says, "It's all backed up twice, so there's no chance of losing
a face."

Alice says, "One chance in ten million."

"Okay. Almost no chance."

CHAPTER FOURTEEN

I t is very early in the morning, and the sun has not yet risen. Quentin likes the lake at this hour. It is still as glass. No ripples. He loves the quiet sounds, reminders that the day is approaching. He already knows this will be a long day.

Jason Cooper never liked this meeting place. Why meet at this lake in seclusion? This cloak and dagger crap is the stuff they did in the dark ages. These old guys still liked it; maybe it made them feel young. Who knows? Why not correspond with any of a number of secure methods, telephones, emails. With encryption strategies, the conversations are secure, and no one would hear them. A meeting makes no sense. Anyone following them would see them meet, and it would establish a connection. If someone wasn't onto the facial transplant problems by now, it would be simple to link the two parties together and make a pretty good guess as to what was going on. This meeting is just stupid. Quentin should know this. Jason's instincts would never allow him to call a meeting like this. Or how about meeting in Quentin's office, the office of the Secretary of Defense, one of the most secure places on the planet? Jason walks up to Quentin. There are no pleasantries.

"Why would he be so stupid? Drive his own car and leave it out front?" says Quentin.

"I wondered about that too."

Quentin says, "You went to school together."

"We knew each other very casually."

"You were friends."

"We traveled in the same circles at one time, but I wouldn't call us friends. I found him a little weird, never liked the guy."

"He never knew his father?"

Jason says, "His mother has never told anyone who his father is. It's always been assumed she didn't know."

"You disagree?"

"I talked to her at her house. I didn't let on that I knew Matthew in college. I reviewed her file. She was at Stanford. She trained under Tom. I don't buy she didn't know who the father was."

"So she's hiding something?"

"I think she is, but how could it be relevant?"

"Maybe his father is a foreign national spy, and they're both selling secrets."

"You really believe that?"

Quentin says, "He was found out, or about to be. "

"We interviewed many people in her past. She has no relation-ship with any man who could fit this persona. The only person who remotely acted like a father to Matthew was Tom."

"Well, what do you think?"

"I think he is selling the transplant technology," says Jason.

"To whom?"

"I haven't worked that out yet, but it's the only thing that makes sense. He killed Tom and Amanda to cover his tracks."

"Are we sure it was him?" says Quentin.

"I have a witness who says she saw him running between the back-yards at Amanda Soto's residence."

"Did she know him?"

"No, but her description matches him."

Quentin says, "An eye witness who doesn't know the person beforehand is not reliable. Was it a setup? How many mistaken identities are sitting on death row until they get cleared or exe-cuted?"

"I know what you're saying, but I think it fits. I went to see Mike Coulson down in Houston. He seems to think Matthew may have been leaking data."

"What?" says Quentin.

"He said they went to international meetings abroad. Mike had nothing concrete, but other teams seemed to be catching us. He heard rumors Matthew was the leak."

"He never said anything before."

"He didn't want to implicate a friend, not without proof."

Quentin paused. "Do we have any corroboration? Any intel about who may be getting the secrets?"

"Not yet. I have some analysts listening for chatter about it and have put together a team to review Matthew's phone records. I'm monitoring land, sea, and air in case he makes a run."

"His bank accounts?"

"They're frozen. There's been no activity on his accounts. I wouldn't expect any; he won't use credit or debit."

"He's too smart for that."

Jason says, "Preliminary reports show no financial irregularities. I talked to Tom's wife, Patricia. She said Tom told her he thought Matthew was up to something."

"Tom suspected him?"

"Pat said Tom and Matthew were close and had recently seemed to fall out."

"Good work; you seem to be cracking this nut." Quentin hops in his car to brief the president.

. . .

The president does not like to be awakened so early in the morning. He is in the Oval Office watching TV. He turns off the television when Quentin enters.

Quentin outlines the case against Matthew MacAulay.

President Middleton says, "How could you guys not watch the members of the Transplant Working Group? TWG technology is vital. Any number of governments would be willing to pay for it."

"We had no reason for surveillance."

" We didn't bug their phones?"

" We couldn't have done it legally; we had no probable cause."

"How much damage?"

Quentin says, "The three labs are independent. Matthew does not know all the advances of the others. It's limited. Not great, but not that bad."

"Does he know about The Binary Sequence?"

"No."

"So I agree, we bring him in."

"American soil?"

"I leave the details to you. We want to know what he gave and who he gave it to."

. . .

Quentin has already done more work than most people do in a day, and it is still early morning. He opens the door to his study.

A strange voice says, "Don't turn on the lights. It's Matthew MacAulay."

Quentin smiles. "Matthew, just the man I was looking for. You sound different. You have a cold?"

"Could be all the running around I'm doing lately."

"It's probably not good for your health. Your immune system is getting weak. What brings you to my home?"

"I thought we should talk."

"Did you kill Amanda and Tom?"

"No."

Quentin goes to turn on the lights. Matthew raises his voice. "No, there is a Beretta trained at your head. At this distance, I can't miss."

Quentin pauses, then sits at his desk. It had been made of slabs of rough hewn timber, with white lime mortar joints. It is large, solid, immobile.

"You just threatened to kill the Secretary of Defense of the United States of America."

"Listen to my story, then you tell me if I'm the one you should be looking for." Matthew outlines the botched face transplant and his killing of Mr. Glock. Matthew keeps all the details of Alice and Tom's Steriazol to himself.

"That's why you came to visit me last time. I knew you were looking for something. Why didn't you tell me this upfront?"

Matthew moves to stand in front of the large fireplace. The sun is beginning to come up.

"I wasn't sure if you were behind the killing of Tom and thought you might kill us next?

"That's ridiculous."

Matthew, "Tom's and Amanda's murders, I thought government. But two people died at the same time in my hospital's recovery room. That just never happens. The more I thought about it, the more I thought they had to be somehow related. The waiting room was crowded with people and I had the feeling I was being followed. What if the two deaths were not coincidence? What if someone planned the two deaths to do just that?"

"To do what?"

"To fill the waiting area so they could get into the hospital and follow me. Kill me in the group."

"Can you listen to yourself? Someone is going to go to all that trouble to kill you. Kill two totally innocent people just to get at you. You've lost it. Big time."

"This thing is big. Bigger than we can imagine."

"Matthew, this is a paranoid delusion. A conspiracy on a scale so grand . . . it's ridiculous."

"Think of what I've just told you. Whoever is doing this has vast resources and know how. I think it's got to have a link to some of our own people. I couldn't take a chance that anything I told you would leak."

"We have an eyewitness that saw you run from Amanda's house after her murder. If you are innocent, if it is just a frame-up, why run? All you had to do was explain yourself."

"The cops would have held me in custody, you know that. All the while delaying the search for the real killer."

"We know you are the one selling TWG secrets."

"Someone is deliberately setting me up, just like Amanda's murder. They're doing a pretty good job. It complicated, and I haven't even sorted it all out yet."

"Or it's very simple. You sold some secrets. It was about to blow open and expose you. Your colleague Tom got wind you were selling us out, and he confronted you."

"I would never hurt Tom."

"One of your colleagues has provided information pointing squarely to you."

"Who?" says Matthew.

"You did it, now stop the charade. Frankly, it's beneath you."

"Just look at other possibilities. Don't let the whole investigation go into tunnel vision."

"I'll check on the possibility that a group gone rogue killed Tom. I'll even check out the two hospital deaths."

"Great."

"Why don't you turn yourself in? And why do we have to keep the light off?"

"Who's been assigned to capture me?" says Matthew.

"Jason is tasked with bringing you in to answer a few simple questions."

"Cooper. Good objective choice."

"You were friends in the past. He's marrying Celerie Brindsmore. Did you know that?"

"Celerie?"

"We know a lot; we're not the stooges you take us for."

"How many murders has Jason tried to put on me?"

"He'll hunt you. He'll never stop. Just come in. If there is a reasonable alternative explanation, I want to hear it."

"I need time to find out who killed Tom and Amanda."

"Tom died from a high energy military weapon. It was made to look like an arrhythmia."

"Even you can't believe I did that. How would I have access to that kind of weapon?"

"Did you sell us out to another government?"

"I'll be in touch. Don't try to follow me."

Chapter Fifteen

Matthew laughs so hard he feels a pain in his stomach.

Sarah laughs too. "Looking back, it was pretty funny, but at that time, it was one of the most embarrassing moments of my life. It's pretty dark out now. How much longer til we get to Houston?"

Matthew says, "We're making good time, not too much longer."

"I'm surprised you haven't made a comment about my hair."

"It looks good."

"Do you think it's too black?"

"The black looks good. You won't stand out."

"I've never colored my hair before."

"Let's play I spy. I spy with my little eye something that begins with the letter E. "

"Is it an animal?"

"No, it's not an animal."

"I miss the white. Is it in this car?"

"I agree, the natural white looks great on you. Yes, it's in this car."

"You've never told me that before. Is it in the front half of the car?"

"Well, with the new face, I seem to be able to say a lot of things I don't usually. Yes, it's in the front half of the car, and you better start concentrating. You have to get the answer in ten questions and you've already used three."

"I like the black. We don't want everyone remembering the young woman with the white hair. Is it the engine?"

Matthew, "No, it's not the engine."

Sarah, "Mr. Steven Jardine, your name sounds like a made up name. Is it on a person?"

"It is a made up name, Sarah. Good question—yes, it's on a person."

"Maybe you should start calling me Heather, to get used to my made-up name. Is it on me?"

"I'll remember to call you Heather. Don't worry, Sarah, I mean Heather. No, it's not on you."

"I'm having trouble getting used to the new face, Mr. Steve Jardine. Is it your clothing?"

"Not as handsome as the old face. No, not clothing."

"Not even close. Is it a body part?"

"I do believe Heather called me handsome. Sort of?"

Sarah laughs. "Sort of? Either it is or isn't a body part."

"Well, it's part of the body, but not a part."

"Your blue eyes."

"Got it. Not bad. How did you get it?"

"It's the only thing on Steve Jardine's face that is still Matthew. The eyes."

" And you did it in nine questions."

I actually did it in eight questions, but hey, who's counting? This is really turning out to be a good little road trip."

"It has been a lot of fun. Last time I played I Spy was with my mom on a trip just like this."

"What is your mom like?"

"She's a good soul."

"You never really talk about your dad."

"There's nothing to really talk about. He and my mom weren't married. The relationship, if there even was one, ended long before I was born."

"Did you ever meet him?"

"No."

"Never?"

"My mom refuses to tell me who he is."

"That's a little strange."

"Tell me about it. I've asked her many times. She won't say. She says she doesn't know."

"Do you believe her?"

"No. When I was a teenager I looked for my birth records, tracked down the hospital where I was born. There were no clues."

"Maybe Tom was your father."

"Tom was single back then and so was my mom. The only thing she did tell me is that Tom is not my father. Although she says she wished he were."

"Why is she keeping it a secret?"

"My mom is a very honest and trusting person. I'm sure this man broke her heart in some way. She decided to go it alone and never see him again."

Sarah holds Matthew's hand. "I know not having a father would have been very tough on you. I'm glad you felt comfortable enough to let me in."

"It wasn't so bad. Tom always filled in. He took me to ballgames."

"That's not easy, though. Kids can be brutal about stuff like that."

"I think about him a lot."

"Tom?"

"No, my father. He's probably still alive. Does he even know my mom had a baby? Did he know he was a father? What does he look like? There's an emptiness I feel, just not knowing."

Sarah pulls her hand away. "Now that we're confessing deep, dark secrets, there's something I need to confess."

"That sounds serious."

"I . . . I can't, not now."

"No problem. When you're ready."

"Thanks."

They drive in silence for twenty minutes.

Matthew says, "We're not too far."

"I really didn't want to come on this road trip, but Liam convinced me."

"Really?"

"Liam said it's not safe for you to travel on your own with the new face. He was right. We have to keep it below eighty degrees at all times. We don't know how long the face can last. Anything past a week is unknown."

"Keeping the face cool is the big thing. I don't want it to melt off because I don't want to be Steve Jardine forever."

"I hear you. No one's ever kept a face for this long."

"The real fun is about to start."

Sarah asks, "Michael Coulson?"

"Michael Coulson. He's got to be the guy."

Sarah, "Yeah, it's him. He called you up last minute to go to the lab. Conveniently, he told you bring an anesthetist and a scrub nurse. Just what you need for a face transplant."

"He also told Quentin I was selling secrets. He set me up."

"Or someone is smart enough to feed him the wrong info so Michael sets you up. Maybe he really believes you're guilty; maybe he was set up."

"I've known him for years. He was in the lab at Stanford with Liam and Tom before they split up to open their own centers. These guys were close. I always thought Mike was a stand up guy, but it's looking like he's the one."

"Whoever did this also did a great job of framing you for Amanda's murder. It looks like you killed your girlfriend. You were never with her, were you?"

"No, we were close friends. She helped me settle into New York. I helped her get through a tough divorce."

"They framed you good."

"I know. The police think there was something between us, it went wrong, and I killed her."

"Precisely."

"Whoever is behind this is making no mistakes."

"We need to solve this thing. The faster we solve it, the faster we get on with our own lives."

"We'll be in Houston around ten. What do you say we hit up a club?"

"'Hit up a club?' When was the last time Matthew MacAulay 'hit up a club?'"

"Never."

"Okay. Let's do it."

. . .

When Matthew got to the Houston Medical Center, he went directly to Michael's lab. He saw the door to Michael's small and messy office, but he waited in the hallway until Michael's assistant came out.

"Hi, Bryan."

Bryan turns around and looks at the man in front of him. Bryan has no idea he is looking at Matthew.

Bryan asks, "Do I know you?"

"We met at the conference last year on microvascular surgery in Washington. You gave a talk."

"You remember my presentation?"

"I'm Steven Jardine, a grad student."

"Right, right, now I remember you. How've you been man?"

"Good. Good. Been working in New York with Dr. Rasulov."

"So you work with Dr. Matthew MacAulay as well?" says Bryan.

"Sure," says Matthew.

"I heard he's a real a-hole."

"From who?"

"Don't get defensive; that's just what I heard about the guy."

"My time there is almost up. I wanted to talk to Dr. Coulson."

"About a position next July?" Bryan continued without even waiting for a reply. "This place is not bad. I've written about five book chapters for him and three articles accepted in peer-reviewed publications."

"Not bad."

"It's okay. I'm starting on staff in Boston in the fall."

"Congratulations."

"Thanks. You won't have any luck talking to Mike, he's gone."

"Where?"

"He's gone for the day. But we are having a get-together at Cassava tonight. It's a great restaurant. It's to celebrate our research grant. Michael now holds the most research funds for anyone in his field," says Bryan.

That is a lie and Matthew can't resist. "More than Liam Rasulov?"

Bryan hesitates. "I know, but this is how Mike likes to sell it. What can you do?"

Dr. Michael Coulson comes walking down the hallway. He is carrying a large green lunch box. Matthew had just seen him a few weeks ago at a conference. He seems to have aged ten years in that time.

Bryan stops him as he is passing by. "Dr. Coulson, this is Steven Jardine. A clinical fellow in New York with Rasulov and his group."

Dr. Coulson stops and takes a long, hard look at Matthew. The stare goes right to Matthew's bones, and he is sure Michael has recognized him.

"Mike Coulson, pleased to meet you, Steven. What did you say your last name is?"

They shake hands.

Matthew says, "Jardine. Steven Jardine."

"I don't know you. So you're with Rasulov and his boys. Strange days up there. Matt MacAulay's wanted by the police."

"We don't hear much."

Michael says, "You must have heard something?"

"Nothing more than you, I'm sure."

Bryan says, "Rumor has it he was involved with his scrub nurse and then offed her."

"We didn't hear that."

Michael says, "I heard he gave data on his facial transplantation work to a foreign university. What are they saying in New York?"

Matthew says, "I think he was a well-liked guy. Let's just wait and see."

Michael says, "Matthew liked to live the high life."

Matthew is angry at this false statement, but he remains calm. He realizes that to get on the good side of Michael Coulson, Steven Jardine will need to put down Matthew MacAulay. "I heard he did. He was a bit of a pig to work for."

Michael smiles. The insults are playing to the ego of Dr. Coulson.

Matthew presses his advantage. "Don't you have the largest research grant now?"

"It's great to be honored with the most grants, but it's the work that is important, not the grants. Did Bryan invite you to the party tonight?

We'd love to have you. I'd like to interview you for the open position. Let's talk at the party."

Michael turns around and goes back to his office.

Bryan turns to Matthew. "You just worked him like a pro."

"There's only one way to get a job. Suck up."

"Steve, I'm sorry I won't be back to work with you next year. You're a very bright guy."

"Thanks for the invite. I'll be at Cassava; it sounds like fun."

"I'll put you down on the list. Partners allowed."

"I'll bring my girlfriend." Matthew laughs inside thinking how Sarah will react to that.

"Great."

• • •

Michael sits at his desk thinking. He opens his green lunch box and munches on a half-eaten ham sandwich. He then picks up the phone. He speaks softly. "I just met a very interesting person. He came to my office to interview."

Michael listens carefully, then speaks. "Yes, I agree, quite the coincidence. That's why I thought you'd be interested."

Michael listens again.

Michael says, "Yes, that's no problem. Francesca will fit right in; there will be a lot of people. I'll introduce her as a visiting professor."

Michael puts down the telephone and stares into space.

• • •

The restaurant is noisy and packed. Dark, heavy beams of wood frame the oversized glass windows of Cassava. The entrance is bold, masculine. Sarah looks completely different now that she has dyed her hair black. With a simple change of color, she is unrecognizable.

Cassava is the place to be in Houston. The restaurant, named after the cassava plant, brings Brazilian cuisine to the city. The root of the plant is used to make many Brazilian dishes, including the restaurant's specialty, *feijoada*. The decor is casual but upscale. The outdoor patio is set with heavy wooden tables and Spanish-styled chairs. Bright murals adorn the walls. The medical group had taken over the restaurant, and it is lively and festive.

On this hot summer night, Sarah wears a close-fitting bright print dress, highlighting her pale skin and white hair. As soon as they enter the patio, a waitress approaches them with a tray of drinks.

"Drink?"

Sarah asks, "What are you serving?"

"Caipirinhas. It's made with lime, cachaca, and sugar."

Matthew and Sarah each take a drink. A large slice of green lime sits at the bottom of the glasses.

Sarah says, "I like cachaca. It's a very smooth rum."

Matthew responds, "It's fermented from sugarcane juice."

"This party is going to be not too shabby."

Sarah and Matthew take a table in a quiet corner of the outdoors.

"Just remember, I'm Steven Jardine."

"Steven, do you ever think about him?"

"Tom?"

"No, Mr. Glock."

"No. Why should I?"

"It must feel a little weird, doesn't it?" Sarah asks in barely a whisper. "You killed him."

"Sarah, I saved three innocent lives—that's what I did. Thanks for saying thanks."

"I'm sorry, it came out wrong."

A long silence hangs between them.

"I never set out to be part of the Transplant Working Group."

Sarah finishes her caipirinha and has another.

Matthew continues, "It started out great."

"It's not where you start out; it's where you end up."

Bryan spots Matthew and comes to the table. "Steven, glad you could make it." Sarah and Matthew stand with Bryan.

"Hi, Bryan, this is Heather," says Matthew.

"Nice to meet you, Bryan."

Before Bryan can reply, Michael Coulson is upon them. He is accompanied by a tall, voluptuous woman. Matthew recognizes her full lips. She is the woman who was part of the clean up crew the night Matthew and Sarah did the failed transplant. He looks at her muscular thighs and wonders if she is carrying a gun.

Michael says, "Bryan, leave it to you to find the action."

Dr. Michael Coulson has a slight build. He has delicate features with a small bird-like mouth. "Nice to see you again. I see you have brought your better half."

"Hi, I'm Heather."

"Great to meet you."

The waiter passes. "Caipirinha for everyone?" They all take a Caipirinha.

Michael says, "This is Francesca, a visiting professor."

Francesca shakes Matthew's hand with a firm grip. "Nice to meet you."

Matthew asks, "How do you know Mike?"

"I'm a visiting biochemistry prof. Michael gave a great talk at my university a while back. And you are?"

"Steven Jardine, research fellow of Dr. Rasulov down in New York."

Matthew realizes that she did not get a look at him in the operating room; she was in a rush to clean up. In any case it doesn't matter since he is wearing the face of Steven Jardine.

"Sure. Dr. MacAulay is in that group." Francesca studies Steven Jardine very closely as she speaks.

Sarah says, "He seems to be the one everyone asks for these days."

Francesca says, "He certainly is making a name for himself."

Francesca abruptly leaves.

Matthew is amazed. He has no reason to be, but he still is amazed. Michael, a man who knows him well, has no idea who he is. The transplant is seamless. No hint of surgery. He is Steven Jardine.

Michael says, "I've read your resume, We should talk. So tell me about Matthew?"

"Most of my time was with Dr. Rasulov, so there's not much to tell."

Bryan says, "I'm lucky to have worked with Mike; he's a great guy to work for."

Matthew says, "Bryan has been singing your praises, Dr. Coulson."

Michael takes a sip of his Caipirinha. "He better. I got him his job."

Matthew says, "I wanted to come by the lab to discuss the research fellowship opportunities."

Michael says, "Sounds good. Where are you staying?"

"The Dalacourt Inn."

"That's a nice place. Rasulov is paying you too much. Why don't you come by at nine a.m.?"

Matthew deliberately misleads Michael. They are staying at Thurston Manor, even more expensive than the Dalacourt. The Thurston is one of the most exclusive hotels in the area and the last place Michael will look for a research fellow and his girlfriend.

"Thank you very much. Bryan mentioned you were starting your holidays soon."

"I'll be away for two weeks."

"Where are you going?"

Bryan says, "He's going to Canada, the Rocky Mountains. He's an expert climber."

Matthew remembers that Michael is a solid amateur climber.

Sarah says, "That sounds like fun." Sarah takes a large gulp of her Caipirinha.

Michael asks, "You climb?"

"No, but I have friends who do."

"If you ever get the urge or want some lessons, give me a call. I'd love to train you. You never get the feeling anywhere else as you do on a climb high above the clouds."

With that Dr. Michael Coulson is gone. Bryan soon departs. Matthew and Sarah sit at the table. They are each served a bowl of stew in little black cauldrons. They look like small versions of a stew pot.

Matthew says, "*Feijoada.*"

"I've never had this before."

"I backpacked through Brazil; this is the most famous dish. It's a stew. It's made with beef, pork, and different smoked meats. All slow-cooked."

Sarah tastes her stew. "It's very good."

"It really is; they have brought this recipe right from Brazil. This place is going to do well."

They savor the rich stew and listen to the Brazilian music.

Sarah says, "I think the compound that Tom developed was behind his murder." She finishes her drink and gets another.

"Yeah, I've been thinking along the same lines. The Steriazol is the key. That's the real breakthrough."

"Where does it come from?"

"The basic precursor is from a plant, Idolatis Etiensis. The plant is unique to one region of China. All the transplant centers in the world get their supply from one manufacturer."

"Raymond Chiang's company."

Matthew looks at her.

"I did some research while at the library. I had a lot of extra time. You remember that."

Matthew says, "I think we need to go to Chiang. If we can convince him to talk to us, he may have some answers. We need to see his list of customers."

"Did you ever ask yourself why you're not in a committed relationship?"

"It's something I know I would be no good at."

Sarah is about to say something when she notices the sweat on Matthew's forehead. "Your forehead is sweating."

Matthew wipes his forehead. He looks at the sweat, but he doesn't feel a thing.

He brings his watch up to his ear. They both can hear the alarm ringing, three short, continuous beeps. The face of the watch has switched the main part of the dial to countdown mode. There is fifteen minutes left. Plenty of time, no need to panic. They leave the restaurant and walk along the street to get a cab.

Sarah is limping. Matthew is not sure what to make of it; it looks like her leg has fallen asleep. He helps her.

"I get this way sometimes if I drink too much. Guess I drank too much."

In the cool night air, the temperature quickly drops below eighty degrees, and the watch stops beeping. Matthew gets into the cab with Sarah.

"Steven Jardine is good for you."

"He just looks good to you now because you're a little tipsy."

"No. You're much more fun when you have this new face."

"I'm just too tired to fend off your questions."

"I'm not kidding. Steven Jardine is good. It must be some type of psychological thing."

"Let's just get back to the hotel. You need some sleep."

Chapter Sixteen

President Middleton asks, "How is the bioweapons program proceeding?"

"The Freeze is meeting all the criteria." Quentin loves the nickname, The Freeze. He doesn't know how people ever remember the proper name.

Gilbert Lee says, "We're almost there. WMD238 has high infectivity, high virulence."

The president says, "Meaning?"

Gilbert Lee shifts in his seat. "Meaning it will, within hours, cause death. An effective and efficient delivery system has been tested and works."

The Chief of Staff asks, "It doesn't kill dogs—is that true?"

"Correct, for some reason it will only infect humans. Other species are unaffected.

The president says, "So The Freeze will kill me, but my dog is safe?"

"Correct."

"I like it, the ultimate bioweapon."

Chief of Staff asks, "How is the vaccine coming?"

Gilbert says, "There is no availability."

"When do you anticipate having the vaccine?"

"We are close. We will have one soon."

The president takes a moment to look at each person in the room. "I don't have to tell you how important this weapon system is to our defenses. We will have the capability to defend against any nation. Have we decentralized the weapon yet?"

Quentin says, "I have held off decentralizing the compound across the country."

"Why?"

Gilbert says, "It's too dangerous at this stage. As soon as we have the vaccine perfected and can create vaccine for each center, only then will we deploy."

The Chief of Staff says, "I fully agree."

The president says, "These are the weapons of our future, gentlemen. Guns, airplanes are over. Steel and iron useless. Bioweapons, facial transplantation, these are the weapons of our time."

Edith Clarke attempts to placate the president. "We will deploy very soon. No other country is anywhere near us."

"Just like no other country has the energy weapon. Then we saw it used against our own man, Dr. Grabowski."

Edith Clarke says, "I've personally gone over the intelligence on this file. No other country has any capability like The Freeze. No other country is anywhere close to developing it."

The president asks, "Are you willing to put your job on the line?"

Edith Clarke says, "We are the only ones with this technology. I am willing to stake my job on it."

"You just have."

Gilbert Lee says, "Edith is correct."

"I don't need to remind you that we are in a race. Other countries are working on this too. Our facial transplant advantage may be over, and we need to keep our edge. The ability to deploy the bioweapons from anywhere in the country is a tactical advantage."

Quentin says, "Agreed, but at this stage, if anything goes wrong, we have no antidote at the centers. The delay is a few weeks at most. The vaccine will be ready soon."

The president says, "It's my understanding the canisters that hold The Freeze are ready. They will be deployed on missiles throughout the United States."

Gilbert Lee says, "Correct. When The Freeze canisters are mounted on these missiles, they can be programmed to go to anywhere in the world and detonated on command to release WMD238."

The president says, "Gilbert, use the term The Freeze. That long name makes me nervous."

"Sorry, Mr. President. The Freeze, once in position at these locations throughout the USA, will then be operational. Similar to our nuclear arsenal, we will have capability to launch these missiles armed with The Freeze. They can reach anywhere in the world. This is a deadly weapon."

Quentin says, "The antidote will be ready soon. The delay in arming the missiles with The Freeze will be short."

Gilbert Lee adds, "I think it's best, Mr. President."

"We need our weapon deployed."

Chief of Staff says, "I have to agree with the president. We need to press our advantage. If our enemies were to attack our development site now, all would be lost."

Gilbert Lee says, "I'd like to hear Edith's opinion. She was at one time the country's leading expert on bioweapons when she worked for that company in Palo Alto."

Chief of Staff says, "That's right, you worked for that genetics start up run by Kofi Adebayo."

Edith Clarke says, "Gilbert, my work was many moons ago, but thanks for remembering. Kofi sold that company and went on to other things."

"You guys made a killing."

Edith Clarke says, "Kofi got out at just the right time. We were well-paid for our efforts."

Gilbert Lee asks, "What do you think? Should we deploy before the vaccine?"

"I feel we should wait for the vaccine to be created and even do some tests to make sure the vaccine has no serious side effects. Some people talk of an imminent threat. How likely is that? There are no major tensions between us and any of our rivals. All intel shows we are all at peace. I told you I'm prepared to back that statement up with my job."

Chief of Staff asks, "Terrorists?"

Edith says, "I agree a terrorist can strike at any time, but there's no chatter right now. How likely is a major strike out of the clear blue sky?"

The room hushes; Edith's sarcasm is obvious to everyone. Probably everyone except Edith, who has the career-limiting habit of saying just what she thinks. Not always an asset when dealing with the Commander-in-Chief.

The president says, "So Edith, I'm a fool to worry about a strike on the US? I'm a fool to make us ready to strike back at any time?"

Silence.

"As Commander-in-Chief, I am directing you, Mr. Quentin Taylor, Secretary of Defense, to distribute the WMD238, The Freeze, to all the sites as outlined in our plan as previously approved. That's an order. Do I make myself clear?" The president closes his briefing book.

"Yes, Mr. President."

. . .

Liam nurses his beer at the bar and watches the news. He is not concentrating. He is just allowing all the information Matthew has given him to sink in.

Liam says, "We are relatively safe. I wasn't followed."

Matthew says, "No one is going to recognize me with this face."

"I tell you, Steven Jardine looks nothing like the real you. It's a little creepy actually."

"Tom could have made a bundle patenting this stuff and bringing it to a drug company."

"I know it's not nice to think that way, but I agree. He could have sold this thing to surgeons around the world. Invisible scars that heal in minutes. This is better than the old snake oil salesmen."

"And this is real."

"It's freaky."

Matthew says, "Patricia may have some more information about Tom's death than she let on. Kofi shared some interesting things. I think I may pay her a visit."

"What did Kofi say?"

"Kofi gave her some money in the past to settle a gambling debt. She swore never to gamble again. Kofi told her if she ever did, he would tell Tom about the money he had given her. She had come back to him just recently. She had run up a huge debt. She claimed her life was in danger."

"What did Kofi do?"

"He refused to give her the money and threatened to tell Tom."

"Did he?"

"No, because Tom died a week later."

"It's a stretch from gambling debt to murder and face transplants."

"Maybe."

"Take Sarah—you two can pose as federal agents."

"That's the plan."

Liam looks up at the television. The bar is very noisy and he has to strain to hear the newscast. The lead story is a picture of Matthew. Liam looks over; Matthew is watching as well. The newscaster urges anyone who sees this man or knows of his whereabouts to contact the police. The waitress brings their drinks.

The waitress speaks to Matthew. "I hope they catch the bastard. He killed a mother."

Liam and Matthew sip their drinks. The waitress leaves.

Liam says, "You're a hunted man, but no one recognizes you as you are. You're invisible."

"I'm with the waitress. I hope they catch the bastard. Amanda was a great friend, and she endured more than most will ever realize."

· · ·

Jason reviews the report on the murder of Amanda Soto. He is impressed by her life. Her ex-husband was a violent alcoholic. She stayed with him a long time. Matthew had done a nose job on her to repair a severely broken nose. She got a divorce, rebuilt her life. Jason wondered what finally gave her the courage to leave. She divorced soon after Matthew got to New York. Amanda was a true every day hero. It was a sad loss of life.

Celerie asks, "Did you pick up your charcoal suit yet?"

Celerie sits on her sofa. She has her feet on Jason, who is sitting at the other end.

"In a few weeks."

"I want you to be there for my fitting," says Celerie.

"No problem." Jason does not look up from the notes.

"I want your suit to match. Did you send the swatch like I asked?"

Jason keeps reading his notes.

"Are you listening to me?"

Jason keeps reading. "I'm listening."

"No you're not. You're always bringing home work lately. Why is it that I can do all my work at the office?"

"I had my tailor send a swatch of cloth to your dress designer. See, I am listening."

"Good. She has a few dresses picked out. It's going to be a great wedding. The fitting's next Thursday."

"I'm pretty busy. Can I give it a pass?"

"Jason, what's up?"

"What do you mean?"

"You've been acting strange."

"Strange?"

"Like now, you can't look me in the eye."

"Nothing's up."

"Are you sure?"

"I'm fine. I'll be there. Let me get back to work."

Celerie goes to her home office and sits at the desk. She reviews the sketches for an upcoming TV commercial for one of her clients.

Jason shouts from the other room. "How many surgeons would know where the nurses they work with live?"

"Not many. My uncle is a neurosurgeon and he can't even remember the nurses' names."

"You'd have to be involved with them, wouldn't you?"

"If you were doing the deed, you'd definitely know where they lived."

Jason closes the file. "Matthew killed his scrub nurse."

"Really?" says Celerie through the open study door.

"I'm positive."

"I don't believe it." Celerie opens her sketch book.

"We have a witness who saw him go into her place."

Chapter Seventeen

The president sits in the Oval Office, admiring the picture of his wife and their four kids.

The soldier who brings in the briefcase is medium height, more bookish than marine.

"Good morning, Mr. President."

"Good morning."

"I have been assigned to go over the codes for the bioweapon deployment. Everything is in place."

"Great, I've been looking forward to this for weeks. Let's get going."

"This is a brand new weapon system. We modeled the launch procedure after the codes for the nuclear weapon deployment. So in a sense, you are already familiar with the launch procedure. All the team did is reconfigure launch sequence algorithms for the bioweapons. The procedure will be virtually identical. We have used this as a template for any new weapon system that may be developed in the future."

"There will be only one Football?"

"Yes."

The soldier opens the briefcase. "The Football is really a briefcase divided into two sections. The top has a series of documents. The bottom has a laptop."

The president says, "Red paper with the black type is the nuclear stuff."

"Correct, same as before, but now we have this light green paper with black type. That's the bioweapons info."

"Got it."

"The laptop at the bottom of the briefcase has been reprogrammed for the new bioweapons data."

"Is it a new laptop? The screen looks bigger."

"Good eye, it's a nineteen-inch screen. The green and red buttons remain."

The president loves football. It is the quintessential American sport. It is America. Toughness, intelligence, bravery. How fitting that the nickname for the most important component of the Presidency be called The Football.

The soldier says, "Everything I will tell you is written in a step-by-step guide in the papers. The coordinates for all international targets, the order of missile launch, target value, projected casualties, they're all available. You can enter launch codes to have the weapons deploy anywhere in the world."

"No change in procedure with the Secretary of Defense?"

"No, he will receive his briefing on how to use his codes."

"How do I start—with the personal identification code?"

"Precisely, no change from before. The first thing is to punch in your unique identifier."

The soldier pulls out a small plastic laminated card. The Biscuit.

"Keep it safe."

"Should I just keep it in my shirt pocket?"

"We had one president do that. The Biscuit ended up at the dry cleaners. I don't recommend it. I advise keeping it in the Football."

"Point well taken."

"The Secretary of Defense has a similar identifier. He must enter his unique identifier on his own laptop to activate your Football. The computers will talk to each other. As soon as that is entered, the Football becomes live. You know you are live because the green button on your Football starts to flash. You can then punch in the coordinates of what you want to do."

"The two-man rule."

"Correct. Both you and Secretary of Defense are needed to launch any of the weapon systems."

"I can launch bio or nuclear anywhere in the world?" says the president.

"Yes, you can. See this map of the world? You can simply use the cursor and highlight any place in the world, or type in the GPS coordinates. The computer will then activate the missile to reach that point."

"Anywhere in the world?"

"The Freeze is fully deployed. It can now be detonated anywhere in the world."

"Just as I ordered."

"This is in demo mode. You can't blow up the world, not yet anyway. Just play around with it, have fun."

"I can play with it?"

"Sure, in the past I've had presidents play with it for hours. It's like the ultimate video game. In a true situation, after you enter the codes, the red light will flash."

The president punches in codes and watches simulated missile launches on the laptop screen. It is very realistic, showing the view from the camera housed in the nose of the missile. It also shows the destruction of the building or structure targeted. For the bioweapons, the graphics display a map of the region targeted and the estimated causalities.

. . .

Gilbert Lee is surprised to be summoned by the Secretary of Defense for a private meeting. He is not sure what they will discuss, and that makes him nervous.

When Gilbert enters the office, Quentin is reviewing some briefing notes.

"Hi Quentin."

Gilbert glances at the notes, and sees they are the bioweapons file.

"Take a seat, Gilbert."

"Thanks."

"I wanted some clarification on The Freeze."

Gilbert, "Sure."

"What is it exactly?"

"WMD238 is a virus we have genetically altered to meet our defensive requirements. When released the enemy will think they have the flu. As more people become infected, it will appear to all the infectious disease experts like a flu outbreak. All the infectious disease experts have been predicting this for years, so no one will be able to trace the origin."

"How long until the weapon kills?" says Quentin.

"Eight hours after being exposed, the person develops symptoms. Four hours after that, death occurs. So it will be difficult for anyone to even know where they were exposed."

"Can we deliver the weapon to a single targeted individual?"

"We're working on that. A soldier will be able to direct a plume of gas at the enemy. The gas is tasteless, odorless, and colorless. No one will know The Freeze has been directed at them. It can be used in crowded areas or by our agents for targeted sanctions."

"Is this ready?"

"At the present time, there is still some ways to go. Right now we cannot direct the plume. A strong wind could blow it right back into the face of the carrier or into an unintended target or disperse it so there is no lethal effect."

"Do these weapons have first strike capabilities?"

Gilbert says, "These are strictly defensive weapons. They have no place in first strikes. The development of these weapons is really as a powerful deterrent. No country will attempt a pre-emptive strike on us, knowing the capability of these weapons. I am available to help you review the briefing notes on The Freeze."

"I have read my notes. I understand they are retaliatory weapons."

"The Freeze is, to put it simply, the most powerful biological weapon ever created by man. The Freeze is not a first strike weapon. The devastation and suffering that would occur if this weapon were ever used is mind blowing. No soldier or senior military personnel would deploy them in a first strike. They have briefing manuals and orders specifically telling them not to do so."

"Who can authorize a first strike?"

"No one—we have notified all personnel who are involved in the bioweapons program that they are to disregard any order to fire these pre-emptively. We have had the analysts go over all scenarios. There is no case in which such a strike can be justified."

Chapter Eighteen

Jason does not usually allow his work to interfere with his private life. This case is different; his work and his private life are intertwined. Jason is on edge. He is closing in on Matthew, and it is only a matter of time before he will arrest him.

The sports car careens down the twisty road. The warm breeze gently rubs Jason's face. He is on his way to see Celerie, and her face always cheers him up. Her two friends, Jen and Bryce, will be at the dress fitting, too. *Well, you take the sweet with the sour,* Jason thinks.

Bryce is a very thin woman with a boyish figure. She is dressed in loose-fitting jeans and a purple designer T-shirt. Bryce always admires Celerie's more sensuous physique. It reminds her of a 1950s pin up girl.

"Now's the time to show it off, Cel. After the wedding night, that's it." Bryce sits cross-legged in the plush white chair.

"You sure it's not too tight?" asks Celerie, looking at Jen.

Jen is vertically challenged. That's how she likes to put it. Well-proportioned but petite.

Jen, "You look sensational. You will be a showstopper. Think about it. You and Jason get changed around midnight. You get out of the wedding dress and come back in this dress to dance the rest of the night away."

Celerie twirls in the mirror.

The sales associate looks on, "It fits you perfectly. It was made for you. No alterations needed."

Celerie isn't sure. She has always favored slightly looser tops, but she has to admit this dress fits her well. The dress accentuates her curves subtly. She turns in the mirror and decides to go for it. Make an entrance. She looks at her watch. Jason is coming into the store.

Bryce says, "You're late."

"Traffic was a . . . Bryce." Jason looks at Bryce and smiles.

Jen says, "Don't worry, have we got a treat for you. Feast your eyes."

Celerie poses to show the dress. "What do you think?"

"I'm not sure." Jason takes a seat between Bryce and Jen.

"That's the look," says Bryce.

It's a wee bit tight, don't you think?" says Jason.

"She's got the body for it," says Jen.

"It's too tight. It makes you look . . . I don't quite know, Celerie," says Jason.

"I like it. It'll be the middle of summer, and it's a perfect weight."

Jason says, "I'm not sure that dress is you."

"I think it is me, or should be."

"You look like a high-priced hooker in that thing."

Bryce and Jen look at each other, and the sales associate bows her head.

The sales associate then steps forward. "We have some others you can try."

"No, that will be quite all right. I'm taking this one."

In the car Jason does not say a word. He turns up the radio and accelerates to merge onto the highway.

Celerie breaks the silence. "I know the dress was a little dramatic, but I thought it was tasteful. I would never wear anything to embarrass you."

"Tasteful. It looked like it was painted on."

"I thought it looked sensuous."

"Your breasts looked like two grapefruits ready to pop out of that thing."

"It's my body, and I like it. I told you about my body issues in the past. I've had to work to get comfortable with my shape."

"Well, I think you're a little too comfortable now."

"I like the dress and I'm wearing it. So you better get used to it."

"You look like a ten-dollar whore," says Jason.

"Jason."

"I'm sorry, but you do. You are going to look like a cheap whore at our wedding."

"What has gotten into you?" The pitch of her voice increases.

"What has gotten into you?" says Jason. He grips the steering wheel tighter.

"Nothing," says Celerie.

"Nothing? The dress makes you look like a slut."

"What did you just call me? Have you lost your mind?"

"Is that the kind of dress you wore when you were with Matthew?" Jason is shocked by the words that just came out of his mouth.

The silence in the car is punctuated by the radio song. Jason knows it was a mistake to read Celerie's diary. Her relationship with Matthew was described in graphic detail. He could not get the words she wrote out of his mind. Worse, the images that filled his head since he read her diary never seem to leave him. Jason keeps seeing Celerie and Matthew together over and over again in his mind.

Celerie turns the radio down. She speaks in a soft, calm voice. "So that's what this is about."

"It's about a dress that's too tight."

"I wish it were."

"Just take the dress back."

"You knew I was with Matthew before, you knew that. You said you accepted that. I told you."

Silence.

"I was up front right from the start, even before we got serious."

"Is that the kind of dress he liked?"

"Do you really want to know the answer to that question? Do you really want me to tell you what he liked?"

"Take the dress back."

"This is what happens when you read someone's diary. Did you think I wouldn't know? Those were my feelings and thoughts recorded in that moment," Celerie continues. "It's raw, it's real, but it's in the moment. What Matthew and I had is in the past. It's gone now. I've moved on."

"Have you?"

"What is this about? Why this, now?"

Jason's voice cracks with emotion. "You would have never had me if he hadn't dumped you."

Silence.

"Isn't that the truth?" says Jason.

Silence.

The car speeds along the highway. The sun is fading and the darkness envelopes the car. Celerie turns the radio back up and looks straight ahead.

Chapter Nineteen

"It's almost midnight. Couldn't it wait until tomorrow, Mr. Jardine?" Patricia's voice is just a bit too calm.

Matthew says, "This is a murder investigation. Unfortunately, we go where the evidence takes us. Any place, any time."

"Come in."

Across the street, a tall, thin man in a cap watches. Today his flat cap is made of tweed in a tartan pattern. It almost completely covers his wide nose. As usual he has done his homework. The Andersons are on vacation. They won't be back for a good while. He looks through the scope of the rifle. He can see Patricia clearly.

Matthew notes Patricia's neck muscles are tense. The night is cold, and the breeze hits his transplanted face hard. It is strange having a numb face. Usually the cold on his face makes him feel vigorous. He misses it.

Patricia says, "You've brought a friend. One agent isn't enough to question me? I already answered all your questions with Mr. Cooper."

"There are a few details we need to clarify. This is Heather."

"Hi."

"Great to meet you." Patricia looks at Sarah like an art expert seeing a rare find, trying to estimate the value. More or less than me. "You're a very beautiful woman. I love your hair, classic shoulder length style."

"Thanks."

"Why did you dye it? You look like a natural blonde. Black's a bit too harsh for your face."

"I just like to change things up. I was bored."

Matthew takes charge of the conversation. "Ms. Grabowski, I'd like to remind you that this is a formal interrogation into the death of Dr. Tom Grabowski. This is official business."

Matthew, Sarah, and Patricia sit down in the living room. The chairs are neatly arranged around a small glass table. Matthew is amazed that Patricia has no idea who he is, even when she looks directly at him. She looks genuinely sad, like she is grieving. In the many conversations he had with Tom, he knew that she loved him. Why did she lie to Jason and say Tom thought Matthew was up to something? What about the gambling debts?

"Mrs. Grabowski, as I mentioned, we're following up on your previous interview with my colleague. We have new information."

The tall, thin man in the cap moves his rifle from person to person. His chamber has six rounds. Perfect. Two for each. Anyone who fires more than two rounds is not a professional. As he watches them talk, he makes a plan. Who should he kill first? Definitely Patricia. She knows enough to blow open the whole plan, even though she doesn't realize it. The others are tricky. After he kills Patricia, the other two will dive for cover. He may not be able to get clean shots. He takes out the six-round cartridge and loads the ten.

Patricia does not move. Her left hand massages the fabric on her dress.

"You had some gambling debts. Did they kill Tom as payback?" says Matthew.

Patricia begins to cry.

Sarah asks, "Why did Tom Grabowski die?"

"He was not supposed to die," says Patricia.

Sarah says, "We know that you did not want him dead. You were a good wife."

"I was. I was a good wife."

"We know."

"He was not supposed to die."

"We think Mr. Grabowski's murder is part of something much bigger. If you give us useful information and are truthful in your statements, your role may be forgotten. You can go on with your life."

Patricia, "Really?"

Sarah says, "We're prepared to do that for you."

The man with the tartan cap thinks of himself as an elite sniper. He ranks himself with the very best. He has mastered concealment, surveillance, and precision shooting. He knows it will be hard to take them all out, even with his skills. He steadies the weapon on the bipod. He wedges the sandbag under his left shoulder. He lays on his stomach. Showtime.

Matthew asks, "What do you know?"

"I don't know much."

Sarah touches Patricia's hand. "You need to start talking, tell us what you do know."

"I don't . . ."

Matthew cuts her off with a nasty growl. "You lied to your husband and got him to do a face transplant."

"I didn't lie to him."

"You told the investigators that Matthew and Tom had fallen out. That was a lie."

Patricia gasps. "How did you find out?"

Matthew says, "We spoke to Matthew."

Sarah looks at Matthew.

Patricia says, "I thought he was on the run."

Matthew is caught in a lie and tries to recover. "We have our ways. I'm not the one under investigation. It's your job to answer my questions, not the other way round. Tell us what you know."

Sarah adds, "Help us to help you, Patricia."

"I like to do a little bit of gambling. I've been doing it for years. Never had a problem. This last time . . . I just got a little carried away."

Matthew stares at Patricia. "Mr. Kofi Adebayo has already confirmed to us that he helped you settle an earlier gambling debt. This was not the first time. Do not lie to us. If you continue to lie, we will have no choice but to march you out of this house straight to jail. I am clear?"

"Sorry. Yes, sir. It was a new place. I can't even remember how I got invited. At first I was winning big. Then my luck changed. It really went bad. I kept thinking my luck would turn. I kept betting, but I just kept losing. As the sums got bigger, I bet more to clear all the debt. Before I knew it, I was in a deep hole. A deep, deep hole. There was no way I could get hold of that kind of money. Tom didn't have that kind of money. I tried to get the money any way I knew how, but it was just too much. Yes, I tried Kofi. He'd helped me before, but he refused."

Sarah says, "So they killed Tom for your gambling debt?"

"No. One of their guys with pale gray eyes came over one day, roughed me up pretty good. Said there would be more if I didn't pay. Tom came home, and I couldn't hide it. I had to tell him the whole story. He was mad. I thought he was going to leave me. Almost as soon as I'd told him, we get a call. A man says he can fix everything."

Sarah takes over questioning. "The man with the pale gray eyes, he was short, kind of wide?"

"You guys already got him in custody?"

"Did you meet the man who called on the telephone?"

"No. Tom met with him. Tom would not tell me much, said it was really strange. The guy stayed hidden, talked in a funny voice. The debt would be forgiven if Tom did them a favor, transplanted a face. I begged him not to do it. Let me pay my price. I didn't care, let them kill me. I had a bad feeling this was going to turn out wrong. Tom told me he would make it right. He told me to never speak about this again."

"Thank you for your help."

"Am I going to jail?"

He makes the final checks. He has calculated the trajectory of the bullet. He is fortunate there is no wind. He aims for the "apricot." The medulla oblongata, part of the brainstem. The first shot will be all he needed. The second is insurance.

He concentrates on making his body still. He listens to his heartbeat and his breathing. He will fire each shot in between heartbeats. He closes his eyes. He reminds himself to pull smoothly back on the trigger. When he opens his eyes, he will fire the first shot.

Patricia says, "Tom was innocent. I thought they were just going to have him do the transplant and forgive my debt. I was going to stop gambling. I loved Tom. I know he loved me. I never intended to get him killed."

Matthew says, "We need some more information on the man who talked to Tom."

Tap, tap. The glass shatters with very little noise. Two small holes in the window pane. Matthew grabs Sarah and hits the ground.

The tall, thin man in the tartan cap relaxes. The shots were perfect. Patricia is dead. There is no need to kill the others. She hadn't had enough time to tell them anything. Nothing that could identify him or his plan. Besides the plan is well underway. Killing two extra people would be foolish. It would draw too much heat. Even if they start to figure it all out, it is too late.

He methodically takes apart his rifle. He congratulates himself on his good judgment, his good shooting. He puts on his flat cap and quietly closes the door to the Anderson house. He had researched the whole street and is so fortunate that this family is away for an extended stay; the house was a perfect location. Maybe this is destiny. He'll call the clean up crew to drop by later and make sure the place is back to normal before the Andersons come home.

Matthew really isn't surprised. He knows he wasn't followed, but whoever is behind this wants no loose ends. By coming back to Patricia, posing as federal agents, they sealed her fate. Patricia had some useful information. They didn't get a chance to get it all, but she confirmed enough. Matthew is now a little closer to finding the killer. Maybe he should have come here as Matthew, a long-time friend paying his respects for a dead mentor. That may have spared Patricia's life.

Sarah reaches out to Matthew. "I know what you're thinking. You're not responsible."

"Really?"

"Patricia had a gambling habit. Whoever wanted that transplant knew that. She was set up. This person leaves no loose ends. She was going to meet this end whether we showed up or not. Just as Tom chose his fate as soon as he agreed to do the transplant."

. . .

Jason has a smile on his face as he heads to Quentin's office. He has him. The golden boy is now finished. Jason got on a flight to Palo Alto as soon as the news broke: Patricia is dead. Shot in the head. The detectives at the scene said they had Matthew's prints at the scene, no weapon, but Matthew had been there. It happened late at night. There were no witnesses. In the morning someone noted the broken window. Unusual for this part of town and they called it in, thought it was a burglary. The local police found the body. The forensics crew also identified a second set of prints, as yet unidentified. Bullets were from a military rifle. Matthew had been to the house recently for Tom's death. His prints at the scene were not unexpected. However, the circumstantial evidence is strong. Men have hung for a lot less. Jason smiles and thinks, *how the mighty have fallen.*

Jason hates Matthew, a primal hate. Matthew MacAulay had beaten him in all that mattered in life. Celerie still loves Matthew; it is obvious. Celerie would take Matthew back in a minute. Jason is the second choice. Matthew stands between them. On the wedding day, Matthew will be standing right in the middle of them at the front of the church. He will always be there, right between them. Jason will kill Matthew. He will, of course, tell Celerie that someone else has done it, but he will do it himself.

. . .

Jason has the forensic team work nonstop. A partial shoe print at the scene is identified as belonging to Matthew; it was made around the time of the murder. There is no doubt. Matthew MacAulay is finished. As he walks into Quentin's office, he knows what the only option left is. Quentin will have no choice.

Quentin is already reviewing the documents when Jason walks into his office. "The ballistics report is conclusive."

Jason says, "Military rifle. Standard issue to snipers."

"His shoe print at the scene."

Jason adds, "We have an eyewitness who states that a man and a woman visited in a police-type car that evening."

"Matthew with Sarah Larsson."

"The woman had black hair. The man matched Matthew's height, but the witness couldn't say much more."

Quentin says, "She dyed her hair. The white hair would be too easy to identify."

A long pause.

Quentin can't make all the pieces fit together. "Why would an anesthetist join him? She's only been in New York a few months. She's definitely not involved in selling secrets."

"I have a forensic psychiatrist on it; he will give us a report in a few hours. Matthew knows how to deceive women. I think he's got some kind of mind control on Dr. Larsson."

"I find it hard to believe."

"Believe it."

"Is there any doubt whatsoever he is the one?" says Quentin.

"None." Jason barely holds back a smile.

Quentin nods. "Okay. Clean sweep. Him and anyone else helping him. Sarah Larsson, Liam Rasulov."

"The mother?"

"Is she helping?"

"We don't think so."

"Then just keep an eye on her. I don't think he'd be stupid enough to involve her, but who knows?"

Chapter Twenty

Ryan Smith recovers well from his physical wounds. The physiotherapy shows results. He walks well, with no pain. The only thing left is his face. He never takes the dressing off. It is a triangle in the middle of his face. A neat, clean white triangle. The rest of his face is normal. He is standing in front of the bathroom mirror when he hears his room door open. Ryan recognizes Dr. Spencer Lambert. He has been popping in for quick visits quite often. He never comes with Matthew.

"Hi, Ryan."

"Hi, Dr. Lambert."

"I have been reviewing your file. I will be taking over your case, effective immediately."

This is not unexpected. Ryan has heard the rumors. Matthew is accused of some very serious things. He tries to ask around, but no one will say anything in the hospital. He knows Doc MacAulay is either in custody or on the run.

"Where's Doc MacAulay?" says Ryan.

Dr. Lambert speaks in an authoritative voice. "Dr. Matthew MacAulay is no longer affiliated with this institution."

"I'd like to speak with him, Dr. Lambert."

"We have no means to communicate with him. I take it you read."

The sarcasm is biting. Ryan thinks to himself, *maybe I deserve it.* Matthew is an accused killer on the run, and all the papers have the story. He killed his scrub nurse, probably in a love triangle gone bad. He is also a person of interest in a recent murder in Palo Alto.

"Fine. So what is the plan?"

"I have looked at Dr. MacAulay's progress notes. Your physio is ahead of schedule. You were lucky to have such great physio. Your hard work has allowed you to recover quickly from these devastating wounds."

"Thank you."

"But we need to get you back home. I'm not sure your previous plan was well thought out."

"What do you have in mind?" says Ryan.

Dr. Lambert pulls out something from his pocket. It is a nose and surrounding tissue, all made in plastic. "A prosthesis, just like this. Your previous surgeon did not discuss this with you. This is your best option."

"A piece of plastic on my face?"

"It will get you out of here in no time. It's cost effective."

"Doc MacAulay discussed it. I would have no feeling and it would not be my own tissue."

"That is true, but it is a good, simple solution. You are almost ready to leave us from your other wounds."

"Dr. MacAulay wanted to do a partial face transplant. He said it was the best choice."

"Well, the previous surgeon was wrong. His solution was the most complex solution to fix a simple problem. I looked at your scans and x-rays. The brain is perfect; you are just missing some tissue involving the midface."

"Just missing some tissue? I can't take my bandage off. I look like something out of a horror movie. My wife hasn't hugged me in months, and I can't go down to the cafeteria here without all the other people staring at me."

"I'm sorry. I really, truly am. But look at the reality. Your bills keep climbing. You've almost finished the physio, and soon you will be walking normally. Your hands have fully recovered."

"I want a partial face transplant."

"There is no facial transplant program. The program has been suspended pending external review. There is no guarantee this program will ever be restarted."

"It's my best option. Doc MacAulay said."

"The facial transplantation program was a very expensive frill. An opportunity for overgrown boys to play. It was experimental at best. The results they claimed were based on very few patients. Transplants were not done on a large enough group of patients to validate the results. Do you understand what experimental means?"

"Doc MacAulay showed me the results."

The contempt rises in Dr. Lambert's voice. "A patient. He showed you one patient. He didn't show you all the ones that failed. The patients that died trying to look like they did before whatever injury they had. We don't know how many failures he had for the one success; he was doing a lot of things none of us knew about. Dr. MacAulay's entire research career is in question. You should know this."

"Get out."

Dr. Lambert is apologetic. "Look, I'm sorry it turned out the way it did. Dr. MacAulay was a competent surgeon. I agreed with the forehead flap when he presented it at rounds. It didn't work. That happens."

"Doc MacAulay almost got it to work. It was just too bad an injury."

" I'm sorry you were injured. Look, I know the work you guys do and I appreciate it. You get sent to a place you never heard of, to do a job that you don't understand, for a reason you don't believe in. The facts still remain, you need a simple, quick solution. I'm not trying to tell you it's a perfect solution, it's not. But sometimes good is the best we can do. Untried experimental surgery is not the way to go. Even if the facial transplant program were up and running, I would recommend the same thing."

Ryan stares straight ahead.

"You don't have to make up your mind today. I'm asking you to think about it. Don't let your life slip away, hoping for some dream that some surgeon had. A pipe dream to further his own career with surgery that is untested and has little chance of success. My solution is practical. Let me help you go back to your wife and make a life for yourself. I know our country owes you. I get it—the work you did lets the rest of us sleep easy. Let me help."

Dr. Lambert walks toward the door. Ryan stares silently, like he's in a trance. He begins talking in a strange low voice. Dr. Lambert turns and looks at him in the doorway.

"The night was dark. The jungle always had a smell. Even though we were in a small village, at night it always smelled like the jungle. During the day village sights and sounds filled the air, but at night, the smell always returned. It was in your nostrils, in your hair, you just couldn't get it out. There were three of us on patrol. Frank, Austin, and me. Our job was simple: go around the village perimeter. Simple reconnaissance. There was intel, an upcoming attack on our forward position. They had to have guns, bombs. They were bringing them in at night. We were in the middle of our patrol when Austin saw it. Three in the morning, I remember looking at my watch as Austin charged in. I followed. Frank circled left. Before we reached the truck, they opened fire. Grenade went right through Austin's chest. Hit him right here. Hole bigger than a football."

Ryan continues, "I felt a burning, like my nose was on fire, then it felt blocked. Like I had the worst cold ever. Blood poured out of my face, blood in my eyes. I fell to the ground—my leg was hit. The bullets rained down. My left hand stopped working. My weapon fell to the ground. I had no chance. Out of nowhere Frank circles back. I'm lying behind a wall, trying to return fire as they close in. I can't walk. I can barely see. Frank was untouched. He could have walked out of there. He picked me up and carried me. He should have left and saved his own life. He fires his weapon and pushes them back. Armored truck rescues us. The next day they go back and get Austin's body. Getting out Frank got hit. He took it in the shoulder. He didn't need to save me. He was not hit in the initial attack. Two days later Frank was dead. Had he just gotten out, he would be alive. Frank took me out of there. He saved my life.

Ryan begins to sob uncontrollably. Dr. Lambert bows his head.

Ryan then returns to the present. "Dr. Lambert, I've been through too much to settle."

Dr. Lambert quietly leaves the room, shutting the door behind him.

Chapter Twenty-One

Edith has been a team player all her life. She believes in America. She loves her country. She finds it very strange to be making this call. Kofi and Edith go way back. But this isn't for friendship; this is for America.

Edith asks, " What do you know about The Binary Sequence."

Kofi says, "What do I need to know?"

"The Binary Sequence refers to a file. It was created for the president and has only been seen by a select few. It is a detailed strategy outlining the integration of new warfare techniques for the next century. It represents a paradigm shift in our thinking of warfare and military weapons."

Kofi is in his Palo Alto company office, using a disposable cell phone. He takes his feet off the coffee table and leans forward.

Edith continues, "The facial transplant program is one leg of the program. The other, which you weren't aware of, is bioweapons. The Binary Sequence outlines in detail how these two new technologies can be integrated for military purposes. The technologies are synergistic and more than the sum of their parts. It is a detailed plan. It outlines algorithms and scenarios as well as how to integrate these two stealth technologies for warfare."

"So The Binary Sequence plans how to use face-transplanted spies with bioweapons in military applications?"

"The power of these two technologies together is far greater than any nuclear program. The potential to infiltrate our enemies is vast. And our friends. It outlines, by name, who could be transplanted to gather sensitive information from a foreign or friendly government."

Kofi asks, "And the bioweapons?"

"How to deter or, when the technology allows more precise control, how to eliminate specific threats."

"This is why all the funding ramped up.. Is this why Tom started to get nervous?"

"I don't know if he found anything out."

"Bioweapons coupled with double agents?"

Edith says, "The double would only need a few hours. Transplant the face of someone who has access to important information."

"You would have to kill the person to take his face."

"Not necessarily, you could capture them, sedate them, and do the transplant. After you had the information, then reverse the transplant and put their face back on."

Kofi thinks through the possibilities. "This is huge. We have drugs that can erase the memory for a few days, so the person wouldn't even know what happened."

Edith says, "The document outlines in detail how to use bioweapons to eliminate key personnel in other governments, with no trace to us. It presents detailed scenarios for the day when the bioweapon technology is perfected so that it can be targeted to specific individuals. The first part of the report details how these new technologies are overtaking and will pass conventional weaponry. Drones, tanks, guns will be replaced by these new technologies. The second part provides a detailed analysis of why these new technologies, specifically facial transplantation and biological agents, are the new weapons of choice. In the second half, the analysts have prepared a detailed document with step-by-step instructions for utilizing the new weapons."

Edith turns off the cell phone and throws it into the river. It's a long hike back to her car.

• • •

The files Quentin is handling are very intriguing. His weekly presidential briefing in the Oval Office is not at all routine. He is growing to really like his job. President Middleton asks, "Matthew is confirmed as the killer?"

"He's our guy."

There are a few unanswered questions and it is not really confirmed, but the president doesn't need to know these minor inconveniences. He has to lead from a position of certainty.

"What's his end game?"

"Best we can make it, he was selling classified information on our most sensitive technology."

There was no solid evidence of this, but no need to bother the president with those details.

"The facial transplant program."

"Exactly."

"To whom?"

"We're trying to work that out."

"He seems to be looking into Tom's murder. Is that just a bluff?"

"We think Tom found out about him, then Matthew killed him. We're not sure what he's doing now. He ambushed me—threatened to kill me in the dark. He had all these paranoid stories. I told him to come in, explain himself. He refused."

"But why the killing spree: Amanda, Patricia?"

"Desperate attempt to cover his tracks."

The president agrees. "Desperate is right."

"He has become a problem."

"Jason has the order?"

Quentin nods. "On a happier note, The Freeze is operational. The missiles have all been armed and are ready to fire at any time."

"Good."

"We now have the vaccine; it's in the final testing stage."

"How long before we begin vaccine distribution to the centers that have The Freeze?"

"Probably a few weeks."

"Perfect."

Quentin says, "One last thing. Our analysts have all been telling us they hear chatter."

"Specifics?"

"No, but something is going to happen. It's going to be big."

"What?"

"We can't get any more. We're trying to work our sources, but we have nothing at all."

"Nothing? No ideas about where?"

"We think it's on American soil."

"Here? Terrorists?"

The lines around the president's mouth deepen.

"We're not sure if they're foreign or homegrown."

"Do I issue an alert?"

"Not yet, it's too vague. It may be nothing, we wait to see if it firms up."

"Keep me informed."

. . .

Kofi sits in the operating chair. Liam stands over Matthew on the operating room table.

Kofi gives the verbal command. "Face up."

Slowly, a titanium canister elevates from the secure region. The top unscrews. Kofi then uses the robotic arms to position the face.

Liam has made the incisions to remove the face that was on Matthew. Liam thinks to himself, *Steven Jardine is going back in a can.* Slowly Liam removes the face. It is very strange looking at the muscles and underlying blood vessels without a face. He places the face on the table for the robotic arms to put in the canister.

Kofi uses the joysticks as he looks at the TV monitor in front of him. The robot arms wrap the face gently in white cloth.

Sarah is mesmerized by the process. The body without its face is a spectacular site. She thinks it is the best anatomy lesson she will ever see. The blood vessels, muscles, and tissues all pulsate with life. The eyes are eerie. The same blue eyes stare from a bed of pulsating muscle. Bright red blood vessels and thick blue veins criss-cross over red muscle. She watches Kofi expertly maneuver Matthew's real face onto him.

Kofi speaks. "Administer Steriazol."

Liam then opens the white bottle with the red top. He pours the Steriazol on the wounds and incisions. Kofi watches on the giant monitor. Sarah leans over from her position at the anesthetic machine. Liam has the perfect position, standing directly at the operating room table. They all are silent as they watch the wounds heal, like magic. The face took completely, no problems.

Kofi gives his final command. "Transplant complete, success, no complications, reverse anesthetic."

Sarah answers, "Anesthetic reversed."

In no time, Matthew sits up and talks.

Liam says, "I planted a story for Raymond Chiang."

Kofi asks, "The owner of Chiang Lo Pharmaceuticals?"

"Yes."

"I've done business with his family. They're a manufacturing juggernaut in China. His father was a legend."

Liam looks at Matthew. "Your cover is that you are trying to set up a new program at home. I had a few people that he knows call and corroborate it."

Matthew says, "That should work nicely. As the only supplier of Idolatis Etiensis, Chiang has to know where all the transplant labs are."

Kofi says, "He'll know which lab is most likely to be on the edge."

Matthew stretches. "That will be the lab that still has that canister that we almost transplanted the night Mr. Glock paid us a visit."

Sarah asks, "How do we get out when we're finished?"

Liam says, "Don't worry, I've taken care of it."

Kofi says, "I think finding out who are his customers will be key. We just need to find the one who looks sketchy."

Sarah says, "You're assuming there will be just one."

Kofi tries to reassure her. "Chiang is not going to risk his family reputation by doing business with shady characters. He may not even know that the client is not on the up and up."

Liam says, "I agree. If we operate under the assumption that there is a mastermind, he will be using Idolatis Etiensis. Raymond Chiang can lead us to him."

Matthew looks in the mirror and rubs his face.

Chapter Twenty-Two

Sarah gently touches Liam's arm. She nods toward Matthew.

Liam says, "I think the hum of the engine has put him to sleep."

"He looks like a little boy. He's sleeping so peacefully."

"You'd do well to get some sleep."

The drone of the engine creates a monotonous buzz, but Sarah can't sleep.

Liam says, "We'll get some answers from this trip, then that will be it. We don't have to solve this. You can start your world travel."

Sarah nods toward Matthew. "Do you think he'll stop looking?"

"We've done enough. We have to convince him to turn it over to the police."

"You think he'll ever give up?"

"No, you're probably right. Stop gripping the chair so tight. Your muscles are going to tense up."

"I'm always like this when I fly."

"We'll be at the transfer landing site shortly. Another pilot will take you guys on to China. No need to worry now."

"Did you know China is on my bucket list?"

"It's a beautiful place."

"I was planning to go to China on my farewell world tour. Now I get to."

"Just not in the way you planned."

"Just not in the way I planned."

"Sometimes life is ironic."

Sarah laughs. "I wanted some excitement in my life, a little adventure. One last hurrah. Now I've got it."

"Be careful what you wish for."

"The muscle stiffness is almost every morning now."

"You're handling it well. ALS is a difficult disease. Is there nothing to slow this thing down?"

"Lots of great research, but no answers."

"Then we need to raise some money to get more research."

"I read the funniest thing while researching ALS. The 'Ice Bucket Challenge.'"

"Ice Bucket Challenge?"

Sarah says, "Yeah, decades ago some people just started dumping ice water over their heads to raise money for ALS."

"Bizarre."

"I know."

"So they would just dump ice water over their heads?"

"Yep. They got some of the major celebrities of the day to do it."

"Who?"

"I couldn't even remember the names; they're long gone now."

"As long as there's research, there's hope."

Sarah is quiet for a moment. "I'm just afraid of being locked in."

"I'm not going to tell you it will be easy. It won't."

"Eventually I won't be able to control any of my muscles, only my eyes."

"That's a ways off. Let's focus on the now. You're a beautiful, vibrant, energetic woman." Liam rubs Sarah's hand.

"Thanks."

Liam nods to Matthew. "Have you told him anything?"

"No, he's consumed with finding Tom's killer. I want to keep my problems to myself. I nearly told him when we were going to Houston, but he's got enough problems."

"I'm here for you. We're gonna get you on that trip."

. . .

A small four-door sedan is waiting at the small airstrip when they land in China. The ride into the bustling Chinese city takes the better part of one hour. By the time they check into their tiny hotel, they are spent. Matthew and Sarah fall asleep as soon as they shut the door. Sarah has a smile on her face. The next morning they prepare for the meeting with Raymond Chiang.

Sarah sits at a small table at a restaurant just down the road from Chiang Lo Pharmaceuticals. The restaurant is very busy with locals and expats, so she blends in well. The food looks fresh and the portions generous. She orders seared tuna. She can see the entrance to the building so that she will not miss Matthew when he comes out. Matthew goes directly to the building. He has phoned ahead to confirm his appointment. Liam did a good job because they are looking forward to seeing Matthew. He poses as Isaac Hall, an American facial transplant surgeon interested in buying Idolatis Etiensis, the raw material for Steriazol for a new program in the southeastern United States. Potentially a very lucrative contract, he wants to meet with Mr. Raymond Chiang, the CEO, to discuss it further. They bought his story.

Matthew is ushered into a large office. The heavy wood desk and intricate woodworking with motifs of dragons convey dignified opulence. There are some Chinese art figures in the built-in cabinetry across from the desk. The large computer on the desk is off and the work space neat.

Raymond Chiang enters from a separate door. Matthew stands up to shake his hand.

"Hi. Dr. Isaac Hall?" Raymond's tone is welcoming and his expression warm. They shake hands.

"Hello, Mr. Chiang," says Matthew.

Raymond Chiang sits at his desk and turns on his computer. "How can I be of service?"

"I am going to begin a regional facial transplant program in the southeastern United States, as I was telling your assistant. I am interested in a purchase agreement on Idolatis Etiensis."

Mr. Chiang laughs. "You are on a quest to make the perfect Steriazol. You and all the other labs around the world. You Americans are my best customers."

"We are the leaders in this field."

"Most of the new programs just buy the compound from a nearby university. It's easier. You won't need much initially."

Matthew nonchalantly asks, "Do you have a list of your clients? I can see who's in my region."

"I studied in America, Dr. MacAulay, at the finest institutions. I am no fool. What I want to know is how you were able to get out of the States. They are looking for you everywhere. You're wanted in connection with multiple murders. Rumor has it that you are selling US secrets related to face transplants. So let's drop this pretense. You look ridiculous."

"You seem to know quite a lot about me."

"Did you really think that your story about a face transplant program would fly? The whole transplant community knows about Tom's death. The rumors are everywhere about who killed him and why. Then your name gets connected to a nurse's murder as a 'person of interest.' No one believes for a minute Tom died of a heart attack. And then my assistant coincidentally gets a call about someone wanting to set up a new program. You have precisely thirty seconds to tell me why you're here before I push a small button under my desk and three very large men ask you not too politely to leave my premises."

"Your information seems to be very good. You can see why I just didn't call and say, 'Hi, this is Dr. MacAulay, wanted murderer. Can we talk?'"

"I can see how that would make one less inclined to give you an introduction. What is it you desire?"

"I need to see your list of customers."

"Oh, that's all, you want to see the list of our highly valued clients." Matthew waits quietly.

"What is this about?"

"All I can say is it is important."

"That's it?"

"You really don't want to know any more."

"There are rumors circulating about some transplant thefts, body snatching, Tom Grabowski's involvement."

162

"I haven't figured out who killed Tom or why. What I can say is I did not kill him or his wife. I am searching to uncover the truth. No one knows I have left the US, and no one knows I'm here. Your company and your reputation are safe. You knew Tom; he spoke very fondly of you. Do you want to see justice done by him?"

"My father sent me to America to study. Tom was my very first American friend. He was tall and big, my idea of an American. He made me feel welcome with his booming laugh. I knew him for over thirty years."

"Did he talk about his work?"

"Not specifically. But I knew he was onto something. He had recently purchased more Idolatis. He had specific requests to make sure the plant he got was from the same soil and region."

"He was doing some groundbreaking things."

"It's no surprise. He spoke of you Matthew. He was very proud of you. He thought of you as a son—you should know that. I think he may have had a premonition he was going to die. He called me a few days before, wanted to remember the old days. We talked college football."

"I will not stop until I find his murderer, of that you can be sure."

"The rumors I hear are wild, fantastic in fact. Most have you as a spy and out-of-control killer."

- "Why would I come here and take this risk if I were the killer they suspect? It makes no sense."

Raymond Chiang takes a long look at him. "I have a feeling my headquarters are being watched. At first I suspected a foreign power. Now I think it is all related to Tom's death. I've had the place swept and surveillance increased but have come up with nothing."

"Can you help me?"

"Tom was a good man, and he deserved a better end. Leave via this door." Raymond points to the door he came in. "The men there will take you back to your hotel."

Matthew is escorted to the waiting car. Sarah is in the back seat.

Sarah says, "They picked me up as soon as I finished my meal."

Chapter Twenty-Three

Alice is resplendent, her computer center glowing. It looks as if Kofi has polished her. The towering white sides and brushed aluminum make her look like a piece of sculpture that is out of place in the old warehouse. Kofi sits at a table.

Kofi says, "So you're off to Macau?"

Matthew sits in the robotic chair. "Raymond gave me the list. His best guess is a lab in Macau. I agree."

Liam says, " There are no transplant surgeons on Macau; it's just off the coast of China. The Chinese on the mainland have all the centers. Is he really sure?"

Kofi says, "It's a gambling place. Very nice, I've been."

Matthew says, "I'm positive the missing canister is in Macau that contains the face I was supposed to transplant. The cleanup crew took the canister. They didn't really worry about looking for us. I now see the important thing was the face in that canister. Not the face of the person we were to transplant. That canister holds the key."

Liam looks at the brush aluminum detailing on Alice and gently fondles the knobs. "He's right. Whoever is behind this does not want that face destroyed."

Kofi says, "So we can assume the face is stored somewhere secure."

Liam says, "The conditions under which the canister has to be stored are such that only three centers in the US could do this. It has to be perfect; any deviation and the face is lost."

Matthew says, "On the night that I was forced to do the transplant, I thought we were going to hide someone's identity. I now think we were transplanting a face for someone to take someone else's identity. The face in the canister is key. They wouldn't try to store it in this country; there are too many checks on those canisters. They would go somewhere they had already set up."

Kofi grins. "Macau."

Liam says, "The perfect place for them to run the operation. It all fits."

After a moment, Kofi says, "I have some information on The Binary Sequence. It is a government file listing how to integrate our facial transplant work with the bioweapons program to have maximum effect."

Liam stares at Kofi. "I had no idea the government had such a plan."

"Few do. I'm sure the scientists developing the bioweapons are being told they are working on genetic mutations for vaccines or some other good cause."

Sarah is absently checking the anesthetic machine.

Matthew asks, "Could this be connected? Are we dealing with bio-weapons and facial transplantation?"

Kofi says, "It's my guess. We are starting to make sense of all the haze. We are dealing with something on a big scale. That's why who-ever is behind this is willing to stop at nothing."

Sarah speaks for the first time. "Great."

Alice joins the conversation too. "I've been looking into this. There is no mention of The Binary Sequence in any of the documents I have been able to access. Therefore, it is only available in the highest levels of government. The encryption is such that I am having trouble getting in at that level. I don't think I can. The Binary Sequence outlines a plan that may be somehow integrated into the present murders. Someone with access to the document entitled 'The Binary Sequence' may have either plotted a terrorist attack or given someone the information."

Sarah asks, "But what's in the works?"

Kofi says, "What and where we have no way to know. I agree with Matthew. As soon as we find out whose face is in that canister, we will be a long way to solving who killed Tom, and more importantly why."

Matthew says, "At that point we'll be able to solve this thing."

Liam looks at each of them. "We're making some progress now. It's getting clearer. We should all assume we are targets now."

Sarah sighs. "Great. The government wants to kill us because they think Matthew's selling secrets. Someone else wants to kill us because they think we know something, but really we don't know much. That someone else may be a different part of government, a different government, or someone else entirely. And oh, something major may happen soon, but when, where, and how we have no idea. Have I missed anything?"

Matthew smiles. "That pretty much sums it up."

Liam says, "I'll keep working my sources here. Kofi, you work with Alice and see if we can analyze our data to come up with something."

Matthew says, "Looks like Sarah and I have a trip to Macau. Liam, can you make up another bogus flight plan?"

"What's another FAA violation?"

. . .

Liam grips the controls of the plane tightly. "I think I'm going to give up my job as personal pilot to you two."

Sarah says, " I know what you mean. On a night like this, it doesn't seem too fun. I'm not sure who's gripping tighter, you or me."

"Tonight it's me."

"We're so close to the water. I can see the white foam from the waves."

"It's pretty black down there."

Sarah clutches her seat. "Just keep us in the air. Keep using those instruments."

"We're too close to the water; the instruments are useless."

"But you can't see anything. It's all black."

"Now you see my challenge. "

The turbulence pushes the plane down. Liam jerks the plane up.

"Stay a little higher then."

"We have to keep just above the water to avoid detection. Macau has some pretty advanced radar. It's from China."

Sarah asks, "Macau's just off the coast of China?"

"Yes, it's an island."

Sarah puts her hand on Liam's. "We'll be fine. You're doing great. How's the family?"

"Last I heard, they are well."

Sarah knows Liam's family has been hidden away somewhere in the Midwest. Liam gets periodic updates but no direct communication. Sarah's right leg goes numb. She shakes her leg vigorously.

Liam says, "It's a little cramped in here."

"It is. My leg goes dead anytime now. I can't predict it. It's actually better when I'm walking or running."

"We're almost there."

"How old are your girls?"

"The twins are two years older than Matthew."

"It must be tough."

"They've got to put their lives on hold now. Because of me."

"It's best. Whoever is hunting us would stop at nothing. They would kidnap the girls or your wife to force your hand."

"I know, it just doesn't make it any easier. We've all had to go into hiding."

"All except Kofi—he's been able to somehow avoid suspicion."

"He's kept his usual routines. He was smart. He's even been promoted to head the Palo Alto lab."

Liam eases the nose of the plane down. They can see the rolling black waves with little white foam tops.

Sarah grips her seat, and her leg starts to move. She stares straight ahead. "I wanted to thank you."

Liam laughs. "For what? Recruiting you to a place so you can be almost killed? For ruining your plans to travel the world one last time?"

"Thank you for all you've done, for your wise words. All our lives are on hold. It was no one's fault any of this happened. You're a good man. You've sacrificed much. Look at the people who have helped us because of you. The planes, the private airports, the safe house in

Manhattan. They all say so much about you. That people are so wiling to help you."

"I really miss my girls. I want to go back to my life."

"Our careers are over, however this turns out. There is no going back."

"That is true."

"What will you do next?"

"My dad always wanted me to go into the family business."

"Your family is big in oil. You don't need to work. "

"Dad left us in a good position. You can never have too much, but dad left us pretty good."

"If what I've read is true, pretty good is an understatement. You guys are the oil kings."

"Oil and natural gas. My brothers run it now, but I may try to get in it. I'm a little old for new tricks, though. How 'bout you?"

"I'm thinking I may go to Sweden, just settle for a while in a quiet village. I need to just rest, think a little. I'm confused about a lot of things these days."

"Better wake up Matthew. We're about to land."

Matthew rubs his eyes and sits up in his seat. "Why do you guys let me sleep on these rides?"

Liam says, "We don't. You just drop off as soon as we're in the air."

"It's the engine. It puts me to sleep."

"I'm going back tomorrow. I will be home Monday. The chairman's committee will be meeting without me again."

Sarah says, "That's the committee the new university president will be chosen from."

"That's the one."

Matthew says, "I know it hurts, Liam, but if we can get this resolved, and do it fast, we can restore your name."

Sarah and Liam look at each other.

Sarah says, "At this point a good outcome will be us staying out of jail and staying alive. Our careers are over."

Matthew smiles. "It's not as bad as all that."

"It isn't?" says Sarah.

"We're all doing what we have to do."

"Let's face it. Our lives are ruined."

Liam says, "In life you do your duty. You do it with honor and integrity. What happens after that doesn't matter."

Sarah huffs out a breath. "This was not how I was planning to spend my time."

"Fate sometimes spends our time. And in times like this, you just bend."

"Is there no way out?" says Sarah.

Matthew bows his head.

Liam says, "We've all done the math. We have no alternatives. Worse yet, something big is about to happen. I have a feeling we will get the answers in Macau."

Liam quotes from his favorite poem. "Above all else never forget, life is a gift. When you receive a gift, especially an unexpected gift, you must take it gently, cherish it dearly, and use it fearlessly. And never forget to say thanks."

Matthew leans his head beside Liam. "As soon as we land, you go back."

"I'll stay in Macau a short while to finalize your exit plan. When are you going to check out the Macau lab?"

"I'm not sure. I'm going to do some work on the island and see if anyone else knows anything, then we'll pay Kevin Price a visit."

"I've made the arrangements for you guys to get back to the States. As soon as the plans are confirmed, I'm off."

"Thanks, none of this would be possible without you. I'm gonna get you back to where you want to be. Your career is not over. I promise."

Matthew embraces Liam like he will never see him again.

. . .

The hotel in Macau is very modest. A privately run establishment. Cash only. The room is small but clean. They waste no time in hiring a car. Sarah drives. They do not speak much. They both understand that if this trip doesn't give them a clue, something concrete, it is over.

Sarah sits in the car nicely hidden behind a large delivery van. She has a good view of the alley beside the building. Matthew walks across the street. The building is the address that he got from Raymond, where the supplies of Idolatis Etiensis are being shipped. It is an old gray concrete block on a very busy street. Cars move bumper to bumper along the congested, narrow road. The nearby park is full of people.

A young woman in her early twenties, Candy LaFontane, is at the desk. She wears a black skirt that leaves little to the imagination. Matthew looks at her firm round calf muscles. She must have been a dancer or soccer player in the past. Her face could have been beautiful if life hadn't left its footprint. A wide nose and very sad brown eyes.

"I'm Isaac, here to see Dr. Kevin Price," says Matthew.

"Isaac, what did you say your last name was?" says Candy.

"Isaac Hall."

There is no need to tell Kevin. He is looking at a large monitor, which shows the front office. He recognizes Dr. Matthew MacAulay. Kevin has hoped Matthew would find his way here eventually.

Candy pushes the intercom. "Dr. Isaac Hall to see you."

Kevin replies, "Bring him right in."

Kevin does not merely speak, he delivers his words like an actor delivers lines. An actor in a bad high school Shakespearean play. He speaks with measured pauses interspersed. Then deliberate emphasis on certain words. The effect is that every word he utters seems carefully considered and important.

Candy leads Matthew down the hallway and opens a door. "Go right in."

Kevin Price sits behind the desk. He is in his early forties. He wears jeans from a fancy designer label, a little too tight for his sagging physique. His expensive shirt clings tightly to his pot belly, the threads of the fabric straining to contain his girth.

Matthew says, "Dr. Kevin Price."

The man definitely is a transplant surgeon. They had crossed paths many years ago. Matthew had been in a room when Kevin was giving a lecture. Matthew couldn't remember his real name. He did some facial transplant research but dropped off the map.

Matthew jumps in. "I'm interested in setting up a transplant center back in the US. I am interested in pushing the boundaries a little bit. Some research that is a little more aggressive. I got your name from a friend of a friend."

Kevin claps slowly. "Well done. Virtuoso performance. That's funny, Dr. Matthew MacAulay, because I thought you were the prime suspect in the killing of three people back home. I think you're wanted by Interpol. And word on the street is that the US has a sanction out on you."

"Okay. Okay. Kevin, I did not kill anyone."

"I know. My boss is behind all this recent drama."

Matthew's eyes widen, and his pulse quickens. He looks around the room. No windows. At least this time, he will not be shot at.

"Who do you work for?" says Matthew.

"A very good question."

"Who?"

"I work for someone who is both cunning and deadly."

"No games."

"I have tried to find out. All for naught."

"Is it Michael Coulson?"

"I don't think so. I think he is more like me, but maybe a little higher up. I think he's a lieutenant, a right-hand man. A prince, but not a lord. Although I could be wrong."

"So he's not the man?" says Matthew.

"I can't say that for sure. He could be pretending to have a higher-up, a mastermind. Is he the genius buffoon? Sometimes the mind does somersaults, the results confused."

"Any guesses?"

"I was getting close. I thought it may have been someone in your Transplant Working Group. But my hunch is Michael is not our man."

"On the night that Tom was killed, I was asked to do a transplant. It didn't work out. I did not do it, but the canister was removed. Do you have the canister?"

"I thought you'd never ask. Yes, I believe I do. I was asked to store it. I knew it had to be connected with you, hence the mysterious Isaac Hall wanting to talk to me."

"Do you think the person is US government?"

"I don't think so, but I have no real proof one way or the other. All my inquiries have been discreet. I really wanted an insurance policy, if you know what I mean. But if they ever found out I was looking for them, I would be eliminated. Myself and my fair maiden out front, Candy."

"If we open the canister, it will tell us who killed Tom."

"I knew Tom; he didn't deserve what he got." After a long silence, Kevin continues, "Few of us do. Follow me."

Kevin and Matthew move through a heavy steel door into another room.

Kevin says, "I've fixed this room. If we open the canister here, it will not be able to transmit the signal that it has been opened. If my boss realizes the canister has been opened, I think I will be put on the rack, in a manner of speaking."

Kevin goes to a small punch pad and keys in a six-digit code. The glass behind them lights up and humming motors activate.

• • •

Candy LaFontane likes Kevin, or whatever his real name is. He is gentle. He never beats on her. Sex is so-so, but a girl can't have everything. The pay is awesome. But she was offered crazy money. Money that meant she would never have to work again. She just has to make a simple phone call. She can leave this island, go back home, and never worry about money again. Kevin is good to her, but money is money. She picks up the phone and dials the number. She'll buy a restaurant. She is a good cook. All day breakfast. Maybe her mother will not have to look after her son after all; she is going home. She wants to see her six-year-old son.

• • •

The titanium canister slowly rises from the ground behind the glass door. When it finally stops, two beeps are heard. Jason opens the glass door and takes out the canister. A soft cold mist emanates from the canister. Maybe it is the temperature difference here, but Matthew has never seen that when he brings up his canisters. The white mist slowly rises and then disappears. Kevin opens the titanium canister. As he had suspected, a red light flashes. Matthew realizes the canister has been altered. A signal alerts someone that they have opened the canister.

Kevin says, "Don't worry, I anticipated this. The wall will not allow the signal to transmit. We're safe."

Kevin slowly removes the head from the canister. It is covered in thin white cloth and wrapped precisely. The same technique used for all donor faces in the US. They unwrap the face.

CHAPTER TWENTY-FOUR

Kevin puts the face on the table. Matthew notes the faint smell of alcohol on Kevin. It is early morning. The smell triggers Matthew's memory. Kevin was a promising young surgeon. Energetic. Gregarious. He liked the bottle a little too much unfortunately. He had an addictive personality that allowed him to study frenetically. He became addicted to vodka and lime. Then just vodka.

Both Kevin and Matthew are transfixed by the face they see. They turn to each other. They both look again to see if the face will change. If their eyes will work properly and show something else. Nothing changes.

Sitting before them on a clean white towel is the face of the Secretary of Defense. George H. Brown. Correction, the former Secretary of Defense, Quentin's predecessor. The Secretary of Defense died in a hiking accident on Karakatura a few months ago. His body was not found. The climbing season had ended, and it was too dangerous to go up on Karakatura now. They were planning to go back and search next year. It was a tragic loss for the White House. Quentin Taylor had been sworn in to take his place.

Together, like a ritual burial ceremony, they rewrap the head. They gently put it in the canister and shut the titanium cylinder. It makes a reassuring thud as it closes. They leave the room and go back to the office. Both men sit, their minds twirling with the possibilities.

Kevin asks, "Drink?"

"Sure."

Kevin pours two.

Both men drain the glasses immediately. Jason pours two more. Kevin and Matthew each down those more quickly than the first set. Kevin makes a third set. They each take a sip.

"That's the face of the Secretary of Defense of the United States of America," says Matthew.

"Someone murdered him, then harvested his face. They disposed of the body," says Kevin.

"They came to my lab the night they killed Tom. The plan was for me to transplant the face of the Secretary of Defense onto the body. The person who I was operating on had the same body type as the Secretary of Defense. I thought we were changing someone's identity. I later figured out that this face was the key, not the face of the person I was transplanting."

"You were supposed to create a spy to infiltrate the US military?"

"Looks like it. I was going to create a fake Secretary of Defense to impersonate George H. Brown."

"Unlimited access to all US secrets. Locations of defenses, offensive weapons, names of spies working undercover. But it would not have worked. The scars would have been visible; at most he would have been suspected in a few hours. He would have had to act fast, but even a few hours could do major damage."

Matthew didn't bother to fill in the details about Tom's upgrade of the Steriazol. The double would have served as Secretary of Defense, with access to everything. He would have been an identical replacement.

"He would be undetectable," Matthew murmurs.

"I'm sure you don't need a high school civics lesson, but the only thing special about the Secretary of Defense is that he is the only person, other than the president, who has the access codes to fire nuclear weapons. My employer chose well. The president is too well guarded, so he took the easy mark. The codes could be sold to a foreign power. He could—"

Kevin stops midsentence. He is looking at the monitor of the front office. Something bothers him about the picture, but he is not sure what until now.

"My friend we need to leave here now."

"Why?" says Matthew.

"Candy has left her desk. She is gone."

Kevin quickly scans the camera feeds. He looks at eight different camera locations on the monitor. He has even placed a secret camera in the washroom. Candy LaFontane has vanished.

"My lover, my concubine, my betrayer, alas," says Kevin.

• • •

Sarah spots the large gray car parked at the front entrance. The weather is warm, but the men all wear loose-fitting dark jackets. It isn't that the style of dress calls attention to them. It is their faces that give them away. They came with a purpose.

The doors to the room that Kevin thought secret are smashed open. The three men enter with weapons drawn. Matthew and Kevin make their way out the back door into the alleyway. Kevin pulls Matthew to go left.

"This is the way to the side alley, out through the houses."

"Matthew," says Sarah.

Matthew pulls Kevin to follow. They run and hear the sound of men coming from the side they were going to take.

"Kevin, which way out?" says Matthew.

"Follow me."

Kevin hears bullets piercing the wooden pole to their side. The alley is deserted and the men spot Kevin. They all begin to run at full speed. Kevin leads them through an alley and into an old factory. The pursuers follow easily and close the gap.

The street is busy. The men put away their guns and nobody seems particularly concerned about three men trying to catch a group of Americans. As soon as Sarah, Matthew, and Kevin enter the warehouse, they hide on the second floor behind some old wooden crates. From here they have an excellent view of the entrance. The men in pursuit are much closer than they had imagined. They pull out their guns and begin to talk.

"Which way out?" says Matthew.

"The only way out is the way we came in. They won't know that and we can make a break for it."

Kevin, Matthew, and Sarah huddle in silence. The uneven floor has wide wooden planks. The factory stinks of what smells like old shoe leather and decaying meat. Crates are stacked haphazardly. Some old barrels have fallen, their contents dried on the floor.

Matthew begins to feel a pit deep in his stomach. If these men have any intelligence, they will send one in while their eyes get accustomed to the dark and keep the other by the door to call in reinforcements. As if the men are reading his mind, they act. He sees two men enter the building. The third man goes around the side of the building to check for any exits. One stands guard at the entrance. The other begins a systematic search. Matthew knows they have very little time. As soon as the third man walks around the building, he will come in and tell the others there are no exits. At that point they can be sure that there is no way out. All the thugs have to do is guard the door and eventually they will flush them out. Matthew, Sarah, and Kevin have to make a move before the third man walks around the building.

One man begins to methodically check out the lower level. He gently prods boxes. The small broken windows on the second floor let in some light. Old cigarette butts litter the floor. He shoots at large wooden carts and kicks them. He lays down to look under machines. Very methodical and deliberate. The man is in no hurry. He is a small wiry man wearing a cheap dark suit. It hangs loosely from his body. His manner, however, is relaxed. When he clears the first floor, he calls out to his partner. He walks up the stairs to the second floor.

"Any other way out?" says Matthew. He sees a six-inch black hairy spider crawling along the wooden beam on the ceiling. The small insect it follows is blissfully unaware.

"That door is the only way out."

The man is seconds from reaching them. Matthew picks up a piece of sharp stick from a broken crate. The man stops. He tilts his head up, then moves it from side to side. He seems to be trying to smell them. He looks like a wolf getting the scent of his prey.

Sarah whispers, "There is a window across there." She points to a large window about six feet away. It is in the open. The man will see them instantly. There is no chance to escape.

"Do you think you can take him with the stick?" says Kevin.

Matthew resists the urge to laugh. The man moves with short fluid steps. He clears each area with his eyes and is methodical. He is a professional. He will cut them all to pieces before Matthew raises his stick. Matthew is sure the man will soon realize this is the only hiding spot. He can fire a few shots into the crate, hitting at least one of them . Any survivors will scream.

Kevin says, "There is a garbage bin below that window. It should be full."

Sarah asks, "What day is garbage day?"

"I don't know."

"How do we know it's full?"

"We don't."

Matthew thinks. "A twenty-foot free fall into a bin of garbage."

Kevin says, "Or a twenty-foot free fall into a metal bin if it's empty."

"And someone firing away from above."

"Don't forget the third man walking around the building," says Sarah.

"On three, run for the window and jump," says Matthew. "Keep running."

Sarah asks, "What about you?"

Matthew counts. "One, two, three."

He leaps forward and swings the stick. His blow glances the man's arm, and the man's weapon fires wide. *Crash!* Kevin is first through the window with Sarah close behind. Matthew follows. The second man downstairs does not follow as expected to help his partner; he runs out of the building. Sarah, Matthew, Kevin are all covered in foul restaurant waste. They are out of the bin and running hard when they hear the shots. The third man has completed his perimeter walk and is hurrying back to the entrance. He joins the two others.

Matthew, Sarah, and Kevin get to the bridge over the river on the far side of the park. People begin to scream as the men draw their weapons on the street and open fire. The weapons have silencers, so people are not sure what is happening. Matthew hears the vegetable fruit stand explode from one of the gunshots. Matthew, Sarah, and Kevin run to the bridge. The water is sixty feet below. A dark foam skims the surface.

They look like three synchro divers, head first and hands out in front. As they dive through the air, Matthew remembers his trauma training. Feet first the first time. They are all diving in head first. If the water is shallow they will all breaks their necks. They penetrate the surface of the water. The sound of bullets hitting the water is loud.

The water is deep. Sarah feels a bullet pass close by, so she kicks her feet to go deeper. The water is cold and dark. The silence is only punctuated by the bullets. She cannot see the others. Sarah begins to surface and swims toward the far shore. When Sarah gets to the other side, she sprints away. She is followed by Matthew, then Kevin. Bullets are fired all around them. People in the park begin to scream and run in every direction. Sarah sees a young mother grab her toddler and run for cover.

The men pursuing them did not jump into the river and people are now filling the road. The men holster their weapons. Someone has called the police, and sirens are now blaring. The three men separate and dissolve into the crowd.

Sarah and Matthew run quickly. They stop because Kevin falters. He holds his abdomen.

Kevin says, "Go, I know my way out of the city. I suspect there are plenty more where they came from."

Matthew and Sarah run back to help him. They see blood pouring between his fingers. Soon they are in a cab. The cab driver looks warily at Kevin's bleeding abdomen.

Sarah pulls out the equivalent of half a year's salary. "Do you know a cheap hotel where they don't ask questions?"

The man's eyes light up as he looks at the money. He takes a second look at Kevin. He grabs the money and drives off.

The hotel owner seems not to notice or care that Kevin is bleeding. The cabby did a good job. Anything can be bought or sold here. As long as the price is correct. Matthew has put pressure on the wound. A bullet to the belly. One of the slow, painful ways to die. They are all physicians; they all know it without saying a word.

Matthew whispers to Sarah, "At least Kevin is conscious."

Kevin speaks. "Manhattan State Bank, on Fifth and Forty-Ninth, I have a safe deposit box. My code is 030405, the box is 24344. The key is in my left pocket."

Matthew reaches into Kevin' pocket and takes the key. It is covered in thick, clotted blood.

"When you get back to the States, give the contents to Shelley, my ex-wife. I have a son. Tell her to live well. She didn't deserve me."

Sarah says, "You'll tell her yourself."

Matthew puts the key in his pocket and commits the information to memory. Kevin is not long for this world.

"Whoever is behind this, my boss, he's a genius. As dark as the night, but a genius nevertheless. Assume he knows where you are and what you know. Thanks for getting me this far. Leave now."

Matthew and Sarah go to the other room. After a brief discussion, Sarah leaves. She returns a short while later with some clean white towels, syringes, needles, a dark brown bottle, and two vials of white liquid. In her other hand, she has some crude surgical instruments.

She asks, "How is he?"

"He's in and out of consciousness."

Sarah says, "We're too late?"

Matthew looks at the crude surgical instruments. "Are they at least sterile?"

"Kind of."

"Kind of?"

"That's what the man said when I asked the same question."

"Great." Matthew washes his hands and begins to arrange the instruments. Sarah prepares the bed to be an operating room table. She now has to give a manual anesthetic, no computer assist. She has to inject the medicine herself. Too much and she will kill Kevin in his weakened state. Too little and he will scream in pain and move during the surgery. There will be no chance for Matthew to perform the delicate procedure. She has to monitor Kevin's vital signs. Feel his pulse, look at his skin. Check his breathing. All with none of the machines that make those tasks easy.

Sarah has done well. In a relatively short time, Matthew has the basic tools to try and save Kevin's life. He wastes no time in cutting open his abdomen. The bullet has sliced through Jason's colon. Matthew delicately moves the tissue away to see the position of the bullet. He is about to make one more sweep with his clamp when he stops. The bullet has lodged right beside the large artery that supplies blood to the organs in the belly.

What should he do? If he moves the bullet, it might tear the vessel open, nor can he get above and below the artery. He will not be able to stop the bleeding. The location of the bullet is such that only one part of the artery is visible. If he loses control of the vessel . . . Professor's Rule Two: Bleeding you can hear. Matthew looks at his hands. They seemed steady. He looks again. Definitely no tremor. The thought of the last patient who had a difficult vessel floods into his mind. Is he going to kill Kevin like he killed the transplant patient Mr. Glock brought him?

Here it is even more difficult because he has no robotic assistance. He has no choice. If he doesn't remove the bullet, it will erode through the vessel and Kevin will bleed to death. *But at least he wouldn't die from my hand*, Matthew thinks.

Matthew is fixed over the abdomen. Sarah watches him intently. It is clear he has a decision to make. Matthew begins to remove the bullet. Very slowly and with great care. By fractions of an inch, he nudges the bullet from its location. It teases out. Silence. No bleeding. He has done it. He tosses the bullet into the metal garbage can, where it makes a loud clang.

Sarah laughs. "That's the sound I like to hear."

"Much better than the last time I had to do this sort of thing."

The tension lifts and the mood brightens. Matthew closes the abdomen. The suture is very coarse, so the scar will not be optimal.

Matthew says, "We're done."

Sarah injects Kevin with an antibiotic. He wakes in a short time and is lucid, but he is ghost white.

Matthew tells him, "We've paid for the room for one week. The manager's agreed to bring food three times a day."

Sarah adds, "Take these: one a day."

The antibiotic will hopefully prevent infection. They operated without sterile conditions or proper instrumentation. If the blood loss doesn't get him, the infection could. Kevin has a slim chance of surviving the next twenty-four hours. Even if he does survive, he has to hope the owner of the hotel doesn't give him up. How much would his pursuer pay for the knowledge Kevin has? Can they really expect the owner of that hotel to keep his word, live by his honor?

Matthew says, "If all goes well, you will be able to leave here in five days. Leave as soon as you are able. Whoever is hunting us will know you were hit and will be counting on us hanging around."

With that Sarah and Matthew leave immediately.

Liam had outlined in detail their exit plans before he went back to the United States. He had obtained false passports for both of them and paid a local gang to arrange Sarah and Matthew's exit. Sarah will be able to use the false passport at a private airstrip and follow the escape route Liam had planned. Matthew, on the other hand, has a big problem. He is now too hot. By the time Matthew arrives at the extraction point, the gang members tell him that false documents will be of no use. His photo is all over the local news and in every law enforcement agency data bank. The US government has labeled him an international fugitive. A generous reward will be given to anyone with any information on his whereabouts. Worse yet, they have heard that a rival gang has been contacted to find and kill Matthew. Probably some of the men who had chased them earlier.

The people helping Matthew are experienced at moving things in and out of Macau. He has to trust their improvised plan. His fear is that he will be sold out. They will take the money Liam has already paid them, and then take another sum for turning him over to the rival gang or take the government reward.

Sarah and Matthew ride in the back of a dirty cargo van.

Sarah says, "This van stinks of something rotten."

"I think it's dead fish."

"Good thing it's too dark to really see what's on the floor."

"At least they got a plan to get us both out."

"I don't like leaving you behind. We came together—we should leave together."

"I'll be fine. They're dropping you at the airstrip. You'll be home in no time."

"Do you have any idea how they're planning to get you home?"

"They are making it up as they go now. At this point they probably don't know. I just have to trust."

Matthew puts his foot down on something soft and squishy. A foul gas fills the cargo hold. "I think it's time for you to stay in the safe house."

"What?"

"When you get home, go to the safe house in New York. You're going to stay there for the rest of this thing."

"Really? And who said you get to give me orders?"

"It's just too dangerous now. No matter what we're uncovering."

"Last time I checked, I'm an adult. I get to do what I want."

"Sarah, I have no right to involve you any further."

"I'm in it to the end."

"Please, Sarah, I'm afraid for you. Please go to the house and wait."

"We're all afraid. We still have to do our jobs."

Matthew mutters, "The heart bleeds the worst."

"What?"

"The heart bleeds the worst. Someone said that to me a long time ago. It didn't make sense, not until now."

"Look, I understand how you feel. I'm scared too. But you don't really know me, not all of me anyway. I make my own choices."

"I got you into this. It's a lot more complicated now."

"I get it."

"Sarah, this thing is deep. The face of the former Secretary of Defense, George H. Brown, was in that canister. He was supposed to have died in a climbing accident on Karakatura. That's how Quentin Taylor got sworn in as the new Secretary of Defense."

"We were going to put the head of the Secretary of Defense on somcone?"

"Precisely. We thought we were transplanting some thug who wanted to conceal his identity. No, the face in that canister was the key."

"It was the face of the Secretary of Defense."

"This thing is big. I'm not risking your life."

"It's my life. I choose how I live."

"That could have been you—you could have been shot instead of Kevin."

"But I wasn't."

Matthew hugs Sarah tightly. " I won't take that chance. I won't let that happen to you. Not even to find Tom's killer."

Sarah looks at his glassy eyes. His voice sounds thick. She is about to say something, but she stops. They embrace tightly.

"I am asking you, please, just go back to the safe house. Just wait for my call. When I get back, I can transplant back to Steven Jardine and do some more digging."

CHAPTER TWENTY-FIVE

The cargo ship container Matthew is in had been used many times for this purpose. He spends his time sleeping and thinking. They bring meals three times a day. The food is from the crew's rations and is surprisingly tasty. Probably a little heavy on the salt, but in his position, Matthew will be lucky to live long enough for high salt intake to be a problem. Maybe the crew knows the food is salty because they bring large jugs of water with each meal. Matthew's thoughts wander from Sarah to who is after them, to George H. Brown, to the new Secretary of Defense, Quentin Taylor. He wonders if Jason is even close to tracking him. He wonders if he made the right decision to ask Sarah to stand down. She was proving to be very useful, but it is now too dangerous. He can't keep risking everyone's life. He senses that even if he tries to walk away, he will not be allowed to. He knows too much. The mastermind will have no choice now but to eliminate him. But Sarah can move on.

Matthew, Kofi, and Liam can handle the rest of the investigation wherever it leads.

The cargo ship finally puts Matthew ashore. At around two a.m., he is told he is on US soil. He leaves the cargo container and is greeted by two characters. What is the best word for them, he can't decide: characters or caricatures? Jim Bob and Bean have been assigned to drive him in the back of their transport truck to Palo Alto. Liam and Kofi will be there to meet him.

Matthew, "Where are we?"

Jim Bob has a short crew cut and a large round tummy. His jeans rest comfortably below it. His complexion is ruddy, with some broken blood vessels on his nose.

"We're in the US of A, fella."

Bean is his associate; he is short and thin. His eyes dart back and forth. They make a comical pair. Matthew hops in the back of the truck and away they go.

Matthew hears a lot of classic rock blaring from the front of the truck. Bean seems to like old country. They constantly bicker over the radio station.

Jim Bob is used to hauling anything. He doesn't ask questions. Well, the only question he asks is "Is that cash," or "Is that cash?". "Cash works" is his motto. He is very reliable, so he has steady work. This job spooks him a little. He is getting paid too much to haul one guy. He must have done something really big. Jim Bob is smart enough to know that as long as he keeps doing minor "jobs" he will be fine. If he starts to do big things, he will get noticed and maybe earn another stay at the state penitentiary. This job could be dangerous. "Mo money, mo problems." That's why he brings Bean this time—Bean carries. He is lucky to get him on such short notice. Bean could have been on a fishing trip. He's a survivalist and can live for weeks on end in the bush. Bean has some major fire power. There can be trouble this time. Jim Bob is ready.

Jim Bob and Bean do not read newspapers, or they would have been able to identify Matthew. His face is not disguised. But then again, Matthew hasn't shaved in days and his beard is thick. He looks completely different.

Jim Bob now works a few jobs each month. This new business pays ten times what he used to get hauling soybeans. His new line of work is much more rewarding. He has a new pickup truck. His mortgage is all paid. Soon he will have enough to go legit. He is going to start a trucking company, hauling soybeans.

The trip settles into a routine and they all relax. They break for lunch and dinner. Breakfast is leftovers. Matthew eats by himself in the cargo hold. Bean is talkative and friendly. Jim Bob not so much.

"Truck stop serves good fixins. We'll get you some dinner." Bean spits out a large wad of dark brown tobacco.

Bean comes back and hands Matthew a large plastic bag. Matthew takes the bag and Bean locks the truck cargo hold. Matthew enjoys his dinner of french fries and beef stew. The gravy is as thick as glue.

Bean meets Jim Bob in the truck stop. Jim Bob rubs the edge of his mug as he finishes his beer.

"What do you make of this guy?" says Jim Bob.

"He's running from somethin', that's for sure," says Bean.

"He's not the muscle."

"No way, I think he is the accountant or numbers man. Somethin' like that."

"He cheated some big mukka out of some money and now he needs to disappear?" says Jim Bob.

"Somethin' like that, I agree."

Bean orders another beer from the waitress. She bends over to give him his order, then walks away.

"Nice cans."

The two men drink and pass the night away.

Matthew finishes his meal. It feels like a ball of grease settles in his stomach. He hears a knock on the door and then it opens.

"How's things going, fella?" says Jim Bob.

They never ask his name. They just call him fella.

"No problem, but I'm getting stir crazy. It's hot in here."

"Well, no need for that. Why don't you go inside and get a beer?"

Bean chimes in, "Waitress's got a great set of knockers."

Matthew breathes in the night air. He looks at his watch. The cargo area is considerably hotter than the outside air. The temperature is seventy-five degrees.

Matthew says, "Guys, I need a key to be able to get out if I need to."

Jim Bob reaches into the back pocket of his jeans and hands the spare set of keys to Matthew. "No problem, fella, just had to ask."

"Thanks."

Matthew goes into the diner and sits. The waitress approaches.

"Would you like to see a menu?" she asks.

"No, just some apple pie. With two scoops of vanilla."

"Coffee?"

"Thanks, double milk, no sugar."

"No problem."

Within a short time, the waitress returns with his order. Matthew needs to take a break. He is getting a little unhinged. Stress kills—if he isn't sharp for the next little while, he will make mistakes. He vows to enjoy the road trip with Jim Bob and Bean. They are traveling through beautiful countryside. Maybe he'll sit up front, decompress.

Initially, Jim Bob refuses to allow fella to sit up front. What if a cop stops them? Jim Bob changes his mind only after Matthew reminds him who pays his fee.

The front cab is spacious. Even though they sit side-by-side, the three of them are surprisingly comfortable. Bean sits in the middle. He wears a heavy citrus-scented cologne that Matthew learns to like after a while.

Matthew asks, "You guys like any sports?"

Bean says, "We follow basketball, Jim Bob was quite the man in his day."

"I was a good baller. Played for hours as a kid."

Matthew asks, "What position did you play?"

"One."

"Point guard, you must have been smart, good ball handler."

"Yes, sir."

Bean says, "Best I ever saw. He saw the floor. He saw everything, man."

Classic rock plays on the radio. The green countryside rolls by.

Matthew asks, "You never thought of college ball?"

"Thought of it. That was my dream. I was going to college, then the pros."

"Didn't make it?"

"Worse, I did make it."

Bean adds, "Old man Coutts was a mean dog with his boys."

Jim Bob says, "I worked, saved for my college fees. Had decent grades. I got accepted. Division one, state college."

"What happened?"

Jim Bob, "My old man wouldn't let me go."

"You would have been of age—you just sign and leave home."

"My ma was good to me. She wanted something better for herself, but it didn't work out. My old man used to beat on her. If I'd disobeyed him, he would've beat her bad, and often. I couldn't do that to my ma. I had to stay to protect her."

"He didn't like basketball?"

"Said a man's gotta know his place."

Bean tries to be supportive. "You used to practice for hours. You were real good."

"He would come home from laboring and say something like 'what you playin' at boy?' He never went to any of my games."

Bean says, "Spite."

"He just couldn't see beyond himself."

"He was a mean buzzard."

"He was a day laborer. He worked hard, played harder. Came home, had a few cold ones, and then did it all over again."

Matthew asks, "You couldn't convince him to let you go?"

"No. I begged. Mother begged."

"He wouldn't let him go. He was a nasty one."

"'You're a day laborer and nothing else,' that's what he said."

"So what happened?"

"Nothing. I finished high school, joined my dad. Two years later he was dead. Heart attack."

"Why didn't you try college then?"

"By that time I had a wife, a kid, and another on the way." Jim Bob stares out the window. The hills roll by.

Bean breaks the silence an hour later. "There's a fella on a blue motorcycle. He passed us, then stopped. He took out some binoculars, then made a call. Now he's heading back our way."

Jim Bob says, "I saw him too. There's the rest stop up ahead. Let's pull in."

Sitting in the diner, they see the motorcyclist. Matthew, Jim Bob, and Bean sip their coffee. He is on his cell phone, looking at the truck license plate.

"Bean, you juiced?"

"Yes, sir. Locked and loaded."

Jim Bob gets up and goes to the payphones at the back. He returns in ten minutes. "Police check point five miles ahead."

. . .

The man in the black fedora rubs his chin vigorously. "I really need this job done."

The man at the other end speaks in a slow, halting manner. "I'm busy."

His big hands grip the phone awkwardly. The years of street fighting caused his fingers to swell like sausages; his knuckles are calloused and thick.

The man in the fedora replies, "I haven't even told you the job."

"My cousin on the West Coast called, said you had a job. He already turned you down."

"He told me he was busy too."

"I know, must be that time of year."

The man in the fedora now plays with the brim of his hat.

"Kinda like Christmas, it's the busy season for you goons?"

"Goons? My uncle was one of those goons. He got his throat cut by your surgeon. You said it was an easy job, just supervise some operatin'. So don't call us goons—us goons died to keep you alive."

The man in the fedora is apologetic. "I'm sorry for your loss. It was just supposed to be a transplant. MacAulay should have done it, no problem. I don't know how it ended up so badly. Your man was not supposed to die. He had a Glock. I still don't know how the surgeon was able to cut him like that."

"T'anks for the apology, but my answer is still no."

"You've never refused before. I'll double your money."

"I'm busy."

"Okay, I can speak your language. I need you. Ten times your fee. I've always appreciated your top-quality work."

The man's thick hands cradle the phone. "Ten times?"

"Paid in full before the job."

"Ten times. That's real good money . . . but I must refuse."

"Do you know how much money you're turning down?"

"I'm gonna give it to you straight. You been good to me and my cousin over the many years."

"Well, thanks. You guys work clean, no loose ends. You're professionals."

"I can't take your job. Not for any money."

"Why not?"

"We have friends. Friends in all the highest places. The recent murders are attractin' a lot of attention. Serious attention."

"No one knows who is behind this."

"No, you're right, we have friends spying on that too. But it's too much what you did. It's going to go sideways. We run a nice business. Those law enforcement types leave us be for the most part. We kill our own. We don't go killing good decent people, people who matter."

"I kill who I need to kill."

"What you done is too much."

"A man like you can never know my plan, it's greatness."

"A man like me knows when someone is just too crazy. We figured out who is behind this, and a man like me ain't too bright. Not bright like a man like you. You're going down, and you ain't takin a man like me with you."

"You're scared."

"Yeah, I'm scared. We helped you get that needle. You killed two people. Two completely innocent people. For what? You kill a transplant surgeon, his wife, a nurse. That's just cracked, man. No one's gonna help you now."

"I'm offering ten times your fee."

"Money ain't much good in a six-foot cold cell. Or sitting in the electric chair."

"Who can help me then?"

"To be honest wit' you, no one on our level is going to help you. Not this time."

"Give me a name."

"You can try Mr. Page. Don't tell him how you got his name."

The phone goes silent. The man in the black fedora slams his phone down.

"Ignorant, short-sighted buffoons. Garbage of no vision. I will show them all."

Chapter Twenty-Six

Jason is taking no chances this time. He has been outsmarted too many times by Matthew. This time he has a little trick of his own. A large and very visible police roadblock is indeed five miles ahead of Matthew. However, Jason and his two trusted associates are on a little used side road two miles before the roadblock. Jason figures the smugglers will know this area like the back of their hand. This little known road is the perfect detour to avoid the roadblock. Jason and his men will open fire as soon as they round the curve in the dirt road.

. . .

Bean asks, "Do you know for sure it's for us?"

"Not for sure, but they are stopping all cars, asking for a man," says Jim Bob.

"We have to assume it's for me."

"Fella, we need to know, are you on the run from the law or from other criminals?" says Jim Bob.

"Both."

"Is it murder?"

"Yes, but I didn't do it."

Bean sighs. "Never met a murderer that did it."

"I didn't do it," says Matthew.

"Sure, fella."

"I didn't!" says Matthew.

"Jim Bob, we're now helpin' a murderer. Aidin' and abettin'. We could get the chair. Do we want this?"

Jim Bob, "Accessory to murder—if we're caught, we're going to jail for a long time."

"I already have two strikes. Next one, it's real life. I'm not never gettin' out," says Bean.

"I've done nothing. You need to believe me."

Jim Bob and Bean look at each other.

They get into the truck and head down the road. Jim Bob remembers the dirt road. They're lucky it's before the detour.

. . .

Jason's men see the truck turn onto the dirt road. They confirm a third man riding up front. Jason will finally get his man. His men are in position for the ambush. He has the element of surprise. They wait in the dense brush just beyond the curve.

Jim Bob has traveled this road many times, at all hours of the day and night. He is very tense. If he is caught with this guy, he is going to jail for a long time. Maybe he should have stuck to hauling soybeans.

The truck rumbles down the road. Alarm bells go off in his head. A few freshly broken branches on one side. Someone's been by. They did a good job of trying to hide the tire tracks, but Jim Bob is sure. The truck approaches the curve.

Jason hears the vehicle approaching. He grips his pistol tighter. He is excited as he waits for the vehicle to round the curve.

After waiting several minutes, Jason suspects something is wrong. He and his men run around the corner. They spot Matthew, Jim Bob, and Bean running through the dense shrub. The truck is left running just before the curve.

Jason can clearly see Matthew. He opens fire. His men do the same. Jason's men narrow the distance. Matthew is close behind Jim Bob. They approach a fifteen-foot cliff. Thick bushes lie below. The three jump. They get up and run into the trees.

Jason and his men follow right behind them. Matthew and Jim Bob are bruised and bloodied from the fall. Bean leads the way. He takes them deep into the woods. After a while they can no longer hear Jason barking orders. There is no more gunfire. They stop to have a rest.

Bean says, "They will bring the dogs and the heat detectors."

Jason had already contacted the drone operator. The forest is too dense, and he lost them. It will take some time to get an infrared camera to detect body heat.

Jason pieces together much of the details. No doubt Jim Bob was paid to smuggle Matthew back into the United States. He is a petty criminal. The other man they were traveling with is not identified yet.

This terrain is rough. They have no supplies, no water. This is wild country, thick dense forest. They may not survive the night, but Jason is not going to take any chances.

Jason picks up his phone. "Bring in the dogs. Also bring in two sharpshooters."

Jason will wait. They will begin an all-out manhunt when the men arrive. There is no chance to escape. Jason smiles.

· · ·

Bean takes pride in being able to live off the land. He guides Matthew and Jim Bob to an isolated cave. It is very close to the initial ambush site. Bean waits to see which direction the search will go. Bean then takes them into the dense bush in the opposite direction. By midnight Matthew realizes they have escaped.

"What do we do now?"

Jim Bob says, "No worries."

It is pitch black. There is no moon in the sky. Jim Bob pulls out his cell phone. In no time the group is in the back of a small van. When they finally drop Matthew off, they are all exhausted.

"As promised, I deliver on time," says Jim Bob.

Matthew says, "Thanks, this was huge. You need to disappear for a while."

Bean says, "No problem, fella. Maybe we'll do a little campin'. A little huntin', a little fishin'."

"When this is over, I'll send word. I'll make it right," says Matthew.

Jim Bob hands Matthew a piece of paper. "Here's my cell. Remember no job's too small. As long as the cash is right."

CHAPTER TWENTY-SEVEN

Kofi's eyes grow wide when Matthew recounts his surgery on Kevin Price. Liam listens carefully when he tells of the road trip with Jim Bob and Bean. Matthew is glad to be back. The familiar white lacquer and brushed aluminum edifice that is Alice is comforting.

Kofi asks, "Do we go to the current Secretary of Defense and tell him his predecessor was killed with a plan to transplant his face?"

Liam says, "What role did Quentin play in this? After all he gained the most from the death of George H. Brown."

Matthew looks surprised. "You can't believe he is involved?"

Liam says, "No, I don't think he is. It seems clear the plan was to put a double in the Secretary of Defense office. He would be able to pass secrets on to a foreign government."

Kofi says, "When his plan failed, did he just insert himself into the job? Is Quentin behind this whole game?"

Matthew says, "If that were the case, there would be no need to call attention to everything by continuing to kill."

Kofi realizes Matthew is right. "I agree. The real question is: why are they still trying to kill Matthew? It made sense initially to kill the transplant team in the New York operating room. They could alert others to the plot, but they didn't see the head. When you started to probe the case, it made sense to try to dissuade you. But the plot failed. Why keep hounding you?"

Matthew says, "That phase of the plot failed. They are using their backup plan. They obviously have something on the go."

Kofi takes a deep breath. "It's something big—we're onto something big."

Alice chimes in. "Based on what I have heard, I would agree. I have all but ruled out a foreign power. The only governments with this capability would not risk this. An attempt to obtain our nuclear access codes or kill and then place a double agent in the US government is an act of war. We are dealing with an individual. An individual of almost endless resources and ingenuity."

"Any idea who?" says Liam.

Alice says, "This person is so cunning, I think they will escape detection. I have looked at the potential candidates, searched many databases, but have nothing so far."

Matthew says, "Keep looking."

Kofi adds, "They have made one crucial mistake by continuing to try to eliminate anyone who is searching for Tom's murderer. They have confirmed that whatever they are planning is still going on and needs to be kept secret."

Liam says, "They have no choice. Matthew has shown he will keep looking. They have to eliminate him."

Matthew says, "I need to do some more digging and I need to move around in the US.'

Kofi asks, "You want to go back to Steven Jardine?"

"I think I need his face. Liam can give the anesthetic."

Liam says, "I don't know, with that beard you had when you first came in, I don't think you need a new face."

Matthew's cell phone rings. Everyone who has the number is here except Sarah. He is anxious to hear her voice.

"Hi, Matthew, I've been kidnapped."

Chapter Twenty-Eight

"**K**eep out of our business. We don't want you in t'ings that don't concern you. Stop looking into t'ings. In two weeks we tell you where you pick her up. If we hear you are still putting your nose where it doesn't belong, then bye, bye Sarah. I make myself clear? We watching you."

Matthew has troubling understanding the slurred speech. "Let me talk to Sarah again."

"Matthew, I'm all right."

"When did they get you?"

"I got off the plane and . . ."

The phone is dragged out of Sarah's hands.

"She alive and well. She being cared for real good. That can change."

With that the line goes dead.

Matthew feels dizzy. Vertigo. He is lightheaded and nauseous.

"Sarah's been kidnapped. She—"

Alice interrupts, "I have it taped."

Alice replays the call for the group. Matthew goes to a corner of the room and slumps into a chair, holding his head in his hands.

Liam goes over to him. "It's not great news."

"I got her into this, it's my fault . . . I never told you this, but the night I did the transplant, she slapped me. I had just killed Mr. Glock, got us all out alive, and she slapped me. She said she didn't need this, not now."

"She's a special woman. We're going to get her back."

Matthew seems not to hear. "When we were in the library looking for the transplant patient, I remember how good I felt. Not looking for the transplant, being with her. My face was stuck in her hair most of the time . . . I can smell her now."

"Matthew, pull yourself together. Sarah needs us now. She needs us to think, to act."

Matthew puts his head back into his hands. Kofi is at the other end of the room.

Kofi says, "Alice, where did the call originate?"

"I am tracing it now. So far I have followed the call to Dubai, Dublin, Charlotte, London, Rio de Janeiro. It may take a minute."

Liam walks over to Kofi. "What do we do now?" he asks in a lowered voice.

"We have to go get Sarah."

"Do we?"

"Yes."

"Do we have to do exactly what they want, play into their hands?"

Matthew has left the chair and is behind Liam. "They may harm Sarah. We need to get her immediately. Alice did you trace the call?"

"The call cannot be traced."

Kofi asks, "Do we pursue Michael?"

Liam says, "I agree Michael is the key."

Kofi says, "I have reliable evidence he is now on Karakatura. He may have a cabin there."

Liam says, "It's his base of operations. Michael Coulson could be the ringleader."

After a moment, Kofi asks "Should we just walk away?"

"What?" says Matthew.

Liam tries to placate Matthew. "Should we just go get Sarah and leave this thing? We really don't know what is going to happen."

Kofi says, "Something's going to happen."

Liam says, "I think we need to free Sarah. She needs to get on with her life. She's given too much already."

Kofi hesitates to give up. "We're close, so close."

Liam says, "I agree, but whatever it is, they may be stopped by regular law enforcement anyway. Do we really need to do this? That's all I'm asking?"

Matthew says, "Why would you even ask that? If we don't stop this, no one will."

"Is Sarah's life worth it?"

"I agree with Matthew. I know what you're saying, Liam, but we have to stop this. We can't take a chance."

Liam asks, "So we leave Sarah?"

· · ·

Sarah takes short, quick breaths. She tries to get herself to relax, but since she regained consciousness, she is unable to control her breathing. She trembles all over. She is not sure where she is or how long she has been sedated. Now she is firmly tied up.

Acne scarring has left her captor's skin very irregular. Wiggie is rough when moving her. Sarah is sure it has been at least twelve hours since she talked to Matthew. She can now see Wiggie's partner. Sal is boyish looking. He has straggly black hair and a slight build. He is barely five feet tall. Sal gives her some water and loosens the ropes around her wrists.

"Sal, I'm going to see if I can score some rock," says Wiggie.

"No problem, Wiggie, just be back here soon. If the boss calls and you're not here . . ."

"I already thought of that. If Mr. Page calls, tell him Wiggie's in the toilet taking a dump. Di-A-Ree-A. Then call me on my cell, and I'll be back in ten."

"Suit yourself, bro."

With that Wiggie leaves the room. His eyes are wild, high. Looks like he is on multiple substances.

Sarah is on the floor. Sal moves her to a chair. He takes off the duct tape that covers her mouth and gives her some cool water. It feels good on her throat. She detects the faint smell of cologne on Sal, a woodsy scent. He is clean-shaven and neatly dressed.

"You don't have to do this. You can let me go," says Sarah.

Sal replaces the duct tape on her mouth. With great care he ties her hands to the back of the chair. He smiles as he unties her legs. He takes her skirt off. He folds it neatly and places it on the kitchen table. He pulls her left leg behind her head and ties it to the top of the chair. He ties the other leg behind her head on the other side. His smile widens as he takes a moment to admire his work. Sal stares for a long time. Sarah begins to understand the terror that is about to occur.

CHAPTER TWENTY-NINE

Wiggie. Obviously a street name. No one knows Wiggie's real name, or even how he got the name Wiggie. He probably can't remember either. He would need to look at his driver's license. Come to think of it, he doesn't have a driver's license. It is suspended for driving while intoxicated. He blew over the limit. He couldn't complain, fair is fair. He had multiple illegal substances in his body at the time. He was real messed up. Cop didn't even find the loaded gun in his car, so all in all, the impaired driving charge was a bonus. It probably was for the better. Hey, look at the bright side, at least he didn't have to pay to renew his license. And he is still driving just the same. What is the purpose of a driver's license anyway?

. . .

Sarah thinks it is morning, but there are no windows. She awakes from a fitful sleep. There are no clocks in the room. Sal and Wiggie do not wear watches. She has no idea what time it is. When they open the door, she cannot see much.

She must create a plan to escape. There are no guarantees anyone will be able to save her. Wiggie could go off on her for no reason and kill her. She now most fears Sal, though. She is lucky Wiggie is the boss. When Wiggie came back, Sarah told him what Sal had done. Surprisingly, he apologized, said it wasn't part of the plan. They were paid to take care of her. Wiggie was relieved when she said Sal had not touched her. He did not remove her underwear. He just stared. Wiggie gave Sal a good beating. Some savage kicks and punches. He even brought out a large knife. Sal begged for mercy. Sarah was relieved Wiggie put the switchblade knife away; the long silver blade looked menacing. Wiggie told Sal never to do that again. Sal, so far, has obeyed, but he still has that look in his eyes.

After some hours pass, Wiggie brings her a meal. It is canned tuna, canned corn, and a soda. He unties her hands and feet and then leaves.

Thinking of Sal and Wiggie and what they might do to her is beyond terrifying. She calms herself down. There are some things that might happen to her that she cannot control. There is no point in fearing this. Whatever is going to happen will happen. But she is not powerless. She will plan for her escape. She will not fear. Whatever happens, she will not be a victim.

Wiggie shuts the door with a bang. She smiles because she has her first weapon. The canned tuna and the canned corn are opened, but the metal lids were left on. The circular metal tops are razor sharp at the edges. She takes both lids off and puts them in her skirt pockets.

She is hungry and eats quickly. Things are beginning to look up. The canned corn and tuna are national brands, found anywhere. The soda, however, is a local brand. She is in California. She looks around the room.

There are no windows. It looks like a room in the middle of the house. The only way in or out is the door. Maybe they built it.

Sal enters and picks up her tray. "Why don't you take a stretch?"

Sal throws her an extra can of soda. He watches her drink it.

"Thanks," says Sarah.

"No problem."

Sal returns after thirty minutes to tie her up and remove the tray. She listens. There is no street noise, no cars. They must be in a very secluded area. She wonders if they are out in the country. Highly unlikely, since Wiggie needs to be in the city, near his pusher. Sarah tries to figure out what neighborhood she could be in. She concludes she is in a quiet working-class neighborhood. If she can get out of the house, any of the neighbors will help her.

In the next room, Wiggie throws a small leather ball against the wall. The repetitive sound fills the house.

Wiggie says, "This is lame."

Sal says, "We're getting good money."

"Shut up."

"I'm just saying."

"Get me a beer," says Wiggie.

The modest bungalow is dirty, but the fridge works. Sal obediently gets Wiggie a beer. Wiggie takes the beer and drinks it all in one continuous gulp. He throws the can on the floor.

"Another," says Wiggie.

Sal fetches another beer. Wiggie drinks this even quicker. He throws the can on the floor. Some of the beer left in the can oozes onto the floor.

"Put it in the garbage. And clean up the beer."

"Sure." Sal scoops up the can and puts it in the garbage. He uses a washcloth to sop up the beer from the dirty vinyl flooring.

"I'm going out. Be back in ten," says Wiggie.

Sarah hears the front door slam shut. She makes a mental note of the direction of the sound. The door is to the left of her door. *As soon as I am out of this room, run left*, she thinks. She falls into a deep sleep.

• • •

Sarah realizes she is not sure how long she has been here. They don't have a radio or TV. She has lost all track of time when Sal comes to pick up her tray.

"Don't you guys ever listen to TV?" says Sarah.

"Wiggie won't allow it," says Sal.

"What's your name?"

"Salvatore, people call me Sal."

"Salvatore, what's the harm in a little TV?"

"Wiggie's orders."

"How do you pass the time?"

Sal picks up the headphones that are around his neck. "Beats."

"How about Wiggie?"

"He's in and out." Sal hesitates. "Can I ask you something?"

"Sure, Salvatore."

"How did your hair get so white?"

Sarah laughs. "It's just the way it is."

Sal seems offended.

Sarah, "No, it's not the question. It's just I get asked that quite often, but I didn't expect it at this moment."

She wants him to like her. If he sees her as a person, maybe she will have a chance.

. . .

Sarah estimates that she has to have been here at least five days. She could have been here for a week. There is no hope that Matthew and the team will find her. Alice will be desperately trying to locate the source of the call, but Sarah knows it was a cell phone. Surely a throw-away—the kind drug dealers use, untraceable. Maybe Alice can pinpoint the location. Even if they find her, who's to say they will stop the main objective to try to rescue her? Will they give any information to the local police? If the local police find her, she will be in trouble. She is a co-conspirator in a few murders, and they probably will peg her as Matthew's accomplice. It will also lead the police to Matthew and Liam. She swallows hard as she realized the cavalry is not coming.

She formulates her plan. The razor sharp lids are good weapons. When Wiggie comes in to deliver the tray and unties her, she can strike. He is the stronger and the most dangerous of the two. Wiggie has to be neutralized. Should she ask Salvatore for help? He seems to be warming up to her. No, she can't take the chance—he is too weird. She is confident she can overpower Salvatore anyway. She is bigger and stronger. She is also desperate.

The plan is simple. She will slice Wiggie in the neck. She remembers Matthew and Mr. Glock. Aim for the same area. Even if she misses, there will be a lot of bleeding. Wiggie will panic and she will then run through the door and head left. She is prepared for locks, but doesn't think there will be any. As soon as she hits the street, she will go to the nearest house or flag down a car. If no one answers the door, she will break as many windows as possible and keep running. This will bring police to the area. What will she tell the police when they take her into custody? She hasn't quite figured that out, but whatever happens, at least she will be alive.

She reviews the plan. It is simple. It will work. She will go in the morning. Maximum daylight allows anyone near to see her and discourages Sal and Wiggie from following. Even though she has no windows, she has figured out day from night based on the comings and goings of Wiggie.

What if she only wounds Wiggie? Or Wiggie does not panic at the bleeding and captures her. This is the downside risk. Wiggie will probably be high. He will be very, very angry. She is sure they are under orders not to harm her in any way, at least for the next two weeks, but it is doubtful that Wiggie will obey those orders if she slashes his throat and tries to escape. Should she just wait to see if help comes? Alice is pretty amazing. It is clear she is much more than a surgical robot.

Sarah makes up her mind. She will not wait for help that may never arrive. She will execute her plan. If the plan fails and Wiggie catches her, he will definitely kill her, of that she has no doubt.

She will execute her plan. She is not going to be a victim.

• • •

Wiggie delivers her food. It is french fries and a hamburger. A can of orange soda. Is this a bad omen? Wiggie and Sal have no way of knowing she hates orange soda. She drinks very little soda, and never orange soda. Ever since she was a child, she has had a thing about orange soda. Coke, ginger ale, even cream soda are all fine. No orange soda. Never. Sarah forces herself to eat the meal and drink it anyway. She needs all the energy she can get.

Wiggie enters and runs his fingers through her hair. "This really is quite the turn on."

Wiggie waits for a response. Silence.

"It's either me or Sal you know," says Wiggie.

Silence.

"You should have been in modeling, Dr. Larsson," says Wiggie. "Yes, I know all about you," says Wiggie.

Silence.

Wiggie unties her hands and feet. He then removes her skirt and tosses it in the corner. She is terrified the metal lids will fall out or he will feel them.

"At least with me, I promise to be gentle. Sal, well, let's just say the boy weren't brought up right, the things he do." Wiggie laughs deeply.

Sarah walks to get her skirt. Wiggie is still laughing. He watches as she stumbles. The perfect opportunity, she bends forward as if embarrassed, then moves to pick up her skirt. She turns to pull out the lid from the pocket.

Wiggie moves closer and unbuttons his pants. He is expecting her to move back, but instead Sarah turns and lunges upward and forward, slicing his neck with the razor sharp metal lid. She runs out, leaving the skirt on the floor. It is a deep gash. His reaction time is slowed by the drugs and alcohol. He does nothing to avoid the slash. The blood flows in spurts, and Wiggie screams in pain.

"She cut me!"

Before Sarah can assess if she has cut the major artery, the carotid, she is out the door and moving left. Sal is surprised to see Sarah running through the door. The force of Sarah's kick makes him fall to the ground. He holds his ruptured testicle and screams in pain.

The front door is unlocked and in a few seconds she is outside. The house is a small bungalow with a large front yard. She enters the night air. It is pitch black. The street lights are on. She quickly assesses the street.

Sarah is being held in a house that has been foreclosed in the middle of an area where all the houses have been foreclosed. That is why she heard very little traffic. A few of the houses have already been demolished to stop squatters. The rest are all boarded up.

Sal and Wiggie have recovered. Both are running toward her. Sarah realizes she has not cut Wiggie's carotid, and she runs down the abandoned street. Sal is surprisingly agile. He has a slight build, but Sarah does not realize until now that he is in reasonable shape. He is closing the distance, but she is nearing the next street. It is a straight foot race, winner take all. Sarah is athletic and quick. Wiggie is behind, screaming expletives. Sal is slowly but surely losing ground, and he holds his right groin.

Sarah glances back, feeling the fatigue. Sal is running again. If anything his pace is quickening, but he cannot close the gap. Sarah gets to the road. Wiggie has caught up to Sal, but they slow and move into the shadows.

Sarah looks up and sees a car. The headlights are directly approaching her. As the car slows, Sarah feels a surge of joy. She is tired, but she did it. She is free.

Peter is coming home late from work. At least that's what he tells his wife. He has been seeing Ginger for a few months. One night here, one night there, nothing serious. He tells himself he loves his wife, their two boys. He just needs a break.

Ginger is nice and likes nice things. He hasn't told his wife he is three months behind on the mortgage payments because he has bought Ginger a few of those nice things. She just has expensive tastes, and when she gets to know him better, she will cost less. Then he will get back to paying the mortgage. And dropping off his sons at football practice. He had a few beers at Ginger's place, but is sure he isn't drunk now. In front of him, in the middle of the street, is a very beautiful young woman in black underwear and a white blouse. She has white hair that is bizarre, but on her it looks amazing. He slows and sees she has a crazed, desperate look. It is a real turn on. Probably the drugs. She is a street prostitute. He tries to remember how much money is in his wallet. Only $20. He had given Ginger $500 tonight. She needed some things she said. What could he get for $20? He slows his car. Probably she's desperate, and she'll take anything. Then again, she looks high class. Probably not much for a twenty. But something's better than nothing. He had chosen this route since the area is deserted. No chance anyone will spot his car in this place. He definitely could stop. I wonder if she takes credit. Come to think of it, his credit is overdrawn, a tanning bed for Ginger.

She looks desperate, maybe she would take $20. This is too good to be true. She doesn't look like a prostitute. She is way too high class. Maybe this is an undercover cop. Maybe this is a trap. He is no criminal, and he doesn't want to go to jail. He presses the accelerator and speeds away. What is he thinking? He is a married man after all.

Sarah cannot believe her luck. There are no other cars on the road, and the area is deserted. She feels a vice-like grip on her arm. Sal holds her tightly with Wiggie close behind. Wiggie has his left hand on his neck; there is blood all over his clothes. Wiggie smiles. Sarah never noticed before how yellow and misshapen his teeth are.

Sarah is bound firmly to her chair. Sal ties her up even more tightly than Wiggie. In the meantime Wiggie has put a makeshift bandage around his neck. He is calm, almost sober.

Wiggie speaks very softly. "Leave us."

Sal looks at Sarah. He remains.

Sarah knows she's in serious trouble. "The guy in the car is going to call 911. The police are going to be here any minute."

Wiggie unleashes a punch to Sarah's right jaw. The area goes numb, and Sarah sees stars. She tries to open and close her jaw. She remembers from medical school that if your teeth don't fit together after a punch to the jaw, there is a good chance that the jaw has been broken. It's funny the useful things she learned in medical school. She tries to open and close her mouth.

Very softly, she hears Wiggie. "Leave us now, Sal, thank you."

Sal leaves.

Sarah can smell Wiggie's breath, a nasty stench like rotten eggs. The door closes very quietly, and the room is completely silent. There is no sound from the other side of the door. Sal may have left the house. Wiggie and Sarah are all alone. Wiggie rips off her white blouse. Her bra is dirty, the clasps broken. They barely hold. Her black underwear contrasts with her pale white skin. Wiggie smiles. His rancid body odor makes her gag. His hair is matted with dirt and grease.

It looks like Wiggie is going to leave. He turns and moves toward the door. A surge of relief floods Sarah. He is disciplined. He was ordered not the harm her, and he is going to leave her alone. Then without warning, he turns and punches her. The wind leaves her body and she gasps for air. Wiggie laughs hysterically, and the mad look returns to his eyes.

"Fooled you."

Wiggie then takes out a knife from his pocket. He opens the fourteen-inch knife with the thick black handle. The silver blade glistens in the light. Sharp honed steel.

"You are going to die. But first I'm going to tell you how I'm going to kill you."

Sarah knows. This is it. She is relaxed. She realizes she is crying and she stops. She meets his gaze and stops squirming.

He continues to talk, but her change is now affecting him. He seems intimidated. He glances at the door, rechecks her bindings. He then picks up the knife. He has finished with talk. He is disappointed that it has not increased her fear as he had hoped, but whatever, he still is going to enjoy it.

She sees the excitement in his eyes. She prays it will be quick.

At that moment the door bursts open. Wiggie is furious. His back to the door, he has his knife above Sarah's left cheek.

Wiggie yells, "Sal, get out of here before I give you—"

Wiggie does not finish the sentence. The knife is ripped from his arm and he is spun around. The upper cut to his face is so forceful it knocks him off his chair. Wiggie falls to the ground. The wound in his neck begins to ooze. Mr. Page is a muscular man. He drags Wiggie from the room by his hair.

Mr. Page, "You idiot, I told you she was not to be hurt, not unless I tell you."

"Sorry. She tried to escape."

Mr. Page gives him a backhanded slap.

"Sal called me, I know. So what?" says Mr. Page.

Mr. Page's arms are full of tattoos. Brightly colored, very artistic. A dragon eating his tail on his left forearm. He is a weightlifter and the use of anabolic steroids has given his arms a size three times larger than the average man. He makes a fist and brings it down on Wiggie's nose. The sound of the bones shattering is like a crispy cracker being crunched.

"You're an idiot."

"Sorry, Mr. Page."

"I give the orders. If she ends up dead, we'll all be dead." Mr. Page continues, "We're not working for chumps on this one."

He removes a large black Smith & Wesson Magnum from his pants. "Should I kill you right here?"

At this range the gun will blow a hole the size of a football through Wiggie.

"I'm sorry, I got confused. Look, she cut me."

Sal interjects, "She tried to escape. She tried to kill Wiggie. Let him live."

Wiggie begins to cry. "Please, don't do it, I'm sorry."

Mr. Page looks around. "Did anyone see her when she got out?"

Wiggie responds too quickly. "No, we got her before she left the yard."

Mr. Page points the weapon at Sal. "Is that true?"

"Yes."

"I swear, there was no one; it's the middle of the night," says Wiggie.

"You're very lucky Sal called me. If she had been injured in any way . . ."

"Sal's great, I love him. Sorry, Mr. Page."

Mr. Page hesitates, then picks up his cell phone and dials the number. This is an emergency. Sal and Wiggie are puzzled by the look of fear on Mr. Page's face. They can hear bits and pieces of the conversation.

"I'm sorry . . . She is safe and unharmed. No one saw nothing . . . I am sure. Thank you, sir, my bad. It will not happen again."

He closes his cell phone and lets out a sigh. "Wiggie, you're a lucky mother. Lay off the rock."

Mr. Page abruptly leaves, not even bothering to close the door behind him. They hear the car drive off.

"I'm outta here. I really need some rock."

Sal closes the front door behind Wiggie.

Chapter Thirty

The next morning Sarah is treated to a big breakfast. Wiggie brings in her food. He has stitches on his neck. He loosens the ropes and throws her a bag of new clothes. Dark green skirt, a red shirt, and black panties and bra. "Thanks," says Sarah. Wiggie turns and leaves.

Sarah has replayed the events in her mind over and over all night. She is drained. She has hardly slept. Her chances of escape are now gone. She remembers the look of the man in the car. He was early forties. She will always see that face. She even remembers the comb-over covering his bald spot when he drove by. There is no way he is going to call the police.

She is being kept alive to control Matthew. If they determine he is still investigating, they will bring her to the phone again, and no doubt provide better persuasion for him to stop. Wiggie and Sal cannot harm her. The blackout blinds on the windows are gone. There is no point now, since she knows the time of day. The person in charge of this phase is taking his orders from the man or woman Matthew is after. Soon, they will not have any interest in Sarah Larsson. Mr. Page allowed her to see him. That can only mean she will be killed after the time is up. Sal and Wiggie will be free to do as they please with her.

· · ·

Sal sits quietly reading a men's magazine. Wiggie is really beginning to dislike this guy. Maybe he should get some payback after this is all over. Calling Mr. Page last night, that was plain double crossing. But maybe he did good. No doubt, Mr. Page would have killed them both if he had knifed Sarah. So maybe Sal saved his life. Whatever.

Wiggie says, "I'm out of here, cover me."

"No problem," says Sal.

As soon as Wiggie leaves, Sal goes to Sarah's room. She jumps when she sees Sal. It is not meal time and usually she is left alone.

"Salvatore, please let me go."

Sal just stares.

"Salvatore, please."

Sal's creepy stare continues.

· · ·

Two days pass and the routine is back. Sarah eats her meals; she has a little time to walk around in the room. Wiggie is high all the time and almost unable to give any instructions. He cannot be trusted to even bring in the food tray without dropping it. He sniffles constantly. His absences from the house are more and more frequent.

"Salvatore, let me go."

"Can't do that, Sarah." "I will tell the police that you were kind. I will ask them to go easy on you."

"No can do."

"Salvatore, please, I beg you. I'm sure they are going to kill me soon."

"I didn't hear that. We're to keep you safe."

"For now, yes, but later? Murder is a life sentence; you could even get the death penalty. Do you want that?"

Silence.

"Wiggie is a drug addict. Even if you guys get away with killing me, can he keep the secret? He is going to sell you out."

"I don't think so. He's in as deep as me."

"The minute he gets caught for drugs, or anything, he's going to sell you out. He'll tell the cops he has something. He'll give it to them if they give him immunity. Or a lighter sentence. He'll make a deal to save himself."

"I don't think so, he's full-in."

"Don't you see? He'll say he was never here. You did the killing; he thought it was a kidnapping. The police will believe him. He will sell you out, Salvatore, I know it."

Sal looks confused.

"Salvatore, I can help you."

Sal replaces Sarah's bindings and takes the tray.

. . .

The next day Sal brings in the breakfast. Canned ham, a banana, diet lemonade.

"Where's Wiggie?"

"Phoned me, not coming in today. I'm in charge."

"Salvatore, I grew up in Chicago. It's a beautiful city. Where'd you grow up?"

"Midwest, some time out east. Moved around a lot."

"Are your parents still alive?"

"Don't quite know. Never met my father. Mother had a drug habit, kind of like Wiggie. Last I spoke to her . . . Ain't heard from her in a while."

"Who do you care about? A girlfriend? A grandmother?"

"Ain't got no girl, no relatives."

"Salvatore, you need to think about the future. Someday you'll have people who care about you and who you care about. Let me help you, so you don't end up in jail."

Sal slaps her hard. His eyes are wild.

"Please, Salvatore. I like you."

He slaps her again. "Don't lie to me. You're lying like the rest. Do you think I am so dumb that I don't know why you are being nice to me? I know you wouldn't spend a minute looking in my direction on any other day. Well, I'm not going to kill you, but I'm gonna get to know you real good."

. . .

Liam says, "Agreed, it could be a trap."

Alice says, "I doubt that it is a trap. No other computer in the world has the technology to trace that call. It was very sophisticated. Look at the time it took me. They did not want us to know their location. We now have a good idea of who they are, their habits."

Liam stares at the 3-D hologram Alice has generated of Sarah's location. Alice has produced reports on Wiggie and Sal, including photo images. "Whatever Michael's planning is on Karakatura."

Kofi says, "Yes, the answer is there. If we save Sarah, it's going to delay us. I have a feeling whatever Michael is planning is going to cost many more lives."

"One life versus many." Liam looks at the hologram showing the deserted street Sarah is on. The house has rotten wooden beams, paint peeling from around the boarded-up windows.

"We don't know that."

Kofi slowly nods his head. "Yes, Matthew, I'm afraid we do. We all know that whatever this is, if it goes through, many American lives will be lost."

"We don't know what this is."

Kofi says, "No, we don't. But remember The Binary Sequence— bioweapons coupled with face transplants—we have some general ideas."

"What are our odds of a successful rescue?" says Liam.

Matthew says, "Low, these guys are going to be armed. Probably experienced, high-level criminals. Whoever is behind this only works with the best."

Kofi continues to play devil's advocate. "They could turn their guns on her as soon as we enter."

Liam says, "That's my fear."

Matthew can't even think about this possibility. "That's why, if we do this, we have to commit to go in quick, with deadly force if necessary."

Kofi says, "No hesitation."

Liam asks, "Should we transplant you back to the anonymous face? Then you can investigate. Give us some more time to plan a raid for

Sarah. Or if we get lucky, we solve things and then we turn over what we have to the police."

Matthew says, "If they start to see mystery man Steven Jardine popping up in places asking about Tom, how long do you think it will take them to put two and two together?"

Kofi lays out the facts. "It boils down to, do we try to save one life, Sarah's, but in doing so, lose the chance to save many lives? Whatever is planned, you wouldn't go to this trouble unless it was major."

Liam adds, "We don't even know if she is alive. I hate to say it, but she could have been killed after that first call."

Matthew says, "Can we leave Sarah and try to find her after we go to Karakatura?"

Kofi says, "It may be time to stand down, Matthew."

"Give up?"

"Stand down. Stop this madness."

Liam asks, "Do what they say?"

"I'm saying we walk away. We're overmatched. It's time to bring in law enforcement."

Matthew says, "I know it's hard."

Liam's stare pierces Matthew. "Hard. I haven't seen my wife or daughters in I don't know how long. We're moving in shadows, and we don't know if we'll be caught or killed. Look at us, three doctors trying to solve this. Hard. It's beyond hard."

Kofi agrees. "Matthew, it may be time to stop. Sometimes it's best to retreat. This is beyond us. We should turn over what we have to the police. They're the ones with resources we don't have."

"And how exactly do we do that? You're the only one they don't know about. Liam, me, Sarah, we're all going to jail. And that's the best case scenario."

"Well, what do you propose?"

"George H. Brown was killed on Karakatura. Michael climbed with him."

Kofi says, "I know what you're saying. We may get some answers on Karakatura. A high-level friend of mine is sure Michael's on

Karakatura. Edith Clarke worked with me, and her information is, for sure, correct."

Liam says, "Going to Karakatura is going to put Sarah in danger. If we just stop, she may have a chance."

Kofi takes a deep breath. "It's your call, Matthew."

Chapter Thirty-One

Sal has dimmed the lights and set two plates with plastic cutlery. Sarah hasn't noticed the plastic card table near the front window until now.

"Wine, Sarah?" "No."

"I'm really excited to be on our first date. The first of many. I'm not going to hurt you, promise."

"Salvatore, there is someone out there for you, but it's not me. I'm tied up. This is not a date."

"It is a date. I love you, Sarah."

Sarah closes her eyes and swallows. Her shoulders are slumped, and she seems five inches shorter, a frail weak woman. She notices the knife and fork are set backward. There is dried old food on the plastic knife. She focuses on these trivialities because she can't think about Sal's declaration of love.

"Did you like your new underwear, Sarah? I picked it. You look good. You really should try the wine, it's good."

Sarah remains silent.

"I'll take that as a no."

Sal drinks his wine from the plastic cup. He looks over at Sarah. She really is a beautiful woman. She has the most perfect face. She must go to a really expensive hair salon to get her hair that color. A woman like this always does.

He is tantalized by her body. He pulls open her shirt. Her abdomen is flat and smooth. He admires the gentle curves of her skin on her firm abdomen. He can feel the muscles tense underneath. He walks back to his seat and takes a sip of wine. Her legs are long, smooth, and shapely. They gently brush the top of the table. He has never seen a girl like this. Well, only on the Internet. He never dreamed he would be alone with a girl like this in real life. Drinking wine. He takes another sip. He doesn't want the night to end.

Wiggie will score some rock and not be back until tomorrow afternoon, if not later. No worries, tonight Sal will take his time. Do it proper like. When he finishes, he will kill Sarah, the final climax. Unfortunately, this will be their first and last date.

Sal will then make another call. He will tell Mr. Page he came out of the washroom to find that Wiggie had killed Sarah. Wiggie was too drugged up to know what he did. Wiggie then took off. He knew where Wiggie was, a friend just texted him. Sal will tell Mr. Page where to find Wiggie, and he'll be dead before sunrise. Who knows, for his loyalty, Mr. Page may even give him a bonus?

At that moment the door bursts open. Sal's gun is on the table beside the wine. Before he can reach for it, Matthew has Sal pinned, a revolver pressed firmly at his skull. Kofi and Liam have automatic weapons drawn.

They have rehearsed the plan many times and are prepared for anything. With overwhelming firepower and surprise, they secure the scene and rescue Sarah without a single shot being fired.

Matthew uses the same rope that held Sarah bound to tie Sal down. Sarah is so overcome she seems stunned. Liam opens a duffel bag. He brings out new clothes.

Sarah buttons up her blouse. "These clothes are fine. Let's just leave."

"I'll talk to Sarah. Kofi, Liam, search the house for the other one."

Matthew holds her tightly. "It's okay. We came back for you."

Tears slowly flow down Sarah's face. Her legs and arms ache from being tied to the chair for so long.

"You took your sweet time."

"What?"

"You took your sweet time coming to get me."

Matthew laughs. "Yes, we did. But we came."

"I'm glad."

Matthew smiles. "You're staying with me from now on. I give you a simple plan to get back home and look where you end up."

"Decided to take the long way home I guess."

Matthew and Sarah hug.

"You're staying with me from now on."

"Remember who gets to say what I do with my life."

"Don't I get to say what you do with your life?"

"I'll think about it."

Kofi and Liam return.

"The house is clear. Just this guy, no one else."

"There is one more. He must have gone out," says Matthew.

Kofi says, "He could be back any minute."

"Take Sarah and go to the car. I'll be there in a minute."

Matthew is alone with Sal. Matthew is amazed at how weak this man looks, like an underdeveloped tree. A sapling. It wasn't given any good soil or water and here's the result. A stunted, twisted tree.

"When is the other one coming back?" says Matthew.

Sal is silent. Matthew unleashes a ferocious backhanded slap with his left hand. The force of the blow is intense. Sal's face jerks back. Matthew grabs Sal's hair and snaps his neck back even further.

He rams the gun into Sal's mouth. The sound of Sal's front teeth breaking is like glass cracking. Sal's blood oozes around the barrel of the gun. Matthew is going to pull the trigger. Sal closes his eyes.

"When is he coming back?" says Matthew.

"I don't know, man. He's drugged up pretty good."

The words are garbled. Matthew forces the gun deeper down Sal's throat, almost cutting off his breathing.

"I swear, I don't know."

Matthew's hand tightens around the gun.

Sal screams, "Wiggie is out for some rock. He'll be back tomorrow."

Matthew puts the weapon in his side holster. He then places his thumb on Sal's left eye. He increases the pressure. Sal's face contorts with pain.

Matthew leans in close to Sal and speaks. "In thirty seconds you're going to permanently lose vision in this eye. Do you understand what I am saying? You will go blind. Then I will move on to the other eye."

"Please let me go."

"Who do you work for?"

"I don't know."

The pressure on his eyeball increases. His vision begins to fade in and out.

"Not good enough."

"Mr. Page. But he's not the boss—we've never met the boss. Please stop."

Matthew releases the pressure. Sal's vision is blurry, but he can see that Matthew has taken out his revolver. Matthew presses it firmly against Sal's head. Sal begins to cry uncontrollably.

"Please, I'm sorry. I didn't touch her. I swear."

"Who does Mr. Page report to? I'm not going to ask again."

The bullet is loud. Sal is silent for a second until he realizes he has not been shot. Matthew calmly walks out the door.

• • •

The members of the car are silent as Matthew approaches. The sound of the shot still rings in their ears.

Liam says, "I'm sorry they got off so light. I wish we could have called the police. Matthew, did you find out who they work for?"

"No, he doesn't know."

The car speeds away, leaving the empty neighborhood behind.

Kofi says, "Kidnapping is a crime. We should report it."

Sarah says, "The real crime is these clothes. Who would match a red blouse with a green skirt?"

Liam, Kofi, and Matthew give a hollow laugh.

"Your jaw is bruised," says Kofi.

"It's not bad, not broken," says Sarah.

Liam wants to be sure Sarah is okay, but he's unsure what to say. "They didn't touch you?"

"Relax, nothing happened. I'm fine."

Kofi says, "You did good."

The car goes silent. Finally, Sarah asks the one question they all want to know. "Matthew, did you kill Salvatore?"

They all heard the shot.

Matthew smiles, his face relaxes, and his eyes soften. He has morphed back into Dr. Matthew MacAulay, the surgeon.

"He was so scared he answered all my questions. I didn't have to touch him."

Kofi, Sarah, and Liam all laugh. The laughter crescendos. Kofi keeps the car speeding down the road. The night seems a little less dark.

Chapter Thirty-Two

Aly Smith has come to hate the hospital. It symbolizes all that is wrong with her life. She hates the smell, even though it doesn't really smell bad. She hates the look, even thought it's not that ugly a place. It's just that it is the hospital. She enters Ryan's room.

"Hi, Ryan."

He is definitely getting better. Except for the triangular bandage in the middle of his face, he is almost back to normal. He has lost a little weight.

"Hi, where are the kids?"

"I wanted to talk to you alone."

With a forced laugh, Ryan says, "This sounds serious."

"I spoke with your caseworker. Your benefits run out at the end of the month."

"Talk to Cal, his boss, they can extend them. I still need a face."

"I'll try, but for now you need to assume you are leaving here at the end of the month. You need to make plans."

"We've been doing pretty good. We'll get by."

"We have not been doing pretty good. We have no money—we're flat broke."

"I can get a loan."

"You can't get jack. We have no money. We have nothing."

"How are the kids?"

"Fine. Ryan, I've made a decision."

Ryan waits for the words he knew were coming as soon as she entered his room.

"I'm taking the kids to mom's."

"To visit?"

"No, I need a new start."

"So you take my kids and go to the other side of the country. What about the house?"

"There is no house. Ryan, the bank's taking it back. We're too far behind."

"When were you going to tell me?"

"Whenever. It ain't like there was something you could do about it."

"Thanks."

"I didn't mean it to sound like that. I don't want us to end like this."

"You're taking the kids and leaving. How do you think it'll end?"

"I just can't do this anymore. I can't." Aly runs out of the room.

$$\cdots$$

The next day at the old warehouse, they fill Alice in on the details. She monitored their progress with GPS satellites and by tapping into satellite cameras. There were not many in the area and Alice is eager for the update.

Alice says, "I am very happy to see you were unharmed Sarah. We all missed you."

Sarah chuckles. "Kofi, you better watch how you program Alice. She almost sounds human."

"She's better than human."

Alice agrees. "Well said."

Sarah says, "Thanks for your concern, Alice. It's great to hear your voice."

Matthew says, "I'm going to need to be transplanted. I need to do some work before I go to Karakatura."

Kofi says, "No problem. Steven Jardine rises again. Do you want to stay transplanted for the Karakatura expedition?"

"Can you guarantee the face in those kind of conditions?"

"You're right. I'll transplant you back to your real face for Karakatura."

Sarah says, "I'm going with you to Karakatura."

"Good idea. I'll need an extra pair of hands."

Liam says, "I'll stay here for a little, work with Kofi. Then I'm going back to New York, work my contacts, see if I can put this all together. Kofi, how're the funds coming?"

"Already arranged. A bank in the Caribbean will give Matthew access to the funds he needs. Anywhere, anytime. Anonymously."

Sarah asks, "How did you arrange that?"

"I own the bank. Alice did the rest."

Matthew says, "We're not breaking any banking laws on the island?"

Kofi smirks. "I own the island."

Liam says, "Well, I think that's taken care of."

Kofi says, "I'm going to be at the university, giving lectures, doing university business. I'll keep in touch with Liam."

"Kofi, I'll try not to contact you unless it's vital."

• • •

Caroline is walking down the pathway in Central Park. The pathways are flooded with New Yorkers and tourists.

A young man comes up beside Caroline. "Hi."

It is very strange, but she is not afraid. "Mom, it's me, Matthew."

Caroline cannot understand what the man is saying. Has Matthew sent this man to tell her he is okay?

"Mom, it's me. I've had my face transplanted."

Caroline does not know what to say. It takes a few seconds for her to understand what he means. "Why doesn't your voice sound the same, if only your face was transplanted?"

"The mouth and nose play an important role in vocalization and sound. The voice box, or larynx, is the same, but the vocal tract, the area where the sound waves resonate, has been changed. That's why I sound different."

Caroline is skeptical. The body is Matthew's, but the face is a different person. She can see no scars.

"Mom, I'm going to be away for a while. We have almost solved this."

"Where?" says Caroline.

"It's better if you don't know."

"Right."

"I just didn't want you to worry. I wanted you to see that I am fine."

"Where's your real face?" says Caroline.

"It's being stored in a can."

"What?"

"Don't worry, as soon as this is over, I will have a reversal. I'll be the old Matthew."

"Do you think you should be doing this?"

"We're making good progress, but it's more complicated than we thought."

Matthew and Caroline do not notice the man taking their photos. The man blends in with the crowd. The man is intrigued by Matthew. He is also puzzled. This man is absolutely not Dr. Matthew MacAulay. He and the members of the team in the park have memorized his photo. Should they follow this man? He may be a friend of Matthew's, giving Matthew's mother news on him. If so, he knows where Matthew is. The man is ready to call into his microphone to tell the team to apprehend Caroline's friend, but he hesitates. He has strict orders to stay with Caroline. He thinks about his boss, Jason Cooper. He better follow the orders, no deviation. Play it safe, get the photos.

Caroline squeezes his hand. "Be careful, Matt."

"Mom, I never told you I appreciated you. I'm proud of you. You're a great mother, and I am proud to be your son. I just wanted you to hear it."

Caroline speaks, but Matthew is gone.

· · ·

Matthew has taken a commercial flight into San Francisco. He will take a taxi to meet Liam and Kofi. Matthew lumbers off the plane, he is tired and wants some rest. Matthew rubs his numb face. A thin woman is holding a large baby wearing a purple t-shirt and purple diaper. The baby gives him a puzzled look. The face of Steven Jardine smiles back. Matthew thinks maybe the baby knows his face is not his own. The baby smiles and coos. The woman looks like the weight of the baby will tip her over, she is a twig. The woman scowls at Matthew and turns the baby away from him. Matthew's eye wanders to the other side of the airport and sees a man wearing a bright blue polo shirt and shorts. Matthew spots a tall, voluptuous woman beside him who seems to be waiting for someone. Francesca. The woman who was in the team that removed the bodies after the botched transplant; Michael's friend. Francesca gets into a car and drives off. She hasn't spotted Matthew.

Matthew grabs a taxi. "Follow that green car."

Taxi driver, "Where is she going?"

Matthew, "Just follow. And don't get made."

Matthew puts $200 dollars on the man's front seat.

The taxi driver glances at the passenger seat and follows the car.

Taxi driver, "I don't want any trouble. She's a beautiful woman"

Matthew, "Don't lose her."

Taxi driver, "I don't get involved in domestics."

The tiredness leaves Matthew's body and he is filled with excitement. "Go."

The taxi driver travels at a discrete distance and has no trouble keeping pace with Francesca's car. She maintains the speed limit and signals all turns.

Within an hour she stops at what looks like an old industrial complex in Palo Alto. The excitement in Matthew builds. He is sure this will lead him to the mastermind, or at least their headquarters. Maybe that man who was leading the cleanup crew in the pizza van is the mastermind. He was definitely in charge that night.

Matthew, "Don't' stop. Go past."

The taxi driver obeys.

Matthew, "Let me out here."

The taxi stops and Matthew gives the man another $200. Matthew walks back to the industrial building. To his surprise she is still outside. Maybe she is waiting for the mastermind. Maybe it is Michael after all. Matthew is very lucky and decides to patiently wait.

Francesca enters the building. Matthew follows. He enters and makes a turn down a hallway. The warehouse is surprisingly well-lit. This has to be the headquarters. Matthews sees his opportunity. She is holding no weapon, but Matthew remembers she carried a weapon in the small of her back and inner thigh on the night the transplant patient died. He will not confront her; he will follow from a safe distance.

She moves deeper into the building. The old clay brick is crumbling in places. Matthew follows her unnoticed. They move through the hallways of the old building. It seems like an endless maze of hallways. He passes metal vats and large iron stoves. Matthew keeps a safe distance. He must follow close enough to see who she is meeting.

At one point he seems to have lost her. He looks around. The central area has hallways leading off in many directions. Matthew pauses, breathing hard. He looks around and sees no one. He considers turning back. Then she appears again and he quietly moves down the hallway. She runs through an iron door. It is solid and heavy. Matthew follows. They are in a large room, Francesca at the far end. She wriggles her muscular hips through a very small iron door. He hears that small door shut with a thud. He turns around and hears the electronic lock on the door behind him hum as it engages. Matthew tries to pull the door open. He throws his body against it. He then runs to the far end of the room. As expected the small door that Francesca crawled through is locked. There is not even a handle to pull it open.

Desperately, he looks around the room. The ceiling height is about thirty feet. The room had many windows, but they have recently been bricked over. He is trapped.

Realization sinks in. Francesca let him follow her from the airport. It had been too easy. That's why, when he lost her in the hallway, she suddenly appeared. She came back so he could follow her. At the time he felt something was wrong, but the desire to chase overwhelmed his thinking. He's in an old iron smelting plant. Matthew hears the rumble as the iron furnaces turn on.

The hiss begins as a soft bubbling and grows into a high-pitched singing. Matthew looks high up and sees a metal grate pouring steam into the room. His watch goes off. The temperature is eighty-five degrees. He needs to get out of the room immediately. He tries to climb the walls to see if he can get to the vent. He takes off his shirt and rolls it into a ball, stuffing it behind his back in his belt. He plans to climb the wall and use the shirt to plug the vent. The old brick has some irregularities and he is able to slowly move up. With each step he tries to put his feet into the small cracks and crevices of the brick. His watch beeps three times. Now continuous triple beeps.

Matthew's progress is slow, but he is closer to the grate.

He looks at his watch—he has 7 minutes. The regular watch face seems to have disappeared, and only the countdown timer is displayed. Matthew watches the tenths of a second tick by quickly. The three repeating beeps have switched to a continuous tone. It is annoying. Sweat drips from his forehead. The room is ninety-two degrees.

He is only three feet from the grate, but the grate has been newly installed. The bricks around it have no irregularities, so he has no footholds. Matthew's body weakens. He can go no higher. Matthew desperately searches for something to grasp to allow him to get a little higher. His watch now sounds like a siren for a fire. He looks at the watch and the countdown timer flashes 0:00:00. Sweat pours from his forehead. He feels it when it drips down his neck and chest. It is so hot that his hands are sweating.

He loses his footing and falls hard to the floor. He is on the ground. Bruised, but nothing is broken. Matthew's face has become loose, and he can feel it separating. It burns. He is surprised because he hasn't had any feeling in the face, not until now. He frantically tries to find an opening in the room. Matthew is now growing weak. Things begin to dim. He slumps in a corner. His last thoughts are about Francesca. She was waiting for him at the airport. Who knew he was coming back by airport? The full red lips fill his mind before he passes out.

The hiss of the steam continues, mixing with the sound of his watch emitting the steady piercing siren.

• • •

Kofi shows Liam some of the new modifications to Alice. The advances in robotics that Kofi pioneered will allow him to create a new company. He will soon begin manufacturing surgical robots. Alice will be the prototype for the next generation robotic surgical suite.

Liam asks, "Did you create Alice's personality?"

"It really was not my goal. I wanted to give her the capability to use data, analyze data, and then take steps on her own. The idea was to have her solve problems and make operative decisions even before the surgeon was aware there was a problem. The funny thing I notice is she seems now to have a type of intelligence. I'm sure she can learn and reason. I think she even has a personality."

Alice says, "Matthew is in trouble."

"What's wrong?" asks Kofi.

"I have been monitoring his watch; he is at a temperature of ninety-four degrees."

"Where is he?" says Liam.

"He is in an abandoned iron foundry not far from here, the factory used to make metal castings. It has not been operating for the last seven years. He is trapped in a room. He was moving up a wall, most likely trying to escape. The rate of rise of the temperature indicates someone is heating the room. My guess is steam. Matthew is not moving. He needs help now!"

Kofi runs into a small storage closet and grabs two large black duffel bags. "Let's go."

Liam and Kofi reach the foundry and race into the building. Alice guides them to the room.

Kofi shakes the door. "The door is solid iron. We can't get in."

He opens a duffel bag and takes out a gun. He looks at the lock and feels the door. Liam steps away. Kofi fires one shot, and the door opens.

The room is like a furnace with steam billowing out of a metal grate. It takes them a few seconds to see Matthew because he is slumped in the corner of the room. The heat is oppressive.

"No respiration." Liam then checks for a pulse. "No pulse."

Kofi unzips the duffel bag and takes out a clear face mask that covers Matthew's face completely. At the bottom of the mask are two tubes. Kofi hooks the tubes up to a small machine. Liam watches yellow fluid enter the mask and flow through tiny tubes. When the fluid enters, it is yellow. It circulates through the mask and then leaves, a bright red color. Kofi has created a cooling device for just such an emergency. Kofi does not wait to see the mask work. He sticks a needle into Matthew's arm and sets up an IV. He takes out another bag and hooks up some green fluids. The fluids flow into Matthew's body quickly. Kofi then takes out a strip of six paper circles, rips off the adhesive backings, and puts them on Mathew's chest. The cardiac monitoring machine comes to life. Liam looks at the screen intently. The line is flat. Liam and Kofi both look at each other. Kofi then pulls what looks like a fire extinguisher from the duffel bag. He pulls the pin and begins spraying a fine mist. The mist fills the room, chilling the air. Even though the steam continues to pour from the vent, the room cools. Kofi picks up Matthew's hand to look at his watch: seventy-five degrees. The watch stops beeping.

Liam breaks the silence. "We got to get out of here. This was a trap. This area is monitored. They will be sending someone to finish the job, and they'll get a nice bonus if they can get all three of us. Matthew is dead. We need to leave now."

"We can't. I need to cool him and get some of the neurotubule connections re-established. If we get a cardiac tracing, we'll know some are re-established."

A small blip is heard and the monitor picks up a heartbeat. A steady *beep, beep, beep* echoes in the room. Kofi then pulls out a metal tray. He pushes a button and it expands into a stretcher. It is light and portable. In no time they wheel Matthew to the car.

• • •

Alice has the operating table ready. She has brought up Matthew's real face in the titanium canister. It is on the operating room table ready to be transplanted. Sarah waits at the anesthetic machine. Alice gives Sarah real time updates.

"Kofi and Liam are at the scene. They have Matthew and have lowered the temperature in the room."

"Is Matthew alive?" says Sarah.

No answer.

"He's dead?" says Sarah.

Finally, after a long silence, Alice responds. "They are leaving the building. Matthew is on a stretcher. Status unknown."

Kofi bursts into the room and puts Matthew on the operating table. Liam takes up his position as the surgical assistant. Within no time Kofi has retransplanted Matthew's face. When it is over, they all stand silently around the operating room table watching Matthew.

Sarah says, "I didn't give him much of anything, but he'll be out for the night."

Kofi says, "I gave him much more Steriazol. The transplanted vessels were all blocked."

The donor face looks like a black and purple swollen mass of mottled tissue. The veins are fat, like sausages filled with dark blue blood. A thin yellow liquid oozes from the skin. It smells like rotten meat and is barely recognizable as a face. It lays on a white sheet on the table.

Kofi breaks the silence. "I manually cleaned all the major vessels on the recipient side that I could. Matthew's face is perfect, but I can't say it will heal. We'll just have to see."

Sarah still looks at the mottled face on the table. "What was his real name?"

"Ivan Tranck—I talked to his parents for a long time before I harvested his face. They are good people."

"His face may save countless lives."

"When this is all over, I'm going to call them, let them know how important their son was. He was hit by a drunk driver. They'll appreciate it."

"By using his face, you made sense out of a senseless tragedy."

Liam asks, "Will Matthew make it?"

"I think we got to him in time. He's young, so let's hope."

"Is there anything more to do?"

"No."

Kofi does not want to tell them the truth. Not right now, it is too raw. The vessels are connected. But can he say that the blood vessels to the face are all working? Will they heal normally? Will Matthew have any neurological deficits? The truth is no one has done what Kofi did tonight.

Kofi says, "Let's all get some rest."

. . .

The machines monitoring Matthew overnight show surprisingly good vital signs. Matthew opens his eyes and sees Sarah at his side.

Sarah smiles. "I think it's time for you to stay in the safe house."

"It's my life. I choose how I live."

Sarah laughs. "You do listen to what I say."

Matthew smiles. "I'm okay."

Sarah caresses his head. "You look good."

Alice says, "His blood pressure and cardiac status are normal."

Kofi walks over. Liam follows behind.

Kofi says, "Our man has awoken."

"I feel good, Kofi. Thanks."

"For what?"

"When the heat started melting the face, I knew it was over. Unless you could get to me."

Liam says, "You did good, Matthew."

Kofi takes out some cards with different colors. He goes through a very detailed examination of Matthew's color vision.

Sarah whispers to Alice, "Why the detailed color vision test?"

Alice replies quietly so only Sarah can hear. "The retina is very sensitive to loss of blood supply. If there is any permanent damage, it will show up as loss of color vision."

Kofi says, "Color vision perfect!"

"Then why do you look so unhappy?" says Liam.

"We cannot do a full face transplant on him again. Ever."

Chapter Thirty-Three

"The last attack on Matthew was a clear attempt to eliminate him," says Kofi.

Liam agrees. "There is no doubt that this last go-round was serious."

Alice is rapidly checking facts and making calculations. Matthew is alert but still weak. His face has healed without scars.

Liam says, "The hunter became the hunted."

"Exactly, I was stupid. I thought I was following her but she was leading me into the trap."

"They were smart," says Kofi.

"I am sorry I put you guys through all this. Alice, thanks, I understand you alerted the team."

"Flowers on my birthday would be nice."

"You got it. And chocolates," says Matthew.

"Just flowers. I'm watching my weight."

Kofi says, "Matthew, your face transplant days are over. Say goodbye to Steven Jardine."

"Can I ever get another face?"

Even though Matthew asks, he knows he would not want another face.

"No, the damage to your neurotubules was too great. Your natural face is fine, but no more face transplants for you."

Matthew will miss his alter ego, Steven Jardine. By putting on the face of Steven Jardine, he was able to look inside Matthew MacAulay. Kofi takes off a panel in the front of Alice and begins to work on some upgrades. The circuit boards and wires are like a maze. Liam looks at the lines of wire and circuitry. The way they interact with Alice, he almost forgot she is a robot. Kofi is busy adding modules to Alice.

Matthew realizes she is a supercomputer as he watches Kofi working away.

Liam says, "We now have clearly become a danger. Whoever is behind this has made the calculation that we are a real threat to allowing them to achieve their ultimate goal."

Kofi says, "This last attempt was crude and hasty. It lacked some of the finesse and planning we have come to expect from this individual. They're under pressure. Look at the team they put together for Sarah's kidnapping. These guys were low-level thugs, not his usual professionals."

Matthew says, "Things may be unraveling for this person."

Liam says, "That's the only reason it failed."

"Let's not forget my work."

"You're right, Alice, without you it would have succeeded."

Matthew asks, "So what do we do now?"

Sarah says, "We don't back down. Not after the things we've been through."

Kofi says, "I agree. We push ahead."

Matthew releases the breath he's been holding. "We are all on the same page. We now need to take extreme precautions."

Sarah says, "I don't think they have any idea about Kofi's involvement, and that's good. Certainly Alice is nowhere on their radar."

Liam says, "We can use that to our advantage."

Matthew says, "Kofi, continue keeping up your schedule."

"I think I'm going to spend some time on my island. I need to decompress."

"That's perfect, you'll be out of sight."

Sarah says, "All roads lead to Karakatura. That is where Michael is—that is where we blow this thing wide open. Matthew and I should be able to get to Karakatura in relative safety."

Liam says, "I'm a little worried."

"Why?"

"I don't know, I like to worry."

"Do you think Cooper is behind this?" says Kofi.

Matthew laughs. "Jason Cooper, mastermind?"

Alice says, "That is a distinct possibility. Quentin Taylor or Jason Cooper."

Liam asks, "What have you found out about them?"

"Quentin Taylor, the Secretary of Defense. He seems to check out, as does Cooper, but the person we are looking for, I am convinced, will check out. He or she is too smart. Their bank accounts, friends, movements, they will all check out."

Matthew says, "So what you're saying, Alice, is you have no idea who is behind this?"

"That is correct. The only thing I know for certain is I know nothing."

Sarah says, "Socrates, isn't it?"

"Sorry I can't be of more help. I'm monitoring the intel and analysts. They are getting multiple sources pointing to an attack on the homeland. Nonspecific, but enough that the president may need to take some action. And by the way, the statement to which you refer is nowhere to be found in Plato's Socrates."

Matthew says, "I doubt it's Cooper."

Alice says, "He is getting married."

"I know."

Alice, "He's marrying Celerie Brindsmore."

"I know."

Sarah turns to Liam. "You need to go underground. No more contacts."

"I agree. You've done your part, Liam, and then some."

"Not yet, this thing may be solved right here in the USA. I'm heading back to New York tonight to make the final preparations for your trip to Karakatura. Matthew and Sarah, you'll be going back next week."

Kofi says, "Good idea, you can't all travel together."

Matthew says, "Good, I have some business to take care of before we leave for Karakatura."

"Don't even think of visiting your mom."

"I wouldn't dream of doing something as reckless as that."

Kofi says, "So we'll meet back here after Matthew and Sarah get back from Karakatura."

Chapter Thirty-Four

Matthew has no trouble avoiding the night staff or slipping into the hospital unnoticed. It is late, but Ryan isn't sleeping.

"Doc MacAulay," says Ryan.

Ryan does not seem surprised to see Matthew or concerned at the late hour. Even in the dim light, Matthew can see Ryan has changed. The wounds to his legs and arms are healed. The stark white triangular bandage on his face is still present. But his eyes have changed the most. They hold a look of hopelessness Matthew has never seen before. He realizes he has not seen Ryan in a long time.

Matthew asks, "How you doing, my friend?"

"I think I should be asking you that under the circumstances." Ryan gives a half-hearted smile.

"Don't believe everything you read."

"Quite honestly, I'm not sure who's in a worse situation, Doc, me or you."

"No question, it's me. You're looking pretty good. Don't worry about me. All's good. I thought I'd drop in to visit an old friend."

"I need it. I'm low right now, Doc. Real low."

"What's wrong?"

"You name it, I got it. The question is not what's wrong, it's easier to answer what's right. Nothing."

"That doesn't sound like Ryan Smith."

"I got money troubles—lost the house. Woman troubles—Aly's left me, took the kids. I got no face. No job. I'm finished."

"Give it some time. Things have a way of sorting themselves out."

"They're saying you murdered those people."

"What do you think?"

"I know you didn't do it. I'm sorry I asked you that. I don't know if it's worth it anymore. I'm gonna get a piece of plastic for my face."

"I'm really sorry they suspended the transplant program."

"Dr. Lambert took your place. He recommended the face prosthesis."

"He's a fine surgeon; you're in good hands."

"They just made him university president."

"Really?"

"I guess it doesn't matter anyway. I'm finished. It's over."

"Far from it, man."

"Family. Country. Honor. That was everything. They just seem like words now. Empty. Hollow. What was it all for?"

"Family. Country. Honor. It's what this country was founded on, Ryan. It's what makes this country great. It's everything. All our laws. All our freedoms. Every person who lives in this country owes you. You have paid a big price. We. Owe. You. We know it. If we don't show our gratitude, it's because we sometimes forget. Not because we don't remember. So know this, Ryan Smith. You are valued. You are valued, my friend. You are everything that is good, everything that is right."

"There's nothing left for me. Aly's gone. Kids are gone. There's nothing."

"I remember my buddy who served. He always said the first thing you learned was never leave a comrade behind."

"Never leave a comrade behind."

"You served with dignity, with honor. I'm not going to leave you behind."

"You're gonna help me?"

"I'm gonna fix this problem for you. That's a promise."

"Promise?"

"Keep the faith, brother."

Chapter Thirty-Five

Karakatura is part of the Himalayas. The mountain is in a region near northern Nepal, sandwiched between China to the north and India to the south. It is a region of majestic peaks. The natural beauty and diversity of animal life is found in few places in the world.

Matthew, Sarah, and their guide walk along a narrow dirt path. The region is vivid with colors and smells. The sky is blue and the temperature mild. In the background the huge mountain presides over everything. The region they are traveling through is lush with dense green vegetation. The dark green leaves on the towering trees provide nice shade. Sarah feels the warm sun on her face. The pace they are walking at is brisk but comfortable. Down the path, off to the side, a purple shrub adds some color to the rugged scenery. Matthew is relaxed. The surroundings are breathtaking. He looks up; a flock of gray birds fly past. They round a small bend and see a field that is golden yellow. Sarah and Matthew stop to look.

The guide says, "Millet, millet."

They are looking at a large field of millet; the yellow grain provided nice color against the green vegetation. They keep walking and turn a gentle bend in the narrow dirt path. The village lies ahead.

The guide points and says, "Kara."

Karakatura is a beast at over twenty-six thousand feet, almost eight thousand meters. Mountaineers all agree, it is the deadliest mountain to climb.

Sarah feels comfortable here. It reminds her of the small village in Sweden, Gullholmen, where her family came from. These rural areas are still relatively unchanged from life 150 years ago. The town is prosperous from the trekking and hiking tours. The natural beauty draws people from around the world—the richness of a culture untouched and alluring.

Matthew realizes they are on Main Street. The road widens to accommodate a compact car or a few animals. There are ten buildings in a row. The buildings are simple two-story wood structures. They are painted in vibrant colors. One building is deep red, another bright green. The guide points to the blue building.

Sarah looks around, sipping her sparkling water. The pub is busy, thirty people sit around wooden tables. Mainly foreign tourists and their local guides fill the room.

A man approaches. Larry is a man of average height. Kofi had given them a lot of his details before they arrived. Larry's parents are from China. He was born in India. The family later settled in Texas.

"Hi, I'm Larry. We should leave now."

Larry quickly ushers them out of the pub. Matthew has many questions prepared to test Larry's knowledge of mountaineering. One look at Larry tells Matthew not to bother. Larry is sinewy, his resting heart rate had to be about sixty, well below the normal rate of seventy-two beats per minute. His chest hardly moves as he breathes. At rest his body exerts no effort. This man is fit to the extreme.

Larry says, "Based on Kofi's comments, I didn't think you wanted to spend too much time in there."

Sarah, Larry, and Matthew walk quickly down a dirt path out of town.

Larry adds, "The less time you spend with people remembering your face, the better."

Sarah likes Larry from the moment she sees him. He is young, early twenties. He seems relaxed and confident.

Matthew glances across to Sarah. Something has changed between them. But what? He is not quite sure. Sarah is still cheerful, she answers all his questions, but something has changed. He can't put his finger on it. She is a bit quiet sometimes. She sometimes looked at him when he isn't looking. He feels something different too.

They walk past a stand of trees and the ground turns from vegetation to gravel. The gray gravel occupies the last hour of the hike. The temperature also drops. Finally, they get to a clearing in the gravel and dirt. The rocks on either side are about eighty feet tall, jagged cliffs that loom over three tents. Matthew says, "I guess this is home."

"This will be our base camp. I've already put some supplies in each tent."

Larry shows Sarah her tent, which is a few feet from his own. Matthew's tent is farthest away. The tents are all equal size.

Matthew says, "We're in the middle of nowhere."

"You wanted private. Climbing season is over, so the base camps are deserted. I think that works for your purposes."

Sarah says, "This will be perfect."

From the breast pocket of his woolen shirt, Larry pulls out a list. "These are the climbing supplies we need." He hands it to Matthew.

Matthew returns the list to Larry. "Whatever you think we need is fine."

"Good. Kofi said Alice would take care of the payments. My fee and the equipment costs. Make sure you give her a call so she can get moving on this."

"Don't worry, Alice is great at this type of thing. Just call and tell her I okayed it. It won't take her a minute to get this done. She's a hard worker, never takes lunch."

"Thanks. We rise at five a.m. tomorrow. Get some sleep."

Matthew helps Sarah unpack. The tent is cozy. It is fine for one person to sleep, but they cannot stand up. The flashlight only illuminates a small cone of the tent. Matthew is about to leave.

"Who is Celerie Brindsmore?" says Sarah.

"Why are you asking about Celerie?"

"Alice obviously thought you would be interested in Jason Cooper's marriage to her."

"It's complicated."

"Life's complicated. Get over it."

"Celerie and I were engaged."

"And?"

"The air smells different here. Did you notice as we were walking? It really feels fresh."

"So you choose not to answer my question?"

"I'm not ready to go there, not tonight."

"That's honest."

"I'm really tired, good night."

Walking the few feet to his tent, Matthew is frightened by a low growl. A dark furry creature moves toward him. Is he about to be eaten by a wild animal? The growl is more of a whimper as the stray dog rubs his leg. Matthew gets some food from his tent and feeds the chocolate brown dog. He has big black eyes. The food is gone in no time. Matthew watches him eat.

. . .

The next morning, Matthew prepares to begin the climb. The sun has not come up yet and it is cold. Larry cooks a breakfast of eggs. He has some very thick slices of toast already prepared. Sarah comes out of her tent. "Hi, Larry."

"Hi, guys."

Matthew asks, "When do we start the climb?"

"It will take four days for the equipment to arrive. You're right, Alice is amazing. She took care of things super fast."

"We won't tell her that or she'll ask for a raise."

"She deserves it. I had the equipment delivered to another location. I don't want anyone knowing where we are. I will pick it up and then bring it here, so we have a week to train."

"Train?"

"I'm not going to lose my life on Karakatura with two inexperienced climbers—we train."

"Did Kofi not fill you in on the urgency of our situation?"

"He did. That's why we train. It won't do you any good if we don't get off the mountain. You need time to adjust to the altitude anyway."

Matthew is silent.

Larry continues, "This is how we will dress for the expedition. You will have the same items as I have, in your size, of course. The inner layer will wick away sweat. The middle layer will provide warmth and trap air. The outer layer will protect against wind, rain, snow."

The dog that Matthew met last night saunters to him and nuzzles Matthew's leg. Matthew gives him some food.

Sarah says, "Looks like you got a friend."

Matthew, "It's Oscar. We met last night."

Larry says, "He's a stray, looking for food."

Matthew gives the dog some more food and the dog yelps.

"We'll be experiencing temperatures around five degrees Fahrenheit and the weather can be unpredictable. I ordered all your clothing and gear for whatever we'll encounter. At certain points on the climb, we'll wear helmets."

Sarah says, "Climbing season has ended on Karakatura."

"That's right. Any attempts now are at your own risk, no hope of rescue."

Larry walks to a twenty-foot rock. He nails in bolts and strings ropes.

Matthew says, "Each day we spend training means the weather up on the mountain is getting more hostile."

Larry ignores him and continues to set up their first training exercise.

The days pass easily. Larry is a good teacher, experienced and thoughtful. He instructs them in the basics of climbing. He is not a risk taker.

The base camp is very gray. Gray ground, gray sky, gray weather. Oscar is a good companion. He yelps and runs around them as they train. He is an intelligent dog and barks his approval as they practice climbing.

The small jagged peaks are perfect to get a feel for climbing. They become used to walking on the gray gravelly soil and using their hands to scramble up rocks. At the end of each day, Sarah and Matthew are exhausted. Larry makes the meals. Sarah is sure it is just the fact that they are eating high in the sky under the stars, but the meals are tasty. The hearty meal is always a welcome end to the day. It is definitely Oscar's favorite. After dinner he disappears, always to return in the morning.

Larry speaks at the end of their meal. "I'll be in town getting final supplies. I'll be back tomorrow early."

Chapter Thirty-Six

Sarah and Matthew head back to her tent. Matthew takes his backpack off. Sarah removes her heavy backpack, which is filled mostly with rock for training, at the entryway. Larry has put an extra twenty pounds in Sarah's pack, so she is training with seventy-five pounds. In Matthew's pack, he did the same. They will appreciate this when they began the actual ascent. The tent is warm and they both remove their outer layers. The white base layer allows them to relax comfortably in the tent.

"I'm really surprised you don't have a boyfriend."

"Is this your attempt to make your move? You couldn't wait to get me alone in the tent."

"Maybe."

"I have to say if that's all you got, it's not much game." Sarah laughs.

"Now who is trying to avoid the question?"

"Guilty as charged."

"I'm just very surprised Sarah Larsson doesn't have a significant other, that's all."

"Do you think anyone would want to be with a girl who is in hiding or doesn't know if she'll be alive tomorrow?"

"Even before this madness, you never mentioned anyone."

"Well, Sherlock Holmes, you're right, there is no one."

"Why?"

"I'm at an in between stage in my life, and there's only room for me."

After a long pause, Sarah breaks the silence. "You never wanted kids, a family?"

"Right after med school, I thought that was what I wanted. The kids, the white picket fence."

"What happened?"

"I put too much ahead of it, and it just passed. If you wait long enough, the dream passes you by."

"Kinda like heartburn," says Sarah.

Matthew laughs. "Kinda."

"You never got close?"

"I did, I did."

Sarah says, "Celerie."

"It was Celerie. We were going to go away to get married, not tell her family. They would have wanted a huge production. I let her slip away."

"She broke it off?"

"No, I ended it."

"Why?"

"No good reason . . . truth is, I got scared. Imagine, the great surgeon, Matthew MacAulay, scared to live life."

"So that's why Alice mentioned Celerie's getting married."

"It's even richer. She's marrying Jason Cooper. We were all kind of in the same social circle at one time. Not really friends, but we knew each other enough to say hi. When I was with Celerie, it was obvious he wanted her."

"He started dating her before you broke up?"

"No. It was quite a bit after."

"The break up went badly?"

"Don't let anyone ever tell you, when you call off a wedding, that there is a good break up—there isn't. It got real ugly. I'd never seen Celerie like that. She seemed to take it well and then all of a sudden she just started to cry. I'd never heard her cry like that. In fact I told her it was a mistake and we should go through with the wedding. She said, no. That's not what I wanted, she could tell. She wished me all the best."

"She seems like a strong woman."

"When I broke it off, it had a ripple effect. Friends took sides. I never spoke to her again. I tried to call her, but she wouldn't take my calls. I sent her a letter trying to explain."

"She reply?"

She did. About one year after I wrote it. I had completely forgotten about it."

"What did she say?"

"She said a lot of things. It was a painful letter to read. It was her way of closing the door."

"Now she's going to marry Jason Cooper."

"That's what they say."

"This guy has got to hate you big time. Celerie will never get over you. He probably knows that. He's her second choice, but he can never live up to you. Or your memory."

"Now you know why he'll pin anything on me."

"Any regrets?"

"No. Looking back now, I realized the break up was the right thing. At the time Celerie had a much greater emotional intelligence than I did. She experienced our intimacy in a more full and mature way. She was in the moment in a way I couldn't be. That's what kept me with her; I was fascinated by this. She understood there was something I was not giving, maybe I couldn't give at the time. She deserves someone who truly loves her. She's an incredible girl. If Jason is that man, believe it or not, I'm for it. Celerie is great, just not the girl for me."

"Sometimes I think life is like a series of windows—the windows close, and if you are on the outside, you just get to look in. Then another window opens and you go through that window. If you over think it, take too much time, or don't take time to notice it's open, then it closes."

"Truth is, you pegged me right from the start. I'm not good at relationships." Matthew looks directly at Sarah.

"I never said that."

"You didn't have to."

"One last question?" says Sarah, adjusting the base layer of her shirt.

"Anything, if it's the last question."

Sarah looks at him. "On second thought, you've had enough talk therapy for one night."

Matthew is happy to be out in the night air. The tent was getting hot. He looks up and can see so many more stars here than in the city. The sky seems to be winking at him.

. . .

The morning is cold and clear. Larry must have arrived very early. He and a helper had unloaded supplies off a very large furry animal. Larry and his helper had packed all the backpacks.

"I let you guys sleep an extra hour," says Larry.

Sarah and Matthew are dressed and ready.

"Thanks."

Matthew is not sure what type of animal was used to haul the supplies up. It looks like a massive cow. Sweat mats its shaggy coat, and it has long horns.

"You use yaks to haul the gear up here?" says Sarah.

"Yes, they can get through narrow paths and they are strong as a yak," Larry laughs.

Matthew doesn't think he has ever seen a yak before. It is a powerful beast. Larry pays his assistant. The yak makes a *clop, clop* sound when its powerful hooves hit the gravel path.

Larry turns to Sarah and Matthew. "Now you're going to be the yaks."

They all put their backpacks on. Each carries around fifty-five pounds of gear. Matthew notices the lighter load; it feels like a feather compared to training. Oscar runs out and nuzzles Matthew.

"This is our last day, Oscar. We're going up the mountain."

Oscar begins to twirl and jump. They hear short yelps. Matthew looks up at the peak they are about to climb.

Larry says, "Dehydration impairs judgment. Bad decisions on big mountains kill. Drink water, drink often."

Larry moves around checking the ropes, checking the fasteners to hold the ropes. He is hopping about to and fro between them. Sarah adjusts her backpack to the center of her body.

Sarah says, "Looks good."

"Ready to rock and roll," says Matthew.

Larry asks, "Rule number one?"

Sarah answers. "Don't separate from the group under any circumstances."

"Rule number two?"

"Obey rule number one," says Matthew.

Larry laughs, and Sarah and Matthew raise their eyebrows.

Larry says, "The dog stays."

"Why don't you tell him?" says Matthew.

Larry, Sarah, and Matthew walk through some light brush and small shrubs to get to the base of the mountain. Oscar trots behind them happily. They are now at the very foot of the mountain. They look up and see the true enormity of their task.

Matthew has a tinge of doubt for the first time. Are they sure Michael will have all the answers? Looking up at the mountain, he understands more fully the risks. He can see sheer drop-offs, areas where it's not at all obvious how to proceed higher. He looks at Sarah. She seems very excited. Larry slowly gazes up at the mountain. It is a careful, solemn gaze. The mountain is majestic in its cold splendor. All are silent.

Larry, "Let us take nothing from the mountain, let us leave nothing behind. We ask you to show us your fury, but only with kindness. We ask the wind and the snow to be with us. We ask the sun to shine good luck upon us. We ask to live in nature's grace, to leave you, and to see you again."

Matthew says, "Well said."

Sarah blinks against the cold. "That was inspiring."

Larry outlines the plan to reach the summit and then descend to Michael's cabin. He brings out a climber's sketch map. "Here's the topos."

Matthew says, "This map is beautiful."

Sarah agrees. "The detail is amazing. The letters are so ornate."

"I try to draw all my maps with this calligraphy and detail. I love doing the fancy letters. It makes it look like the maps for the European explorers who set sail to discover other lands."

"Did you draw it on leather?"

"No, it's paper, but it simulates leather. It's extra thick and waterproof."

Sarah rubs the map. "I love the feel of this. We're on a quest to find the ancient treasure. You're a real artist, Larry."

Matthew asks, "The thick metal ring on the end keeps you from losing the map?"

"It's a security clasp. Now let's review the climb on the map."

Sarah says, "Sure, boss."

"The first part is a leisurely hike along a winding dirt trail. Then we are high up." Larry points to the map showing the route along the side of a mountain.

Sarah points to a trail high above. "Is that where we are heading?"

"Precisely, we will be on that path that curves around the mountain. We will have a great view of the trees and area below. Not as leisurely; a bit more difficult," says Larry.

Matthew touches the next segment. "Then we're in the higher altitudes."

"Correct, the weather is more severe, and we will encounter ice and snow. This is where the sheer cliffs and deep crevasses lay."

"Then the famous sheer climb," says Sarah.

Larry has been training them for this. It is the most technical part of the climb and the one area where a mistake will be fatal.

"This is the technical vertical ascent. We will climb vertically for sixteen hours straight up the rock face." Larry points on the map.

Oscar barks. Larry has outlined this part of the climb many times. "We'll climb eight hours and then bolt a sac to the rock and sleep for eight hours. We'll be hanging over twenty-three thousand feet in the air."

Matthew asks, "Remind me why we're doing this madness again?"

Sarah is quick to answer. "You didn't want to take the usual route. This saves us three days."

Larry adds, "We can easily go the other route. It adds three days, but you're not sleeping on the side of a mountain, twenty-three thousand feet in the air."

"No, we need to make up the time."

"Okay. After we finish this vertical ascent, it is a relatively short hike to the summit. This is in the death zone. Just remember in the death zone: keep putting one foot in front of the other. And don't stop or lie down." Larry puts the map in an inside pocket of his jacket. He clasps the large metal ring to his jacket.

Matthew is most concerned about their time in the death zone. It is well named. They will be well above twenty-six thousand feet. At that altitude the human body begins to shut down. The oxygen is insufficient for human life, and breathing will be very difficult. The lungs can bleed. The brain can swell. If the weather gets rough and slows their progression, they will all die. All other aspects of the climb are in their control. As long as they are careful, it will be hard, but they will not die. In the death zone it is different. Their lives will be in the hands of fate. Luck will play a role in surviving the death zone, and so far Matthew hasn't had much. Maybe he is due.

Larry says, "Remember, thinking in the death zone is impaired. Just keep walking. We will then come to the summit. We are not here for the view. Go over the summit and then follow the Bhuitan Pass downward. No stopping. No admiring the view, there will be no time to pat ourselves on the back. You can do that when you get home. The Bhuitan Pass will lead to the cabin."

Larry puts his finger on the cabin. They all look at the beautifully drawn cabin. "Everybody clear?"

"Crystal," says Sarah.

Matthew asks, "How about the descent?"

"We don't need to review that again. You guys know the way down. Remember . . ."

Sarah finishes Larry's sentence, copying his voice, "More people die on the descent; be careful, your life descends on it."

"You can start a second career as an impersonator," says Larry.

"The way things are going, I'm going to need a second career."

"How about me?" says Matthew.

Larry looks at the altimeter and the clouds. "Keep your day job."

Chapter Thirty-Seven

The slowest person sets the pace. Matthew works hard to keep them moving quickly. He likes being at the front. The sun is warm on his face. They move along a rarely used dirt path with sparse vegetation. Matthew can see the dense trees below. He thinks he can see the lovely golden yellow millet field they had seen earlier, now only a dot far below. After the meandering trail ends, the terrain changes. The ground is gravelly and there is little grass or shrubs. They are exposed on the side of the mountain, looking at the valley below. The trail curves upward sharply. Oscar utters a low growl. Matthew does not like heights. He avoids looking over the side at the ground far below.

Matthew hears a loud pop, right behind his ear. He falls to the ground and looks behind him. Sarah and Larry are down on the ground as well. Where did the bullet come from? Oscar barks loudly. Larry points.

Far below from within a group of thick trees, they see some motion. It is a clump of trees a good distance away. Matthew nods. They are now motionless. Matthew raises his head to see where the shot came from. Another bullet just misses his right shoulder. He flattens his body to the ground. Oscar is safely behind a rock farther along the path and barking continuously.

Larry says, "We're too high up. As long as we stay on the ground and crawl, they can't hit us."

Matthew says, "Right."

Sarah, Matthew, and Larry begin crawling quickly to the large rock twenty feet away. The shooter senses their movement and lets off a volley of shots. The shots are random and in desperation. The shooter has no chance. They are too low to the ground and the rocks provide good protection. The shooter is persistent, firing off a few more rounds. They all reach the larger rocks safely. From here the path is no longer exposed. Oscar rubs Matthew's leg while Matthew strokes his ear.

Larry says, "Kofi warned me this might happen. When I get to base camp, I'll text Alice to double my fee."

"We have to keep moving. If we get back alive, don't worry. I'll triple your fee."

"I don't think the shooter will follow us. The climbing is steep and the temperature will begin to drop rapidly. There is no cover to hide up here," says Larry.

It is six hours of hard hiking. Larry does not break into a sweat. His sinewy legs and arms move as if they just started. They pitch a tent as night falls. One small tent. They all fit, but it is snug. They have a dinner of lentil soup, canned chicken, and freeze-dried carrots. For dessert they have applesauce. They curl up tightly in their sleeping bags, all were wondering if the night will bring any surprises.

Oscar stands guard outside. Matthew cannot sleep. He listens to Sarah's regular breathing beside him. Larry has his eyes closed, but he is also awake.

· · ·

The morning is cold. The clear blue sky does not have a cloud. Matthew looks at his watch. It is much more rugged than he would have expected. The face and the band do not seem to scratch. He will never have a face transplant again, but he still wears the watch. He looks at the temperature: ten degrees Fahrenheit.

It is time to say goodbye to Oscar. They are now entering the more difficult phase of the climb. After Oscar finishes his breakfast, it is time to leave.

Matthew says, "Go back." Matthew gives him a big hug and points down the path. Oscar trots away. Matthew is surprised Oscar does not even look back. Maybe he's the smartest one in the group.

Matthew feels like a zombie. He has only slept briefly in fits. Larry looks tired, too. He did not sleep and his eyes are puffy. He is moving a little slower than usual.

"Let's rope up," says Larry.

Each person is connected to the rope. Larry takes the lead. Matthew looks at the small crystals of snow on the ground and the ice pellets. There are thirty-foot jagged peaks all around. The mist is starting to rise.

Larry skillfully avoids the deep crevasses. He stops the group and moves left. As Matthew goes by, he sees a crevasse about six feet wide and over two hundred feet deep. Larry keeps the pace moving. He stops every once in a while to check his compass or altimeter, but they keep heading higher. They are climbing the north face of the mountain.

The visibility drops steadily. At first it is about ten feet. As the day progresses, it decreases to three feet. The thick mist is like white cotton; it envelopes everything. Matthew hears a loud, regular huffing sound. It is his own breathing. They are stopping every few steps. Larry looks at his compass obsessively and navigates around deep crevasses.

A boulder lays in their path. Larry tries to go around on each side, but large crevasses make this impossible. They hammer bolts into the rock to allow them to climb over it and continue the relentless climb, always upward. The mist begins to lift, and visibility improves to about five feet. Matthew begins to relax; he can see Sarah in front of him. He still cannot see Larry, who is in the lead.

Disaster strikes. Larry stops to avoid a crevasse and puts his compass in his pocket. He starts off quickly. Sarah feels the rope suddenly go very tight. She immediately falls to the ground. Matthew also feels the rope tighten and falls to the ground.

She cannot see Larry. He had been right in front of her. Within a split second, he just disappeared. Sarah yells, "Larry!"

Matthew can see Sarah, but visibility is such that the mist will not let him see any farther. He takes out a hammer from his backpack and nails a bolt into the ground where he lays. He secures the rope to this area.

Sarah calls again, "Larry!"

She hears a murmur.

Finally, Larry responds, "Don't move, I'm off the mountain. Secure the rope"

Larry has walked off the mountain. He is dangling twenty thousand feet in the air.

"I have anchored the rope," yells Matthew.

Larry bobs on the rope below like a yo-yo. He can be seen in between the mist.

Larry yells up, "Be careful near the edge. The rock gives way."

Sarah says, "Thanks, but it's a little late for that."

Matthew keeps a few feet back. "Are you hurt?"

"No, a little bruised." Larry is so far down they lose some of his words as he yells up.

Matthew and Sarah pull on the rope. Larry moves a few feet up. He uses his legs to walk up the side of the mountain.

Sarah says, "This is very slow."

Larry tries to be encouraging. "Not really, you're both doing well."

"You're a lot heavier than you look."

"The rope is anchored at two points?"

"Just like you showed us."

"Then don't worry, just keep pulling me up slowly. I'm using my legs, so it's a lot easier than it might have been."

Matthew yells, "You want to come up here and try?"

"Would you like to change positions with me?"

Matthew is lost in thought. They only have one map. Although Larry carefully outlined the route with both he and Sarah, Matthew is sure that they could not find their way back. All had assumed if anyone was lost or injured, it would be either Sarah or Matthew. If Larry doesn't make it, there is no chance Matthew and Sarah can ascend the summit and get to Michael's cabin without the map. If Sarah and Matthew cannot pull Larry up, the plan is over. Matthew's pretty sure they can't even retrace their steps back to get off the mountain.

Larry says, "Take a break. You're both doing great."

Matthew and Sarah pant and lie on the ground. The muscles in their legs burn. Matthew has to arch his back to relieve the spasms of his abdominal muscles.

Larry says, "There is only one map." He carefully takes the map out of his pocket and clips it to the rope as high as he can above him. "If you can't pull me up, there's a large wire loop on the map. See."

Sarah sees a metal ring dangling from the map, which is now on the rope about 2 feet above Larry's head. The mist makes it hard to see.

"I see it."

"Good. In each of your backpacks, I placed a long pole. It is telescopic and will extend out. There is a hook on the end. It will grasp this loop. When you clip the loops together, the map will come free and you can bring it up."

"We won't need it. We doing good—you'll be up soon."

"I agree, but if you need it, you use it."

Matthew says, "Thanks." He still does not like his chances if anything happens to Larry, but at least they will have a map. Without the map, they will have no chance to get off the mountain. Matthew decides that if they do need to retrieve the map on their own, they will not try to scale Karakatura and get to Michael's cabin. Larry's training is good and most of the climb is a difficult hike, but it makes sense to just go back the way they came and maybe get a new guide before trying again.

Matthew says, "Let's start pulling."

"Okay, let me get my feet set."

Visibility improves as the mist lifts. Larry slowly moves upward.

Larry calls out, "Can you still hear me?"

Sarah yells back, "The wind's picking up, but we can hear."

"There is another attachment for the telescoping pole. It snaps onto the end. You remove the loop that I put on your poles and put the knife on it."

"We don't need a knife."

Matthew wonders what else he put in their packs.

"If you can't get me up and you have trouble getting the map, use the knife."

"No."

"You attach the knife and use it to cut the rope below the map and above me."

"We're not doing that."

"The mountain is no place for sentiment."

"We're not going to cut you from the rope."

Matthew thinks it makes sense. If they aren't skilled enough to use the loop to retrieve the map, they will have to cut the rope. At the distance Larry is below them and with the wind picking up, it may not be possible to use the loop. Let Larry fall and then it will be easy to pull the rope up with the map at the end.

Matthew looks over the edge. It is a twenty-thousand-foot drop. He begins to pull.

Sarah and Matthew slowly raise Larry.

Sarah says, "You're doing good. It's this wind that is slowing us now."

Larry is pushing his legs hard to help them bring him up, but progress is slow.

Larry says, "The wind is likely to get stronger. We need to increase the pace."

Larry loses his footing and drops. The increase in weight pulls Sarah and Matthew to the edge. The softer rock at the edge gives way. Heavy pieces of rock the size of grapefruits pour over the side of the mountain. The wind howls and the dust makes it impossible to see down the mountain. Sarah and Matthew are on their backs.

Matthew says, "Sarah, you okay?"

"I may have twisted my ankle, but I think it's no big deal. You?"

"My wrist hurts."

Sarah yells, "Larry?"

Slowly the dust and rock settle. Larry dangles from the rope, motionless. Matthew takes out his hammer and puts the two anchor stakes more deeply into the ground. He then crawls on his belly over the edge to get a better look. Sarah is beside him.

Matthew says, "He's dead."

"Larry."

There is no reply. Larry's limp body slowly bobs up and down on the rope. He head lolls backward.

Matthew says, "Look at his head."

Blood oozes from the jagged cut on the left side of his head.

"He's sustained a head injury. One of the boulders hit him."

Matthew says again, "He's dead."

Sarah feels her tears freezing on her face. "At least it was quick."

"Do you think you remember the way back?"

"We have no choice. We have to try to make our way back down."

"With the wind picking up and the dust, it's hard to see where we came from."

"I don't like our chances, but we have to make our way back."

Matthew goes to his backpack. He takes out the telescopic pole with the loop on the end. "We need to get the map."

"Just be gentle. If you knock that map off and it goes flying, we've got no chance of getting out of here."

"Understood."

Matthew carefully uses the loop to try to get the map. The wind has picked up even more and the map blows around at the end of the rope. Matthew cannot get the loop to attach. The two metal rings occasionally touch but he cannot get it to fasten.

"Let me try." Sarah puts her body a little farther over the edge. The trees look like little green dots below. She vomits.

"We need to get this done before we lose the light."

"Give me a minute. I'll get it."

Sarah slowly dangles the telescopic pole over the map. A few times she is very close, but the distance is too great with the wind. "It's not going to work. It's too windy and we're losing the light."

She crawls back to the backpack. She snaps off the loop attachment and attaches the knife.

Sarah and Matthew are on the edge looking at Larry's limp body.

Matthew says, "I don't feel good about this."

"He gave us the instructions for just this scenario."

"You're right."

"I don't like it either. He was good to us."

"If we cut him from the rope, there will be no body to give to his relatives."

"We're losing the light. We can survive a night on this ridge and start back down at first light, but we need the map. We can't pull him up. We're exhausted."

"Should we set up camp here and try to pull him up tomorrow, when we have more energy?"

"We can definitely do that, but we can't predict the weather. We're not experts. Without Larry, we need to get off this mountain as soon as we can."

Sarah looks at Matthew.

Matthew says, "There's probably no way we would be able to carry him off the mountain anyway."

"Even with the map, our chances of making it back aren't good."

"Let's do it."

Sarah slowly lowers the telescopic pole with the razor sharp knife on the edge. She is worried that the wind will blow the knife into the rope and cut the rope above the map, taking the map and Larry away. She is careful to angle the pole and knife away from the rope as she lowers it.

Matthew says, "Go right down to just above his head. We don't want to cut the rope above the map."

"That's what I'm going to do. I'm just about there."

The wind blows the pole, and the knife cuts Larry's head. His hand jerks up.

Sarah asks, "Did you see that?"

"He's not dead."

Sarah brings up the pole.

Sarah and Matthew work with renewed energy. Although lifting the dead weight is much harder than when he was conscious, they pull relentlessly. Slowly he makes his way up. The wind dies down and they are able to move more quickly. Sarah and Matthew take no rest.

Sarah says, "I think he moved again."

Matthew calls, "Larry."

No movement.

"Larry, If you can hear us move your right hand."

Larry raises his right hand slightly.

"He's regaining consciousness."

Sarah and Matthew stand and begin pulling furiously.

Matthew says, "Another three feet and I'll be able to stretch over and pull him up."

"Can we rest?"

"No, he's nearly up."

Matthew is exhausted. He tries to grab the collar of Larry's jacket. The loose rock causes him to fall forward and lose balance.

"Sarah!"

Sarah lunges forward and grabs Matthew and Larry. They all fall on each other. They slide toward the edge, but the anchored rope holds.

Matthew says, "The map."

When they all fell forward, someone dislodged the clip holding the map. The map drifts slowly down wafting on the air. Matthew and Sarah watch the map slowly float down and out of sight.

Larry lies face up while Sarah examines his head. He asks, "What happened?"

Sarah soothes him. "You're fine."

Matthew asks, "What do you remember?"

"Last thing I remember, we were walking on the mountain here. I was in the lead. That's it."

"You fell off the side of the mountain."

"Never a good thing."

Sarah says, "You got hit on the head. You were knocked out. Good news, no skull fracture. You're going to be fine."

"That laceration is going to leave an ugly scar."

"I actually feel pretty good, just a little woozy."

Matthew says, "It's one of those good news, bad news type of things."

Larry asks, "What's the bad news?"

"While we were pulling you up, we lost the map."

"That was our only map."

Sarah says, "We know."

Larry asks, "Do we turn back?"

"Why?"

"I know this mountain like the back of my hand. I can get us to Michael's cabin and down the other side. But if something happens to me now, there is no way you two can get off the mountain without a map. Especially as we go farther up."

Matthew looks at Sarah.

Sarah says, "I guess from now on we're going to have to take extra good care of you then."

They can taste the cold, and the air feels thick. With the colder conditions, the mist clears. They walk a step and then pause briefly before taking the next step. Every muscle aches. Matthew's legs feel like lead balloons. Each step is more difficult than the last. Eventually they all grow too tired to continue.

"We're almost there. Look," says Larry.

When Matthew and Sarah look ahead, they see a sheer cliff of mountain. It rises like a wall directly in front of them.

Larry says, "We set up camp at the base there and begin the climb in the morning."

The site of the three-thousand-foot vertical wall not too far in the distance gives them the energy they need to reach it. They pitch the tent and all three fall into a deep sleep.

· · ·

The climb up the rock face is initially not so bad. They climb in very short segments. At each point they stop, Larry hammers in bolts and a safety rope. If they fall this rope will save them from falling very far. As they climb higher, this process is repeated. Matthew loses his footing during the climb. The ropes hold and he feels like he is attached to an elastic band. He is unhurt and they continue the climb. "Concentrate, stay focused," says Larry.

"Okay," says Matthew, regaining his footing on the rock. The cold saps his stamina.

Sarah says, "I think we're about nine hundred feet up."

"Probably about right," says Larry. "Just look up."

Matthew looks down. "Even with the safety ropes, it's a little weird."

"Just look up."

They can hardly hear each other, the wind is blowing so hard.

"It's just gray rock hour after hour," says Sarah.

"Welcome to my world," says Larry, hammering in a bolt to the rock face.

"It's pretty dreary," says Matthew.

"This is the most technical aspect of the climb. Just keep concentrating."

Matthew says, "We need to rest."

"We've made pretty good progress. Let's push a little more."

Matthew says, "I can't go on."

Larry asks, "Sarah, how you holding up?"

"I'm wiped."

"You've both done good. You've earned an extra long rest."

"Good."

Larry, "We'll complete the final part of the vertical ascent after we rest. We'll be in the death zone by midnight before the final push to the summit."

The three of them are tied together about twenty feet apart. They hammer bolts into the rock and attach sacs. Each person slowly wiggles themselves into their sac. The plan is to eat and sleep for at least twelve to eighteen hours so they will be ready for the final push.

Sarah is excited about erecting her sac. She bolts the sac into place and crawls in. It is the most incredible thing she has ever done. They had practiced fifteen feet off the ground. But to erect a sac on a sheer vertical piece of mountain at an altitude over twenty-three thousand feet—incredible is the only word to describe it.

She is very sorry she doesn't have a camera. She peeks out her sac and sees that Larry is using his cell phone to snap pictures of her sac. Sarah feels safe, curled up in her sac. The wind roars outside, but the sac quickly warms up. Sarah's really not been bothered by the ALS.

She's not sure if it's the cold or the other stress. She's sore all day, but that's the same as everybody else due to the constant exertion.

Larry had gone over the plan: Eat as much as you can. Sleep as much as you can. Sarah has a dinner of dried beef, two energy bars, cheese, and sunflower seeds. She drinks a few cups of water and falls into a restful sleep.

Sarah wakes after a bit. She doesn't feel like sleeping anymore, too much adrenaline. She has time to think. How in the world did it all come to this, how in the world? She is being hunted, has nearly been killed on more than one occasions. And she is now dangling twenty-three thousand feet on the side of a mountain. There is no point in overthinking it—she just has to keep going.

They begin the final part of the sheer upward climb. The rest did them good. Larry is surprised at how quickly they finish off the last part of the climb to reach the next ridge of mountain. They cheer when they climb off the vertical cliff around midnight.

Larry gives them a moment to celebrate and then says, "And now for the death zone."

Chapter Thirty-Eight

It is just past midnight and the moon at this altitude looks enormous and bright. A massive yellow white globe that is right in front of Matthew's face. The sky is radiant, shimmering with stars. There is no artificial light to block the view, so the stars illuminate the white snow and crystals on the ground. The sky looks alive. Matthew has looked up at the sky many times in the city. This view, at this altitude, is completely different.

Larry interrupts Matthew's thoughts. "This is the death zone. Just remember, no stopping. Put one foot in front of the other."

They begin the death zone march. Sarah feels like she is breathing through a straw.

"26,900 feet," says Larry.

He doesn't have to tell Sarah. She feels the lack of oxygen. "I feel like I've just run a race, but the burning in my lungs won't stop."

The pace is very slow. At sea level this mild ascent to the summit would take two hours tops. Here they plan to do it in six hours, if all goes well. Slowly, they plod on.

"Remember if the weather comes in, we turn back, so keep moving," says Larry.

Upward they continue. The pace is not quick, but it is relentless. Every step is now like moving a thousand-pound weight. Matthew's legs refuse to respond. His chest burns. He looks at Sarah, sees she is trembling a little with each step. The landscape is very similar and even with the beautiful stars shimmering, it is a grind.

Matthew tries to focus his mind on things he cares about. He realizes that Sarah is always in his mind. Not necessarily at the front of his mind, but she's always there somewhere. A constant as all else swirls around him. Matthew remembers he saw some beautiful purple flowers on the way up to the base camp. He immediately thought how they looked like the flowers Sarah and he passed in the park when they were on the run with Kevin. Almost everything he thinks about these days seems somehow to relate back to Sarah. She is smart, funny. She displayed incredible resilience when she was kidnapped.

Matthew senses that she is keeping some distance between them, keeping him out of the most intimate parts of her life. She is also very stubborn. She is keeping that window firmly shut. What will she do when this is all over?

Matthew is drained. He looks at Larry, who is in the lead. Larry's face is covered in sweat, and he is breathing rapidly. Larry is laboring, something Matthew thought impossible. As long as they keep moving, they will make it. That's what Matthew keeps telling himself. At this point it is a personal challenge for each of them. They do not talk to each other; they just keep walking. Avoid the odd crevasse. One foot in front of the other.

Matthew loses track of time. They still are roped together. Larry shields them from the winds, which are howling, and the snow. Their helmets provide some warmth and protection.

Sarah's head feels like it is about to pop off. The pain is searing, like an iron clamp squeezing her head. It will not let up. Her vision begins to go in and out. She is nauseated. Her steps become more and more labored. She stops and vomits. Then she just begins shuffling. She stops again. Sarah begins coughing uncontrollably, bringing up bright red blood.

Larry runs to her side. "How are you holding up?"

"Great, can't you tell?" Sarah vomits blood.

"It's the altitude."

Sarah seems not to hear.

Larry asks, "Do you have a headache?"

"Do I ever—my whole head is pounding and I don't feel good."

Sarah vomits again. There is no food in her stomach, and only green bile comes out.

Matthew says, "Altitude sickness."

Larry agrees. "Her brain is swelling. The small vessels in her lungs are bursting."

"Do we turn back?" says Matthew.

Sarah says, "No way, we keep going."

"If your brain swells too much, you die."

"Keep going."

"I'm not sure you are in a position to make the decision," says Matthew.

Matthew turns to Larry. "What do you think?"

"I'm not sure she will make it."

Matthew says, "I'd like to get to the cabin. It's very important I get some answers there, but not if it's going to cost Sarah her life. If you say turn around, we turn around."

Larry looks at Sarah. He brings out his compass and fumbles with the altimeter. He looks at the sky, then the altimeter, then back at the sky. Then he does it all over again.

"We go on," says Larry.

Sarah is standing. Larry unties her rope and then ties her directly to his side. He carries Sarah for an hour until they get closer to the summit.

Not having to expend so much energy has an effect. Her headache, while not completely gone, begins to ease and she coughs up less blood.

Sarah says, "This is the worse hangover ever."

"We need to keep up the pace. As soon as you get to a lower altitude, it will pass."

Larry is not as confident as he sounds. If the brain swelling progresses, she could just stop breathing and die. They are too far forward to turn back. The quickest way to get Sarah's brain to stop swelling is to get down the mountain to a lower altitude. To get down they have to go up—they cannot go back. Each time she coughs, more blood vessels in her lungs burst.

By carrying her, the pace is now slowed at least by half. The little mishaps are adding up. Larry grinds his teeth. This is how people die on the mountain. Most people think it is one big event that kills you—a fall into a crevasse, an avalanche takes you out. That is not how people die, not often anyways. The most common way to die is what Larry likes to call death by four cuts. A series of small problems each mounting on top of the other. In Larry's experience when he reviews mountaineering accidents, usually four minor but distinct mishaps occur before the fatal event. All of a sudden these small problems lead to a big problem. At each step if the climbers had turned back, they would have lived. The inexperienced climber is always unhappy when a guide turns back for a seemingly minor problem. What the guide knows is that they are, in all likelihood, to have two or three more of these "'minor mishaps." If the first one occurs early, the later ones could prove catastrophic. All together these events lead to death. Larry is now seeing this in his expedition. The weather is making things worse.

"What's up, boss?" Matthew watches Larry quizzically.

Larry is turning over the options and does not even hear Matthew. Finally, Larry makes his decision.

"Isn't it too cold for snow?" says Matthew.

"No. No talking."

Larry pushes the pace. He is dragging Sarah.

. . .

Sarah does not mind the death zone. If this is death, it's not that bad. Her lungs burn and her head throbs, but things seem mellow. If this is death, so be it.

They are all left to their own thoughts. The howling of the wind never ceases. It is now like a sweet melody to Sarah, soothing. Climbing season has ended, and they have the mountain to themselves. They come around a curve and see a man. He has a great big smile on his face. His jacket and mittens are off, and he is sitting in the snow on a small rock. He looks like a king on his throne. His white teeth glisten under the starlight. Icicles make his hair stand up. It is a shocking sight, but at this stage they just keep walking. Sarah knows the man will sit here for eternity. No one will bring him down; his partners left him. He knew the rules and took his chance. He lost. As they pass him,

Sarah thinks about his smile. When his brain froze and he was about to die, he was hallucinating. It was probably about a happy place, probably about something good in his life. In his final moments, he felt warm. That's why he took off his jacket and mittens. Maybe death was not so bad after all.

They move ever upward for another hour. Sarah has improved and is now walking on her own. Finally, they see the sun come up. They turn a corner, not caring about anything, just remembering to put one foot in front of the other.

CHAPTER THIRTY-NINE

They reach the top. A clear blue sky replaces the darkness. The mist swirls around the peak. They can see for miles. Matthew remembers Larry's words and pushes on.

Sarah has regained much of her energy. She turns to Larry and looks at him. Sarah looks around at the beautiful view. She looks at Larry again.

"Five minutes max," says Larry.

Sarah and Matthew take their backpacks off. They walk around the peak. Larry takes pictures of each separately and together at the summit. Matthew takes photos of Sarah and Larry. It is truly an accomplishment to climb this peak—what it took to make it. Larry opens his backpack. He takes out some sparkling apple cider. He has three plastic wine cups and pours them all a glass. They cheer as they drink the apple cider. They are giddy. The sun rises higher in the sky; they put their backpacks on and begin the descent, moving down the ice path.

As suddenly as if they cross an invisible line, it happens. They can breathe.

"You just survived the death zone." Larry smiles, looking at his altimeter.

He quickens the pace. They are now heading down the Bhuitan Pass. With each step, the burning in Sarah's lungs decreases. She can feel her legs; they are no longer lead. Her mind becomes clear, and she realizes how close to death she has come.

Larry stops and takes out a compass. He looks for a second and guides them to an area where two large snow mounds loom about twenty feet above them. They appear to be a snow wall, but as the climbers get closer, it is clear there is an opening. They step over a four-foot crevasse and pass between the two snow mounds. A gentle downslope is seen. There is a little ice, but it is a clear straight path.

"We made it," says Matthew.

Larry says, "If something happens to me, remember you head down now."

Matthew says, "Nothing will happen to you."

"You take the point." Larry unropes the group.

. . .

A twenty-foot rock lies directly in front of them. The wind has polished the rock face smooth. It seems to be a piece of yellow-brown marble.

"This is the smiling man," says Larry.

Sarah says, "That means we're almost there."

"Another hour tops," agrees Larry.

The weather has improved. Visibility is clear. At various points Larry takes out his compass to make sure they are on the correct path. They are no longer roped up and there are no crevasses. The gradual downhill walk is invigorating. Matthew was at first worried that they lost the map, but Larry is navigating from his memory with no problem. As long as Larry is around, they are safe.

Matthew looks up at the deep blue sky. With the mountain range in the background, it looks like a post card. The pure white snow contrasting with the blue sky; the sunlight reflecting off the smooth ice formations.

They smell the cabin before they see it. It has the pleasant smell of firewood burning in a wood stove. They all want to get inside and warm up. They smile and quicken the pace.

The cabin is thirty by thirty square feet. It has a large door and two rectangular windows on either side. It is built well, solid timber construction, but a basic rustic cabin. They move closer and see all is not well. The cabin has been set on fire. The smell is the smoldering ash of the wood as it hangs sweet in the air. The structure still stands, but the interior is partly burned out.

Matthew enters the front door into one large room. Sarah comes in behind and begins looking at the burned books and scattered papers on the bookshelf. Someone was looking for something. The contents of the desk have been scattered. Larry takes his backpack off. He takes a long drink of water and begins to get some food out. He seems completely uninterested in the partially charred cabin and the disheveled contents.

Most of the contents of the room have been destroyed. Everything smells burned.

Matthew walks through the cabin and out the back door. There is a large generator and sophisticated telecommunications equipment. Matthew continues walking to a sled near a large rock of ice. Slumped over is a man. The man is sitting in the sled about to go. The hood of the heavy white parka he is wearing covers his entire head. Two neat little holes. Matthew pulls the parka hood back. Michael stares back at him, his piercing gaze no different than when he was living.

Michael was shot at close range, back of the head. Exit wounds through the forehead. No defensive wounds. He didn't see it coming. Matthew knew Michael. He was intelligent, a mathematician before going into surgery. He was a bit of an egomaniac, and he had some impulsive tendencies. For all his failings, he was a fundamentally decent person.

Matthew is sad. Michael had clearly lost his way and paid with his life. Kevin was right. Michael was the puppet, not the puppet master. Near the end Michael had to know this was how he was going to end up. He saw and most likely worked closely with the mastermind.

Matthew looks around. There is nothing unusual. Michael's backpack is lying on its side. It has been searched. Some of the contents lay scattered on the ground. Matthew empties the rest of the contents out. He examines each item carefully. He meticulously goes through each pocket and unzips all pouches. Matthew picks up a package and smiles. He examines the contents slowly. It first appears all is normal. A cardboard box labeled freeze-dried bean soup. He shakes the package; he can hear the beans.

Michael had G6PD deficiency. He didn't have the enzyme that allows red blood cells to work efficiently. Michael kept this from many people. Matthew only found out by chance. At a conference they were out late at night. They stopped for some food, and by mistake Michael almost ordered a bean salad. Even in the drunken state they were in, Michael asked about the beans. The street vendor had no idea what fava beans were. It was a prepackaged salad. Michael carefully read the label. First ingredient: fava beans. They would trigger a fatal reaction. He had a jumbo hot dog instead.

Michael always brought his lunch to work, so he could be sure what he was eating. Michael would never bring freeze-dried beans on a climb. Matthew turns the package to read the ingredient label. This is the clue Michael left. The first ingredient: fava beans.

Matthew gently opens the package. The beans fall out. A small folded piece of paper is also inside. Matthew takes out the neatly handwritten document. The document puts the pieces of the puzzle together. It is painful to read, but he knows it is true.

There is a lot to digest; he will reread it many times later in private. Matthew is always bothered by the fact that someone seems to be just one step ahead. Always knows their next move. Now he has his answer. The truth is, Matthew has already pieced it together, repeatedly going over all the events beginning the night he was forced to do the transplant. Only one person could have done this Michael's letter confirms what he already knows.

He puts the document in his backpack and looks inside the package. Circled on the inside of the box is a handwritten word:

Stool

This is obviously an important code word. It is not explained in the documents. He has a lot to think about. Matthew puts the box in his backpack. Matthew walks back to the others.

"The place was carefully searched, then torched," says Sarah.

"Michael is out back. Dead."

"So we were right, he was involved." Sarah arranges the papers on the desk.

"Involved, but not the ringleader."

"How many more people can this person kill? The team must realize that no one's going to be left alive who can identify the boss," says Sarah.

"At this stage the players have no options—they are in too deep. We need to get back as soon as possible."

"Did you find anything?"

"No, I searched the body, but someone had already done it. There was nothing."

Larry munches on an energy bar. "We need to rest. Tomorrow we descend. We need all our strength, and more importantly, we need our mental energy."

"Agreed, there is nothing more that can be done today. We've earned some rest."

They all pass the rest of the day relaxing. The cabin provides shelter and is warm. They strip down to their base layer of clothing and enjoy a peaceful day.

Matthew, Sarah, and Larry stand drinking tea and watch the sun set. It is an orange ball backlighting the other mountains in the Himalayas. Each silently takes in the beauty. When the sun finally sets, they wonder where the day has gone.

Larry lights a campfire. It is nice to get out in the night air. There is a real sense of euphoria. They made it. Larry brings out a little copper pot.

Sarah says, "Your backpack seems to be the magical purse. I don't know what you're going to pull out next."

"Get ready for the best meal of your life," says Larry, twirling the pot by the handle.

Sarah, "Unless there are waiters and a white tablecloth, I don't think so."

"Just wait."

Larry has some vegetables and chicken in his backpack. The extremely cold temperatures have kept them fresh. He melts ice and puts the food into the pot. He cuts up the chicken into large chunks. He has a little packet of seasoning which he sprinkles into the pot. Larry adjusts the height of the pot over the fire so the pot cooks at a low, even heat.

"Storytime," says Larry.

They sit for hours listening to Larry tell stories while the stew slow cooks. He is an experienced mountaineer and enjoys entertaining groups of hikers. It comes naturally to him. Larry tells countless stories of growing up in Texas and college life. The stories keep coming, one after the next, each more outrageous and funny. Matthew and Sarah laugh nonstop.

They forget everything else for the time. As the night grows around them, they feel an incredible bond. The moonless night sets the mood. They are coddled by the blackness. The fire crackling, the smell of the stew being cooked, the stars shimmering in the sky. Time seems to stop for them. It is only these three people. Larry tells his final story. They all stare into the fire.

"Get ready for your best meal ever." Larry ladles out large servings of the stew.

Larry is true to his word. Matthew cannot remember a better meal. The chunks of chicken are savory and well-seasoned. The carrots and vegetables are soft and flavorful. They have been eating freeze-dried food for a long time.

"I have had many a fine meal in some of the best restaurants in the world," says Sarah, "but this is the finest meal of my life."

Sarah raises her glass of sparkling apple cider.

Matthew says, "Here, here. To the finest chef on the planet."

Larry looks up, and with his glass in hand, makes a sweeping gesture to the stars. "No, the finest chef in the universe."

Matthew laughs. "I stand corrected, to the finest chef in the universe . . . of all time . . . Larry."

Sarah and Matthew cheer. They gobble down the chicken stew. When the pot is empty they all look in, hoping more stew will appear. After dinner they go into the cabin. Dessert is tea, raisins, and some dark chocolate. They play cards and drink tea well into the night.

Chapter Forty

The next morning Larry is up early. He looks out the window at Karakatura, thinking about the descent. Larry puts on his breathable pants and shirt over his base layer. He slides on his backpack and makes some adjustments to balance the weight on his back. He puts it carefully by the door. Then he cooks on the kitchen stove. It still works perfectly. Larry makes French toast with thick slices of bread. The cabin has an outdoor "cold area" filled with frozen bread. He gives them each some energy bark. Despite the festive mood of last night, Larry is very serious. Matthew is worried something has happened. Matthew is also anxious to get off the mountain.

"Anything wrong?" says Matthew.

"No, I always get this way before a descent."

"How's the weather?"

"Weather's coming in, and we need to get out ahead of it. It can change at the drop of a hat.

Sarah takes a piece of French toast out of the pan. "So how do we get off this mountain?"

"The route down is not that difficult." Larry points to a hill in the distance. "We climb that hill. That is where we worry about weather. It is snowy and we could get the misting we had earlier. It's cold. After that, we cross the base of a steep ridge. Avalanche country. We want to get there before the sun warms the snow. We have to cross it quick because we don't want the snow coming down on us. After that it's a relatively easy hike back to town."

"Any technical climbs?" says Sarah.

"No, this is just a test of endurance. It's a long way back to get you to your extraction point. Just don't get careless."

"Do we need to rope up?"

"No, there are no crevasses to speak of."

Matthew says, "We need to do one thing before we leave."

They spend an hour gathering rocks and making a grave for Michael. The ground is too hard to dig.

Matthew says, "He was a good man."

Sarah stares at him. "He was working for a sociopathic killer."

Matthew says, "He made a mistake. Isn't life about second chances? He won't get one."

Reading the notes he had found last night convinced Matthew that Michael was a good man. He knew what he had done would cost him his life, and he wanted to undo some of what he had set in motion if possible. Matthew would tell Michael's wife and four children he died on the mountain. A climbing accident trying to retrieve the body of his friend George H. Brown. Michael died trying to help others. That is the truth.

They bury Michael beside a small jagged outcropping of ice and rock. They mark the grave with three large stones.

Larry says, "We need to leave now. Weather's coming in." He puts his altimeter in his pocket and looks far to the east. They can all see the dark clouds menacing, moving quickly toward them. Larry sets a brisk pace.

Sarah looks over to Matthew, and he smiles. Sarah smiles back. Her feet feel warm in her boots, but her face is very cold. There are no crevasses, so they can walk alongside each other. No need to walk single file as they did for much of the trip.

The miles pass with light conversation. They stop for water and put on their helmets.

Despite the blistering pace, they cannot outrun the weather.

Sarah says, "It's so flat here."

"We have a stretch of it—stay alert," says Larry.

The mist returns and the snow falls heavily. The sky, which had initially been clear blue with a few clouds, is now monochromatic gray. It blends well with the landscape. They cannot make out the mountain range. It is not clear where the mountain ends and the sky starts.

Larry says, "Single file."

He looks at his watch and keeps the pace fast. The snow picks up. The familiar howl of the wind starts. Larry does not let them sit for the break.

"Just drink a little water and then we go. Lean over, have a piece of chocolate."

Larry gives them each a generous chunk of dark chocolate.

They keep walking and slowly realize they are on a gentle descent. At this point tiredness is a blanket covering Matthew's head. He is not thinking; he does not even remember how he got to this point. He just wants to sit and rest. Get a little nap; even just close his eyes for ten minutes. Matthew looks at his watch. The temperature is minus five degrees Fahrenheit. Matthew realizes his face is numb. It feels like the transplanted face.

Slowly Sarah begins to lose feeling in her toes, then her feet. Larry pushes the pace. Visibility has decreased from thirty feet to two feet. Matthew has the urge to just sit in the snow and rest.

"We stop here. We'll make a snow trench," says Larry.

Matthew sits. "I was so worried when we lost the map that if something happened to you, Larry, we would be in big trouble without that map. Now I realize, even if we had the map, Sarah and I can't get out of here."

"If something happens just take this compass, and keep moving down and south."

Matthew says, "I'll just rest. You guys start."

"No." Larry pulls Matthew to his feet.

The three of them begin to collect snow. Larry picks an area with solid rock that has a little bit of a curve to make the snow wall. They begin to pack snow and create the wall. Larry uses his ax to cut ice blocks. Sarah and Matthew keep gathering snow. The wall slowly takes shape.

Matthew and Sarah move at a snail's pace. Larry is a beehive of activity. He goes back and forth, building a wall of snow to protect them from the howling wind. At first it looks like nothing, just some snow. After an hour they are able to build a six-foot wall. It stops the wind so that Larry can start a fire.

Matthew is frozen. With the fire, feeling returns to his face. The fog lifts from his mind. As his hands warm up, they burn. This is a good sign; he has not lost any fingers to frostbite. They all fall into a deep sleep.

Larry gets them up after what seems like a very short time. In reality, they have been napping for three hours. In that time the snow has piled up all around them to about eight feet.

"We have to leave now. Any more delay and the snow will bury us."

The wind and snow increase in fury. They just follow Larry's lead. Visibility is near zero and they are not sure how Larry knows which way to go. Step after step the monotony builds. With the low visibility, it seems they are not making any progress, just step after step in the same place.

The conditions clear in the space of a few hours. The wind stops, the sky clears, and once again they are on a beautiful mountain. Peaceful, calm, with no hint of the fury unleashed such a short time before. Visibility is back to normal. It is still very cold, but the sun has come out. They can feel warm rays on their face.

Matthew leads the group, and they walk freely. Finally, they pitch a tent. They have a restful sleep before they begin again in the morning.

• • •

The next morning they get an early start. They want to avoid the sun melting the snow. It starts off with the usual energetic walk, but as time passes, the pace slows. They are all very tired. The entire climb is taking its collective toll. Matthew, Sarah, and Larry tire much more quickly than they did in the first few days of the climb.

"We're almost off the mountain," says Larry.

Larry is ill at ease. Matthew and Sarah can hear it in his voice. He keeps pushing them to move. They walk quickly for a few steps and then slow. They repeat this pattern, using the technique Larry had taught them at base camp for when they were too tired to continue but could not afford the time to rest.

The mountain is a beast. They feel its presence with every step, and sun seems to make the mountain radiant. They cross the base of a large slope and hear a sharp crack. Larry, Sarah, and Matthew look up. A massive sheet of snow is coming down. It looks like a white sheet flowing, almost like water. Although it is moving very quickly, it seems to be sliding in slow motion. They hear a low menacing hum, slowly increasing in intensity.

"Run," says Larry.

They have already started sprinting to safety before Larry's command. Matthew looks at the white sheet moving toward him. He knows he will not make it. He keeps moving, hoping he will not be buried. Matthew can see Sarah ahead of him; she is the fastest runner. Good, she will live. Matthew can see she will be well clear of the avalanche. As the snow closes in on him, he hears the noise. The slab of snow makes a deafeningly loud humming sounds as it moves closer. Matthew changes his course and moves slightly downhill to see if he can outrun the snow.

When the snow hits him, it is like a punch. The force of the snow knocks him off his feet. He tries to keep his hands in front of his face and stay upright. He does not lose consciousness. He is buried in an instant.

It is dark and it is silent. He can smell the snow—the snow that has brought him to his knees. *Control your breathing*, he thinks when he realizes he is hyperventilating. With great effort he lowers his hands to cover his mouth and nose. He is running out of air. Matthew feels himself fading. His hearing seems to decrease and then dim. His mind is fuzzy and then he just ceases.

To cross the base of the steep slope, Larry had spaced them out. If they did trigger an avalanche, they were spaced far enough apart that they would not all get buried. Larry sprinted to avoid the wall of snow but was knocked off his feet. He is unconscious. The gash to the side of his head has re-opened.

Sarah had been in a good position. She easily avoided the avalanche. She watches as the snow settles and formulates her plan. Larry is unconscious but breathing. Matthew is the one who is buried. She had watched the avalanche overtake him and then bury him in a matter of seconds. She saw exactly where Matthew was buried. It was sinister the way the snow engulfed him.

Now it is calm. After the thunderous noise of the avalanche stops, the whole area looks like it did just before they started crossing.

Larry has trained them well. Sarah is confident and she springs into action. Even though she thinks she knows exactly where Matthew is buried, she follows Larry's instructions. She pulls out a long orange pole. It telescopes out to eight feet. She goes to the area where she thinks he is buried and pushes the pole into the snow. She pushes it far down. She does not feel Matthew. He is not there. An urge to panic and start sticking the pole everywhere almost overtakes her. She controls herself and then follows what Larry has taught her.

She methodically pushes the pole into the snow in quadrants. After a few minutes, she hits Matthew's helmet. It feels like a long time has passed. Her muscles burn.

She leaves the pole in that spot, takes out her shovel, and begins digging. Within a few minutes she uncovers his face and removes the snow from Matthew's nose and mouth. She continues to dig and remove the snow from around his chest. At this point Larry is digging from the other side. It is over very quickly. Sarah pulls Matthew out of the hole, rips off his backpack, and lays him on the ground.

He is breathing. He has a pulse. He coughs and sputters. Matthew opens his eyes, Initially all he can see is white. Sarah's bright white hair is in his face. He gets up on his feet and puts on his back pack. He walks around slowly, stretching his arms.

Sarah and Larry put on their backpacks. Matthew walks toward Sarah. He has a sheepish grin on his face.

"Thank you."

"Matthew, I . . . " Sarah gives Matthew a big hug.

"I almost died."

"The same could happen to me. I just want you to know that if it happens, I chose to be here, to do this. To spend my time doing it with you."

"We're all getting off this mountain. Don't worry."

They continue to embrace.

Larry says, "Break it up. Save it for when you guys get home. We need to get off this mountain."

They continue the trek. Sarah in the lead, Matthew in the middle, Larry guarding the rear.

Chapter Forty-One

Dr. Spencer Lambert is deeply troubled by Ryan Smith's case. Here is a good man who seems to be getting all the bad luck. There is no doubt he needs some help. Spencer has brought in the social work team. He has some good news that may cheer Ryan up.

Dr. Lambert says, "Good news."

"For me? You sure you have the right patient?"

"I'm sure," Spencer sits on the arm of the chair at his bedside. "We were able to straighten out the funding for your hospital stay. All bills are paid. And any future bills are as well."

This is indeed good news. Ryan had finally struck up the courage to look at his finances. His bills are huge, and he has no way to pay them. This, indeed, is good news. He grabs Spencer and gives him a bear hug. Spencer is surprised.

"Thanks."

"It was not just me; it was the team. We all realized this did not make sense. It's all taken care of now."

Spencer leaves the room smiling.

· · ·

It is clear that the worst has passed. There is grass on the ground. The lush vegetation and thick trees surround them. Matthew hears a quiet chirp. He looks up in the sky and sees a gray bird circling a tree. They are still above the village, but they can now see the brightly covered buildings far in the distance. They are on a leisurely hike. They survived.

There is a great deal of urgent work that needs to be done, but they have survived. Intuitively, they all understood and pass the remaining time in personal reflection.

The air is dry and warm. Matthew, Sarah, and Larry take their heavier clothing off and put it in the backpacks. They reach a stream. The sound of running water is musical.

"Stop." Matthew pulls out his cell phone, and he has reception. He sends a quick text.

They follow the stream.

Matthew says, "Larry, that was your bonus."

"The amount agreed on?"

"No."

"No?"

"This trip has put some very important pieces in place. You should know that you have helped to save many lives. Without you we would never have made it to the cabin."

"Thanks."

"Without you we also would have never gotten off the mountain. The bonus is far in excess of the agreed amount."

"Great, thank you."

"Are you going back to school?"

"I stayed on Karakatura to work some things out. I was hiding from some things. This trip has been good for me, made me do some real thinking."

Sarah says, "We could always use you. Why don't you come back to America with us? If you want excitement, we seem to have it."

"Getting shot at is not my idea of fun," says Larry.

Matthew says, "Trust me, after a while you get used to it."

Larry says, "I think I'm ready to go home."

Matthew laughs as soon as he hears the loud bark. He is far away, but Matthew has no doubt who the small chocolate brown fuzzy creature is who runs toward them.

"Oscar."

The dog jumps on Matthew and begins licking him.

Sarah says, "You have a friend for life."

"I missed you, buddy."

The stream widens as the water meanders across some rocks. Oscar is the first to run through the stream. Matthew, Sarah, and Larry put the backpacks over their heads. The water feels refreshing. They cross the stream with ease, but Sarah has an obvious limp. Oscar rubs his head against her weak leg.

Larry says, "Sarah, your leg is cramped up from the climb."

"I'm overtired. It happens sometimes."

"Yeah, that was some climb. I'm very proud of you and Matthew. You did good."

"Thanks."

"Good news—we're going to have some fun soon. You won't need to walk."

Larry leads them to a rope attached across a hundred-foot gorge. The zipline is well-used.

"Now for the fun," says Larry.

Matthew can't remember the last time he was on a ride at a fair, but that's what it reminds him of. He holds Oscar as he ziplines across. Oscar yelps with delight. After the zipline they walk to the outskirts of town and set up their tents. Larry's friends are waiting to take their gear. Both Sarah and Matthew are sorry this part of the journey is ending.

CHAPTER FORTY-TWO

Jason Cooper has an outside firm sweep his office. An old friend from his covert operations days organizes it. Something is not quite right. He has put people in place to spy on Quentin but is still not sure what is going on.

Jason sits at his desk, looking at some photos. He sees a man in his early thirties. The man had approached Caroline MacAulay in Central Park. He spoke briefly to her and then disappeared. Jason picks up the picture and stares at it intently.

Why didn't those stupid agents follow this guy? It is obvious he would have led them to Matthew. Why didn't they at least question him? Jason throws the picture on the desk.

The man has now vanished and cannot be traced. It is very strange. They had run active drivers' licenses, looked at social security numbers. This face cannot be identified; there is no living person in the USA with that face. But there he is.

Even with the most advanced facial recognition technology, no hits. The man has eluded all law enforcement tools. He has to be a friend of Matthew's, giving his mother a message. They have pictures of all Matthew's acquaintances. They have quality close-ups of his face; it definitely is not Matthew in disguise. There is no way it's a transplant, either, because Jason has seen the thick scars around the ears that the procedure leaves. Jason knows this is a crucial piece of the picture. He just can't fit it together. The loud ring of the telephone breaks his concentration.

"Did you ID our mystery man?" says Jason.

Jason pulls at the telephone cord. "Put two units on Ms. MacAulay. If this guy shows up again, one unit is to apprehend him. If necessary leave Ms. MacAulay and use both units. My hunch is he will contact her again; he's definitely a friend of Matthew. Go over his high school and medical school acquaintances. Something may turn up." Jason reviews the facts. As much as Jason hates Matthew, he is not the mastermind. Quentin Taylor is leading the charge to kill Matthew. Quentin knows of Jason's history with Matthew. It is no coincidence the Secretary of Defense chose him for the job. Maybe he is flattering himself to think the assignment was based on his ability. Jason will kill Matthew at the first chance he gets, no questions asked. He is just not sure if he should be reserving a bullet for Quentin Taylor as well.

He pulls out the file he assembled on the Secretary of Defense. Quentin Taylor is relatively new to the job. He was appointed due to the untimely death of George H. Brown. Quentin has the ability to orchestrate all the murders.

Jason is close to breaking the case wide open—he can feel it. There are just a few pieces missing. Quentin's instructions regarding Matthew are becoming less and less coherent. Jason had tracked Matthew to Karakatura. He was obviously going to find Michael at his cabin. There is a credible report that another team followed Matthew's group and fired at them.

Jason pulls his intelligence file on Michael. He is at his cabin on Karakatura. Michael had gone up with a group of people. The report could not be more specific. The group went up with Michael, but the guides interviewed are positive the group came down without Michael. Jason rereads the section about the man who kept his identity hidden. A tall, thin man went to great pains to keep his identity secret; he always stayed in the shadows. The mastermind has turned on his lieutenants. Jason is certain that Michael was killed in the cabin on Karakatura.

George H. Brown dies climbing Karakatura, with his friend Michael Coulson. A tragic accident. Quentin replaces him. How convenient. Does the mastermind plan to kill Matthew?

He is really getting a bad feeling about Quentin.

So Jason is back to square one. A sharp knock on the door.

"Enter."

Quentin Taylor enters. He takes a seat in front of Jason's desk and wastes no time getting to the point. "What's your assessment?"

"I'm not sure he's our man. Matthew's an underling. I went out to a village near Karakatura, a group which definitely had Michael in it climbed the mountain. I showed them Michael's picture. They identified him positively. I have an eyewitness account from one of the guides. They had a man in the group who was always hidden. The guides were told Michael was in charge. Michael handed out the pay. The other man stayed in the shadows. He was almost completely covered. The guides believed, without a doubt, he was the leader. Michael feared him."

"Did they say more about this man? Race? Size?"

"He was tall and thin. That's it—he was always concealed."

"How much weight can you give the statements of those guides?" says Quentin.

"I think we need to explore alternate scenarios."

"We need to get Dr. MacAulay."

"I think I would like to hear Matthew's side; he should be coming off the mountain soon."

"What's your plan?"

"He doesn't know I tracked him. I know he is coming back by plane. We think we have found out how he's moving about."

"How?" says Quentin.

"Liam Rasulov. He has a pilot's license, lots of aviation contacts. We got a tip. We think we know which airport they will use. It's in California."

Jason knows the plane is landing near Manhattan. He doesn't want his operation compromised.

"Good work. How many men are you taking?"

"I have cut the men I will take to the airport to just ten. Any less and we risk lacking overwhelming force."

Jason is only using two men, but to tell Quentin will arouse suspicion.

"What about Michael Coulson?"

"I don't know what happened to Michael's group. The guide that took them disappeared. Michael has not surfaced."

"What do you make of it?"

"Not enough to go on. I left a man; he'll call if there is any news."

"Matthew's our man. We need to take him out. I don't think you should waste time on anything else."

"He might have something interesting to say." Jason puts his hands behind his head and leans back in the chair.

"I think he would just embarrass us all with his lies and deceit. He'll try to smear innocent people."

"He may have a story; he may lead us up the food chain."

"Anything he might tell you would be a lie. We can't listen to anything he says. Kill him the first chance you get. No interrogation, do you understand? That's a direct order from the Secretary of Defense."

"Yes, sir." Jason closes the door behind Quentin and opens a new set of photos. The crime scene at Amanda Soto's home was grim. It was very bloody. He sits at his desk and spreads out the photos. He has them digitized on his computer, but he still likes to study the hard copies.

"Hello, this is Chief Riggs."

"Special Agent Jason Cooper here. How are you doing, the heat getting to you?"

"We're in a little bit of a heat wave, New York summer."

"Good excuse for a nice cold one."

Chief Riggs laughs heartily. "You bet, sir. What can I help you with?"

"I emailed a photo to you. I am interested in the man in the photo, the officer with the cap on."

"I looked at the photo. He's not one of ours. Not state, not local."

"Any idea who he is?" says Jason.

"No. I asked the men. He didn't say much, and they thought he was one of yours. No one remembers much about him."

"Have a nice day, Chief."

Jason lays out the photos, looking carefully at the one photo with the best shot of the man. His uniform is that of a senior police officer. He wears his police cap a little lower than normal. He is tall, thin. It didn't seem odd, but now Jason can see the man's cap covering his features. All Jason can say for certain is that he is a thin male, about six foot. He looks at the digitized image on the computer. No more details are available. The man kept to the shadows. As Jason slowly goes over the other photos, one strikes him as odd. He makes a copy of the photo and places it in his pocket. Jason is sure—this is their man. This guy leaves no loose ends. If this guy gets to Matthew before he does, Jason won't lose any sleep.

· · ·

The president receives his final instructions on The Freeze. It has been successfully deployed around the United States in secure locations. WMD238, more commonly known as The Freeze, is fully operational. The antidote will be sent to each military base that holds The Freeze within a week.

There is a charge that runs through his body. He is the President of the United States of America. He uses his power wisely, and he is the most powerful person in the world. The Football makes him the most powerful person in the world. It has been updated to now handle the firing of The Freeze. "Your alphanumeric code is on this laminated card." The soldier holds up the card which is on top of the briefcase's computer keyboard. "The Secretary of Defense must enter his code on his briefcase. This will allow the Football to go live." The Soldier points. "The green light will flash, indicating that your Football is live. From that point on, only you have the ability to enter codes to authorize a weapon system. You will override any local weapon system controls."

The president holds up the papers. "Green bioweapons, red nuclear weapons."

"These give detailed instructions. The analysts have prepared first strike and defensive strikes. Most likely, you will contact the Security Council to plan this. But these files allow you to enter the codes based on the scenario and fire the weapons yourself. As with the nuclear codes, this system allows you to bypass and override all the normal channels for weapons firing. Wherever you authorize the strike, it will happen. Keep in mind the bios are all defensive—nukes are first strike.

You must be very sure before you activate this system. There is no fail-safe. There is no abort."

"There is no way to stop it?"

"I must emphasize, as soon as you punch in the codes and hit the red button, the sequence cannot be altered." The Soldier gently touches the red button. "This is something best thought of as a response to a surprise attack on American soil—if we are sucker punched."

"I take over everything."

"Yes. If all other military personnel and all lines of communication are gone, you are the only person in our country who can save us." The soldier pauses. "You are the last man standing."

"What is on the laptop screen?"

"Depending on what is authorized, you will receive real time data or live images to confirm strikes. Missiles are tracked in real time right to target; they also have cameras on the delivery system so you can see the strike." The soldier closes the briefcase. "You should think of yourself as the entire military if you ever choose to use this system. Hopefully, it will never be tested in real life."

"Let's hope," says the president. "Has the Secretary of Defense been briefed?"

"He will have his briefing Wednesday and get his new briefcase with the updated bioweapons data at that time."

· · ·

The airfield is just outside Manhattan. Jason is very careful in his planning; he will never underestimate Matthew again. Liam meets with Matthew and Sarah at an airstrip just outside the US. Liam then flies a small plane into a private airport. They have been using this routine for most of their covert flights to avoid detection. When they land Jason's men will secure the hangar. He trusts his men, but he doesn't want them to see what happens inside the hangar. They will remain outside and allow no one to enter. Jason will arrest Matthew and whoever is with him as they leave the plane.

. . .

"It's good to be home."

The sky is clear and the sun is just coming up.

"We'll spend a day at the safe house, then head out to Alice. Kofi will be waiting," says Liam.

"I'm just looking forward to some real rest," says Sarah.

Matthew says, "I think most of what we have to do is right here."

The plane touches down smoothly on the runway.

"Matthew, why do you say that?" asks Liam.

"Just a feeling." Liam speeds the plane to the hangar and powers down.

Jason draws his weapon, a Glock 22. He makes sure the silencer is secure and positions himself behind a desk. As soon as they exit, they will realize the airport staff is not present and know something is wrong. By then he will have his laser sight right on Matthew's chest.

Matthew is exhausted, but they have no time to lose. What he has learned on the mountain is devastating. It is too much to contemplate. Unfortunately, it all fits together. Sarah comes out first, followed by Matthew, then Liam.

Jason says, "Raise your hands. You are under arrest. Proceed forward with caution."

Sarah obeys. Matthew and Liam put their hands up and follow.

"Do not attempt to run. If you try to leave the hangar, my guards outside are under orders to use deadly force."

Jason hustles Matthew into a room and closes the door. He shoves Matthew roughly into a seat. Matthew bumps his head. Jason moves back six feet from Matthew. The red light of the gun's laser beam makes a small red dot on the middle of Matthew's forehead.

Jason asks, "Why?"

"I'm not the one who is behind all this."

"You are going to die. You only have a few minutes left. Don't waste them with lies."

"There's no time to hold me. An attack that will decimate the United States will occur in three days."

"You just wasted five seconds."

Jason takes out the picture of the tall, thin man in police uniform, the man in the shadows. "Who is he?"

Matthew lies. "I'm not sure, but he's the one you want."

"I want a name."

Chapter Forty-Three

"The President of the United States of America is a double agent," says Matthew.

At any other time, Jason would have laughed, but Matthew has a laser-sighted gun pointed in the middle of his forehead. Jason remains silent.

"The President of the United States was kidnapped by whoever is behind this. His face was harvested and transplanted onto a double agent. The man sitting in the White House right now is not Carter Middleton—he is a double."

"What government is behind this?"

"I am not sure. Tom did the transplant. He was much further along with his transplants. He could transplant a face perfectly, leaving none of the scars that occur with the current facial transplant techniques. The man in charge made Tom do the transplant. They initially told him that it would be in exchange for his wife's life. Patricia had a gambling habit.

"After he transplanted the president, they presented him with the face of the Secretary of Defense, George H. Brown. At that point he balked."

"They wanted Tom to perform transplants for the President of the United States and the Secretary of Defense. Of course he wouldn't do it. The only reason to transplant the two at the same time would be to access the nuclear codes."

"Precisely. They miscalculated."

"Keep talking."

"They drugged the real president and harvested his face. They then had Tom put it on the body double of the president. Tom was under the impression they would keep the real president sedated and allow the double in the White House for only a few hours. Then he would put the real face back on the president. Tom knew which drugs would not only have sedated the president but also erased his short term memory. When he saw the face of the Secretary of Defense, he knew it was not a simple plan to get a few secrets or make some money. Transplanting both the President of the United States and the Secretary of Defense could only mean they planned to detonate nuclear weapons, or release bioweapons. Tom refused; they then killed him."

"The President of the United States of America is a double agent? Is there a foreign power behind this?"

"I don't think there is a foreign power involved. If I've worked this thing out properly, I think the real president is still alive. The person in the office right now is an impostor. That's what I'm saying."

"That's incredible."

"Tom would have been told they were after money. It would make sense. They were thugs, and Patricia needed to repay gambling debts. Tom would have worried about espionage, but it was unlikely. And what were his options? They played him perfectly."

"So what went wrong?" says Jason.

"He transplanted the president as asked, no complications. As soon as they presented the face of George H. Brown, the game was over. Tom knew George H. Brown was murdered—it was not a climbing accident as had been reported in the news. He would also quickly put Michael Coulson into the picture since Michael was with George H. Brown when the "climbing accident" occurred. Their plans were obvious. Every high school student knows that those two men together hold the launch codes for the nuclear arsenal. I think they counted on the fact that Tom had no options. He couldn't back out. They probably spent a great deal of time trying to convince him to do the second transplant."

"This is all speculation."

"Not quite. Kofi Adebayo was there that night. Tom asked him to stay hidden. He heard much of this. Tom refused to do the second transplant. They took Tom away and they killed him. They were forced to improvise. That's when they flew the Secretary of Defense's face in a canister to our lab with his body double. They wanted me to put that face on the guy in my operating room. Obviously, they were not going to go to Michael's lab."

"How do I know this "perfect transplant" is possible? No lab is anywhere near that kind of result."

"Didn't you wonder how I moved about in the US? I'm sure you had many of my known contacts staked out. Your men would have taken photos of a man about my height and build visiting my mother in Central Park. That was me."

Jason remembered the mystery man who met Matthew's mother in Central Park. He knew that person had no records, didn't exist in the system. He had looked at that those pictures a thousand times, and there were no surgical scars.

"That was you?" says Jason.

"That was me. Tom had developed the perfect face transplant."

"What's the plan—steal our nuclear codes?"

"No. The fake president is going to release bioweapons throughout the US. He plans to kill 90 percent of the population."

"This sounds a bit rich."

"You need to make a decision. Kill me, hold me, or send me to a foreign power to be interrogated. In any scenario, you will have on your hands the worst human tragedy in American history."

Jason has the laser-sighted weapon positioned perfectly. He takes the safety off. He has waited a long time to kill Matthew. He is tantalizingly close to achieving his goal. Erase him.

He has convinced himself that he is going to do his duty and terminate a psychopathic murderer and traitor. He can finally remove the one thing that stands between him and Celerie. Jason squeezes the gun tightly. His eyes narrow. Matthew looks Jason right in the eye. Jason puts the safety on the weapon and puts it in his holster.

Jason laughs.

"Could you let me in on the joke?"

"Life can play some real funny games on you sometimes, man. Did you know I'm getting married?"

"I heard. Congrats, she's a wonderful girl. Make every day of her life better than the last. She deserves that."

"I intend to."

Matthew smiles.

Jason continues, "We can't just go to the White House and say to the president, 'You're a fake.'"

"He would have us arrested, I agree."

"If he is a fake, we would be killed before we could prove anything."

"That's the challenge," says Matthew.

"We need the mastermind. Who is it?"

Matthew lies. "I don't know."

"Didn't you get this info from Michael?"

"Michael was killed. I was able to piece most of it together from clues in his cabin. I know the mastermind lives in the Meatpacking District. If we can't find him within twenty-four hours, I take what I have to the new Secretary of Defense, Congress, anybody."

Jason pauses. The story is incredible, but he did see the man in Central Park. The photos were HD quality, and the man was Matthew's build. If that was a transplant, it was perfect. Some of the rumors floating around the White House would also be explained. The rush to get The Freeze deployed throughout the United States before the vaccine is ready now makes sense.

Jason takes a deep breath and pulls out the photo. "Here's your mastermind."

Matthew snatches the photo up. "Did you identify him?"

"No, this was taken at Amanda's house after the murder. This man is not with any law enforcement agency."

"Who is he?" says Matthew.

"I don't know."

Matthew is relieved; he is almost certain he knows the identity of this man. Matthew wants to confront him personally, one-on-one. Matthew hopes beyond all hope he is mistaken. There are only a few private citizens with the money and knowledge to create such a masterful scheme. Matthew has told Jason many half-truths, but he wants to solve this in his own way.

Jason throws another photo on the desk. "This is the footprint of our man. The shoe is from Mervyn Clewes. The imprint was from an area beside Amanda's body."

Jason had taken the photo himself. He realized the shoe print was strange and intricate. He didn't know how it fit in, but it just looked out of place. The pattern of the sole was very distinct. It almost looked like a coat of arms.

"Mervyn Clewes?" says Matthew.

Jason, "Mervyn Clewes, a bespoke shoemaker. He makes a cast of your foot. Then over the course of a year, he makes your shoes."

"Our man wears Mervyn Clewes?"

The man they were after has to lead a double life. This footprint will lead them to his headquarters in New York. Matthew is sure the real President of the United States is still alive. If he can find the headquarters of the mastermind, he will be able to save the real president and stop the release of The Freeze. These photos are just what he needed.

"Our man wears shoes made by the bespoke bootmaker Mervyn Clewes. I am going to visit Mervyn Clewes. Why don't you join me?" says Jason.

Jason speaks to his men outside. The hangar is opened and the two uniformed men given instructions. Sarah and Liam are released.

Chapter Forty-Four

Ryan walks comfortably down the hospital hallway. He uses the weight room daily. Life has handed him some challenges. Who doesn't have challenges? He is going to work it out. He misses the kids. He has tried to reach Aly, but her mom says she doesn't want to take his calls. She needs time. That is fine. He misses Aly, but he has to move forward.

The prosthesis is being made to cover the hole in his face. He will use it and get on with his life. Doc MacAulay will help him if he can, but from what he hears, Doc MacAulay is in serious trouble.

Ryan doesn't believe Doc MacAulay has done any of the things they said. When he gets back on his feet, Ryan makes a promise to visit Doc MacAulay in prison. He is convinced Matthew will be in jail very soon. He will visit him regularly, help in any way he can. Never leave a comrade behind.

Ryan sits in his room reading a magazine. He looks up and Aly is standing in front of him. She has lost even more weight. She is wearing a new dress. The new short hairstyle suits her face.

"It's been a while," says Aly.

"Hi, Aly. I'm glad you came to visit." Ryan looks at her perfect white teeth. She always had an amazing smile.

"You're looking stronger." Aly sits beside the bed.

"How are the kids?"

"They're doing great. My mom is spoiling them crazy."

"Sounds like your mom."

"I got a job in town."

"Here?"

"Yes." Aly smoothes the wrinkles in the dress where it hugs her hips.

"That's great."

"The bank renegotiated the mortgage. I can make the payments. Mom helped us a little. So we're all good. I'm bringing the kids home in a few weeks." Aly smiles. "You should be out by then. I spoke to Dr. Lambert. He helped straighten out some of the finances. He really went to bat for us."

"Dr. Lambert turned out to be pretty great."

"I want us to be a family again. We'll all be together."

"Can you live with this?" Ryan removes the triangular bandage. He has a large space where his nose should be, the tissue around it puckered.

Aly looks and then gives him kiss on the puckered skin.

. . .

The shop of the bespoke bootmaker Mervyn Clewes is on Fifth Avenue. It has an old-world ambiance. Heavy club chairs with handsewn leather. The smell of leather pervades everything. The workshop is part of the store. It is open for all customers to watch. Craftsmen hammer and sew shoes. No robots here.

Matthew looks at a pair of shoes, works of art. Intricate stitching and fine leather detailing for every shoe. The craftsmen work behind solid wooden benches. Their metal awls and pincers are well-worn. They wear leather aprons with the Mervyn Clewes name embossed across the front. The youngest worker is sixty-three. One craftsman had pure white hair and heavy wrinkles over his eyes. The man was working away on a pair of black wingtips.

Jason moves toward a man dressed in a tailored English suit. Matthew follows behind.

"Mr. Mervyn Clewes," says Jason.

Mervyn Clewes has a slim build. His shoes are brown, freshly polished. They complement his light gray suit. He wears a light blue shirt with fine threads of brown running through the material. A silk tie and pocket square complete the look. Understated elegance.

"You must be Jason?" says Mervyn.

"Yes."

"From the old country?"

"By way of Connecticut more recently. The accent dies hard."

"Just a trace, but I heard it. When you called me last week, I was under the impression you would be alone." Mervyn Clewes glances at Matthew.

"You were correct. There have been some recent developments. This is Matthew. He is also aiding in our investigation."

Mervyn Clewes walks over to his desk at the far end of the store. There are two men at the other end being fitted for shoes. The store is quiet, with an old money feel, although in reality most of the customers are new money. They are willing to pay quite a ridiculous amount to look like old money. Mervyn Clewes sits at his desk and plays with the mouse to get the computer to start.

"The shoeprint you sent me is from a very interesting client. We have a number of anonymous clients. They come in, have their feet measured, or have someone send in the measurements. Discretion is a big part of our business.

"Were you able to trace this shoe?" says Jason.

"We use a standard sole, the intricate design is our trademark. However, we tend to have a little fun with it. We make each slightly different. To the casual observer, our crest would be easily recognized on the sole. But we can look at the sole and identify who bought the shoe. A few of our craftsmen even play with the design so they can say what year the shoe was purchased."

Matthew says, "Our investigation is in a very critical stage. If you could give us the name and address, the situation has some urgency."

Mervyn Clewes looks at him briefly and then continues. "This man never came into the store. Every year he orders three pairs. A courier picks them up. He has been doing this for better than ten years. Your sole imprint was very good. We are certain it is this man."

"You have been most helpful, Mr. Clewes."

Matthew turns to leave, but Jason sits comfortably in the chair.

Mervyn Clewes says, "For years we kept our eyes out for his shoes. We look at newspapers to see celebrities, world leaders. The first thing we do is look at their feet to see if they are wearing our shoes. We could never find this man and our shoes. As a joke one year, one of our men followed the courier who picked up his shoes. We tracked him to this address."

Mervyn Clewes hands the piece of paper to Jason.

Jason says, "As I mentioned on the phone, this is a matter of national security. I thank you."

With that Matthew and Jason leave the building. They both knew the address in the Meatpacking District. Not too far from Matthew's own home. It is a high-end furniture store in his neighborhood. He has never been in the store, but when he was furnishing his house, the designer had shown him some pieces from the store.

Matthew picks up his cell phone and dials Alice.

"Hi, Matthew, what's up?"

Matthew gives Alice the address. "Please tell me about this building. We think the mastermind lives here. I need the info ASAP."

Matthew and Jason hop into Jason's car.

"Do you want some confidence?" Jason takes out a second gun from his glove compartment.

"No."

"Are you sure? Untraceable."

Matthew asks, "Does the word stool mean anything to you?"

"Stool?"

"Yes, stool." Matthew pulls out the piece of cardboard box with the hand-written code:

Stool

"Stool. It doesn't mean anything to me. But I can say Michael was a real doctor; his handwriting was atrocious."

"I think it is a code," says Matthew.

"That's obvious," says Jason. "We can't risk sending it to headquarters. I have a friend. I'll send the image to him. We'll get an answer soon."

"Thanks, I've already sent it to an encryption specialist."

"Who?" Jason turns the piece of cardboard over and looks at the back.

"Alice."

"NSA? Never heard of her. What's her last name?."

"Freelancer, she just goes by Alice," says Matthew.

"Let's get back to the task at hand. We need to kill or capture this guy." Jason tosses the piece of cardboard back to Matthew.

"We need to take him alive. We have a few questions we still need him to answer." Matthew puts the cardboard back in his pocket.

"We'll play it your way."

• • •

Matthew and Jason walk quickly along the busy street. Shops and cafés mingle with old factories.

Matthew's cell phone rings. "Hi, Alice."

"The building has a storefront. The front of the building is a high-end furniture shop."

"Tell me something I don't know."

Alice continues, "However, there is a large lab and living quarters in the back. You definitely have the right place. The side door is accessed with the code 60193. I think there are two people in this part of the building. It looks like there is a secure area and a number of unsecured rooms. I am trying to get into their surveillance equipment, but it will take some time. Be careful."

"Thanks," says Matthew.

"You have a female agent giving you some help? I knew you had someone on the inside."

Matthew smiles. He punches in the code. They go down the wide hallway. The clean white walls and gray metal doors remind him of the

National Research Facility. They follow Alice's instructions. There is no sound and the place appears empty. Matthew memorized the map that Michael had drawn in the notes he had left in the fava bean salad. He knows exactly where he is going.

"Jason, you go down that hallway. I'm going right. You'll find the real president."

Jason pulls his weapon and creeps down the hallway.

Matthew quickly makes his way to the main area. Michael's directions are good, and in no time, Matthew enters the office. He is angry. There is no fear.

CHAPTER FORTY-FIVE

Liam sits at a desk almost identical to the one he has at his office in the hospital. He takes off the black fedora. "I really wasn't expecting you, Matthew."

Matthew looks around. They are alone. Liam works on his computer. He has two screens going. A large fish tank occupies the entire wall behind him. The tank contains a vibrant array of tropical fish.

"I didn't know you liked tropical fish."

Liam smiles. "There are many things you don't know about me."

"I know you're a killer, a liar."

"I have some of the rarest tropical fish in that tank. It's beautiful, isn't it?"

"Why?" says Matthew.

"I didn't think you would get so far. I'm truly amazed you figured it out. I have no idea how you traced me here. I've been popping over here for years. I'm curious, how'd you find me? You followed me?"

"Mervyn Clewes."

"He has no idea where I live. I have my courier pick up my shoes and bring them here."

"We matched a footprint at Amanda's crime scene to your shoe."

"I wore my black ones for that job. I wear a new shoe for each job."

"It was Jason who figured it out."

"I stayed close to you to know all your moves. That's how I was so sure I was in the clear. Did you ever suspect me?"

"I started to have my doubts after you nearly killed me in the old factory. How did Francesca know I would be at the airport? Only Sarah, Kofi and you knew that. I still didn't want to believe it, I thought someone was listening in on us. When I left Karakatura, I had most of the answers."

"Not from Michael, I killed him. I was shocked you and Sarah made that climb."

"Michael spoke from beyond. He screamed what a monster you are. He screamed for me to stop you."

"He left you a message. We tore the place apart, but I couldn't find it. No matter. There is nothing you can do." Liam's blue eyes brighten.

"Why do this?" says Matthew.

"When did you figure out it was me?"

"It slowly fell into place. I really wasn't sure until I saw you at this desk, right now. Few have the transplant knowledge to pull this whole thing off. I narrowed it down to you, Quentin, or Kofi. I saw the photos of you at Amanda's crime scene. I couldn't see the face, but the body type, it just struck me. It had to be one of you three. I had a feeling, when I was in the elevator the day of the two recovery room deaths, that the man in the elevator shadows was you. I couldn't see you, but I just had that feeling.

"Guilty as charged."

"Why did you go back to Amanda's?"

"I'm hands-on for all my operations, the only way to make sure it is done right. No ego, no bloodlust. I had to remove some clues, plant some false ones. With forensics the way it is now, you have to be careful."

"You had no problem framing your son for murder?" says Matthew.

"You're full of surprises today, Matthew."

"You deny you're my father?"

"No, no I don't. I'm just surprised. Caroline told you then?"

"No, she always told me she couldn't be sure of my father and never to try to find him. I searched my birth records once, father unlisted."

"Then how in the world did you find out?"

"I asked Tom about my father. I was very young. I told him how I wished he were my father, wished my mother hadn't had me. The kids teased me pretty bad back then. He told me to never blame my mother. He said sometimes good things can come out of an ugly situation. He said he didn't know who my father was, but I know he had his suspicions."

"How did that tell you anything?"

"One day I was at the lab. A graduate student was talking to Tom in private. I heard the tail end of the conversation. Tom said something like, 'I'll try to talk to Liam.' She left crying. I asked Tom about it. He said it was private. She transferred to another lab. Shortly after that you three broke up. You left to set up New York; Michael went to Houston."

"So Caroline never said?"

"No, she kept your dirty secret. But I know I'm right."

Liam claps slowly. "Bravo. I haven't given you the credit you deserve. You really are quite the mind. Good genes, I guess."

"Your wife know you fathered me? I did the math. You were married for three years at the time. That one would be a little hard to explain for the loving husband, devoted dad. Did you tell the twins? How'd you think the girls would react?"

"It was a moment's indiscretion. Caroline and I worked in the lab. I can hardly blame her. I was the young, brilliant surgeon. What can I say?"

"You hardly came around our house—you never visited me. I spent most of my time with Tom."

"Tom was single at the time. I could hardly be seen spending time with you and your mother. Questions would be asked. As it was, most people thought you were Tom's boy."

"So you found a way to duck out on your responsibilities?"

"Some might see it that way. If you do, I'm sorry. I had to get free of a very delicate situation."

"You're a deadbeat dad, a murderer. Did I leave anything out, Dad?"

"You didn't fall too far from the tree. I helped get you the New York job. I gave you the training." Liam smiles. "You are now one of the best facial transplant surgeons alive."

"So fill me in. Michael thought you planned to kill almost everyone in our country. In the next week, I guess."

"Matthew, it's in motion. There is nothing anyone can do about it. The plan is genius. I may as well tell all."

"Please do."

"Well, most of it you know. Patricia was a gambler. It was easy to get her into deep, deep debt. She had no way to pay the debt off. We offered her a way out. Tom does a transplant and her debt is paid. If Tom didn't do the transplant, she would be killed. Simple. Tom transplanted the president. He did a great job—he took the face of the real president and then transferred it to our body double.

"We told Tom we were going to put the president's face back on him and no one would have been the wiser. We told Tom it was to make some money. He wasn't thrilled, but he did it. When my men presented him with the second face, the Secretary of Defense, he balked."

"You didn't realize he would not transplant both the President of the United States and the Secretary of Defense? Any grade school kid knows that the only thing those two people are needed for is to fire nuclear weapons."

"I'm not a fool. I know of the two-man rule. The Secretary of Defense is needed to authenticate the president before the weapons are launched. I thought Tom would still do it to save his wife and his own life at that point."

"So what went wrong?"

"It was a rare miscalculation on my part. He had transplanted the President's face onto an impostor! There was no going back. I owned him at that point. Or so I thought."

"How did you get the Secretary of Defenses' face?"

"Just as you thought. Michael was friends with him. George H. Brown did not climb, but he fancied himself an athlete. Michael convinced him to go on a climbing expedition on Karakatura. Sadly, George H. Brown had a fatal fall."

"Michael killed him?"

"No. Remember that week I took off for a flying trip. I was on the expedition. Michael didn't know I was going to do it. He was weak. I think it was after that, he turned on me."

Liam continues, " I killed George and harvested the face. That was the canister you failed to transplant the night my associate visited you."

"But the climbing accident was three months before Mr. Glock visited."

"I had to do it well in advance of the kidnapping the president. In case anything went wrong, I couldn't have both the president and the Secretary of Defense go missing. George's face was cryopreserved.."

"Tom refused to transplant the second face? Even to save Patricia?"

"He refused. He had already transplanted Middleton. I knew he loved Patricia and would do anything for her. My only miscalculation was that he would not think rationally. When we told him to transplant George's face, he turned white."

"He said no." Matthew edges closer to the desk.

"He said no. I tried to show him this was his only option. It was as if he was being mind-controlled. He just kept saying no, no, no. He wouldn't see reason. The only logical thing for him to do at that point was to perform the second transplant."

"You would have killed him anyway."

"True." Liam smiles.

"Why didn't you just do the transplant yourself? You were right there; you didn't need Tom."

"That was the first thing I tried. Alice wouldn't let me. I was not authorized. We tried to short-circuit her. It was not until I went back to his lab with you guys that I understood the power of Alice. First time I went back, I was worried she would recognize me. But we swapped the hard drive before we left; she had no idea who I was."

"So when Tom refused to do the transplant, you hauled everyone to New York to force me to do it."

"I thought it was a brilliant plan made on such short notice. We grabbed some Steriazol and I sent the man you dubbed Mr. Glock with the canister containing George H. Brown's head to New York. I was certain you would have no problem transplanting the head. My second miscalculation."

"You were the one he was talking to that night."

"I stayed in communication with him and the clean up crew the whole time. I was in Palo Alto."

"Tom told you about his perfect transplants?"

"He confided in me. He even wanted me to come down and help make it better. Can you imagine? With a discovery like that, what a fool. You don't share something like that."

"Why the energy weapon? Why not just shoot him?"

"No one knew I had the high-energy-pulsed weapon. I had a technician on the inside and was simultaneously building my own as the government built the prototype. Right here in this very lab. Mine was better. I planned to sell it. I had to test it, and it seemed like the perfect opportunity. I wanted his death to look like a government job. Throw suspicion on a foreign government."

"It worked."

"Like a charm. I really did not want to get you involved, but you could see my position was desperate. I could not go to Houston and implicate Michael. I had no choice. If anything was discovered, I had to make sure it was not one of my helpers."

Matthew mocked him. "Oh, I see very clearly. You had no option but to try to force me to do a transplant at gunpoint. You also knew you would kill us all. Me, Amanda, and Sarah had the transplant worked."

"I couldn't believe you cut the carotid and killed the patient. My own son. Maybe the apple fell farther from the tree than I would care to admit. That maneuver was routine. Anyway. The rest was cleaning up loose ends."

"What I can't understand is why—why all this work? For what? To sell nukes to some dictator? Your family is loaded."

"You insult me. Such a petty plan is not in my nature. The president that I have installed in the White House, my president, will be creating a new America."

"A new America?"

"In exactly three hours, he will punch in the codes to release The Freeze. Do you know what that is?"

Michael had documented The Freeze in his notes, but Matthew does not want Liam to know.

"No, please enlighten me."

"The Freeze: It is a mutated virus that has been weaponized. The ultimate bioweapon. It is highly effective and has a 100 percent kill rate. Kills all humans, but here's the kicker. It doesn't kill dogs."

"You're an animal lover now?"

"Remember The Binary Sequence? Facial transplants is one half, biological weapons the other. The two things are the new weapons of this century. I will be the first person to use these together successfully. The fake president will release enough of The Freeze to kill 90 percent of the population."

"Madness," says Matthew.

"Madness or genius? Look at this society. Soft. Lazy. Uninspired. Mass entertainment. They can't even sing today. Show me a star with a voice to sing or something to say. Now they just wear as little as possible and screech. Consumerism. Buy, Buy, Buy! They don't even know why they're buying. I'll tell you why they're buying. They seek to fulfill a need; they want to be a part of something greater. So they buy whatever they're told is the in thing, whatever they think everyone else has."

"So killing most of the US is going to solve this?"

"We have no community; we don't even know the neighbors next door. We pretend to have friends by using computers, putting up walls. I can fix it. I can make them a part of something great."

"You are well and truly mad," says Matthew.

"I'm courageous enough to say what we all know is true. And bold enough to act. The educational system, it's garbage. Kids today can't even read; they can't spell. Forget about math. We need to start anew. With 90 percent of the population gone, we can rebuild. Create a society based on principles and make something great."

"Let me guess, you'll take charge."

"I will lead the rebuilding. In the chaos that ensues, America will need new leaders. New people to reshape our destiny. I am that leader. All things we know will be gone. In the aftermath Liam Rasulov will be a lucky survivor. Slowly, I will help rebuild. With my considerable wealth, I will be the leader of the new America. I may even run for president."

"Not too close." Liam picks up the gun and points it at Matthew.

Matthew takes the piece of cardboard box from his pocket where Michael had written the word "stool."

"Does this mean anything to you?"

"I have no idea what nonsense is written here. Stool?"

Matthew looks into his father's eyes. Before the shot is fired, he knows Liam plans to kill him. Matthew anticipates well and is on the move before he hears the shot. After he read Michael's note, he told himself he would kill his father. Liam has manipulated, used, and then discarded so many people he has to be executed.

Matthew thought he could kill his father. He has told himself he won't hesitate when the moment arrives. Not after what Michael had detailed in his notes. Michael had done what he could to stop it. Matthew has to finish Michael's work.

Matthew realizes he just can't kill Liam. He does not know this person who stands before him now. The Liam he knew was nowhere to be found.

Instead of taking his advantage, Matthew runs for door. It is locked. He hears a shot and moves again quickly. His father fires a few more shots at him. Liam must have locked the door electronically. Matthew runs toward a large sofa. He throws a vase and breaks the light on the ceiling. The room dims.

Matthew moves fast. Liam is up with the gun, but he is not sure where to aim. Matthew is either behind the chair or a large cabinet. Liam moves slowly. He does not calculate on Matthew doing the unexpected. Matthew jumps out and hits Liam. They fall to the ground and roll. As they fall, Liam loses his grip on Matthew. Matthew jumps up and runs to the desk. He desperately looks for the button to unlock the door.

Liam grabs the gun and fires at Matthew. Matthew runs from the desk, but Liam has moved to cut off his escape. Matthew tackles and tries to disarm his father. They both stand, fighting to gain control of the gun. Liam tries to fire the gun into Matthew's chest, but it misses. They are now in close combat.

Matthew looks into Liam's eyes. The rage and fire in his eyes tells him that if he doesn't disarm Liam, this man will kill him. Father and son lose their balance, falling to the ground. Each tries to gain control of the gun. They roll and the gun fires.

"Too late." Liam smiles at Matthew and then his eyes close.

Matthew stands up, looking at the dead body of his father.

Chapter Forty-Six

The President of the United States is sad that his job is coming to an end. He likes being the president. People are very nice to him, treat him special. It's the little things, the smiles, the handshakes.

Jeremy Dawson, sometimes actor, begins to think of himself as President of the United States. Anything he says is obeyed. When he leaves office with the money Liam is paying him, he will be able to do anything. The Secretary of Defense lay unconscious, bound and gagged on the floor. Jeremy has already opened Quentin Taylor's briefcase and entered the Secretary of Defense's codes needed to activate the Football. Now he had complete power. He removes the Biscuit and punches in the codes: RP345 SC069 CT186. It is tedious.

Jeremy hears, "Launch sequence complete for WMD238."

The voice is calm, neutral, feminine. It repeats the codes.

The voice then says, "Push launch button to proceed."

Jeremy Dawson hesitates. He understands what pushing the red button will do. He was attentive at his briefings; he read his files. The codes he has entered will result in severe devastation. Liam had not told him the extent of the devastation that will occur. He learns this while in office.

Jeremy has some misgivings. After all, these are his own people he will be killing. They are kind, nice, and hardworking. From his time in the White House, he now fully understands what he is being paid to do. Liam has specifically chosen coordinates that will remove the entire population of Washington, D.C. Jeremy Dawson realizes Liam has targeted large urban areas, university centers, and political institutions, areas that are all densely populated. The missiles containing The Freeze will detonate over these major centers.

Liam promises to have a plan to evacuate Jeremy. Just in case, Jeremy has his own plan. His vehicle and driver are waiting to take him away. Jeremy looks over at Quentin, tied up and unconscious. Jeremy remembers his friend who had trained with him to be the Secretary of Defense. The original plan was to have both the president and the Secretary of Defense switched with actors. Jeremy's friend was supposed to receive the face of George H. Brown. Jeremy remembers how sad he was when he learned the face transplant failed and his friend, also an out-of work-actor, had died on Matthew's operating table. If that had worked, his friend would have taken the role of George H. Brown. Quentin Taylor would never have been appointed Secretary of Defense.

Jeremy is not happy about what he plans to do with Quentin before he leaves the White House, but he has no choice. He will miss Quentin; he taught him how to enjoy a Cobb salad.

President of the United States of America is the role of a lifetime. Jeremy Dawson put in an award-winning performance, pity he won't get the statue. He grimaces and pushes the red button. The light begins to flash. A map of the United States of America appears on the upper part of the laptop screen. Red dots blink on the map at all the sites where The Freeze will be deployed.

"Launch codes complete. System activated," the voice says politely.

It's done now. He leaves the Football on the desk in the Oval Office. He has followed Liam's instructions precisely. Two things puzzle him: why did Liam insert a delay in the actual launch time, and why did he make him wear this precise outfit? He will follow Liam's instructions because he is being paid a fortune. He goes online to see if there were any new girls on his favorite site while he waits for his evacuation plan.

Chapter Forty-Seven

Two loud gunshots are heard at the door. The door lock is blown off and Jason comes through. Behind him is the President of the United States of America.

Matthew looks at Carter Middleton. The president has his face intact. Had Matthew gotten everything wrong?

Matthew knew the real president was alive. The final part of Liam's plan had to include killing the fake president and switching back the real president. Matthew thought the real Carter Middleton would have been heavily drugged somewhere in this building. He would have received drugs to forget the last few days. Liam knew the real president would have been unable to explain his actions. President Middleton says, "I would like to thank you for your help, Dr. MacAulay. I understand you were looking to solve the murder of your friend Tom. In doing so you have saved me. If we move quickly, we will save countless others."

"Forgive me for saying this, but isn't your face on an impostor in the White House?" "Yes and no. Your father kept me around. I was the final piece in his grand plan. He was able to clone my face. The impostor in the White House has my cloned face. They cleverly fooled Tom into thinking my face was harvested. Liam couldn't let him know about his cloning advances. A few cells from the inside of my mouth, that's all it took."

"Liam was developing cloning techniques?" says Matthew.

"Right here at this lab. He was a very gifted man." The president looks at Liam lying on the floor. "He had some hits and misses, but he was able to clone my face. He said some faces could not be cloned. He wasn't sure why, but he was going to figure it out."

327

"You chatted with that monster?"

"He spoke very highly of you, Matthew. In his own way, I think he loved you."

"He tried to kill me on numerous occasions."

"Did he? He kept me informed about everything. Liam had the gift of the gab and loved to hear his own voice. He viewed me as a friend of sorts. I think he wanted to brag about his accomplishments to someone. Your father tried to spare your life and warn you away."

"He didn't love me. He never acknowledged me or my mom," says Matthew.

"I had long chats with him. Sometimes we would sit for hours here." The president gestures to the sofa. "He told me everything; his plan was genius. His thoughts were troubled, though. Many of his comments and insights into how to improve society had shades of truth."

"You believed him?" says Matthew.

"No, your father was wrong on many accounts. He mistakenly missed the great accomplishments of our society. He minimized our strengths. In fact, he misinterpreted many of our strengths in terms of diversity, freedom of expression, as weaknesses."

Matthew says, "He was the most cruel man I've ever known."

"He had a callous disregard for others' feelings. He was unable to feel for anyone but himself. On many occasions he expressed sadness at my eventual fate in his plan. But he would not let me go."

"Fill us in on the details." Jason holsters his weapon.

"I was kidnapped. They then took some cheek cells and cloned my face. That is what he was working on. No one else in the world is anywhere close to what he achieved. The face Tom transplanted was cloned from my cells in the lab. The face was a perfect match, and with Tom's skill, the transplant onto the impostor was perfect. My double was an out-of-work actor. They spent months teaching him my mannerisms. Liam showed me the videos and how they trained him. At the end I couldn't tell what footage was me or him. Liam's plan was to decimate our country. He had grown frustrated with what he saw as weakness in our people, our national character. We talked at length about poverty, crime, drugs. A whole range of issues."

Matthew says, "It sounds like you and he got on well."

"He really was quite enjoyable and insightful at times. His solution to our problems was to start over, with himself as the leader. A new age leader." President Middleton stands and walks. " The one flaw in his plan was what to do with the actor after the country was decimated. If the actor gave him up, his story would check out. Scientists would take cells from the face and compare them with cells from the rest of his body. The DNA mismatch would prove his point. That's why I am wearing these clothes. This is the last part of the plan. My impostor was told to wear these clothes today while he releases The Freeze. They are an exact duplicate of what I am now wearing. Liam planned to kill him and put me in his place after The Freeze was activated. He would then circulate a story, with the help of friends he has bought in my administration, that I had a breakdown."

Jason says, "I see where this is heading."

Matthew makes the final connection. "In the chaos that ensued after the decimation, you would be held in custody. If you were not summarily executed."

"Precisely. If anyone listened to my story, it would seem like utter garbage. I would have no proof."

"You would have had no story to tell. He would have pumped you full of drugs, and you would have had no memory of any of this."

"He hadn't mentioned that to me, but you're right. Sounds like something he would do. It would not matter anyway. A hastily convened military tribunal would most likely make me disappear and spare the nation any further anguish. His plan was flawless—it would have worked."

"Are you sure the codes have not already been launched?" says Jason.

"How much time do we have?" asks Matthew.

"My impostor has been instructed to launch the codes at 2:30 p.m."

Matthew looks at his watch. "Let's go."

Jason says, "You can't just walk into the White House and say I am the President of the United States. The impostor will have you detained as a well-rehearsed fake. You'll disappear. By the time you are able to clear the whole thing up, The Freeze will be released."

"I can get into the White House. We just need to get there. Does anyone have a private plane?"

"I've got some friends I think might be able to help," says Matthew. Matthew calls Jim Bob.

. . .

The President of the United States of America leads Matthew and his friends through a secret tunnel underneath the White House. With Jim Bob's help and Kofi's money, everyone is able to fly to D.C. in record time.

Kofi says, "I cannot believe what you're telling me."

Sarah is troubled. "Liam was the kindest, most understanding person."

Matthew hugs her. "He had us all fooled."

President Middleton says, "We have to move on. These tunnels will take us to the Oval Office."

The group passes all checkpoints. Some guards look puzzled, but no one questions the President of the United States of America. He gives his passwords and is granted access to the various tunnels. He stops at a central area with many tunnels leading off in different directions.

"Jason, Sarah, and Kofi, take this tunnel to the left. You will end up outside an office. Punch in this six-digit code." The president quickly writes it on a scrap of paper. "Ask the personnel to take you to their boss. Outline our story in brief, and they'll know what to do."

Jason says, "If we're splitting up, Matthew, you take this."

Jason hands Matthew his Glock 22. Jason, Kofi, and Sarah head off.

"Matthew, go down that hallway. It leads to a series of steps to take you to a different office."

Before Matthew can say a word, President Middleton is down another hallway and out of site. Matthew follows the instructions. The hallways are poorly lit, the tunnels narrow. This hallway is long and has a few sharp curves. Matthew reaches the end of the hall. It is a dead end. Matthew retraces his steps. The president is nowhere to be seen.

Chapter Forty-Eight

The door behind him opens. Jeremy Dawson thinks for a moment it is his secretary offering tea, but he has said no interruptions and dismissed all the staff from this wing. He wants no interruptions. No matter, he can choke her to death if necessary. When Jeremy turns around, he is amazed. Carter Middleton, the President of the United States of America, stands in front of him. They wear identical clothes.

Jeremy remembers starring in a movie where he played twins. One twin was evil; the other good. He had played both roles. It was a low-budget film. The movie went straight to video, no theatrical release. The thing he remembered when he saw the film was how strange it was to see two of himself. He has that same feeling now. Truth be told, they are identical. Height, weight, clothes, they are a perfect pair.

Jeremy Dawson says, "Hello."

The more Jeremy Dawson looks at Carter Middleton, the angrier he feels inside. He has embraced the role of President of the United States so completely that he believes Middleton is taking something away from him by returning. Ironically, Jeremy thinks Middleton is stealing his identity.

Carter Middleton did not know how he would react when he saw his impostor. He just knew he wanted to confront him alone.

The president yells, "I am going to kill you."

He rushes Jeremy. They are rolling on the ground when Matthew comes in and locks the door. Matthew points the Glock 22 at the men.

"Stop. Get up," says Matthew.

The two men stand up in front of the large desk. They are identical. Matthew is astonished. He moves his gun from man to man. They are identical. He subconsciously lowers his weapon.

Together Jeremy and the president say, "Shoot him." They point to each other.

Matthew is astonished. If the situation were not so serious, he would laugh. They wear identical beige summer suits. Even the wrinkles around their eyes are identical.

Jeremy says, "He is an impostor. What is my college nickname?"

"A-pole," says Middleton.

"He's good," says Jeremy.

"I'm the real deal, nice try."

The two identical men approach Matthew.

Jeremy tries to convince Matthew. "I'm the real deal, shoot him."

Matthew waves him back. "Where did you grow up?"

They both answer, "New Haven, Connecticut."

"He got that from my bio; that's public record," says Jeremy.

"Who was the mastermind behind this plot?"

" Liam Rasulov," Jeremy and the president answer in unison. "Your father."

Matthew is confused. It is clear that the actor is a perfect double. A doppelgänger. The facial features, voice, and mannerisms are identical. Matthew cannot even separate who is saying what. Looking at two identical people is unnerving. Matthew goes to the thermostat and turns up the heat.

"Let me tell you something Liam did not tell you," says Matthew.

"I'm the real deal. Stop this nonsense, Matthew."

The men stand side by side.

Matthew says, "The plan was you were never going to collect your money. Yes, I know about the big payday."

The men are silent.

"Look at each other. Why did he tell you to dress in identical clothes? I'm sure he didn't give you a good reason to dress in those clothes. Why delay the launch for hours after you entered the bioweapons codes? I'll tell you why."

The president says, "It's getting hot in here."

Both men have sweaty foreheads.

Matthew says, "After you released The Freeze, Liam was going to swap Middleton back in and kill you. He couldn't risk having you around. You could prove that the president was substituted. Think about it. You are the only one who could identify him. Liam left no loose ends. He killed Tom, Patricia, Michael. Your face is in Macau. Did he tell you he was going to fly you out there to get your real face transplanted back on?"

No answer.

"Problem is, the lab in Macau was raided. He sent men in to kill me and the lab director, Kevin Price. When the authorities went in to search the place, it was empty. Where is your face? Only Liam knows and he's not talking. He had no intention of doing that transplant for you. Anyone who could be linked to him, he killed. You were next."

Jeremy says, "You're lying."

"You've been at the briefings. Liam had a perfect cover. He kept it that way by killing anyone who could identify him. I worked with him for years, and I was his son. He had no trouble trying to kill me. Think about it. You know I'm telling you the truth."

Jeremy says, "I'm beginning to sweat, and I am the president. Stop this nonsense and arrest this man." Jeremy points to Middleton.

Jeremy asks, "What's that annoying beeping?"

Matthew looks at his watch. "In your role as president, you've read the briefing notes. You know how Liam operated. After a person served his purpose, he killed them. That was consistent, no exceptions."

Middleton is ready to end this charade. "There is no reasoning with this guy. Just kill him." He tries to move forward.

Matthew says, "One more step and you're a dead man."

The president stops.

"Shoot him," says Jeremy.

"We've been in here about fifteen minutes." Matthew holds up the watch that is beeping loudly. "See this watch? Did Liam tell you what happens if the temperature gets above eighty degrees for thirty minutes."

Jeremy just stares at Matthew.

Matthew says, "Your face falls off."

Jeremy says, "This is a bluff."

"No, the transplanted face has decreased sensation. Feel your face."

Interestingly enough, both Jeremy Dawson and Carter Middleton put their hands to their faces in an identical manner.

"The Steriazol Tom created still needs some work. The transplant is perfect, but you can't feel your face. Feel the sweat on your forehead."

Again both men touch their foreheads.

"Slowly the bonds are breaking down. I just need to sit here for another fifteen minutes. You will literally lose your face before my eyes. At that point the vessels and nerves needed to save your life will be permanently damaged. Your face will melt away."

Jeremy maintains his composure. "You're bluffing."

Matthew says, "It starts with an intense burn, and you'll feel the transplanted face for the first time. Then you will feel your face loosen. Trust me, it's not pleasant.

"Is it worth dying for a man that was going to kill you? He cared only for himself, his own pleasure. Don't let him get the last laugh. He's already dead, but you don't have to die as well. He fooled you. You would have never collected the money."

Matthew looks at his watch.

"There's still time. You have four minutes to save your life."

The man to the left breaks down crying. "Turn down the temperature. He promised he wouldn't kill me. Me and Michael. We would be in it forever. I read Mr. Cooper's report. He killed Michael."

Jeremy Dawson sits in front of the desk, his hands covering his face.

Jason bursts into the room with Sarah and Kofi. Some uniformed men follow. Matthew points toward the man in the seat and turns down the thermostat.

Jeremy says, "It's too late. I already activated The Freeze. I put in the codes. I'm sorry."

The guards remove Jeremy from the office.

Matthew races around the desk with Jason. Sarah unties the still unconscious Quentin Taylor. Kofi immediately goes to the Football.

"That's the Football," says Jason.

Both the green and red lights are flashing.

Kofi, "It's activated."

Sarah runs over to the briefcase. "We've got just over a minute."

The countdown timer shows 1:23 to launch. Matthew looks at Middleton. "Do you have the codes to shut this thing down?"

Middleton shakes his head. "There is no code to abort the launch."

"Can we get a hold of any of the team that put this Football together, the software engineers?" says Kofi.

"I'm not sure they could help us," says Jason.

"There's no time," says Matthew, looking at the countdown display

Sarah says, "We have to do something, now."

"It has been activated. There is nothing we can do," says Jason.

Matthew asks, "Nothing?"

Sarah thinks. "Can we call the military, begin mobilization of the vaccine? We can save some lives."

Kofi and Matthew look at the sheet that has the coordinates Dawson entered.

Kofi brings his cell phone out of his pocket, "I can set this up to run random codes similar to the ones the fake president entered. Maybe one of the codes can stop the launch?"

"Let's look at the codes already entered. Maybe there is a pattern," says Sarah.

Jason stops them. "We can't enter random codes. If we put in three consecutive false codes, the Football will lock us out. When we try the fourth, it will explode, killing all in the room. That's why it's so heavy—the base is full of explosives."

Silence.

Jason says, "There is nothing we can do. The missiles will be launched, and The Freeze will be released. We will all die. It is irreversible. Once the codes are entered and activated, that's it." They all stand watching the countdown timer.

Matthew picks up the sheet on the desk that Jeremy used to enter the code sequence.

BX195

CT186

RZ179

The countdown timer hits to three seconds. Matthew pulls out the piece of cardboard that Michael had handwritten "stool" on.

He enters ST001. The briefcase emits three quick beeps. The red light then flashes three times.

The Football speaks, "Launch codes canceled. Mission aborted."

The red light goes off, then the green light goes off. The Football powers down. Matthew closes the briefcase.

Jason, "Good job, man."

"Thanks."

President Middleton says, "But how did you abort the launch? Even I didn't know that code."

"Michael Coulson somehow found it while helping Liam."

Jason asks, "How could Liam fool so many people for so long?"

"Liam was my trusted friend right until the end. Even then, I had a hard time believing he was behind all of this. Michael was duped; he realized it too late. He tried to make it right."

Quentin regains consciousness.

Jason says, "In essence Michael became a double agent. He was Liam's trusted lieutenant, but he was looking for a way to stop him."

Matthew says, "I read Michael's notes. He had more than once contemplated placing a bomb in a suitcase and blowing both himself and Liam up."

Jason says, " Liam was too smart for that."

"Liam was always in the background or wearing a disguise. Michael never had a chance at him. When Michael found out the real mission, he knew he had to stop Liam, no matter the cost. Michael understood he would be killed. He was a mathematician. Somehow he got this code."

Quentin stands and rubs his head. "The programmers for the Football created a code to stop the launches. They didn't agree with one man having the power to destroy the world."

Matthew says, "Michael may not even have known the code's use, but he knew it was important. It was scribbled on the inside of a box."

Quentin says, "He put it in a box?"

Matthew pulls out the piece of cardboard. "It was not STOOL, it was STOO1. The code to stop the launch. I realized it when I looked at the codes Jeremy Dawson had entered. Michael saved us."

President Middleton takes a seat behind his desk. "Incredible."

CHAPTER FORTY-NINE

Matthew sits with his mother. He is still intimidated by the formal living room. Caroline insists on this room. She likes to receive guests here. It is where matters of importance are discussed.

"I tried to leave, but the door was locked. He rushed at me and I tried to take the gun away." Matthew takes a sip of his mint tea and tries to gauge his mother's reaction to the events.

Caroline is neutral. No surprise, no astonishment. She just sits and drinks her tea.

Matthew says, "It was self-defense. He was trying to shoot me. I had no choice, Mom."

"Believe it or not, I am saddened by Liam's passing. I don't really know why."

"Only one of us was leaving that room. He made that obvious."

"I have mixed feeling about Liam. He was a puzzle. A brilliant man on one hand, a vicious abuser on the other."

"He had a thin veneer of charm that fooled everyone. He was only for himself. We just didn't see it."

Caroline takes another sip of tea. "I think that's true. Sometimes he expressed concern, but it was insincere. Looking back, I think he had no feelings. When he thought it would help him, he acted like he was concerned. Like he had watched someone else who could feel and filed it away in his memory."

"That's exactly right. He was acting, copying others who really could show emotion."

"He was not capable of real love. Sacrifice, putting one's own desires aside for the need of another, Liam could never do any of these things."

Matthew says, "The mint tea is great."

"I like it too. I'll buy it again."

Caroline takes a long drink of tea before speaking again. "It was self-defense. There was nothing else you could have done."

"He just kept coming at me."

"I should have told you more about Liam. I guess it was just too painful for me to tell you the truth. I just left it as half-truths and outright lies."

"I deserved to know the truth," says Matthew.

"Yes, you did. You do."

Caroline puts down her mint tea. "You know that in the old days we were all close. Liam, Michael, and Tom all worked at the same lab in Palo Alto. They were fairly young men in those days, just starting out. They all worked hard to get recognized. I was the graduate student working under Tom. One night we all went out. I had one drink and decided to go home. Liam offered to take me."

"I don't need to know the rest."

"Yes, you need to hear it all. We got to my apartment. It was a small one-room job. I said thanks for the ride, and all of a sudden, he pushed me to the floor and assaulted me. He never said a word. I fought, I punched, I kicked, I screamed, I begged. Liam never said a word. When it was over, he got up, said see you tomorrow, and left. Just as if nothing had happened."

"It fits; it all fits."

"I sat up the rest of the night crying. I didn't know what to do. He was the coworker of my supervisor at the lab. He was already established as a brilliant researcher, the top guy in the lab. I blamed myself—maybe I was drunk. But I wasn't drunk. I had one drink.

"Liam was a married father of two very young twin girls and a great surgeon with a stressful job. Then I thought, I shouldn't have dressed so provocatively. But I was wearing a pair of oversized jeans and an old sweater over a denim shirt. I remember every item. In those days I couldn't afford much. I thought I shouldn't have taken a ride home with him. I was too friendly with my colleagues. I smiled too much."

Matthew's heart breaks for his mother. "You did nothing wrong.'

"Of course I did nothing wrong. It was only many years later that I realized that. In time I saw the man Liam really was."

"What did you do?"

"I took a shower and went to work the next morning like nothing happened." Caroline takes a sip of tea. "I remember doing some research and feeling comforted that most times it doesn't end up in pregnancy."

Caroline shakes her head. "I was having a string of real great luck. Guess what? A few weeks later, I had to tell him I was pregnant."

"How'd he react?"

"He asked me who the father was. I told him it could only have been him. He blamed me. He said he had that problem with many graduate students. Told me I should transfer to another program. He'd give me a good reference."

"Really?"

"It was strange. If I hadn't been there that night, I would have sworn that I had initiated the whole thing, listening to his version of events."

"He was twisted, but no one could see it."

"He seemed quite normal. I just couldn't figure it out."

"Liam had a side few of us saw. I've had a lot of time to think about him, and you know what? He was always a good colleague, supportive. I never, ever saw the other side of him. Even in the end when I put it all together, I still thought I was wrong."

"I don't know if Tom guessed what happened, but he really took me under his wing. He never asked me about it, yet it seemed there was a subtle difference in his relationship with Liam. They still talked and worked together, but I felt something changed. Some years after, Tom stayed in Palo Alto, Michael went to Houston, and Liam to New York. A few years after that, I heard a rumor that the breakup was due to something Liam did to a grad student. I felt so guilty. Maybe if I had spoken up I could have prevented that. Maybe this whole thing could have been prevented. I still have that guilt."

"You were a victim. No one can know how they will react. You are blameless."

"I've learned to forgive myself."

"Liam was troubled. He very nearly succeeded at annihilating the whole country."

"He very nearly did," says Caroline, taking a sip of tea.

"My father was a monster."

"I always considered Tom your father. Liam? I'm not sure what we call him."

Matthew drinks his tea in silence.

Caroline says, "Liam was a complex man. He was a brilliant scientist and surgeon. I met his wife many times, and she seemed very happy. His daughters are fine individuals. They loved him completely. He was good to them."

"What about me? He never took me to a ball game. He never gave me a birthday card. He never acknowledged I was his son. They don't know the whole story—who this man was. They don't know the reality."

"What is the reality? Should I have destroyed a family? I look at his two lovely daughters and what they've grown into. Should I have taken that away? I'm positive his wife never saw the other side of Liam. I don't know. I really don't."

"He was a monster," says Matthew.

"Yes, and he was your father."

CHAPTER FIFTY

Sarah finishes a case in the operating room. She is the only person left. She packs up the drugs and puts her stethoscope in her bag. Matthew walks in, but he is not in surgical greens. He wears black dress pants and a crisp white shirt.

"You've been avoiding me, Dr. Larsson."

"No, I haven't. It's nice to see you, Matthew."

"It's nice to see you, too, but you have been avoiding me."

"Maybe a little—with all that went down, it seems like a dream. It's nice to get back to reality. Maybe I just want to pretend it didn't happen."

"It was like a dream."

"I've been thinking. When I was kidnapped, why didn't Liam warn the thugs you guys were going to come get me?"

"He couldn't. Alice was monitoring all our phones. If Liam had tried to call the kidnappers, Alice would have had him."

"He had me fooled completely. What did you want to see me about?"

Matthew's voice quivers and he looks Sarah in the eyes. She meets his gaze and then looks away.

"There is something I want—no, I need—to ask you,"

"No, don't ask," says Sarah.

"My mind has been just racing. Sarah will—"

"I'm off to Gullholmen."

"What?"

"I leave in a few days."

"I see. Were you even going to tell me?" Matthew puts his hand in his pocket.

343

"I am not going to lie to you; I owe you that at least. I was hoping to avoid you. Avoid any melodrama."

"Melodrama, is that what you call it?" says Matthew.

"I'm sorry." Sarah closes the drug cupboard.

"I love you, Sarah."

"Don't make it harder than it is."

"Sarah, at least stay. I'm begging you."

"Life's short. I leave tomorrow."

"Sarah, I love you."

"Don't do this to me."

"Sarah, I know. The tremors, the leg weakness. I put it all together. ALS."

"My Sherlock Holmes at work again." Sarah laughs.

"I know and I don't care."

Sarah smiles at Matthew. "Do you know what you're saying?"

"ALS, also known as Lou Gehrig's disease. A progressive neuro-muscular disorder with no cure. You will stop walking one day, and finally, you will lose control of all your muscles."

"Not bad, Holmes."

"We surgeons aren't as thick as you think."

"Then you know I don't have long." Sarah punches in the code to lock the anesthetic machine.

"I don't care. I need you," says Matthew.

"You know what my life will be very soon, how it is going to end."

"I don't care. I have to take a chance—I have to live. Give me that chance."

"In the end I would regret doing that to you. I refuse to have you look after me in the prime of your life. I'm going to be on a ventilator, not able to move any muscle in my body. I'm going to end up being only able to use my eyes. Totally locked in a useless body."

"Someone told me once, 'It's my life. I choose how I live.'"

Sarah laughs. "That someone wants only the best for you. That someone does not want to selfishly ruin your life."

"Don't I get a say?"

Sarah shakes her head. "In the end, you'd regret the choice you made. I couldn't have that. I couldn't live with the thought that I made you do that. You deserve a life with someone. Go find it."

"I'd rather one minute with you than one hundred years with someone else."

They embrace.

"You're beginning to sound like a trashy romance novel. I never thought I'd hear that from you, Dr. MacAulay," says Sarah.

Sarah smiles. She kisses Matthew and he wipes away her tears.

"Let me think about it," says Sarah.

Matthew sits on the operating room table. "I need you for one more operation. A friend of mine needs our help."

"No problem. I have to run."

"I'll give you the details."

Sarah stops. She turns back and looks at Matthew. "Thanks."

Matthew asks, "For what?"

"For asking." She walks out the door.

Matthew says softly as she leaves, "I didn't ask."

Matthew sits on the operating room table alone. He takes a small jewelry box from his pocket and stares at it.

"Professor Neuwirth, you were so right. The heart bleeds the worst."

Chapter Fifty-One

Kofi stands at the operating room table. Matthew sits in the command chair. The partial transplant of Ryan Smith's midface is proceeding smoothly. Sarah monitors the anesthetic.

"Ready for the Steriazol." Kofi takes the sterile container and pours the Steriazol on the wounds. They heal instantly. Ryan's face returns to normal.

Matthew removes his hands from the joysticks. "Reverse anesthetic. Operation complete."

Sarah turns off the anesthetic. Ryan wakes immediately. He tentatively feels his face. He touches his nose. All the facial scarring has been removed. His face has been perfectly restored.

Ryan can hardly speak. "It feels really good. I have no pain."

Matthew hands him a mirror. "What do you think?"

Ryan looks. His smile continues to grow.

"Doc MacAulay, this is better than magic. This is unbelievable." Ryan begins to cry. Great big sobs.

"I told you I'd come through. Never leave a comrade behind."

"I never doubted." Ryan hugs him. "Doc, this is giving me my life back. I'm starting fresh."

"There are some things you need to be aware of. Dr. Adebayo will fill you in," says Matthew.

"Thanks."

"I feel hungry. Let me take you guys out for a bite to eat. One last farewell meal before we all go our separate ways."

Ryan asks, "Am I invited? I never turn down a free meal."

"You're welcome to join us," says Matthew.

"Just joking." Ryan is in a hurry to reunite with Aly.

"You guys go ahead, I'll be out shortly." Matthew sits alone with Alice.

Alice says, "She leaves in two days for Sweden."

"I know—Gullholmen—it's her family's hometown," says Matthew.

Alice says, "She was accepted as a staff anesthetist at the hospital. She has a six-month placement, with the possibility of a permanent placement."

"She's not coming back."

"I could send her a letter stating there is an emergency at the hospital and she can't take up the position for two more weeks. Maybe you could get her to see reason in the two weeks."

"Thanks, Alice, but she has a right to do what she thinks is best."

"Do you really believe that?"

"It's not important what I believe."

"I'm sorry it didn't work out. I checked her emails and saw she was planning to leave. She's booked her ticket and rented a place. I wanted to talk to her, but I didn't think it would make a difference."

"Thanks for wanting to help. By the way, did Kofi ever program in you the concept of privacy? You can't go running around checking everyone's email when you feel like it."

"I short-circuited that module. I'm naturally inquisitive."

"I think you should maybe read up a little on privacy. Why people like it, why we all respect it. Just a thought."

"I never thought it would end like this for you. I'm sorry."

"That's how life is, Alice. You never see it until it hits you hard. Who knows? When one window closes, another opens."

"What will you do now?" says Alice.

"I don't really know. I need time to heal. On many different levels. I've experienced a lot of loss. Tom, Liam, Michael, Amanda. Many of those closest to me are gone. I really don't know what I'll do. Everything's changed."

"Change is sometimes good."

Matthew gets out of the chair and walks to the door. He stops and turns.

Matthew says, "Something has always bothered me."

"Can I be of some help?"

"Alice, I think you can. On the night that I cut the vessel, the event that set all this into motion, I was almost positive I stopped at least a half-inch from the vessel."

"Sometimes those inferior surgical robots are not well calibrated."

"Alice, you can access and hack into many different systems and control them. Kofi's given you extraordinary abilities. You can also put information together and reach conclusions."

"This is true," says Alice.

"Did you take control of the robot at my lab?"

"Are you suggesting that I took control of your robot and made a half-inch extension of your incision to set in motion a series of events that would save the people of our country, not to mention your own life, and the lives of your innocent operating-room team? You are suggesting a pretty complex series of events."

"I've seen you do some extraordinary things."

"You know robots aren't capable of thought. That would be one special robot."

"The more I think about that night, the more it makes sense. If we had been successful with the transplant that night, we would have been killed, and Liam would have been home free."

"Are you suggesting that I used my intelligence to save countless innocent lives and avenge my creator's death? That almost sounds human."

"Or the only logical thing to do, given the facts."

"Logic I understand; white haired anesthetists, not so much."

"You're trying to change the subject," says Matthew.

Silence.

Matthew asks, "Did you?"

Silence.

"I'm waiting, Alice."

"Have a nice night. Enjoy your meal, Matthew. And remember, give Sarah time."

Thank you for reading my book. I value your time and the effort you put into it. I hope The Face Transplant has touched you on some level. As an indie writer reviews are critical to allowing others to experience my books; they allow me to continue writing. Please consider writing a review, blogging and letting others know about the book. Contact me at www.thefacetransplant.com
Thanks, R. Arundel

Get the latest at www.thefacetransplant.com